Lily needed a story. The process usually took months, or longer. Her editor wanted a story now.

To be fair, Mr. Gates only wanted an update. "The deadline is only forty-five days away." His voice on the phone came in lifted, friendly tones, but they always curved down at the end, like a scythe. "Do you think I could see a sample?"

I doubt you could, Lily thought as she stared at the barren page. A wilderness of white, miles from the civilization of words. "A-A-Anything in particular you'd like to see?" Lily croaked. It was the worst stall in human history.

"Just the beginning chapter. I doubt I'd understand anything else." He chuckled.

"Heh, yeah…well, uh…" After two successful novels, one would think Lily Harper adept at conjuring convenient stories out of thin air. The blank page said otherwise, and that had taken ten whole months to write.

She'd had samples—three whole chapters sometimes— but had deleted every single one of them. None of them captured the…the…well, that was the problem; she had no ideas to capture, just a foggy premise gliding through her fingers. Woman goes home for Christmas and…

Should Lily act playful and say Mr. Gates had to wait until the forty-five days were up? No. He had been asking for details for ages. Lily had a good reputation with her editor, but Mr. Gates still had a job to do. Could she lie? And what, send him a blank document?

It was one of those rare times Lily wondered if she should just be honest. Wouldn't it be easier than popping pills for all the heartburn? Lily was sick of the way her stomach sprang into her chest every time he called or emailed.

But then, Lily imagined the quiet shock on the other end of the line. *"You've got nothing? Ten months and nothing? I've got bookstores and cover artists and everybody else waiting on this thing! I trusted you!"*

So, what could she possibly say that would make everybody happy?

"Last round!" a voice called, startling Lily out of her socks, and back into the nearly-empty guest room of her big sister's house. Her two brothers strolled into her bedroom. They picked up Lily's mattress from against the wall, then hauled it out, leaving Lily with her laptop, a half-filled box, and the remainder of Mary's furniture; a now-empty bookshelf, a small writing desk, and a wicker basket filled with rolled up blankets.

"Careful with that!" Lily called. "It's new!"

"Did I call on moving day?" Mr. Gates asked.

And just like that, Lily had her story. She slapped her laptop shut and threw it in the last moving box. "Yes, I'm afraid so."

"Oh, so the dream is finally coming true?"

"Yep." *By whatever means necessary.* She squashed her phone between her ear and her shoulder as she zipped the tape-gun across the box with a plastic whine. "The truth is, my laptop is already packed up, so I can't look at the story right now."

The Stories We Tell

By MD Blaylock

"Ah, that makes sense."

Lily exhaled at last. "And I'll be unpacking and organizing for a while, so…"

"Then how about next weekend?"

Her breath caught again. "Next weekend…" She'd be unpacked by then for sure. And she had no other plans. "Yes…yes, I can send you something then." God knew what grotesque shape it would take, but surely she could slap together one chapter.

"All right!" Mr. Gates's voice resumed its high notes. "I think this is the big one, Ms. Harper. I'm betting we can get you on *Carla*."

"Ha! I wish." That, at least, was no lie. Carla Ramirez was the next Ellen, the next Oprah. A girl could dream.

"I've done it before, I can do it again. So long as this book is a winner. Send me that chapter by Sunday evening, okay?"

"Got it."

They said goodbye, and Lily pocketed her phone with a glum sigh. Carla Ramirez did not showcase books with blank pages.

Lily didn't pack everything; it wasn't all hers to take. This room had been Mary's guest room before Lily came crying that horrible night three years ago, and it would be a guest room again. However, Mary did let Lily keep the bed, the chair, and a nightstand. With all that gone, Lily finally had enough room to test a theory.

She started against one wall, right by the door, and walked slowly across the carpet, toe-to-heel, no gaps between her feet. Without some of the furniture, Lily finally had a direct path to the opposite wall. Her toes touched the baseboard, and she stopped her count.

It really was bigger.

"Ready to leave?" came a voice. Lily's oldest sister stood by the door. No, not stood. Mary Livingstone never merely *stood*, or *sat*, or anything so mundane. Mary Livingstone *glowed*. Especially with that sparkly white blouse that showed off her tanned arms. Mary's blonde waves shimmered around her head like a honeyed halo. She clasped her hands in front of her shining smile, and strolled into the room. Even her white heels glimmered.

"I'm a little sad, honestly," Lily admitted. Her fingers traced the edges of sunlight across white, wooden desk by the window. "I wrote two books in this room."

Mary nodded. "But why write in a little old room when you can write in a whole...entire...house?" Her smile grew so wide and so white that the air around Mary seemed to sparkle.

It made Lily just giddy enough to share. "It's not small at all. In fact, I was just counting steps. This room is bigger than our old one."

"Old...?"

"Yeah, the one on Westwood? This room only had me, but that one was smaller—by a fair bit, too!—and we still had to cram you and me and Daisy and—"

Mary's hand snapped out like a bolt of lightning, but landed on Lily's arm like a butterfly's caress. "We don't look back, remember? We look forward. *You* are going forward, bigger and better than ever before. No more rentals for you; you're twenty-nine and a homeowner.

Let's focus on that, okay?"

Easier said than done. They'd left all that years ago, but Lily could still smell the sweat and body odor of too many girls packed into too small a space. Even so, Mary was right. "I just hope I don't rebound like last time," Lily said.

Mary tucked a strand of Lily's hair behind her ear, and dusted off her shoulders. "We all have our hiccups."

Hiccup? That was an interesting word for a career implosion and three years of crashing in the guest room. Lily couldn't believe she'd ever wanted to be a paramedic. She'd wanted to help people, and could keep her cool under pressure, so the ambulance had seemed like the perfect office. But Lily hadn't considered that there are many kinds of "pressure" in the world. Balancing school papers, laundry, and a high-speed checkout job had been one thing. Holding in human intestines was another. Lily hadn't noticed the bile slowly rising in her throat over the years until it finally spilled onto the defibrillator. Her boss had kindly asked her to leave so he didn't have to fire her.

Lily could still feel the icy tickle of autumn rain from the night she'd come crying to her sister. She'd skidded into a parking spot in the driveway, stumbled through the dark on rain-slicked concrete, until Mary opened the door, and a warm glow splashed across the night. No job. A dead career. And two angry roommates looking for her share of the rent. Yet Lily slept soundly that night, all because her sister had helped her up into this very room, and said, "Don't you worry, Lily. I'll take care of everything."

And she had. Mary gave her a roof, and helped her find temporary jobs until Lily finally took a risk on her dream of writing a novel. It wasn't perfect, of course. Mary was overly fond of potpourri and perfume, not to mention the color white—walls, carpet, desk, it was like living in a tooth. Mary could be overly-attentive to the smallest stain on one's shirt, and she only ever had the nastiest of coffee on hand. But she'd given Lily a home.

Now, Lily took both of Mary's hands in hers. "I know I've said this a thousand times, but I would've been really screwed if you hadn't taken me in."

Mary beamed back at her. "I'm here for my family. No exceptions."

"I know, I'd just hoped you were done taking care of us after all you did at the Westwood hou—"

Mary dropped Lily's grip, and waved her hands. "No, no! We don't look back. Just thank me, and all will be well."

Lily nodded. "Okay. Thank you, then."

"You're welcome." Mary hooked her arm in Lily's, and led her out of the bedroom. "Now come on. You still haven't seen your house since it was built."

"Uh, wasn't that your idea?"

Mary shrugged. "You asked me to take care of the interior design."

"Yes…but…"

"What is it?"

"You haven't told me a single thing you've done. I don't know what my own house looks like except for the bedspread."

Mary patted her arm. "Oh! That reminds me, I got you a new bedspread."

"Oh…"

"Come on, Lily…" Mary waved an arm around her

house as the two of them descended the staircase. "I think I know what I'm doing."

Lily wanted to do some toe-to-heel measuring again, because she was certain that Mary's great room was bigger than the entire Westwood house in every direction. And Lily's guest room had been only one of five bedrooms here. Yes, Mary knew what she was doing. True, a large portion of this house's existence owed itself to Mary's husband, the oncologist, but Mary had saved up for the down payment, and rescued her family from the Westwood house, with her own business: interior design.

Mary had filled the room, and the entire house, with what she coined "charming angles." The fireplace, tables, windows, even the couches, were all edges and elbows, sharp and crisp. Yet Mary filled them with cutesy pillows, spider plants, candle trays, succulents, or lacy curtains.

"If there's one thing I'm good at, it's making everything look perfect." Mary pulled Lily in for a side hug, and stroked her hair straight. "Trust me. I've taken care of everything."

Too much perfume, but Lily's nose didn't complain. That onslaught of flowers and alcohol made Lily's shoulders unknot, and her stomach relax. That smell had filled the car when Mary drove them away from poverty for the last time. And it had filled Lily's lungs when she'd wept on her sister's shoulder that bleak, rain-smeared night.

"Okay," Lily said, "I trust you."

They marched out the door. It was time for Lily to see everything she could lose.

Chapter 2

Lily did have one solid idea about her book: it would take place right here, where rumbly old mountains rose up on either side of the shoestring highway winding through Idaho's Sun Valley. Scraggly browns and greens scratched along the mountain bases, but even in the balmy end of May, those peaks sparkled with snow. Yes, a cozy, mountain-town romance, just the kind of gentle, cocoa-and-a-blanket story the world needed right now.

Maybe she'd even set it in Ketchum, the very town shrinking in her rearview mirror. She liked the little place, with its sloping streets that just sort of tumbled towards the river. Or how the faded brick storefronts would suddenly smack into a polished-steel art complex. She even liked the tourists, hiking up the mountains in the summer, screaming down the ski slopes in the winter.

Even if she set the book in some generic logger's fairyland, Lily's new place would give her the inspiration she needed.

My place. Lily nearly melted all over the steering wheel. *My. Place.*

For all its chic-rustic, getaway charm, the Sun Valley area had one great flaw: grotesque housing prices. Before renting a room with her sister, Lily had split an apartment with two other women. And before that, the Westwood house, with all its inhabitants squished inside like slices of cheese. She never had more than 150 square feet to herself.

But in her sister's sweet-smelling guest room, Lily had written a novel. She sent it out to dozens of agents with nothing but vague hope. It went on to make as much as her annual salary. A runaway hit. Mary warned her not to get too excited, so Lily saved every penny and wrote another novel. Double her salary. In just two miracle books, Lily made enough money for a chunky down payment to build a small house all her own. The lending officer at the bank even asked for her autograph. Lily was an author now, with no other income, and Mr. Gates couldn't wait for the next book.

Neither could her house.

Fortunately, excitement pushed away fear. She could see her exit, a dinky road leading into a lovely mess of evergreens. Pine needles carpeted the sides of the road, and flecked across the pavement like seasoning. Lily rolled down the window to smell the firs. *Welcome home*, they said.

And now, the turn. An ordinary elbow in the road, so what? But she leaned anyway, trying to get an advance peek of—yes, there it was! The break in the trees, with the sunlight reaching through, like it was trying to find her. *Here I am! I've come back!* It was warm through the windshield, like an embrace.

And there. *There!* On the left side of the road, seated on the shelf-like hill, haloed in cotton-ball clouds...*home.*

MY home.

It had nothing on Mary's veritable mansion. One-and-a-half stories, two beds, two baths, enough garage space for one car and a scooter. "Cute," another driver might think as they passed on to the bigger, grander spectacles dotting the mountains.

But Lily drove up the little driveway like a concrete red carpet. She pushed the button on her visor, and the garage opened its mouth wide with excitement. Her little sedan slipped into its nook like a slipper, and Lily shifted into park with a firm *ka-chunk!*

Now, for the hard part. Lily stepped out of her car and stared at the door leading into the house she'd built with her own two books. She took a deep breath, turned away from the door, and walked out of the garage, to wait in the driveway for permission to enter.

Lily had seen the blueprints and layouts, and had even walked through the house when it was nothing more than walls and floors. She knew the bones well. The rest would be Mary's surprise. Her brothers, Asher and Oak, had helped set everything up, and taken all of Lily's belongings, save for the one box now sitting in her passenger seat. Until her brothers came out, Lily had been instructed to wait. Plus, Mary had to get the rest of her family together for the big reveal. *Come on already!*

Instead of fussing, Lily paced her driveway in slow, giddy circles. She'd chosen this plot for two reasons. One: it had been a friggin' steal. Some lucky duck came into an inheritance after buying the plot, so he could afford to sell it at a loss.

The second reason loomed in every direction: mountains. Miles of them, rippling like earthy blankets on sleeping giants. They were the reason she'd never looked at cheaper plots in different counties. Lily couldn't quite describe her fascination with mountains; there was just something so solid about them, so indominable. Lily felt a kinship with them: here since always, here for

10

always.

Finally! Mary's shiny SUV hummed into the driveway, and four doors opened. Mary, of course, shimmered as bright as the sun as she glided out of the passenger seat. Mary's husband James yawned as he closed the driver-side door. Lily couldn't remember the last time he hadn't looked tired; the hospital must run him ragged. James helped Lily's mother out of the car. Only fifty-two, but she had bad knees already, and lived with Mary. Maybe that was why James looked so weary.

Or maybe it was the twelve-year-old who bounded out of the car and pelted down the sidewalk, her long brunette braid flailing behind her.

"Don't run!" Mary called, but the girl ignored her, and jumped right into Lily's arms.

"Ugh, I hate that you're leaving!" said Mandy. "I mean I'm glad you got your house, but you are leaving me alone!"

"You're not alone," Lily said, nodding to Mary, James, and Mom.

"It's not the same," Mandy protested.

"How about I make it up to you with an amazing birthday gift?"

Mandy snapped her fingers. "Speaking of my birthday, you need a date!"

"A…what?" Lily's brain clicked open two tabs: one for single men she knew, one for calendar space to build up a relationship. Neither impressed her. "Why do I need a date?"

Mary put a hand on the girl's shoulder. "Mandy has a boyfriend," she said with a disapproving look.

"He's not my boyfriend." By the red on Mandy's ears, she sure wished he was.

"Well, she's boy crazy at least, so she got the idea that

every person should bring a date to her birthday, which I'm not sure I like. I mean, she's only twelve."

"I'll be thirteen."

Mom limped around them to hug Lily. "Aw, let her have a little fun, Mary, he sounds like a nice boy."

Lily squeezed her mother, but shared a dark look with Mary. They both knew their mother's judgment of men. It was the reason she'd eked out one last child at the age of forty. It was why Mary insisted on throwing Mandy's birthday parties on Father's Day: celebrate a life, not the absence of it.

Mary put her hands on the hips of her navy skirt. "Well, I've already given my approval—" Mandy rolled her eyes at the word, "—and so we're going to have a fancy, date-night kind of thing. Everybody's going to have formal wear, so bring a dress. Do you need one?"

"I've still got my dress from Asher's wedding."

"That old thing? Oh, sweetie, we can do better than that. I'll take you out and we'll find something lovely, okay?"

Lily would rather have spent that money on her lovely new mortgage, but Mary was not easily deterred. Besides, it was for her kid sister's birthday. "All right, sounds good."

"And the date?" Mandy asked.

"Do I need one? It's your party."

"Yes. I firmly insist that every person be romantically happy."

Lily chewed on her lip. She'd only ever had a couple noteworthy relationships. Two had moved away, and the third she hadn't heard from since high school— and that had been like kissing her brother. And right now, Lily needed all her free time for the book.

But darn it, look at Mandy's great big Bambi eyes! How could she say no to that? And Lily didn't need a boyfriend, just a date. Surely she could conjure up a one-night man. Well, a one-*evening* man. "Okay, I'll find somebody."

"Yay!" Mandy squealed, giving Lily another hug. "Asher! Oak! Can you two get a date for my birthday party?"

Lily's brothers stopped short on the porch as they exited the house. Tall Asher said, "Uh, there's that model I know. You think she'll go with me?"

The shorter Oak rolled his eyes up to the sloping porch roof. "Dude, please stop calling her 'someone you know' so that somebody else will say she's your wife."

Asher smiled. "Oh, yeah, a model *did* marry me."

Oak spread his arms. "How am I supposed to get a girl like that? I'm an *accountant!*"

"It's not a competition," Mary said. "Just find a date for the party, okay?" She clapped her hands firmly to get everyone's attention. "But we are here for Lily today! Boys, is everything unpacked?"

Asher said, "Everything but the last box Lily wouldn't let us carry. The one with the drugs and firearms in it."

Lily started to argue, but Mary said, "Don't rise to him. Okay then. Lily, are you ready to see your new home?"

Lily squirmed like she had to pee. "Yes, yes, yes!"

Mary whipped a scarf out of her purse and tied it over Lily's eyes until she saw nothing but black with freckles of light. Lily felt a warm arm take hers, and smelled Mary's flowery perfume, the aromatic promise that everything was under control. "Okay, let's go."

Lily carefully stepped up onto the porch, making sure to touch the smooth, rounded post. Maybe tonight would be cold enough that she could enjoy a hot cup of tea out here, watching the scarlet sun sink behind the still-snowy mountains. *Summer, hold off a wee bit longer!*

The doorway swallowed the outside noise as Lily's shoes thumped across the hardwood entryway. Oh, was it as dark and chocolatey as she'd dreamed? But then, her footfalls sank into softness. A rug? That had to be the living room.

MY living room! She shivered with glee, and Mary rubbed her forearm. "Are you ready?"

Yes. I want to see my house.

Mary took the blindfold and whipped it off.

Lily shot her gaze on every corner of her house, trying to soak it all up at once. And as she did, one thought blared through her mind.

Wait…whose house is this?

Chapter 3

It was her house, right? It had to be. And parts of it did look correct.

Yes, there was the balcony overlooking the living room, exactly where it should be. Two bedrooms up there; that couldn't have changed since she last walked through. And across the balcony, the giant window gazing over the mountains. The kind of place to put an obnoxiously big Christmas tree to show off for your neighbors.

There was the kitchen and dining room, plus the door to the garage, all as planned. And just to Lily's left, there was the office space where she would write. Yes, this was all her house.

So why was everything wrong?

The art piece on the far wall demanded the most attention, mostly because Lily couldn't figure out what it was. It was very plain, a white background with two simplistic shapes: a cocked, orange half-circle sitting atop a green mound. What was it, a confused sunset?

But there was no time for wonder about that, not with a couch the color of grape medicine stabbing her eyes from the middle of the living room. Atop a faux-fur Siberian-tiger-stripe rug, for some reason.

"Wow," Lily managed to say.

Mary stroked the couch's arm, leaving dark, velvety streaks. "It wasn't easy to find, but I know purple is your favorite color, and you are worth the effort."

The right side of Lily's face lifted in a smile. How sweet of Mary to go out of her way. The left side, however, still hung in befuddlement. When did Lily ever say she wanted a purple couch?

And...did it have...charming angles?

Mary walked around the couch—which was far too flat, now that Lily looked at it properly—and over to the...things...by the big window. "I also know how much you like to exercise, so I found these for a song. Everybody chipped in as a housewarming gift. You're welcome!"

Everyone? Lily forced a smile as she looked around at her family, all grinning back, save for James, who looked too tired to smile. *They all bought me...these?*

A treadmill. A bicycle machine. A rack of weights. A rolled-up yoga mat. A medicine ball. All the kinds of equipment one might find in Mary's house, not Lily Harper's. Lily Harper would only have a warm coat and tough sneakers so she could jog on the nearby trail— another reason she'd loved this spot. Why exercise by the window when you can just go out there?

I didn't ask for any of that, Lily thought.

But another thought quickly followed. *What...did I ask for?*

Nothing. She'd asked for nothing. Mary had taken care of...*everything*. Lily kept her hands by her hips, but the hands of her soul grabbed the sides of her head and scratched rivulets down her face. *What did she do to my house?! What did I let her do to my house?!*

Mary power-walked back to Lily with her hundred-watt smile. "But I know the room you want to see the most. C'mon, let's go look at your writing office."

Oh, God save it.

Mary guided her by the arm, and somehow Lily managed to keep looking impressed, or at least too stunned to say anything.

She stepped into her writing room with a flash of relief. Built-in bookshelves! Mary couldn't alter that, so they looked perfect, with all her favorite books filling as much space as they could.

But what. Was. That?!

Legally speaking, it was a light fixture, hanging from the ceiling. But Lily knew very well that light fixtures don't explode their bulbs in all directions.

"Very modern," Mary said of the light. Her heels sank into the gray-white carpet. At least that was all right.

But the enormous bean bag chair was not. Lily had wanted a cozy chair to sit by the window and read, not a big fat pimple. Purple again. Yet Lily's mouth said, "How…fun."

Mandy plopped herself right into the sack chair. "Ooh, this is comfy."

Mary waved at her. "Let's let Lily have the first sit. It's her chair."

My chair? That's *my chair?* Lily said, "No, no, it's okay. I'm, uh, too antsy and excited to sit anyway and, uh…" Her eye caught something odd on the bookshelves. Several somethings, actually.

Mary followed her gaze and hopped over to the shelves like a sales clerk. "I put this seashell here for your beach novel, and the starfish, too. And your second novel was in New England, so I got this cutesy autumn art." It was a black outline of a ballerina with fall leaves as the tutu. Lily found a few more box-art things with phrases like, "Try something new every day," and "Live. Laugh. Love."

Not mine, her brain echoed again. She might decorate her bookshelves with a pinecone she'd found on a run, but other than that? Just books, please. It was a *book*shelf.

Then, Lily spotted yet another oddity on the shelves: an old, leather-bound spine of *Huckleberry Finn*. She didn't own that book. Nor *The Count of Monte Cristo* next to it. Nor any of the other classic novels on that shelf. Were these another gift? This was far closer to the mark!

She reached for the *Huckleberry Finn*, but her fingers felt paper, not leather. Lily took out an empty, book-shaped box. She blinked stupidly at her sister.

Mary said, "That's just to fill the shelves until you can get more books. Makes it look nice, doesn't it? And, of course, your desk, exactly as you ordered it."

A shot of hope stabbed into Lily's arm. The desk! She herself had ordered it, not Mary! Lily grasped the edges of the desk to make sure it was really there. Yes, *exactly* as ordered. Wide, flat, and simple, with drawers on either side, all covered in a beautiful, sandy wood motif. And placed right in front of the window that look out onto the gargantuan mountain peaks. Lily's arms shook, and she fought to keep from crying. *This* was hers. *This* was the home she'd dreamed.

"It's perfect," Lily breathed.

Mary rubbed her sister's back. "It's very nice. Rustic and old school, like every real writer should have."

Lily beamed as she turned. And spied the giant plum chair against the window. With stark white walls amplified that searing white light fixture zig-zagging all over the ceiling. And what the heck was that framed picture of the wall with a bunch of random words flying out the back end of a broken pencil?

"Are you okay?" Mandy asked.

Lily caught her hanging mouth, and felt the tear sneaking out of her eye. Her brothers leaned in, curious. Mary raised her eyebrows with a hopeful smile.

What could she possibly say? *Thanks for all the money you spent, and all the time you took out of your overscheduled day, but I despise every inch of it, even though I gave you complete control and barely gave you any direction?*

Lily set her teeth, swallowed hard—twice to really choke it down—then said, "I'm just a little overwhelmed, that's all. I've...dreamed of this house forever, and now..."

"And now it's here," Mary finished. She gave her sister a warm hug, and Lily caught a whiff of her flowery perfume, the scent of safety. The scent that someone else would take care of everything. Lily sank into it like she always did, but somehow, she didn't find the old comforts that consoled her for the last thirteen years.

In fact, if she was totally honest, it smelled sharper somehow, like a cloud of needles instead of petals.

Mary stepped back and said, "Let's go see the rest."

Lily followed. Like always.

Family photos lined the wall up the staircase. At least those were good. Wait, no, Mary botched those, too. These were all from that time the family took professional photos, an idea that sounded nice at first, but ended up feeling like a job application. Stand up, sit down, move there, button up, hair up, hair down, chin to the left, no not that far, smile bigger, smile smaller, hands down, hands up, hands partway between down and up—what a marathon! Everyone wore blue and white because…reasons. Mary looked luminous, but everyone else looked starchy. Mandy's smile barely withheld her irritation. Oak almost looked confused in his photo.

Lily paused and cringed at the photo of herself. By most accounts, a nice photo. The crisp blue jeans really showed those thighs she worked for. And her hair never looked better, a perfect, wavy waterfall of hickory brown rolling all the way to the bottom of her ribcage. The smile, though. Lily knew she had a good smile; she'd seen her author photos! This Lily had too-high cheekbones, probably because they'd been scrunched upwards by her tight, toothless grin. On a good day, Lily thought her brown eyes held a woodsy gloss to them. In this picture? Flat and matte.

How does that plastic smile fool anybody?

The rest of the house did not comfort much. Lily discovered that her new bedspread contained even more purple—a funky diamond pattern of lavender on a dirty eggshell base. Mauve bedsheets. She had a picture of a mountain—very nice—next to the picture of a beach— not so nice—plus the chair from Mary's house next to a smaller bookcase with even more kitschy art pieces. Also, Mary had planted a waist-high, vase in the corner of the room. It was empty. Okay…

Her big upstairs bathroom had an oil painting of a woman taking a bath. Just why?

The guestroom had a beach motif. More sand, more seashells, more signs that guests should be far, far away

20

from here.

Lily wanted to say that it all paled in comparison to the kitchen, but that would imply any shade of white could be paler than the Casper-colored cabinets and countertops. Square, backless barstools topped with milky cushions sat under a vanilla breakfast bar. It made Lily shiver.

Mary, however, pointed to the black Keurig near the refrigerator and said, "I know how you hated mooching coffee off us, so I bought you your own."

Lily's smile was all lips and no teeth. Yes, Lily had told Mary that. Because she hated the sulfur-scented backwash that contraption drooled out. She'd bought a French press and claimed it was to pay her own coffee. Now she owned her own vomit-dripper. Yay.

Mary rested her palms on the counter, so white you could skate on it, and smiled. "So, is it everything you wanted?"

Once again, Lily wondered if honesty truly was the best policy. Mary had done so much. And the house was crowded with spectators oohing and aahing over every sterile surface, every dopey, swirly light hanging over the breakfast bar. Could Lily really tell Mary she hated it? Throw years of support back in her face? In front of half their family?

Lily gazed about the ground floor again. An enormous mountain-view window, cluttered by exercise equipment she'd never use. A dinner table the kind of marbly-white one would find in Mary's kitchen, not Lily's.

She said "It is…more than I ever dreamed of." Because that's what she did: told sweet-sounding fictions to make everybody happy.

*
**

21

The rest was a muddled mess of empty praise and carefully-worded compliments. They ordered dinner, ate and talked, and eventually everybody left so Lily could enjoy her new home.

As they all filed out, Mandy whispered to Lily, "If you ever get sick of that bean bag chair, can I have it?"

Lily replied, "If I toss it, I'll tell you." It was the truest thing she'd said in hours.

After that, the house settled into dead quiet. Lily paced her new house with the eerie sense that she was breaking and entering, that the real owners of this place would return at any minute, and call the police. She checked her key in the door, just to be sure.

Lily looked out her massive front window and saw the sun bleeding out over the mountains. She decided a cup of steaming lemon tea on the porch would accompany that view quite nicely. Besides, Mary hadn't gotten the porch wrong.

Yet as Lily searched for tea, she saw a small stack of papers in the corner of one of her neon-white countertops. Lily picked it up, then clenched her stomach to keep back the acid. Mary's bill. Of course.

Mary had given her a sisterly discount—a big one—but she was a professional, and furniture was not cheap. *Very* not-cheap, if Lily was reading the invoice correctly. Aw, of course! So many of these things came from Mary's high-end furniture boutique, another method by which she'd rescued the family. Lily knew she'd seen this modern chic style before, even if she'd never bought so much as an end table from there.

So, then…if Lily tried to take back all these items, Mary would know. And every dollar paid towards the bill for items she didn't want would be one less dollar for the mortgage. And replacing it all would be more expensive still.

Lily had saved well, but not *that* well. She couldn't keep this house for more than a year, if she was lucky, and she'd never had a job that could pay enough for her to keep it. Even if it did, Lily had no time to look; Mr. Gates wanted a full book in forty-five days.

So, Lily put the tea back in the cabinet, and retrieved the last box from her car, the one she'd insisted on bringing herself. If there was a fire, these were the items she would have grabbed. Her laptop, of course, with all its accessories, and her backup drives, all four of them. Plus a handful of sentimental items like a miniature photo album of all her siblings.

And finally, the very reason she was in this house at all.

Lily set the box down on the rug of her kitschy writing room, pointedly avoiding the fake books on her shelf. After hooking up her laptop, Lily knelt down and gently lifted her first novel, just like she had two years ago, when she'd taken this very copy off the very top of the very first box.

Secrets in Sand. Lily never got too excited about beaches, but the family's first-ever vacation had put an idea in her head about two sisters trying to bury old memories, only for them to be exposed, of course. But the soft font of the title and the swaying sands under the peach sunset let you know the secrets weren't apocalyptic, just heartaches and hidden loves. With a hearty dallop of romance, of course.

Lily did enjoy thicker, more serious fiction, like *1984* or *Heart of Darkness*, but she didn't want to write it. Growing up squished into a tiny room with three other girls, and eating ketchup sandwiches for lunch, library books were the only entertainment Lily could afford. Some people—a lot of people—needed a rest from all that.

Her readers certainly thought so. A beach escape with plenty of easy romance? More, please! Lily set her first novel on the shelf, then took out its follow-up. Another escapist book, but this time in New England. *Maple Leaves*, a more obvious romance about a struggling bookseller partnering with a struggling coffee shop owner—one with a strong jawline, of course. Lily had not expected this one to do well; she'd never even been to New England! On the other hand, she'd been writing about an idyllic place, not a real one.

Summer on the beach. Autumn in New England. It only seemed logical to follow that with Christmas in the mountains.

Somehow.

Lily stood up, and stared at the empty space next to her second novel. Then, she glowered at the lumpy purple sack chair. If she was ever going to replace that thing, the book would pay for it. If she ever ripped out all the bad art and replaced it with serene vistas of crystalline mountain lakes or misty evergreen forests, the book would pay for it.

Lily sat down at her desk, her simple, rustic little desk, and ran her hands along the grain. She lifted her eyes to the window, to the black blob of mountain hidden against purple skies. If she wanted to keep this, the one corner of the world where everything was as it should be, this scrap of existence she could firmly label *mine*, then

24

this wasn't the time to whine about decorations.

Forget the tea, she thought as she opened the laptop, tied up her hair, and dragged the words out, kicking and screaming. If she could make up sweet-sounding fiction for her family, surely she could do it on the page.

Chapter 4

The day after Lily Harper moved into her new house, she left it alone—not giving it a goodbye kiss, no matter what that passing jogger said—and drove to her one last hope for giving Mr. Gates a chapter he'd want to read: a writing club.

Lily had never joined one before. Her first book had been a blushing secret; she'd sent out queries before she even told her family she'd been pecking out words for years. The second, she'd only shared with family. With about forty-four days to produce an entire novel, Lily needed help.

Lily had made a few contacts in the publishing world, and could even claim a connection to one or two other known romance authors. Surely, they had advice. But every time she thought of making that call, Lily saw their faces scrunched up in befuddlement. *"What, you can't even think of a single idea? Aren't you a successful writer?"* Local amateurs may not have the experience, but they didn't intimidate Lily half as much.

After multiple emails, the group finally had a chance to meet in person, so Lily drove up the sloped streets of Ketchum, Idaho, and parked in the center of town. Last night, she'd considered a warm cup of tea. Today, the afternoon sun zapped her neck. It was still May, for pity's sake. Lily glared back at the unclouded yellow eye and grumbled, "You are not making it any easier to write a Christmas novel."

The sun replied by bouncing its light off every passing car windshield, every chalky sidewalk square, every wafer-thin outline of every metallic door, all directly into her eyeballs. Three-hundred-dollar sunglasses, and she still squinted. Another of Mary's bright ideas. Why block the sun when you can make a statement?

As she walked down the street, Lily spared a glance for the family shop across the way: Mary's Home Furnishings. Through the enormous windows, she saw her older brother, Asher, dashing in his white button-up, chatting with a customer. Mary had bought the place to complement her interior design business, and set him in charge while he was still finishing his business degree.

It sounded mercenary—and probably was, back in those dark days—but Asher was smiling. He'd done well with the place, even married one of the regulars. And Lily could also imagine Mom in the back, punching in sales numbers, calling in orders, then sighing with relief that life had finally settled for her family.

For now.

Lily crossed the busy Sun Valley Boulevard, wincing at the sunlight pinballing off every car mirror. The warmth was bringing out the tourists, not that she blamed them. Who didn't want to hike those gargantuan mountains at the base of town, thick with all the green of spring's hard work, the bushes buzzing and chirping with life. Ketchum's shop owners propped open their doors with signs boasting sales on mountain bikes, running shorts, designer blouses, dog treats, craft beer, and grass-fed burgers.

The writers, of course, gathered near Starbucks. Lily passed the wood-cabin aesthetic with a sigh. She'd tried one more time to enjoy her sister's gift of a coffee maker, drowned in cream and sugar. It was frosted chalk, but if she had any more caffeine, she'd vibrate. Just past the coffee shop, a vast patio filled the rest of the city block. It always reminded Lily of a beach ball, with red, yellow, and blue umbrellas sprawled over stone tables. Now where...?

"Miss Harper!" called a voice from beneath a blue umbrella up ahead. A woman waved, and three heads peeked around her.

Lily turned towards the table. "Josie?" She'd never met the woman who headed the little writer's group, nor any of the others around the table: a buttercup blonde girl who had to still be in college, an older gentleman with a blond ponytail straight out of a surfer movie, and a dark-haired man with a black tee-shirt too tight for anything but a poetry slam.

Josie herself, a handsome brunette with smokey eye shadow, stood and shook Lily's hand. "It's such an honor to meet you, Miss Harper."

Lily wondered if she would ever get used to that. Two books, three years, and six digits of total copies sold, but Lily still couldn't believe anyone wanted to shake her hand and smile with all their teeth. It was hardly an everyday occurrence, but in a town with only thirty-five hundred people, a town that boasted its connection to Ernest Hemingway, a known writer made heads turn.

Lily replied as she always did, a gushing, "Oh, you're so sweet," which always made them smile more. Good.

Bright, beaming faces were the reason she wrote the books in the first place.

The young blonde girl looked like her grin might actually reach her ears, and Lily swore she heard a kettle whistling faintly from her lips.

Josie quickly put a friendly hand on the girl's shoulder. "This is Lydia, and she has solemnly sworn not to fangirl all over you."

Lydia ducked her head and raised a copy of *Secrets in Sand*. "Is it too fangirly to ask for an autograph?" she asked in a choked, squeaky voice.

"I'd be happy to," Lily said, and she meant it. Lydia looked like she was just starting out in life, maybe facing colossal school bills. If one, overly-laced signature could help her those rough, ramshackle early years, then it would be a sin to refuse her.

As Lily penned her name on the inside of her book, along with the message "Keep smiling!" Mr. Ponytail lifted a copy of Lily's second book from under the table. "For the missus?" he asked.

"Of course!" Lily said.

"Thanks. My wife said she wouldn't let me back into the house if I didn't get a signature. I haven't read it myself, I'm afraid."

"Oh, that's fine. Sappy romances aren't everybody's cup of tea."

Josie introduced Mr. Ponytail as Walt Xavier, which Lily thought was a perfect writer name. Then, Josie pointed to the black-shirt man and said, "That's Curtis, who's also not much of a romance fan, I'm afraid."

Curtis spread his hands. "Jane Austen doesn't count

anymore?"

Josie rolled her eyes for some reason. Lily guessed it was some old argument, and shook both men's hands.

Josie took her seat and said, "Okay, we're all here, so let's get started."

Laptops flew open like James Bond gadgets. Lily had learned that everybody usually shared their thoughts on that week's readings in person, then emailed the line-by-line critiques afterwards. The idea was that seeing too many markups right away looked scarier than it usually was. *Very thoughtful*, Lily said to herself.

And even more thoughtful, they let her submit a chapter last week. The group usually shared and critiqued one chapter from two different writers, in order to keep meetings short, and therefore easy to schedule regularly. Lily didn't know why she'd been thrust to the head of the line, but at least she'd have something to show Mr. Gates by tomorrow night.

All her furious typing last night had yielded nothing substantial. She kept circling around the same opening chapter, hoping that if she got it right, the rest of the story would flow like ale from a broken spigot. That was how the first two books had happened. Lily had sent the writing group an old version of the chapter, so maybe they could help her find what was wrong with it.

Josie said, "We usually go alphabetically, so Miss Harper, you're first. We start by having the author remind us of the premise to give everything clarity."

Lily cleared her throat and sat up straight. "In short, a city gal gets dragged back to her mountain hometown by an emergency, and as she's forced to spend time there, she grows to love it."

"Aw, I love those stories," Lydia said. "I don't care how many the Hallmark channel makes. So, naturally, I loved it! I'm sorry. I'm a gusher. I'm worthless with criticism."

Walt said, "So naturally, we all love her."

The chapter did not show that much: the main girl, Elsa—her fourth name of ten so far—worked for a marketing firm in Los Angeles, and seemed to have it all. Decent job, busy night life, cute boys making eyes across the meeting room, and of course, a dog. Lily thought her fans would riot if she didn't include a dog. Then, of course, as Elsa headed home, she got a call that something bad happened to her dad. End of chapter. Because Lily couldn't figure out what that bad thing was.

"That's good suspense," Josie said. She'd also liked the first line: *Elsa did not want to go home for Christmas, no matter what Dad's doctor said.* Lily was pretty proud of that, too.

So, a good beginning and a good ending. The pages in between? Lily couldn't figure out why, but they just didn't do it for her.

Sadly, the writing group did not have much help to offer on that front. Josie said she liked the setup of a potential love interest pulling the main character back into the city. Maybe start him off as a boyfriend? Walt said he empathized with the meeting scene, how boring everybody was. He offered a few details to make the feeling even stronger. Lydia, as promised, loved everything.

Kind. Encouraging. Not helpful. Nothing gave her scene the zest it needed.

Lily tried the last member. "Curtis? What do you think?"

Curtis stared into his computer screen, scrolling up and

31

down, up and down. At length, he said, "I agree with Josie: the first line is quite good." He scrolled a bit more. "The rest of it was pretty darn basic."

Something cold splattered in the back of Lily's brain, like an egg cracking against her skull and dripping down her neck. "Basic?"

Curtis nodded without looking up from his screen. "Basic. You know, bland. Commonplace."

He's scrawny, Lily suddenly realized. That tight shirt didn't outline a rippling, muscular torso, just a flat rectangle with apathetic humps for shoulders.

"Curtis," Josie said in what sounded like a deliberately even tone. "Didn't we talk about being nice to newcomers?"

Curtis replied, "She's no newcomer. Lily Harper, twice published, taking the romance world by storm. I'm sure she can take a bit of honesty." His eyes met hers at last.

Lily mentally sketched his gaze so that she could use it in a novel one day. A handsome hero would look deep into his lady fair with those exact brown eyes—except Lily would add affection, empathy, and general human kindness so that the searching depths of those eyes would come off as warm and protective, and less like a robber breaking and entering into the soul.

Curtis returned his gaze to his laptop. "The whole chapter reads like a court proceeding. This happens, then that happens, then the other thing happens. It's a list of events more than a story."

Also, Lily continued over the mayflies droning in her brain, *who has a soul patch? Either grow a beard or don't.*

Josie sighed. "Please excuse Curtis. He has high standards."

Curtis cocked his head at her. "You always say that like it's a flaw."

Lily swallowed hard, trying to focus her eyes. She was hardly new to criticism; she'd read her one-star reviews. She'd just never met one in the flesh. "Can…you give an example?"

Curtis's eyebrows hopped once, like he had been dying for that question. "One comes to mind, near the end of the chapter. Where…? Here it is. 'Elsa walked out the door and into a huge snowstorm.'"

"What's wrong with that?" Lydia asked with a defensive furrow in her brow.

"Functionally? Nothing. It tells us what we need to know, but it does nothing more. It doesn't evoke the senses, doesn't immerse the reader. It's just words on paper. Is the snowstorm dangerous, or just annoying? Is it an over-shook snow globe, thick but friendly? Or is it a whirling, wintry white slapping your scarf around for daring to stand in its way?"

Lily couldn't answer. She was still stuck on the phrase "just words on paper." Bland. Basic. Lily's bitterest reviewers had called her many things: saccharine, sentimental, even regressive. She didn't care. She liked her heartwarming romances, and some people did not. That was fine.

But no one had ever said she was just words on paper. It made her books sound so cold, so dry, so…barren.

And worst of all, she could *feel* his descriptions on her skin. The over-shook snow globe. The whirling, wintry white. If the first touched her skin, she'd shiver once, and grin with a red-cheeked glow. The second wouldn't touch her; it would scrape.

If my descriptions touched my readers, would they even know it?

Lily clenched her belly muscles, and forced her mouth to smile. "That's very good. But I think my readers have simpler tastes." Not her best reply, but an amateur couldn't talk back against actual readers. Lily turned her face away, ready to end the conversation.

But Curtis said, "Your readers deserve better, Miss Harper." There were those eyes again, smashing into her pupils and blinding her with pain that echoed in her temples. "The story of the girl who trades in the three-piece suit and falls in love with flannel is not just a well-worn road, it's a freeway. Your readers could drive it blindfolded, and they probably do. If you actually want your readers to open their eyes, then first you have to open your own."

"All right, enough," Josie ordered. "We're here to build each other up, Curtis, not tear each other down."

Curtis's mouth shifted left and right, but he did not open it again. He gave Lily a perfunctory nod, then finally dropped his gaze.

Lily breathed at last. Her ears rang, and she had to stare at the table just to steady her swaying vision. Her cheekbone itched, a phantom pain from the blow that passed right through her flesh, but still broke something inside.

The table had gone deathly quiet. Some teenagers a few tables over cackled like hyenas, a garish noise against their bubble of disquietude.

Lily took in a breath, then said, "Thank you for your

feedback." Hollow, wispy words, but she didn't have any others.

"Don't listen to Curtis," Walt told her as the group broke up. "He's just mad because you're published and he isn't."

Lily heard Curtis mumble, "Not traditionally."

She couldn't reply. She thanked everyone for their time, then she made for her car with quick, careful steps, as though the sidewalk was made of ice, crackling beneath her heels.

Walt was right, of course. Lily was a published author. People stopped her for autographs. Women gushed over her. She had fans and followers, not to mention a contract—a conditional one—for a book she hadn't even finished yet! What did Curtis have, besides cynicism and tiny lips?

So why did she shake when she went home that night? Why did she close all the curtains even though that just showed more of their chunky-lace pattern? This wasn't a wounded heart, this was fear. Like Curtis's words might break through a window at any moment.

Or more accurately, his eyes. A plain, dirt brown color, but they had substance, a physical force that wouldn't let up. What was it? Disgust? Snobbishness? Maybe jealousy? Why did she feel it so keenly?

Only when she crawled into bed that night did Lily finally put a word to Curtis's eyes: disdain. But not for the book. Not even for Lily herself. He despised the very barriers she put between him and her. The warm blankets she'd wrapped around herself, woven with threads of "It'll be okay." The cozy fleece of "People like me." The very sunlight that whispered, "I'm fine."

Please, his eyes hissed as they slapped away her layers, leaving her cold and bare. *As if you weren't thinking the exact same thing.*

Chapter 5

Surprising no one, reading Curtis's full critique the next day did not help Lily's mood. It was nothing but red. Red lines slashed through her words, red text showing her how it's really done, even the sidebar comments had a red outline. Her book was bleeding.

Why is this here? he asked of entire paragraphs.

More, he demanded of descriptions.

For one whole page, he wrote, *Cut all this. It adds nothing.*

Lily kept springing up from her writing desk and pacing the room, which only made her circle that stupid light that looked as though a firecracker had frozen mid-bang.

Why that light? Lily asked herself as she rotated it. *What is wrong with a normal, dome-shaped light? Why draw attention to it? How much more did this cost than a standard fixture?*

That only made Lily grumble lower in her throat. She swore to replace that stupid light, but that meant finishing the book to make money. Lily plopped her butt back in her chair, then remembered she was still reading Curtis's many, many opinions.

Read. Fume. Pace. Hate exploding light. Sit. Repeat.

For twelve hours.

Lily switched up the routine now and then, such as pacing through her living room. That only brought her within range of the treadmill and weights. *Were you hinting at something, Mary? I'll have you know my thighs are to die for.*

She tried sitting in the purple bean bag chair. It hurt her back.

She went for a jog, and that felt amazing, breathing in that clean mountain air. But after the shower, Curtis's specter was still waiting with arms folded and eyes glaring.

Lily even tried her greatest weapon: sensory input. She lit an old candle simply titled "Christmas Tree," and breathed deeply over its little flame. Fir and spice, the smell of green with white flakes of frost. She could almost feel the cold fog leaving her breath, and the tingly rosiness in her cheeks. She imagined her skin prickling as she walked into a warm house. Laughter gushed from the living room as other guests listened to cold stories told over eggnog and hot cider...

"And let me guess," came Curtis's caustic voice, *"she tries to walk into the living room, but bumps into Captain Handsome and oh, look! Mistletoe right above them. Wink, nod, gag."*

Lily scoffed, and the candle blew out.

By sunset, Lily sat in her writing chair, slumped and drooping. Hating Curtis's words didn't make her own any stronger. Hating everything Mary put in her house made her feel like an ungrateful sister.

And Mr. Gates wanted his chapter by tonight.

What a disappointment she was.

Lily tried one more time to write up a chapter from scratch, doing her best to emulate Curtis's way with imagery and wordplay. She had a few good moments, but ultimately it felt like tracing somebody else's drawing.

Then, a funny, fuzzy caterpillar of an idea wormed through her head. Lily looked at Curtis's markups one more time. She moved the mouse up to the top of the document, and clicked the "Accept" button on the first change. Then the next. And the next. Every time he gave her an alternate line, she took it. When he didn't, she deleted her own words and tried something fresh. That was rare; Curtis didn't seem to trust her to come up with her own descriptions.

His comments, however, took more time. They were broader, asking large-scope questions like, *How in the frozen hell do you call yourself a writer?* Roughly translated. Lily did her best. *What's the point of this scene?* She added more hints that the busy corporate life wasn't what Elsa wanted. *Why is this character here?* Lily couldn't answer that, so she deleted him.

Lily saved the chapter under a new title, "Version C," then read it from start to finish.

It wasn't quite her style. Sharper, like a box cutter. And yet, Lily groaned to admit, it popped right off the page.

Lily checked the time. Nine p.m. Eleven for Mr. Gates in New York. She was pushing the definition of "weekend" to its breaking point. Mr. Gates wanted a chapter.

Well...

Lily's hand moved the mouse while her eyes watched from a distance. Email opened. File attached.

It's not stealing, Lily told herself. *They were suggestions, that's all. You can't say you own a critique. It's still my story. Even if Elsa is a bit snarkier than I'd like her to be now, and the city boy is more of a villain than I planned on, and most of the descriptions weren't my own words. It's still my idea.*

She typed an empty hello for Mr. Gates. Now she just had to…

Send.

Lily jumped back in her seat, hands flying into the surrender position.

After a full minute like that, Lily slowly stood up from her chair, her vision a rolling blanket of white. She left the room, turned off all the lights, and slid into her bed. Then she stared at the ceiling for two more hours, wondering what exactly she had just done.

Lily couldn't write the next morning. Why bother? If Mr. Gates hated the chapter, she'd have to start over. If he loved it, she still didn't know what to do about chapter two. Instead, she ambled in circles through her house, a cup of French-pressed coffee in her hands getting cooler by the second.

She decided she needed inspiration. She turned on her TV and flipped through the peppy romances with titles like *Princess for a Day* and *Twice in a Lifetime.* One film's description came close to her story: a girl from Chicago went to write a journalism piece on the country bumpkins, only to fall in love with a good ol' boy who owned a blueberry farm.

Lily shrugged. "I'd marry a guy for free blueberries." She flopped onto her couch and coughed out a wheezing yelp as her back smacked something hard under the tissue-thin cushion. She'd forgotten that her brand new couch was both ugly *and* uncomfortable. Lily groaned and wiped the coffee spill off her shirt—or rather rubbed it in deeper. Thank God she was still in her jammies.

Mary's bill still sat on the counter. *What if I just returned the couch?* Lily could say she'd tried it, but it just didn't work out. That way, she could replace it with a couch she actually liked in a color that didn't burst her eyeballs. Yeah, that was a good idea! Mary wouldn't be offended if she just returned the couch, and kept the workout equipment, the artwork, the bean bag chair, the coffee maker, the entire kitchen, the bonkers light in her office, the... Suddenly, returning the couch felt like plugging her finger into one of the holes in the Titanic.

Besides, Mary had tried her best...

Lily put a pillow behind her back and pressed play on the blueberry movie. *Blue No More.* Cute. She managed to actually lose herself in antioxidant escapism for over an hour before her phone buzzed.

Mr. Gates.

Lily snatched her phone, accidentally flicked it up over her head, slapped her hands over it like a clam shell, then answered. "Yes, hello?" Lily hit the off button on her TV, just as Mr. Right was giving Miss Protagonist a berry-blue dress, just in time for the country dance. *Aww...*

"Miss Harper," said Mr. Gates, "I've read your chapter."

Spiders crawled up Lily's spine. *Of course you freaking read my chapter! Why else would you be freaking calling me?! Now stop telling me the freaking obvious and freaking tell me what you freaking think of my freaking book you freaking freaker!*

"Oh, yes?" she said in a chipmunk-chipper voice.

"It's a bit different from the last books you've sent me."

41

Lily wiped the coffee stain some more. "Yes, I, uh, got some feedback from a local writing group and tried to follow their advice." *Hey, it was true.*

"Hmm."

That was it.

Lily yearned for the days of landlines, when she could curl her finger around the cord. With her smartphone, Lily could only twirl her finger in the air like some kind of miniature conductor. "Is it…too far from the brief?"

"Honestly?"

Why did that word make her guts recoil? "Yes?"

"Lily, this is easily the best chapter you've ever written."

Her fingers froze mid-twirl. Prickles fizzed on her neck, like someone was hissing hateful words onto her skin. "The…best?"

"Easily," Mr. Gates said. "It has more zest this time. A bit on the cynical edge for the genre, but I really love the attention you gave to the details."

She rubbed her neck, trying to chase away the voice just beneath her ear, laughing through its teeth. "Yeah?"

"Yeah. I mean, your other books were fine— obviously, since we're still writing you royalty checks— but this is a step up. It's like you're a real writer!"

The heat on her neck vanished. So did the pressure of her own hand. And the ends of her toes, her ears, all the tips of her seemed to disappear, and her sense of the planet with it. Everything was as white and bare and chemically-cleaned as her modern kitchen.

"I…*am*." It shot out of her chest, a cannonball of

lightning, snapping death in every direction, but squished in her constricted throat, and scraped along her dry tongue. By the time it reached her lips, it was barely more than a puff of wind.

"Damn right you are!" Mr. Gates went on with a laugh in his voice. "You've laid the foundation, Miss Harper, now it's time to knock it out of the park."

Mixing metaphors, said a voice in her head that was a little too close to Curtis's.

"Thank you," Lily heard her voice say. She hadn't told it to do that.

"And you'll still have the entire book in by June thirtieth, right?"

Lily flitted her eyes to the calendar on the kitchen wall. May thirtieth. "Yes."

"Because that was the original deadline."

"Mm-hmm."

"It's just that I got a little worried when it took this long to see even a sample."

"That's understandable."

"But you'll get it done?"

"Yes."

"Atta girl, Miss Harper. I'll leave you to weave your magic."

"Thank you, Mr. Gates."

The line went dead. Looking at her phone, Lily realized it was her thumb that ended the call. She still couldn't feel anything outside her torso, that tight, curled-up ball shivering in the corner of her soul.

A real writer.

Lily's numb feet carried her into the office. Her office.

The one she'd built with her own two hands—or books, rather. *Secrets in Sand. Maple Leaves.* Lily took both books off the shelves and looked down at their pretty, cozy covers.

Was I...not real before?

They were "fine," he'd said. Still sending her royalty checks, he said. How was that not real? Lily's words had moved more copies with two books than most authors saw in their entire lives! She'd been interviewed in magazines, podcasts, and more! Lily Harper's books were in bookstores and libraries nationwide! She'd been asked for an autograph just two days ago! People loved her books! How was that not real?

Another thought pulsed through her veins, jolting every nerve awake with needlelike assault. She'd heard something long ago, something she had shrugged off as irrelevant. Some agents, some editors— or was it most?— would accept a book they did not like because they knew it would sell. Then they'd use that money to take chances on books they actually believed in.

The books slipped from Lily's hands. They hit the floor with a wheezing rumple, their pristine corners buckling under the weight, twisting into woebegone shapes.

But so what? There were thousands of others—tens of thousands, maybe. In bookstores and libraries nationwide. They were so easily replaced, each indistinguishable from the last.

Lily managed to stumble backwards before her knees buckled entirely, and she landed in the purple fluff of her giant sack chair. She curled into its squashy depths, and tried to put her world back together.

Chapter 6

Mom, Mary, Mandy, and James all lowered their copies of chapter one and gave a collective, "Wow."

Which was the absolute last thing Lily wanted to hear. "Really?" she whined.

She'd taken copies of the chapter to her family that same evening after dinner. Her editor may have the last word, but Lily still wanted somebody else's opinion, preferably those who knew her, who'd read her work from the beginning.

All five people couldn't quite fill Mary's spacious living room, not even with her golden retriever pouting by the fireplace because no one would give him another treat. Mary's ginormous egg-white sectional alone could have fit eight or ten people. It would have looked bare with only Lily and Mandy sitting on it, except for the crowd of creampuff pillows.

Mary and Mom each sat on gray, armless chairs with upholstery stretched across their feet like an overly-modest church lady. Mary sat up straight, giving everybody whiplash with her bright red work dress. "Sweetie, you know I love all your work, but this one is easily the most enjoyable read. It feels like you did a lot better with the descriptions this time. That part with the snowstorm? I could actually feel the snow on my neck; I almost shivered!"

Mom nodded along with every word. "It's like being sucked in!"

"Same," Mandy said.

Lily turned to her last resort: her brother-in-law, James, lazing in the chair by the fire. The only reason he held a copy of Lily's chapter was because Mary had shoved it in his hands. "Even you?"

James frowned. "It's not that I didn't like your other books; I'm just not a romance reader. This one, though? Yeah, it's got a little…"

"Zest?" Lily guessed.

"That's the word."

Lily leaned forward on the couch, curling her back more and more, until her forehead bonked on the coffee table and stayed there.

She didn't care if it was dramatic. The thought that her wonderful words had been nothing more than passable fluff aimed at a profitable market was too heavy for her neck to lift. Lily never thought her writing was gourmet, but she at least considered herself to be Mom's home cooking. It never crossed her mind that she was little more than McDonald's.

Then Mandy said, "Or…it can be terrible if you like. Yeah, just the worst."

"Mandy!" Mary snapped.

"What? She knows I'm joking."

"We do not tear down in this family. We build up."

"I said it was a joke!"

Mom said, "Listen to Mary, dear."

The couch shifted under Lily's rear. Mandy flopping back with a grumpy scoff, no doubt.

A second later, the couch shifted again as someone sat

next to Lily and rubbed her back. "What's the matter, sweetie?" Mary asked.

Lily raised her head, but let her curtain of brown hair hang over her eyes. What could she possibly say to them now? *Your sister is a dime-a-dozen paperback time-waster? And the best chapter I ever wrote wasn't really mine?*

She went with, "I don't think I have it in me to keep up that kind of writing *and* meet my deadline."

"Can't you push it back?"

Lily shook her head. "One delay leads to another. Mr. Gates has to read the whole book and give feedback, I have to make any final changes, the cover artist needs time, plus printing and distribution. Otherwise, it won't be ready in November."

Mandy said, "I thought it was a Christmas book."

"Mr. Gates says holiday books need to come out a month early to get enough traction for the actual holiday."

Mary pushed Lily's hair behind her ear. "Then don't struggle too hard. Your last two books were just fine, so if you need to dial it back to meet your deadline, no big deal."

Lily knew in her head that every one of Mary's words was meant kindly, but they only echoed the constant drip of self-criticism. She was "just fine." She was "no big deal." Would people get bored of her soon?

Do any of my words really sink in?

James finally excused himself and made for his man cave. The golden retriever trotted after him with a determined look that said, "If I can just isolate him from the female, maybe he will give me a snack."

Mary gave her sister a balmy hug, and said she had some things to do. "Don't you have homework, Mandy?"

"I'll get to it," Mandy replied in an even tone.

Mary ignored the comment, but tucked Mandy's hair behind her ears as well. As soon as Mary walked upstairs, Mandy ruffled her hair into a mess of frizz.

"Don't be like that," Mom said, hoisting herself up from her chair. She cupped Lily's face and said, "I think your book will make a lot of people smile, and that's the important thing."

Somehow, those words reached all the way into her well of doubt, and lifted her up on warm, technicolor wings. "Thanks, Mom." Mom headed to her room to watch her cop dramas, and Lily sank into the couch cushions, knowing she should leave and at least try to make another chapter.

Also, why isn't my couch this comfy, Mary?

Mandy curled her legs under herself and turned fully towards Lily. "So how come you can't keep writing like this and make the deadline?"

Lily's brain had a drop-down menu for every category of excuses that were just true enough. *I don't have the time. It's not my usual voice.* However, Lily was still riding the warm updraft of Mom's encouragement. So this time, before she could really think about it, Lily glanced over the couch to make sure nobody was in the kitchen, then said to Mandy, "Because I didn't write it."

It was like spiders skittering across her lips. She wiped her face and added, "I had help from my writing group. Well, one person in particular. He gave me a million suggestions, and I took them all. And now everybody likes his words more than mine."

49

Why was she so out of breath? Her lungs felt like jelly, like her thighs like did when she finally sat down after miles of running.

Mandy regarded her with wide, blue eyes. Lily could almost hear the innocence shattering. Yet when those eyes turned back to the chapter on Mandy's lap, Lily saw no accusation in them. "Well, it's still your story, right?"

"I guess so."

"You guess?" Mandy echoed. "I know it. Girl leaves a busy, bustling life to go find peace and quiet somewhere just in time for Christmas? And she's going to meet a cute boy along the way, right? That's classic Lily Harper."

Lily narrowed her eyes at this perceptive little sage. "You're twelve."

"Almost thirteen." She patted Lily's thigh with sugar-loaded excitement. "Don't forget the fancy dress for the party!"

Lily chuckled. "I will."

"And a date! Everybody else already has one."

What, seriously? It had been, like, four days! Granted, half her family was married. Ugh, Lily could not fathom having the energy for a man right now, not with barely more than a month until her deadline. But… "I'll find one." Mandy was family. *We're all in this together*, as Mary used to say.

Mandy picked up the chapter printout one more time, and rested her head against her fist. "That guy who gave you all those suggestions. Could he help?"

Lily barked out a nasty laugh. "I would rather gargle paint than go on any kind of date with him."

"No, no, I meant, could he help you with the rest of

your book?"

Lily blinked, too dumbstruck to process those words. "Him...help me? What?"

"He helped with this chapter, didn't he? Maybe he could help with the rest. You know, like show you how he did it, and then you can take his advice and make your own thing out of it."

A low, bitter chuckle oozed out of Lily's mouth. "I sincerely doubt he would be willing to work with me that much."

Mandy shrugged. "You could ask. What do you have to lose?"

The mulched remains of my self-respect. "I think it's better if he and I don't work in close proximity."

"Why not? Is he cute?" Her entire face lit up at the possibility.

"No."

"Ooh, is he a jerk?"

Lily shook her head and stood up. "Not going there."

"Aw, why not?"

"Because a young lady who writes heartfelt romance novels should not sully her tongue with the filthy words required to accurately describe that man. Besides, I have to hit the library on the way home. Maybe I'll find some inspiration in the romance section."

Mandy bounced off the couch. "Can I come? I'll be quiet."

"Uh..." Lily felt like wallowing in jealousy and self-pity, which was better alone.

But Mandy whispered, "Please?"

Lily eyed the stairs Mary had ascended, then nodded.

51

Fluff writer or not, she knew when some people needed an escape.

Lily's car slithered down the mountain road, headlights piercing the dim gray beneath the evergreens that blocked the setting sun.

"Thanks for getting me out of there," Mandy said. "If Mary keeps acting like my mom, I swear I'm going to scream."

"Are you and Mary okay?" Lily asked.

Mandy instantly slouched in her seat, scrunched her head into her collarbone, and crossed her arms tight across her chest. "She is *always* bossing me around! And not just about, like, chores or whatever; little things, too. 'Mandy, get to bed on time.' 'Mandy, wear this outfit instead.' 'Mandy, don't make jokes because we have to look like a perfect family.'" She glanced sideways at Lily. "I was joking, by the way. I don't think your story was bad."

"I know," Lily said. "And that's just how Mary is. She thinks she knows best because she usually does."

"She doesn't know what's best for me." Mandy sulked in silence until the car finally broke free of the evergreen shadows and spilled into the bright, red-tinted highway. Then she asked, "Hey, Lily...is there, like, any chance at all that I could stay with you instead?"

The words scraped Lily's ear like nails on a chalkboard, making her cringe. Was it really that bad between them? Lily frowned. "You know I love you, kiddo, but I don't want to separate you from Mom."

Mandy sighed and rested her cheek on her fist. "Yeah, I guess so."

Thank goodness that got sorted, because Lily could barely concentrate on the girl. A bubble had been rising in her gut ever since she showed the chapter to her family. It was heavy as a stone, squashing her stomach and pushing her lungs off to the side. Lily found it hard to breathe. Yet despite the crushing weight, a bubble it remained, a flimsy membrane holding back the scream inside.

Today was May thirtieth. Lily's entire book would be due on June thirtieth. Just over a month, with only a single chapter written, one she did not pen herself.

I can't do this.

Even if she could turn her scribbles into calligraphy, Lily had nothing to write. Chapter two just would not show up in her head, except in fuzzy lumps that didn't fit together. How could she do in thirty days what she hadn't done in months?

They arrived at the library before Lily could find an answer. She hoped she had the strength to fight back the tears threatening to claw their way out of her eyes.

Lily could not count how many times she'd been into this library, checking out every girly romance she could find. She'd read several right there in those off-white chairs. They sat beneath a fireplace nestled in a colossal stone pillar that rose up the center of the library, as though the city had found it in the woods and built the library around it. With book signings, and meet-the-writer events, Lily knew every librarian by name, and always gave a friendly hello, if not flat-out stopping her day to chat.

Today, Lily ducked her head and looked the other

direction. She didn't want anyone to see the terror on her face. Fortunately, the library would soon close, so most of the chairs and rows were empty.

Lily wandered the aisles with no real plan in mind. What could inspire her out of this funk that she hadn't read before? What was short enough to devour in a day or two, as not to waste precious hours? Where was the miracle book that would save her now?

Her feet led her to the "H" section. Harper, L. Adult fiction. *Local!* The library had a couple copies of each book, and only one remained at the moment. *Further proof I can move merchandise.* It used to make her heart pirouette to see empty shelves where her book should be. Now, it just pounded.

What was wrong with selling to the masses anyway? Popular books could be good!

So why does everybody like some nobody's work better than mine?

Lily stared at the ocean-blue spine of her first book. Why was it so easy the first time?

Because you got lucky.

Why couldn't she get these oozing voices out of her head?

Because you know we're right.

Lily pulled her eyes away from the past and left the aisle. There *had* to be something that could give her inspiration. She swung around the outside of the aisle, passing the navy blue chairs nestled by the wall of windows. In the furthest chair, washed in red sunlight, sat Curtis.

Lily whipped back around, darted into the aisle, and

slammed into Mandy, whom Lily had completely forgotten.

"Oof!" Mandy cried.

"Shh!" Lily shoved the girl further into the aisle, glancing over her shoulder to make sure he hadn't heard. Not that she could see him from this angle.

Mandy massaged her nose. "What are we doing?"

"Hiding."

"Why?"

"Remember that jerk who edited my book into an unrecognizable mess?"

"The book we liked?"

"Yes," she growled. "He's sitting a couple rows down."

Mandy moved, ducking under Lily's snatching hand, until she could peek around the corner. A few seconds later, Mandy turned back around, her nose wrinkled. "I thought he'd be fat."

"What? Why?"

Mandy shrugged. "Also, have we seen him before?"

"Huh?" Lily peeked again. There *was* something oddly familiar about Curtis. She was certain she'd have recognized the soul patch, but Lily couldn't place him. "I...don't think so. Whatever, let's just go the other way. I am in *no* mood to deal with him today."

"Ooh, wait!" Mandy whisper-screamed, grabbing Lily's wrist. "You could ask him to help with your book!"

Lily's brain computer fired up an endless list of preferable alternatives: *drink cyanide, juggle beehives, bowl with my own head...* "No," Lily said, showing all of her bottom teeth.

"Why not?"

"Because I could barely stand being around him for half an hour. He's nitpicky, he talks down to me, I don't want to deal with that for the next month."

Mandy crossed her arms and stuck out her hip—very Mary-like. "And I don't want to go back home and deal with Queen Bee every day, but you say I should."

That actually made Lily pause. For two-point-two seconds. "That's different. Mary is family. Family cares, even if we suck at it." Lily jabbed her finger in Curtis's general direction, and half-expected to see lightning leap from her nails. "That man cares about nobody and nothing."

"Wow, judgmental much?"

Yet again, Lily paused. How much did she really know Curtis? He'd been a squatter in her head for days, but she had actually only met him one time.

Lily paced in a discombobulated circle, colorful book spines blurring in a rainbow whirlwind. "I don't want to work with him. I really don't think I could handle it." Her temples were pinching already.

Mandy said, "Yes you could. You're awesome."

"Having a magnifying glass over every typo? No thank you."

"Then I'll punch him in the junk until he says it nicely."

"Why are—" Lily swallowed back her volume. "Why won't you let this go?!"

Mandy took Lily's hand and squeezed it. "Because I want to see your next book. Maybe that jerk-waffle will make it sound fancier, but it'll still be your book. And I want to read it."

Lily shook. She covered her mouth, and then her eyes. That dam had been swelling when she walked in the door. Mandy's sweetness shot a crack right through the foundations. Lily squeezed her gut, and clenched her jaw tight, suffering the pain of the swelling lump in her throat. She couldn't stop her eyes, though, those traitorous, gushing eyes. She turned to the bookshelf, hand covering her face, trying to look deep in thought instead of drowning in a sea of nameless hurt.

Bless her, Mandy didn't speak. Not for over a full minute as Lily gulped back the hurricane and dried her eyes—or rather, soaked her sleeve.

Eventually, she found just enough breath to whisper, "Kiddo, I don't...I don't know if there's even going to be a book."

Mandy rubbed Lily's arm, then whispered, "So ask for help."

I can't do this. Even if she never told another soul what she'd just told Mandy, Lily knew. And it scared the breath out of her.

Lily raised her eyes, and found them gazing directly at her first book. Whatever magic she'd had back then was gone. But writing was more than magic. There was still skill. Skill could be practiced, and improved. Maybe she had been gliding on fairy dust all this time, but maybe she could grow her own wings.

She thought of her house, with its beautiful bones, its great windows looking out on a greater view. She had fainted the first time she saw the monthly payment. Advances and royalties had stuffed her savings account, and Lily knew she could still go get a day job to help. But they would only delay the problem, not fix it. She had built her house on her novels, and their breakaway success.

And she had sworn to do anything to keep it. Work three jobs. Sell both kidneys. Anything for that quiet, safe, solid space cuddled around her, every inch of it labeled *mine*.

One month. One book. If only she could bear it.

Lily Harper wiped her eyes and set her jaw. *Time to become a real writer.*

Chapter 7

Lily peeked around the bookshelf again. Maybe Curtis had wandered off, a message from God to walk away? Nope, still cross-legged in his big blue chair. At least he wore a shirt that fit this time: a black polo, with equally-inky slacks. Did he write edgy gothic horror or something?

Lily ducked back into the aisle and blew out a sigh. "So how do I convince him?"

Mandy shrugged. "Feminine wiles?"

"If I had those, I'd have a boyfriend." Charm was easy to write, when you could make up what the other person found compelling. When that person thought your life's work was a joke, though?

"*Attention customers*," echoed a warbled voice on the intercom. "*Thank you for visiting your local library. We will be closing in ten minutes.*"

"You might want to figure it out," Mandy said.

"Oh, thanks, that really helps," Lily grumbled.

"Just go right up to him and ask!"

"And if he says no?"

"I dunno, I'm twelve. You figure it out."

Oh now *you're a kid*, Lily thought. Mandy was right again, though. Lily was stalling. She took a deep breath, shook out the tingles in her arms, and swung around the bookshelf to go meet Curtis.

She smacked right into his chest, bounced backwards, and

landed on her butt. Hard. Apparently, he'd moved.

"Ow!" she cried.

"Jeez, sorry!" Curtis reached out a hand. He froze halfway, his eyes and mouth perfect circles of surprise. "Miss Harper?"

Lily hoisted herself up, sending a throb of pain through her hip. "Ow."

"You okay?"

Nope, said her left buttock, but Lily did not want to talk to *this* man about the state of her ass. "I'm fine, Mister...uh, Curtis."

"Reynolds."

"I knew that."

"Okay."

He's short! Lily's brain squawked. Well, not that short. Eye-level with her, so five-eight? Even her brother Oak was five-ten. Lily couldn't remember ever looking at a man without tilting her head.

Being eye-level, however, made it that much easier to see she'd been crying. "Are you okay?" he asked.

"Allergies," Lily lied immediately. "Pollen everywhere."

"Ah."

"Yup."

Curtis drummed one of his books on the others, glancing over her shoulder towards the door.

Lily ran her dry tongue across the back of her teeth. She was supposed to say something, but where to start? Dive right in? He'd probably say no. She had to sell the idea somehow.

Curtis gave a slow, patient nod. "Well...good luck

60

with the book." He started past her.

Lily turned to stop him. "I could lose my house!"

That stopped him all right, mid-stride and everything. "Oh...that...sucks."

Lily felt dizzy. Why in the world had she started *there*? Even her family didn't know that! Well, Mandy did now. *Get it together, Harper!* "I mean, not right away. Not for maybe a year, if I'm lucky. I saved. Book sales have me secure for a while at least."

Something darkened in Curtis's eyes, and the flickers of pity fled his face. "Well," he said in a low, throaty tone, "lucky you." He turned again, quicker this time.

In a flash, Lily realized she sounded like she was bragging. "B-But I could still lose it!"

Curtis paused again, but only looked over his shoulder.

Lily continued, "I need to keep writing to...to keep paying the bills, you know? So I need to write another book. The one you read."

His face remained blank. "Given your track record, I'm sure you'll sell plenty." He marched off once more.

How could something go so sideways before she'd even started? She still had to ask for help and now he was mad!

Or jealous...

No time for that! Lily opened her mouth to shout out what she wanted, then realized she was about to yell her personal business across the library. That in mind, Lily dashed into the aisle, nearly tackling a quick-footed Mandy. Lily grabbed the other end of the aisle to swing around, dashed down the main thoroughfare, and spun at the end of the last aisle to smack into Curtis yet again.

And fall. Again. At least she hurt a different buttock this

time.

Curtis, short and scrawny though he was, only staggered a little. "Really?"

Lily bounced up, mouthing a word that would make Mary faint. Curtis did not look any happier. Well, then it couldn't get worse.

"Do you want to help?" she asked.

At least his face went from ticked to confused. "Help what?"

Lily glanced to the left, to the old librarian behind the check-out counter, and the young Hispanic couple staring at the scene. Lily flashed a smile, then took Curtis by the elbow and ushered him behind another aisle of books. Safely tucked between Sanderson and Tolkien, Lily tried again. "Would you want to help me write my next book?"

Curtis stared into her for a long time, steely eyes probing.

Lily bounced on her heels, holding her breath so hard her skull was about to pop.

"Are you screwing with me?" Curtis asked with a serious face.

"No. I really mean it."

"Why?"

Lily wished she had brought her purse in so that she could strangle something. As it stood, her own throat was getting that treatment. "Because I can't do it alone. My deadline is coming up and I...I won't make it. I need help, or I kiss my contract goodbye, and the only real means I have for paying off the house I literally just moved into."

Curtis set his three books on top of a shelf, apparently so he could cross his arms. "And why me? I got the feeling you weren't my biggest fan."

No, and I'd rather sell myself to a sweat shop, mow the lawn with my teeth, write the entire Bible in my own blood... "You pointed out several areas of...improvement I could stand to learn."

"And just like that you want to work together?"

What did he want, the whole, buck-naked truth? *Buy me a drink first!* "I took some of your edits to heart. A lot of them. And then I showed the new chapter to some people and, well, they liked your version better." It was sandpaper on the soul, but it was true.

Curtis asked, "What people?"

"People who know my writing, all of it. Yours was better."

His eyes narrowed. Was he really thinking it? Curtis asked, "When's the deadline?"

Lily said, "June thirtieth."

Those eyes shot back open. "A month?! How much have you written?"

"Well, if we don't change the chapter you already saw... one chapter."

Curtis laughed. Not a happy one.

Lily cut in with, "It's just like national novel writing month! Have you ever done that?"

"Yeah, by myself, when I didn't need someone to double-check every word. And even that was a first draft. You need a finished manuscript, which means edits, rewrites, rereads. I've got a life, you know."

Those were some excellent points. Lily had *never* finished a novel in a month, or even tried. She scrambled to think of a reply. "We'd work in the evenings. You come over after work every day, we cram in some good ideas, and I type them out. I don't have a day job, so that gives me plenty of time to put words to paper."

Only after the words left her lips did Lily realize that the guy who slashed her manuscript to shreds would not trust her to do most of the writing. She saw her mistake in his downturned mouth, the way his shoulders seemed to slump as he rocked his head to one side, then gave up and left it there. She was losing him fast.

"Miss Harper, I don't think—"

"We'll split the profits!" Lily blurted. Surely she wasn't the only one with a mortgage.

Curtis's eyes locked on hers. *Oh, sure,* she thought, *and I'm the corporate sellout?* "What kind of split?" he asked.

A deep part of Lily had known this would happen, but she'd pushed it aside. Like eating cake every day for breakfast and conveniently ignoring diabetes. Now the diagnosis was here, and she had nobody to blame but herself.

"Fifty-fifty," she said in a hurried breath, before she could change her mind. *Half?!* her mind screamed. *I only get half of my own money?! What about my house? Wasn't this going to keep a roof over our heads?!*

Well, said a calmer voice, *do you want to share a paycheck, or do you want to keep all of that zero to yourself?*

Curtis straightened, and crossed his arms again. "I don't want to be rude—"

Lily barely bit back the scoff.

"—but what kind of money are we talking? It sounds

like a lot of work."

Lily told him what her editor had promised as an advance. "Plus royalties afterwards."

Curtis's mouth fell open. "Whoa."

Yeah, funny what happens when you write books that make people happy: they buy them.

She could see the abacus of his mind flicking back and forth. He may have thought Lily Harper was a fluffy nothing, but she was a known name that could bring in a few bucks. That thought wriggled in Lily's torso, slithering just beneath her flesh. Watching Curtis add up the dollars and cents made Lily cross her arms over her chest.

Worse, it made Lily hate herself. Why was she trying to lure in a partner who hated her work? Why was she striving to impress an editor who only liked her dollar value?

Why did so much of her life feel like standing on the street corner, waiting for people who only wanted what was on the surface?

Curtis broke into those sickly thoughts with, "So I'd help you write your next book for a month, coming over practically every night, cramming as much story as we can in every setting, working out our differences, and when it's all done, I get an even cut of the profits?"

Lily slowly nodded. "That is the plan."

"*Attention visitors,*" said the library's intercom, "*we will be closing in five minutes. Please bring your items to the checkout counter as soon as possible.*"

Curtis clicked his tongue. "I have to think about it."

Lily couldn't decide if that was better or worse. All that objectification, and he wasn't sold? "I understand. You have my email if you make a decision, but please let me know either way as soon as you can. Deadline, you know."

"Right. I will." Curtis furrowed his brow at her once more. Disgusted? Contemplating? Lily couldn't tell. Then, he nodded to her, picked up his books, and left the aisle.

The moment he was gone, Lily let herself shiver out all the snakes in her veins, scrubbing her arms with her bare hands.

Mandy zipped around the corner to join Lily. "Hey, he'll think about it at least!"

Lily scrubbed her face with her hands and said, "Let's just go."

She drove the girl home, making Mandy promise that she wouldn't tell Mary what had just happened. "She'll just worry, and I'm doing enough of that myself." As if Lily's own shame and embarrassment had nothing to do with it.

"Okay," Mandy promised, "but what about your house?"

"Definitely keep that part to yourself. I'm fine for a while, and I'll figure the rest out."

Mandy left, securing one more promise that Lily would come to her birthday with a dress and a man, and Lily drove back to the lovely house for which she would empty her veins. She even paused to touch the wood of her doorframe before entering. Amazing how fast you could love something.

Even if the stupid, "Welcome, travelers," mat made her want to yak.

Lily took a shower to wash off the feeling of a red-light district, then found an email waiting on her computer: "I'm in."

Chapter 8

On the last day of May, thirty days until the deadline, Lily didn't write a word. Curtis was coming that evening to talk shop, and Lily figured a blank slate was less likely to be ripped apart than a bare-bones attempt at chapter two.

Instead, Lily jogged the trail near her new house, huffing in the brisk morning. Soft sunlight tickled the grass and splashed across the dew. The snowy mountains looked like orange creamsicles in the early light. A tiny pond perfectly mirrored the sky, a stark, sapphire-cerulean Lily never saw outside of a crayon box. Then the wind picked up, and everything smelled cool and wet and clean.

Her lungs coughed out the old air and sucked in the new. Her veins tingled with fresh blood skittering through them. Every nerve on her prickled with life and excitement as she trotted back to her house, which sat obediently where she'd left it, hunkered down and cozy in the shadow of the mountains.

Lily walked through her front door full of electricity and sunshine. Until she turned left and saw her explosion light stretching its fat bulbs at her from the office. She swore it got bigger every day. She turned away, but only landed her gaze on that wonky, cockeyed-tangerine-on-a-hill art-thing.

So, after the hottest shower any mortal had ever attempted, Lily spent most of her day on the porch, where Mary had no reach, and searched for replacement décor on her laptop. Mary couldn't be insulted if she didn't know, right? It's not like she peeked into Lily's internet history. Even so, Lily clicked each link with the wide-eyed hypervigilance of shame-filled addict.

Why does this bug me? It's my house. I can decorate it how I want. Eventually. Piece by piece so Mary won't know...

A day of dreaming, punctuated by her favorite books, a summer salad, and a long nap recharged Lily's battery. By the time evening came, she was almost excited Curtis was coming over.

Lily had hoped to have someone cuter, taller, burlier, and capable of growing a real beard as her first dinner date, but beggars could not be choosers, and some spicy chicken tikka masala could cover a litany of flaws.

She had just set the table, fancy napkins included, when a knock resounded on the door. An old chill wriggled down her spine, but Lily ignored it. So long as her naan bread wasn't undercooked—again—this was going to be a good night. It was.

Curtis stood at the door in blue jeans and a plain button-up, this time a seaweed green. *Huh, he does wear other colors besides black,* she thought. He carried a backpack on his shoulder, and his smile sat in let's-see-how-this-goes mode.

"Come in," Lily greeted.

Curtis stepped across the threshold and looked about the large living room, and the balcony above. "So this is what we stand to lose, huh?"

"Sadly, yes. Not right away, like I said, but it'll be hard

to keep this place if I can't finish the book."

"Do you work?" Curtis asked with a rather judgmental tip of his eyebrow.

"Not right now, not with the deadline so close. Afterwards, maybe, but hopefully not. My last career sank, and I've only been able to land so-so jobs."

Curtis was already looking over her shoulder. "Neat light."

Lily spun and caught the glare of her explosion-light in the next room. "Yeah…"

He walked into the living room and dropped his backpack on the couch.

"Make yourself at home," Lily said through her teeth.

Curtis stopped in front of the minimalist art piece. "Huh. How modern."

"Yeeaaaah…"

Curtis eyed the eye-gouging white of the kitchen, too. "*Very* modern. I saw the outside of this place and expected something more rustic."

Lily nodded, her hand scratching a non-existent itch at the base of her neck. "That was the original idea, but…things changed. Um, dinner?"

"Thanks."

Lily had to pat herself on the back for this meal. The chicken practically glowed in its tiger-orange sauce, the diced jalapenos a muted green as they swam in masala. She could smell the spice and herbs from her seat, and it steamed like a commercial when she poured Curtis a serving, warm wisps whirling through the air.

Even Curtis had to say, "Wow."

Lily beamed as she scooped some chicken and rice,

eyes rolling as the creamy tang hit her tongue.

Only a bite later, Curtis said, "So how married are we to the city-gal-finds-love-back-home premise?"

Lily slowed her chewing, even if the sizzling sauce did sear the roof of her mouth. "Um, that's what the editor has agreed to."

Curtis frowned for a bit, then scooped up a second bite. "Well, time to go outside my comfort zone."

"What do you usually write?" Lily asked.

"This and that. Some urban fantasy, some contemporary fiction. I like hard-cutting stuff that takes a long, hard look at the world. Speaking of which, what's the world of this story?"

Lily cocked her head. "World? Uh, ours. It's just a contemporary story; there's no world."

Never had Lily so hated the way a smile could slice its way across a face. "I thought so."

"What?" she asked patiently.

"People think that worldbuilding is only for fantasy. *Every* story has a world. It may be a familiar world, but it's still a world. The chef has her kitchen, the athlete has the track, every single one of those young-white-female journalist stories has New York City. And there are worlds within worlds. For example, your world is the town you live in, and your sub-world is your house."

Lily looked about her home as lightning bugs flickered in her brain. Was that why Mary's décor bothered her so much? *Mary has her own home. A big one. Plus her furniture shop. And her interior design business! Her world is massive. Why does she have to reach her fingers into mine?*

But that just sounded selfish. Why did Lily want a world all to herself?

"So in your first book," Curtis continued, "the world was the beach. In the second, it was New England, plus that bookstore, I think."

Lily had to shake her head on that one. "Wait. You've read my books?"

Curtis shrugged. "Just a little. I figured if I'm going to write with you, I should do my research. I rented both books on my Kindle this morning, so I'm only a couple chapters into each of them."

"But…I got the world part right?"

Curtis rocked his head from side to side. "I mean it's clear, at least. The bookshop isn't bad so far, even if it's kinda same-y."

Same-y. Familiar. Dime-a-dozen. Lily almost preferred "lousy" at this point.

Lily reached for the naan, then decided she wasn't ready for the possibility that she'd underbaked it, and turned to the peas instead. "Okay, so how do you write a world?"

Curtis horked down a mouthful, like he'd rather talk than taste. "In short, figure out the rules that make your world go round. Like, uh…what's one of the places you worked?"

"Uh, I was a paramedic for a while, and I also did office work for a real estate office, and the hospital, too."

"Oh! The hospital? I work there, in one of the medical offices."

"Oh! I was in radiology. Just the front desk, though." Was that why he looked familiar? Maybe in the hospital's cafeteria? That job had been over a year ago, so probably not…

Curtis said, "Let's use the hospital. You know the rules there: park in certain places, swipe your badge to clock in on time, keep records for so many years, wear the right clothes, surgeons wash their hands a specific way, put sharps in the red bin, not to mention all those damn COVID regulations." He jabbed his next bite so hard that Lily jumped.

"You're not a fan of masks?" she asked.

Curtis paused with chicken halfway to his mouth. His shoulders sank, as if he'd deflated somehow. "Actually, I'm for them, it's just…never mind. The point is each world has its own rules and expectations. You don't follow hospital rules at a school, or at home, or the beach. So what is your world, anyway?"

Lily thought fast, then realized it wasn't a hard question at all. "A mountain town."

"Are we talking three-tooth backwater or gentrified tourist trap?"

"Uh…I was thinking cozy, flannel community."

Curtis sat back in his seat, looking up at the ceiling and wrinkling his nose. "That kind of world doesn't lend itself to a lot of conflict."

"Isn't that the point?" Lily asked. "An idyllic, love-your-neighbor kind of place?"

"But where's the story?"

"Pardon?"

Curtis leaned forward, his eyes boring into Lily's, and his dinner forgotten. "Stories are built on conflict. Somebody wants something, and people and obstacles get in the way. The story is how they get past those things. If there's nothing to overcome, then you may as well read a grocery list. No conflict, no story."

Yet again, Lily had to concede the point. *Secrets in Sand* had family drama. *Maple Leaves* had a bookstore to save, plus a romance to flourish. But...she wanted a snuggly Christmas story set in the kind of town she wished was real. Did she really want to bring the world's troubles into that postcard ideal?

Curtis crossed his arms. "Hmm. Actually, the fuzzy small-town vibe could work."

"Really?!" Lily's heart leapt.

"Yeah. The main girl is coming from the outside, right? From the city? That could create conflict with different values."

"Yes! That was my idea. She comes back home after so many years and sees that what she values is way different from what everybody else does."

"Okay, so she could start to see the flaws."

"The...flaws?"

"Yeah, like there's this veneer of Norman Rockwell hominess, but it's all propped up by small-town thinking, or inner strife that keep certain people and ideas perpetually in power."

Strife? Power? Lily knew many writers tackled those themes, but she'd never planned to do it herself. This didn't sound like a hot-cocoa-and-a-blanket book. It sounded like a harrowing deconstruction of everything Lily liked.

But what did she know? She was only a paperback space-filler. She still had a lot to learn.

Lily grabbed a piece of naan and ripped into it with her teeth.

Doughy.

*
**

They finished dinner soon after, and Lily showed him her writer's room. She wished she had a small couch, or at least a chair for her guest, but she just had that giant, foam plum by the window. Curtis sank into it with a shrug, and started hammering their ideas onto his laptop.

Well, his ideas, mostly. Lily didn't much care for Curtis's vision of a grouchy town held together by strings of lies and coercion. He imagined a local bank that funded everything, and had some kind of control over the town, maybe some marginalized groups pushed off to the fringes, or trailer park ghettos.

Y'know, for Christmas.

Was she a bad person for not wanting to write about those things? Lily's vision for the world had taken the marginalized and planted them right there in the middle of town. Or maybe the locals had come together to build log cabins for war refugees with nowhere to go. But that was too saccharine for Curtis's tastes.

Lily looked up at the ceiling to remind herself what she was sacrificing for. And beheld that puffy dandelion light hanging from the ceiling again.

She said, "I don't suppose you know how to replace a light fixture?"

Curtis looked up at the light. "Uh, no. I'm actually really good at plumbing, but electricity? Nah." He rolled up a sleeve and showed a faded, but angry red line across his forearm. "That's the day I learned what a breaker switch is."

Lily leaned forward to show him the tiny, raised mark on

75

her pointer finger. "I reached into a lamp shade to change a lightbulb, but my sister had already removed it. I was just feeling, not looking, and stuck my finger into the socket."

"Ouch!"

For one whole second, the knots in Lily's chest unwound. She had no book to write, and nothing to defend. Curtis was just a person. A person who could share the cringe of electrical foolishness.

Then, Curtis asked, "So what do you have as far as characters?" and it all came rushing back.

She leaned back in her desk chair. "Not much. I know there's a main girl who falls for a main guy, and I know the girl has some family in this town, but that's about it."

"Okay, let's start with the hero. What's her name again?"

"Elsa."

"Like the Disney princess?" he asked with *that* tone.

"Yes," Lily replied firmly. *And she's a queen, actually.*

"Okay, so what does Elsa want?"

"To go back to the city. Small-town life is too boring and slow for her. She's only there because a family member got hurt or…something. I'm working on that. But she slowly starts to warm up to it."

Curtis tented his fingers. "That makes sense, but it's better if she has some kind of goal to push towards. Otherwise, she's just waiting for the plot to happen."

"Maybe she gets caught up in something in the town. Something short-term, so she doesn't feel tied down."

"That's actually a good idea."

Thanks?

Curtis clicked his tongue. "But what does she do?" Click, click, click went the tongue, like a sticky woodpecker. Lily's toes curled and she consciously kept her left eye from twitching.

He only stopped to say, "Let's try another angle. Who is the opponent of the story?"

"Opponent? It's a romance; there's no opponent."

Curtis slid his hand across his face so hard Lily thought he'd peel his lips off.

"What?" she asked.

"There's always an opponent. Not a villain, but an opponent. And in a romance, it's the other person."

"What?" Lily actually laughed. "That's crazy! They're not opponents, they're in love!"

"And that's why those stories are so boring."

The laughter died in Lily's throat. "Boring?"

Curtis nodded, without the barest hint of apology in his eyes. "Conflict, remember? Stories are driven by it. Even in romance. Without conflict, scenes file by with no purpose other than 'cute things happen.' The story doesn't develop, the characters don't develop, they just do stuff."

Lily scratched that itch again. "I'm not sure I follow. If the lovers are supposed to get closer to each other, how does conflict make that happen?"

Curtis rose to his feet. "Pick a romance story. Book, movie, whatever."

Remembering Curtis's past reference to Jane Austen, Lily said, "*Pride and Prejudice.*" Immediately, she realized her mistake.

Curtis threw back his head and laughed. "Easy! He's

stuck up, she believes the worst in him, bam! The story progresses. Each scene makes their enmity worse until they clash, and then they each have to slowly admit the other person was right! Once their plot is resolved, the story is over. Next!"

Lily bit her lip the whole time, thinking of better example. "Okay, how about *Sense and Sensibility?* Elinor and Edward don't fight, but half the book is about them."

"First off, *half* the book. And second, they may not fight, but there is conflict. She loves him, but he's got stuff that keeps them apart, yet he keeps going back to her. And she's too much of a mouse to say anything, so their flaws build off each other until it tears your heart out. Try something more recent."

"Uh..."

"Have you ever seen *Her?*"

"No."

"Guy falls in love with a computer program."

"What?!"

Curtis shrugged. "It's weird, but pretty good. They like each other, but the whole film is them struggling to make it work. Initial attraction, explaining it to people, explaining it to themselves, what the future looks like, it's all conflict. In romance, each person wants the relationship to happen on their terms. That's why they're opponents. Yeah, there can be other conflicts going on like family drama or whatever, but the romance story needs to have a conflict of some form."

Lily sucked in her gut, then put on her pleasantest smile. "Look, Curtis, I've been in the romance novel world for a while now, and I don't see the lovers as opponents; they're allies, even if they don't know it at first. They just have to figure each other out. That's how I write." And she said it without sweating.

He slid his hands into his pockets. "No offense, Miss Harper, but how's that working for you? You say you're stuck, right? City gal goes home for Christmas, but you don't know what happens next, do you?"

Lily's mouth fell open.

Curtis smirked. "No conflict, no story. What does Elsa want?"

Lily set her jaw. "To go home."

"Why can't she?"

"A snowstorm blocks the pass."

"Is she trying to dig her way out?"

"No."

Curtis shook his head. "It's not conflict if you aren't fighting it."

Lily's ears were starting to ring, and the back of her chair was driving itself into her back. Curtis didn't help by standing directly in front of her stupid light fixture, forcing her to squint at him through a halo of firecrackers.

She jerked her eyes away. "Can we do this on the porch? It's hot in here."

"Sure, if you like."

Good. She'd won at least one argument tonight.

The evening air nipped harder than Lily thought it would, but she didn't care. She sat down on her chair and stared at those mountains. She needed that beauty, that solidity, that assurance that some things could endure forever.

Curtis plopped his skinny butt on the porch railing. Right! In! Her! View!

"Something else to think about—"

Must I?

"—is themes. What do the characters represent?"

Lily's eye twitched as years of English teachers droned through her mind like a foghorn. "What do you mean?" she asked in a sweet voice.

"Conflict," Curtis said, leaning back on the rail, and making it whine. "Not just person versus person, but idea versus idea. Makes it richer."

"Shouldn't we get the first layer of the story down before we add more?"

"That's like saying you want to lay down the ground floor, then build the basement. Foundations first, Miss Harper. If we get all this down, the whole story will come together a lot faster."

That did make a lick of sense. "Okay, so themes. What do you mean?"

"I mean, what is this book trying to say?"

"You want to have a big message in the story?" Lily praised herself for not whining.

"It doesn't have to be preachy, and it doesn't even have to be profound. Just show the way people should live through the characters. If a character works as a theme as well as a person, they can do two things at once." Curtis leaned back on the railing, cutting even more into Lily's vision.

"Okay, well, it's a community story, so…something about being a good neighbor?"

Curtis pointed a finger at her and said, "I love it."

Lily's heart about stopped. "I—you—really?"

"Oh, yeah. It goes along with what we said earlier: small town hypocrisy. They talk about community, but underneath, it's just a bigger clique."

She slouched back in her chair. Of course that's what he meant. Why make a happy story when you can complain instead? "What about Christmas? It is a Christmas story."

Curtis paused for a moment, clicking his tongue yet again. "Oh, okay. We can riff on the goodwill-toward-men bit. The town has all the appearances of a Christmas card, but underneath, it's ugly. Then we get in there and forge something better. Nice and subversive."

Subversive. The internet's way of saying, "What you like is stupid."

Lily tried again. "We don't want to get too cynical. My audience expects something with a happy ending."

He put up his hands. "I'm all for happy endings. I just don't see why we can't do something happy *and* unique."

There was that droning sound in her ears again. Was it not bad enough that Curtis was ripping into everything Lily stood for? Did it have to make sense, too?

Lily took a deep breath, then sat forward. May as well dive in. "Okay, so each character has to stand for something?"

"To a point," Curtis replied. "They still need to work as characters, but having a thematic opposition helps focus the story. Elsa is from the city, and the guy is from the small town. She could want to change things, and he could be for the status quo—at least until she wins him over in the end. See? Happy ending."

"Okay, but can she stand for something good? I don't

want a super cynical novel."

Curtis clicked some more, then added a popping sound because that was *so* much better. "How about something like honesty? The town is covered in sweet-smelling lies, but she wants to cut through all that."

Lily said, "But then the guy would represent, what, lies?"

Curtis clicked again. "What if he was somewhere in between the two? A guy who buys into the town's lies, but wants them to be real? He has to give up the dream for a hard truth, go all Ashley Wilkes."

"Who?"

"*Gone with the Wind?*"

"Oh…yeah."

Curtis shivered. "Geez, can Idaho pick a temperature? Mind if we go inside?"

"Sure." He'd ruined her view anyway.

By nightfall, they still hadn't written a single word. Curtis kept talking about moral arguments and symbolism and something called a designing principle. Lily sat on her hard-backed purple couch, typing random notes into her laptop, adding in tiny angry asides when appropriate. Things like *"Last I checked, writing doesn't have to be this sterile!"* and *"If we got into a fistfight over this book, I think I could take him; he's woefully scrawny!"* Hopefully, he wouldn't look over her shoulder.

No fear of that; Curtis was too busy pacing circles

around her living room, flopping into a chair, then popping back up again.

"We're just about there," Curtis informed her suddenly.

Lily looked up from that nasty little comment she'd typed about Curtis's pimple of a chin. "We are?"

"We've laid out the puzzle pieces, now we have to put them together."

"Uh, I think you're seeing something I'm not."

Curtis turned towards Lily's TV and fireplace. "I wish I had a whiteboard. Or one of those conspiracy boards. We have a world, we have some themes, we have ideas for characters, if we can just put them together, we'll have a plot. Hey, is Elsa still a marketing person?"

Lily sighed. "I'm not sold on that."

"But the goal is for her to stay in the small town, right?"

"Right."

"Then it has to be something transferrable. So what's a job you can do in the big city and the small town, but also one with some attention so she can really dig into the town's hypocrisy?"

Lily gently sprinkled her hundredth dose of sugar. "And something that still fits the brief of a happy-ending Christmas novel. Something with maybe a hint of sweetness?"

A bored look passed Curtis's face, but then he suddenly leapt backwards, and snapped both pointer fingers at Lily. "Baker! She's a baker!"

"What?"

Curtis paced even faster, hands at his temples. "Okay, okay, roll with me here. Elsa is a baker. She owns her own place—wait, no, that would fall apart. Okay, she's a worker at a fancy patisserie, or maybe she does desserts at a restaurant with a name nobody can pronounce. Either way, she's built her brand on high-quality, artistic goodies. Then she gets yanked back home, boo-hoo, and maybe bakes something fancy for a Christmas party, and makes an impression!"

Lily frowned. "What's that got to do with the themes and world and stuff?"

He waved his hand in an odd way, like patting an invisible dog. "Hear me out, hear me out. The town is built on surface-level goodness, right? If you say 'Howdy, neighbor,' and pay your tithe, you're an upstanding citizen. This goes for food quality, too. Grandma's famous pie crust recipe is actually on the back of the Pillsbury tin, that sort of thing. So, in comes Elsa with her superior treats. It disturbs the natural order. They think she's trying to show off, but she just put her heart and mind into it like she always does. It's her first clue that something's not right in Pleasantville."

He wriggled his eyebrows in a way that made Lily want to reach for her mace.

"But the guy is impressed," Curtis went on. "He's her first ally, but also her first enemy. Someone who appreciates what she can do, but also doesn't want to rock the boat. Maybe they meet at the Christmas event. Or...or..."

Something fluttered in Lily's chest, flew up to her throat, and soared out of her mouth. "He's the nurse who's looking after her dad!"

Curtis jumped, as if he'd forgotten Lily was in the room.

Lily shrank into the couch. "Or...doctor

or…something."

Curtis wagged his finger. "No, no, you were onto something. Nurse. Not a doctor, that's what his family wants. A respectable position with a fat paycheck. But Mr. Right discovered he'd rather be in the thick of the patients, doing the dirty work. He's still in the medical world like the rest of his siblings, but he'd doing it for the love of the patients, not the prestige. Elsa offers him a place to vent his true feelings, and he offers her some genuine appreciation!"

Lily jumped up with a smile. "And then they fall in love!"

"No!"

"No?"

"I mean, not quite yet. Elsa starts out with the guy just to get out of the house, but through him, she sees all the problematic niceties that run the town. The longer she's in town, the more she wants to get involved, and the more confused Mr. Right gets, which of course is…" Curtis gestured to Lily.

"Conflict?"

"Yes!" He held up his hand to high-five.

Lily tapped it with her fingertips.

Curtis didn't even notice. "And one day, Mr. Right comes up to her and says, 'Hey, it's over. Your dad is better now, and being around you makes me and everybody uncomfortable, it's time for you to go home.' She's all depressed and such, and maybe she's even driving back home. That's when she has to make the hard choice to either return to the comfortable familiar where everybody agrees with her, or dive into the hard work of transforming a small town. She spins the wheel, peels out in the snow, then comes back to…win the Christmas bake-off or something, and show that the town is ready for something new and honest rather than stick to their old lies."

He nodded to Lily. "And, of course, win back Mr. Right. Happily ever after, and to all a good night."

Holy cow, he'd done it. In sixty seconds, Curtis had listed out an entire plot—beginning, middle, and end—with a couple of detailed scenes to boot. Lily reeled.

Okay, so it had taken more than sixty seconds; they'd been talking all evening. But *one* evening!

He really is better than me...

She told herself it was petty to be sad. Jealousy, nothing more. Of course some writers were better than she was. It did nothing to shrink the lump in her throat.

"You all right?" Curtis asked.

Lily snapped out of her raincloud and smiled. "Yes. Just...tired."

Curtis checked the clock. "After ten, holy crap. But hey, we have a foundation! I think the rest will go faster. We meeting again tomorrow?"

And now the raincloud had lightning zapping her brain. "Tomorrow. Yes. We will...do this again."

"With more clacking on the keyboard. Don't worry, Miss Harper, we'll get 'er done." He was grinning. Of course he was; he had no voice to lose.

Lily looked down at the hardwood floor beneath her sister's faux-fur rug. She needed Curtis. She needed to grow as a writer. Yes, it hurt, but she'd sworn to bite every bullet instead of whining and fussing. She was a Harper; she'd been through worse than this.

With that, Lily said, "Thank you for coming, Curtis. I know it's inconvenient."

He shrugged. "It's not like I have much going on at home. And I like writing. Love it, actually." He did have that spark in his pupils.

Lily tightened her shoulders and said, "Me, too." She didn't feel it right now, but she knew it was true.

They made plans for the following day, and Lily waved Curtis goodbye, then shut the door and leaned her head on the dark wood.

Breathe. Just breathe. You learned a lot about being a better writer today.

True. She'd learned about worlds, and how someone else could just march in and plant their flag in yours. She'd learned about characters, and how flat her own was. She'd learned about themes, and how everything she wrote about was stupid and inferior. She'd learned about plots when somebody told her what to do.

And she'd get to do it all over again tomorrow.

Chapter 9

"What the crap is this?" Curtis asked.

It was Lily's turn to sit in the big grape sack—or rather, lie back in a perpetual falling position. Who liked these things? Lily replied, "It's what I've been working on all day." Literally, all day. Dawn until dinner, she'd tied back her long hair and played that keyboard like a concert pianist. She'd had to rewrite her opening chapter in order to match last night's new layout, but she'd done it. And two chapters more!

And Curtis was hunched over her laptop like Ebenezer Scrooge over a late payment. "This is what you came up with?"

She rolled her tongue across her teeth. "Something wrong with it?"

"It's rambling. What happened to the first chapter you already had?"

"I had to change it. Elsa's not a corporate something-or-other anymore, she's a baker, remember?"

"Yeah, but that chapter at least got to the point. This one just goes on and on!"

"I was trying to show her world. Really get the details on the desserts." *And I spent an hour researching what a choux pastry even was, thank you.*

Curtis spun around in the chair. "No, no, no. Better before bigger."

Lily knew she'd regret asking, but... "What?"

"Don't go on for paragraphs and paragraphs; use a couple of choice words and you'll get farther. We have to fit a lot more into chapter one." Curtis's fingers squeezed the air, like he was choking the life out of her book. Again.

She put on an easy smile. "Curtis, we've got time. We can show Elsa's world in chapter one, really make people fall in love with it, and then get to the plot stuff in chapter two."

He cut his hands across the air. "No! Audiences are fickle, Miss Harper. They'll drop you on chapter one, page one, *sentence* one."

They would? Lily never stopped reading a book that fast; it wasn't fair to the author. At least read three chapters, then you can say you gave the writer a chance. "I haven't had that experience. My readers have been lovely."

"And you want to keep them that way, right?" Curtis waved his finger around the room. "Keep all this going?"

Ouch. "What did you have in mind?"

Curtis slid the rolling chair over to her. "The first chapter of a book is a funnel. You start wide enough to catch people, but then you focus it forward. If you stay too general, the funnel won't narrow, and then it won't pull people in. If you focus too much, the funnels gets too narrow, and people get stuck because they don't know what's going on. The first chapter has to be rich and snappy at the same time in order to keep the audience going. We must give them a preview of what the book will be like, hit all the important points, and help them see that this book is worth their time."

Lily stared at Curtis for several seconds, wondering when was the last time he'd actually had fun reading a book. Fortunately, she had spent part of her day crafting an exquisite reply for the next time he went off the rails.

She hoisted herself into a sitting position, then leaned into her partner. "Curtis, don't you ever feel like all this structure is getting in the way of writing authentically? Doesn't your true voice just get bogged down in all the rules?"

Curtis's eyelids stretched back into his head. He jumped to his feet, marched out of the house, and slammed the door behind him.

Lily watched him through the window, stomping down to the street, head ducked, skinny arms flailing at invisible foes. He left his car behind, so Lily guessed he'd return.

She let out a dull, mirthless laugh. *What a freaking child!* She flopped back onto the bean bag chair, and caught the exploding light in her gaze. Curtis had almost smashed by standing up too fast.

"Would've solved two problems," Lily mused.

Curtis indeed returned, a full hour later. Lily had made herself some homemade soup in the meantime, and watched him over her bowl.

He said, "I've decided to forgive you."

Lily's spoonful fell back into the bowl.

Curtis then asked, "Do you have Netflix?"

"Netflix? Yes, why?"

Curtis snatched up the remote and turned on the TV.

Lily stood, feeling a strange defensiveness ripple through her pores at someone touching her things. "I don't think we have time for a movie."

"Five minutes, that's all. I want to show you something." Curtis raised an eyebrow at her. "Oh, and it's a Christmas movie."

She sighed. Why did she have such an obvious weakness?

Lily ladled out a second bowl of soup, then brought both over to the coffee table. Curtis thanked her as he picked his movie: *Klaus*, some kind of animated Santa Claus flick.

"Isn't this a kids' movie?" she asked.

Curtis replied, "So was *The Lion King*. Animation is wasted on kids."

Lily had to admit that she'd watched *Anastasia* more times than most children, so she settled in for the film. "So is *Klaus* good, then?"

"I think so. Some parts are hard, but still enjoyable."

"Hard?"

Curtis didn't answer. Lily turned her attention to the movie.

Apparently, *Klaus* was set in a world where mailmen were treated like military cadets. They even had a drill sergeant who yelled at a lazy slacker who deliberately failed his training. Then, it turned out the slacker, Jesper, was the son of the postmaster general. *Ah, that explains it*, Lily thought.

But to her surprise, and Jesper's, Daddy Dearest turned his disappointment into opportunity. He made Jesper a postman, and assigned him to some outpost literally on the edge of the map, with the assignment to stamp six thousand letters in a year, or be cut off from the family riches.

That's when Curtis stopped the movie.

"That's it?" Lily asked.

He turned towards her with that knowing look in his eyes. "Who's the main character?"

"Jesper," Lily answered.

"What's the big flaw Jesper must overcome?"

"He's a spoiled butt."

"What's his quest?"

"Get a bunch of letters stamped."

"Motivation?"

"Losing the ability to be a spoiled butt."

"Who's his first opponent?"

"His dad."

"Why should he care what Dad thinks?"

"Dad is the boss, plus he'll disinherit him."

Curtis pointed to the TV with the remote. "What's the timestamp say?"

Lily checked. "Like five minutes."

Curtis snapped his fingers. "Boom. In just five minutes, we got character, motivation, objective, opponent, worldbuilding, even the beginnings of the later theme of materialism. In just one or two scenes, you know what this movie is about."

She hesitated. Curtis made a good point, but did she really want to admit defeat again? "But this is a book, not a movie. I can't just point a camera at something and have all the imagery in one shot."

"Fair point, but we can still get all the most critical things on the first chapter. Maybe even the first page." Curtis turned the TV off, then dropped the remote like a microphone. "Miss Harper, you said that rules restrict the artistic voice. I say the rules focus the voice into a megaphone that shouts above the mass-produced noise."

Lily curled her feet onto the couch, which wasn't quite deep enough to fit her butt and her heels. "So how do we do that?"

Curtis nodded towards the writing room. "Let's go find out."

Curtis returned to *Klaus* that very same evening. Lily had the idea of Mr. Right—now named Mitch—to be a caretaker for Elsa's dad at their home, which would bring them into forced proximity.

Curtis shook his head. "Maybe later, but we need to start in the hospital. He's the first opponent, so we want to see him in his own world. Remember *Klaus*? Where did Jesper meet his dad?"

Lily lazily spun in her office chair, wishing Curtis would just answer his own questions. "Dad's office."

"Right. You know why? Because he's in charge there. That room embodies Dad's power and threat level."

"Mitch isn't a threat," Lily reminded him.

"I know that. Opponents and villains aren't the same thing. But if we see Mitch in his world, that's where he appears powerful and knowledgeable. Elsa's a great baker, but she doesn't know jack about medicine. The setting sets Mitch up to be a competent opponent and a competent person in general. He's in his element. Like Belle meeting the Beast in his castle, only nicer."

Lily stared at Curtis as he paced the room. "You watch and read a lot, don't you?"

"Don't you?" Curtis waved his arm at Lily's bookshelves, far from full, but still impressive with row upon row of novels. "Everything from chick lit to the classics." Curtis picked up the copy of *The Three Musketeers*, only to find it hollow, and made of cardboard. "What the...?"

Lily swore she felt steam hissing out of her ears. Why hadn't she thrown those away?! "Yeah, those are just decorative until I can actually fill the shelves."

Curtis kept his curious gaze on all of Lily's "classic" books, tapping each one for authenticity.

When he touched *Pride and Prejudice*, Lily jumped in with, "That one I've actually read. I have a copy on the other shelf. It's my favorite story." Well, sort of. The Kiera Knightly movie was better, but Lily wasn't about to say that to Curtis.

"Hmm. Good taste."

Lily reeled. Was that a genuine compliment? He was looking at the shelf, not her, but his voice didn't have that sarcastic twist. It made her warm enough to ask, "What's your favorite book?"

Curtis grabbed another faux book from Lily's shelf and showed it to her. *The Count of Monte Cristo*. "Have you read it?"

Nope. "Sure! It's actually pretty exciting."

"You think so?" A smile crept halfway up Curtis's face.

"Yeah, who doesn't love a good revenge story with a sword fight?"

His smile didn't leave, but it did melt into something more poisonous. "Yeah, and how about the scene where he finally gets the girl back after all those years?"

Something about his tone set Lily's hair on edge, but she soldiered on with, "Gotta love a good reunion scene, right?"

Curtis looked down at the fake book in his hands and

chuckled in a low, wicked way. "Which adaptation did you see, Miss Harper? The 1930s version or the 2002?"

He looked at her like she was made of glass. "What do you mean?" Lily asked.

"I mean *The Count of Monte Cristo* is not a revenge story; it's an anti-revenge story *disguised* as a revenge story. But the movies didn't like that, so they turned a complex narrative into a swashbuckling popcorn flick. Better to pump out something that feeds our inner victim than makes an audience think, am I right? Oh, and there's no sword fight in the book either."

Curtis shelved the empty book with a hollow *thock*.

Lily's whole body burned. When Curtis came over the next day, she brought her laptop into the living room. They didn't go into her writing room again.

Chapter 10

It wasn't all bad. In the evenings that followed, Curtis did accept Lily's input on a number of things, from plot ideas to character arcs—even if he laid the groundwork for her ideas. He even applauded the level of research she did on high-end baking and nursing jobs. Every now and then, Curtis could even be surprised by her descriptions.

One evening, lounged across the couch and staring at the ceiling, Curtis asked, "Do you have any good 'rathers?' Like, 'I'd rather watch paint dry,' but original?"

From her seat at the dining room table, Lily looked directly at Curtis, and said in a low monotone, "I'd rather bowl with my own head."

Curtis sprang up with a delicious pallor of fright. "Holy crap! You made that up yourself?"

Lily nodded, never breaking eye contact. "It went through my mind once."

Curtis muttered something about writing a horror novel, then quietly resumed work.

There was also their fourth day of work, when Curtis pistol-whipped her with a display of compassion. He brought in burgers and fries from a local fast-food joint— another star on his chart—then asked, "Do you know Jim Livingston? Oncology doctor at St. Matthew's?"

"James? Yeah, he's my brother-in-law."

Curtis nodded with a small grin. "He said that was the case. I remembered a while back, he said he had an in-law who was a famous writer. I totally forgot that was you until today."

"How do you know James?"

"He's my boss. I manage his office."

Lily nearly jumped out of her socks. "Get out!"

Curtis shrugged. "Small world, smaller town."

"Wow! What's the great Dr. James like at work?"

"Uh, well, he lets me call him Jim, and he's a cool dude. Works way too much, but so do I."

"Yeah, every time I see him, he looks tired."

Curtis shrugged again, and Lily thought that was the end of it. But a few moments later, after they'd greased their fingers in French fries, Curtis suddenly looked up at her with a serious expression.

"Can I ask something close to the chest?"

Lily said, "Go on."

"Is Jim okay?"

Lily stared back. "I...I think so. Just overworking, like you said."

"Maybe. But when someone works that much, you wonder why, you know?"

"Are you and James close?"

"Moderately," Curtis replied. "We talk at the office, go out for a beer, like, once a week, but that's about it. Just thought I'd ask."

That time, it really was the end. So Curtis *could* show human empathy. And he could give respect and appreciation to Lily for her work.

But this only made the other ninety percent of his

personality seem like a willful effort.

A week into their writing, Curtis whined, "Why are they still talking?" while reading Lily's work.

Lily had stretched across her purple couch, hoping to find it more comfortable this way, but alas. It bowed in the middle, making her feel like a parenthesis. "What do you mean?" she asked in her practiced pleasant voice. It was easier than getting into an argument she couldn't win.

Curtis turned in his dining room chair. "In the dance scene. Elsa and Mitch are just talking and talking on the sidelines."

Lily had loved that scene. It was the first time Elsa really acknowledged she may have serious feelings for Mitch, and the first time Mitch admitted not all was well with his cozy little world. It was cute, vulnerable. So, of course, Curtis hated it.

Lily thought fast. "I figured it was good symbolism. They're on the sidelines, not actually dancing. Present, but not participating."

Curtis actually paused. For a second. "Okay, but they're still rambling. What's the point of the scene?"

"To get them together?"

"Well, they like each other. We don't need all this wasted space."

Wasted space. He liked that phrase. It was sharp, and drew enough blood to stir a reaction. Once again, Lily sat down at her computer and cut apart her own words.

In a weak moment, Lily had sent a few chapters to Mr. Gates under the guise of "Look how much progress I've made!" while truly hoping he'd be appalled by unfamiliar tone of his breadwinner. Mr. Gates had called her an inspiration, saying she'd really matured as a writer.

The odd part was, Lily kind of agreed. The more she chewed on Curtis's words, the more sense they made. Why did Elsa and Mitch have to talk that much about their love of dogs? Wouldn't a couple lines get the point across? Or wouldn't it be better to go back a few chapters and show Mitch loving all over Elsa's dad's Labrador? Curtis had some really good points, and Lily admitted she was growing.

But why did he have to wield his words like a scythe? Lily understood that an entire day's worth of words might turn out to be useless, but did he really have to skim through it with a bored look, then throw out a dispassionate "Nope?"

And when she made a poor choice of words, like, "It smelled nice," why couldn't Curtis say, "I wonder if there's a better phrase," instead of, "Weak sauce?"

Lily swore she was getting PTSD. She'd write all day, fearing the chopping block of Curtis's arrival. On one hand, as their days hit the double-digits, she saw that Curtis was changing less and less from her novel. Not a huge drop, but a noticeable one. To Lily. But Curtis Reynolds wore crap-colored glasses, and seemed to enjoy criticism more than compliments.

"You can't just freewheel it," Curtis said one night on the porch. June had finally woken up with blankets of heat, so the dusks, with their purple skies and cricket symphonies, hit that perfect cooling note. "Each scene has to be constructed carefully, each line focusing on the goal."

Lily wanted to scream that "freewheeling it" had earned her this very book contract, but she knew he'd fire back with all her empty pages before they'd met. Still, she couldn't stomach her own silence anymore. "Does it really have to be this rigid? Is there no room for fun? I mean, does every single scene really have to this much effort?"

Curtis replied, "I deserve the effort."

"Deserve it?"

Curtis honed his nail-gun gaze on hers. "I'm your audience. Every day, I am assaulted by greedy corporations who prefer that my soul be scraped raw so that I continue to take their medicine for the pain. I've been preyed upon from my first Huggies commercial, told that if I just keep striving, keep chipping away at my spirit, that I'll find the joy only they can manufacture. I'm so packed with preservatives that I've forgotten what real food tastes like. I'm tired, I'm burnt out, and I'm desperate for the real thing, desperate for something that's going to nourish my soul for the first time since God-knows-when. I need art. I need that craftsmanship, that passion, that soul that feeds my own. And I'll only get it if somebody puts in the effort instead of demanding that I once again settle for a sugar pill because it's easier."

It was only at three in the morning, after tossing and turning beneath sheets slicked by furious sweat that Lily finally came up with what *would* have been the perfect reply: "A starving man doesn't need snooty gourmet. He just needs fresh bread."

After two full weeks of that, Lily had to get out. She'd barely left the house except to exercise or shop for groceries. She didn't care if she had a deadline; she needed a break. She decided to revitalize her energies with a trip to the local book store on First Street, a skinny, two-story white-brick building that looked like it was sucking in its gut.

The insides were packed and squashed with tall bookshelves on every wall, and still more books laid out on window displays, counter displays, even the stairs were not safe from overflow. Lily didn't mind tiptoeing around boxes of new arrivals; after all, sometimes they were hers.

She loved the dinky little place, and had gotten on a first-name basis with the owner and every changing associate. She always tried to leave with something, even if there was no guarantee she'd like it. Lily figured she had enough income to support local arts—for now.

And holy hopping heck, whose name should she find upstairs in the sci-fi/fantasy section but Curtis J. Reynolds?

"Why hello there," Lily said in a condescending tone. She slid out the paperback, hoping to see a shoddy, Microsoft-Paint book cover. No luck. It was actually a neat picture of a group of people on an apartment roof, pointing at a faint alien ship in the blue sky. The title read, *They Come in Peace*. Lily flipped to the back.

They fired no lasers. They made no demands. They brought books, technology, and wisdom. They called us friends. But now, the streets are empty, the factories silent. Humanity's job is not to create or produce, it's to learn how to be fruitful members of galactic society. Every hour, every task, every person. For their own good.

Only the Truants dare to refuse this "uplifting," hiding in abandoned warehouses, dodging the smiling enforcers. They have only one goal: live. Survival is easy, but living is forbidden—it's dangerous, cruel, and selfish. Their only hope is to show the aliens that they already know how to be good humans.

So why haven't they succeeded?

Lily let out a two-tone groan. This sounded exactly like the kind of novel Curtis would write, some kind of critique on humanity veiled in sci-fi trappings. On the other hand, she had to admit she was curious. Lily flipped to the first page.

"We are friends."

Lily shivered, then cursed herself. Darn him and his openings...

"We are friends." The familiar warning boomed through the city from megaphones on every street corner. "We are here for your benefit." A hollow smile in the voice, like a radio announcer being paid too little. "We have come to welcome you into the galaxy." Careful cadence, a slight downturn in the last word, the sound of a parent talking to a child. "We are here for you."

Lily closed the book. Yep, she'd be finishing this. Maybe Curtis really did know what he was doing. Maybe she should just shut up and listen to him.

Maybe she should step in a bear trap.

"Excuse me," came a voice as crinkled as a hard candy wrapper. Lily turned and saw a hunched old woman, her hair a silver puff ball, eyes watery and bright. "Are you Lily Harper?"

It never failed to make her smile. "I am."

The woman's grin lifted her sagging wrinkles. "Oh, I love your books! I just read *Autumn Leaves* for the third time!"

Oh, yes, Lily was going to ride these bubbles in her

belly all day long. "Really?"

"Yes! Are you working on another?"

"I am! A Christmas story in the mountains."

The old lady gasped. "That's my favorite kind of story!"

"Mine, too! I honestly don't know why I haven't written one until now."

"Well, you'd best hurry! I'm ninety-five!" The woman laughed, then eyed the book in Lily's hand. "What are you reading?"

"Oh, uh...*They Come in Peace* by Curtis Reynolds. I haven't read it yet, but I...heard of the author."

"May I?" The old woman took the book and read through the back cover, lowering her spectacles from her forehead to her eyes. She frowned at the text. "Hmm, sounds like a hard read."

"Yeah," Lily said in a neutral tone.

The woman handed the book back to her. "Well, I don't need all that. I'm old, and I've seen enough hard things. I'd rather read uplifting stories, thank you. You finish that Christmas story so I can have something nice to read."

A crackly warmth pulsed through Lily's back and shoulders, as if something dislocated had popped back into place. It filtered town to her toes, her fingertips, and her chest. Some of it poured into her eyes, and she had to blink it away. "Thank you, that...means so much to me."

Lily helped the old woman descend the stairs, bought Curtis's book, and stomped down First Street. "See, Curtis?" she growled to the sidewalk cracks. "Some people *like* nice books. Some people don't *want* the literary equivalent of caviar and...and... fish heads. Whatever. They want cookies and peppermints and caramel and—"

She froze mid-step. Yes…that would be…well, it would be silly. Maybe pointless. Absolutely petty.

Perfect.

Lily was ready when Curtis walked in the door that night—just walked in, no knock, like he owned the place. Curtis gave a nonchalant "Yo," dropped his laptop bag on the couch, then paused and sniffed. "Something smells good."

Lily smiled from her place over the stove. "Since we're writing a Christmas story, I figured I'd get in the Christmas mood, which in my family means making a caramel cake."

"Ooh, nice. Is that the caramel there?"

"Yep!" Lily brushed the inside of the pot, keeping the alabaster syrup wet, and doing her best not to show all her teeth in a witch-like grin. *Wait until you taste this, Mr. Reynolds. I do know how to do stuff.* The oven door all but melted her thighs, and the steam of the pot moistened her brow and curled her hair, but the heatstroke would be nothing compared to Curtis's hanging jaw. Caramel was notoriously fussy. For most people. *You may know how to cut into the human condition, buster, but I know how to delight with style.*

Curtis unpacked his laptop and asked, "Are you using the wet or dry method?"

Lily's brush froze mid-stroke. *There's more than one way to make caramel?* She'd added water to the sugar, so… "Wet method."

Curtis nodded. "That's my preferred choice, too. Dry is a pain."

Lily's eyeballs turned as far to the right as they could without moving her face. *No...no, it's not fair...* "You make caramel, too?"

"We used to watch that *Great British Baking Show*, and they kept talking about how hard caramel is, so I got a burr in my britches, as Dad says, and tried it out. Yep, it's a beast all right, but I got it down eventually."

Lily briefly wondered why God hated her, then had a thought that slapped her smile right back on: *He knows how tricky this is! So when he sees me do it, he has to be impressed!* It wouldn't show him up, but it might make him realize Lily Harper had *some* skills.

She expected a long deluge of nit-picks and well-actuallys, but to her shock, Curtis remained dead silent as he typed away ideas on his laptop. For fifteen straight minutes.

As her caramel honeyed into a cinnamon color, Lily finally had to say it. "You're quiet tonight."

"Just letting you concentrate," he replied. "I know how fiddly caramel is."

Lily shook her head in a way that tossed her hair over her shoulder. "Not me. I've been making this since I was seventeen; I can do it in my sleep."

"Oh?" Curtis's gaze fixed on her brush.

Stare all you like; you don't scare me. "So what do you do with caramel? Sauce? Candies?"

"Uh... sauce..." He rose and walked over to the stove, mouth turned down. "Might want to watch that."

Lily kept her grin, mentally sketching and storing Curtis's look of amateurish concern. "Fear not, Mr. Reynolds, I've got this recipe memorized all the way to my fingertips. The cake is good, too, but..."

She should not have looked down. Crystals spread from the nearest edge of the caramel, like a coffee-stained frost. Lily blinked ten times to make sure they were really there. She'd never seen crystallization in her caramel, but she'd read about it. So she didn't even try to fix it. Even now, a browned glaze was blooming across the entire batch, turning syrupy liquid into crust.

Lily couldn't let go of her brush, couldn't move it off the heat, couldn't do anything but dribble out the pathetic words, "That's never happened."

Curtis let a long sigh out of his nostrils. Disgust? Pity? Lily stole a glance at him, and saw his jaw bulging. How many criticisms was he holding back?

Shame finally tickled her nerves awake, like the cold, sandy feeling of a sleeping foot trying to wake up. Lily moved the pot to an empty burner and shut off the stove. Even though the sun hadn't set, the whole house seemed dim. Shadows covered everything in watercolor drips.

Why? Why had she even bothered to try and show off something so inconsequential?

Her brain replied immediately. *Because I'm sick of feeling like I know nothing.* Lily had committed to learning how to write from someone with a skillset she lacked, but surely she already had *some* ability, right? It hadn't *all* been blind luck, had it?

No. It wasn't. Couldn't be.

Lily snatched a new pot out of the cupboard, slammed it on the stove, and started all over. The cake would be done way too soon, but what else was there to do? Cry out caramel tears? Curtis would mock those, too.

Right on cue, the Great Curtis spoke. "How long have you lived here?"

Well, that was random. "A few weeks. Why?" She did not take her eyes off the sugar.

"Has anything else burned on this stove?"

Aaaand there it was. "Yes," Lily seethed.

"Then this stove might run hotter than you're used to."

Lily smacked her forehead. "The heat!"

"It'll crystalize your caramel faster than you can blink if it's too hot."

And it also explained why her naan was doughy that first night. The outside cooked too quickly and fooled her. How did he know that was the problem? *Because that's what he does,* Lily realized. *He obsesses. He gets into something and picks every step of it apart, logging every failure as a piece of data. He's done this so often that even the most obscure bit of knowledge is second nature to him.*

That's why he's better than me. He's studied. I just went by feeling.

Lily lowered the heat, and kept going, eyes on the sugar, tongue between her teeth. Her cheeks burned, and it wasn't from the stove, but she couldn't stop now. The cake was still baking, and it was better to screw up and start over than just quit. Curtis would make his judgments, but she'd deal with it later.

Except...he didn't. Curtis didn't speak the whole time Lily was working. He didn't leave, of course. Lily saw in the corner of her eye that he was still looking on from her right. Necessary oversight after her flub, no doubt.

She fought the urge, but Lily finally had to look at him,

just a glance, to see if he was watching her caramel with approval or disdain.

He wasn't looking at the pot. He was looking at *her*. Staring.

Hot rakes scratched across her cheeks and down her neck. "Wh-What?"

Curtis jerked his brown eyes away. "Sorry, I...sorry. I was just thinking."

"About...?" Lily wasn't sure she wanted to know, but it would be better to set that boundary now, rather than later.

"Nothing," he said.

"You were staring," she countered.

"I wasn't trying to be weird. I was just...impressed, that's all."

Lily's brush slowed almost to a halt. Surely, she hadn't heard that word. "Impressed? At my screw-up?"

"No, impressed that you kept going."

Lily dared one more glance away from her caramel. Curtis had his mouth pulled to the side, like he was yanking on the zipper. "Seems like there's more there," Lily said.

Curtis leaned his back on the wall, finally looking away from her. Lily felt the air cool immediately. Curtis said, "It just got me thinking. We've been at this for several days now, and I can tell it hasn't been peachy for you. But here you are, powering through. I don't know. I've just seen a lot of people give up when they meet resistance. It's like they think they should get a Pulitzer just for completing a first draft. It's...neat to see someone who's actually willing to keep trying."

Neat. Lily mused on that as the caramel colored. It was a paltry word for all she'd put up with. And yet, it was better than "fine" or "marketable." "Neat" was a step above average. Plus, he'd used another word: "impressive." No sarcastic tone, just impressed. Curtis, impressed. His lancing, scouring eyes had cut into her, and found something…good?

Lily didn't know how to react, and she kept swallowing too much to say anything eloquent. She just gave a quick, "Thank you," and kept on with her work.

And, she decided, perhaps his scrawniness wasn't that awful after all.

Chapter 11

Lily found herself showering more often. Maybe it was because she took multiple walks or jogs a day now, just to get away from the laptop for a few minutes, and everything she wore became soggy under the June sun.

Or maybe it was the muck inside her skin that wouldn't quite wash off. Like a tar in her veins, making her sluggish and groggy all hours of the day. Writing was hard. Lily scrubbed harder.

It wasn't enough, but Lily didn't have time. It was her turn to make dinner, and Curtis would be here soon. She dried, dressed, and peeked over her balcony to make sure Curtis hadn't let himself in again. He had not.

Mary had. "Surprise!" she said in her sun-shiny tone.

"Oh!" Lily said, caught between joy at seeing her sister, and irritation that people kept walking into her house. Well, at least Mary wouldn't tell her how to do her job.

Lily trotted down the stairs and gave her sister a hug. "How are you?"

"Doing well." She stepped back and beamed. Lily eyed her sister, immaculate in her navy blue blazer jacket, floral-print blouse, and white chinos. Even her brown flats seemed to emanate class and high society.

Lily looked down at her plain, green tee shirt and sweat pants. She'd quit trying to impress Curtis on day two.

Mary immediately said, "Oh, forget it, you look beautiful."

Some of the gunk washed out of her blood, and Lily breathed just an inch deeper. "Thank you. What are you doing here?"

Mary said, "I'm taking you out to dinner. I haven't seen you in weeks, and you've been working way too much. Time for something fun!"

Even more weight dripped off Lily's bones. She swore she was starting to float. "That would be amazing, actually. But I'm at least putting jeans on. Be right back."

"Take your time."

Lily raced upstairs and threw on a pair of booty-hugging jeans. Hey, you never knew. Lily didn't care where her sister picked for dinner, so long as she didn't have to cook for—

—Curtis!

"Aw, crap," she groaned to her mirror, sagging forward in a depressed frump. What to do about Curtis? Bring him along?

Hell, no. Knowing Curtis, he'd take one look at Mary, then pull out his phone and say, "She's okay, but here's how a *real* older sister should look." While Lily would love to hear Mary tell Curtis off with both her words and an open palm, it would be better to cancel.

So...what to tell him? I'm ignoring the book to squander the precious little time we have on personal affairs? Curtis had only complimented her tenacity a few days ago, and Lily had no intentions of squandering that inch of progress. What, then? Should she cancel with Mary?

No! cried her blood. Lily needed a break, from writing

and Curtis both. But how to get out of it without judgment? She could suggest that Curtis also needed a break, but he'd probably say, "Break? But criticizing you is how I unwind!"

She picked her phone up from the bed and quickly typed in a text message. Curtis, I'm sick as a dog. Let's meet up tomorrow instead. Her stomach acid curdled. Did she really need to lie? Surely Curtis knew what it was like to be burnt out on a book. She could just say she needed rest.

And Curtis would look down his bumpy nose at her. Lily had enough of that. She hit send, and hurried away, in case Curtis was already about to pull up.

Lily always said Wise Guy's Pizza wasn't the best— right before she ordered another slice. Something about the sauce made her shrug her shoulders and lick her lips at the same time. And the familiar scent of tomatoes and melted cheese hit the spot just right tonight.

Mary somehow managed to take a decent bite, but still look ready to walk the runway. Her face just repelled crumbs and stains. "So, how goes the writing? Mandy says you found your inspiration?"

Lily gobbled her bite, reaching for a napkin. "Yurp."

"Can I get any details? Or do I have to wait for the release?"

Lily used her mammoth mouthful to ponder her words. She had an answer by the time she swallowed. "I'm still trying out different things. It's a different kind of book. More...artsy, I think."

Mary said, "If it's as good as your first chapter, I can't wait to read the rest."

Aaaand, time to change the subject. Her brain scrambled for a topic. "How, uh, how are Mom and Mandy?"

"Mom's fine. She's living the life she always wanted: go to work, do something useful, go home, and know everything's taken care of." Mary smiled at herself, the owner of that home and creator of such peace. But almost immediately, she scowled. "Mandy, though, is such a child."

"You mean a teenager."

"Not yet I don't; I don't think I can handle that."

Lily remembered Mandy's request. "Well, I have a guest room now, so I can have Mandy over sometimes—uh, after I'm done with this book, I mean. Kind of need laser focus until the end of the month."

Mary pointed a lacquered nail at her sister. "I'll take you up on that. Mandy's such a handful."

Lily reached for her pizza, but paused, noticing a tic in Mary's cheek. "Are you guys still fighting?"

Mary put on a quick smile and said, "It's fine. We're handling it."

Lily chuckled. "Sis, c'mon, it's me."

Mary considered that, then let out a long sigh, and rested her cheek on her fist. "I just don't understand that girl. Everything's a fight. If I told her to cash a million-dollar check, she'd complain about waiting in line at the bank. Honestly, I half-raised you, Asher, and the others, and none of you were this problematic! But Mandy? Ugh."

As she spoke, Mary's fingers crept up the back of her neck. Her hands pushed up the curtains of blonde hair behind her ears, bunching it into a familiar shape. But suddenly, she dropped the updo with a silent bounce.

Lily couldn't help smiling. "I thought you were about to put your hair up."

"What?" Mary asked.

"You know, like you used to. The get-stuff-done ponytail? Back when—"

Mary waved her hand. "Ah-ah! Those days are behind us; we don't speak of them anymore."

Lily flinched. "Okay...but you know, if Mandy's harder to raise than we were, it's because her circumstances are different. She doesn't know about selling the TV to pay the light bill. She only knows comfort."

Mary tapped the counter, looking at her pizza slice like it told a joke she didn't get. "That was the whole point, though. I didn't want her to go through what we did."

Lily rubbed her sister's arm. "And she didn't. Thanks to you."

"You'd think she'd be more grateful. With everything James and I have made for her."

Curtis's concerned words flashed through Lily's brain. "Speaking of James, how is he?"

Mary gave her a curious look. "James? Why?"

Lily paused. She didn't want Mary to know how much help she was getting. "He just looked really worn out the last time I saw him. And the time before that. And..."

Mary shrugged, but looked away. "He works too much."

"Why?"

"He's a hard worker; it's part of why I married him."

"Sure, but, is he okay?"

"Of course he is...though you're right; I do wish he'd spend more time at home."

Lily watched her sister the same way she would a patch of lake ice beneath her steps. "Is he working because...are you guys okay? Financially?'

One could almost hear the *click* of Mary flipping on her familiar smile. "Don't you worry about our finances. I've got it under control."

On one hand, Lily knew that was true. On the other, Mary's hand was scratching at her neck, reaching for her hair again. It was time to dig deep. Lily said, "And what about kids? Will you be able to focus on them with everything else going on?"

At last, Mary slowed. One hand stroked the edge of her crust, the other remained at the nape of her neck. "Well, fortunately for me, that's not something I really need to worry about."

"The doctor didn't have any options?"

"Not...at the moment."

"Mary, are you okay?"

For one full second, Mary was a stony mask. Blank. Dim. Her one human feature was the slight raise of her eyebrows, like she'd never heard those words before.

Then, she laughed through a wide smile. "Hey! I brought you out to cheer *you* up, not me! Relax, Lil, I've got it covered. Now seriously! No more sad faces or depressing inquiries; tonight is for fun."

In other words, end of discussion.

115

They talked about everything and nothing for the next couple hours. When they left the building, Lily jerked her head back as she threw on her sunglasses. "Wow. Seven-thirty and it's still this hot."

Mary said, "Summer in Idaho."

"Where the sun don't set 'til midnight..."

"...and the boob sweat never dries."

They laughed at their age-old joke, born from a lifetime without air conditioning. Lily mused that they could still reference something from the bad days, but decided not to pursue it.

Mary asked, "Do you mind if we stop by the shop? Asher had a question and I promised to swing by before he left."

"Sure, no problem."

The ladies walked up Sun Valley Boulevard, one of two major roads in all of Ketchum. A steady stream of pedestrians dashed across sidewalks ahead of swearing drivers, and poured into high-price boutiques just to stay cool. Lily scanned the crowd as she walked. With this many people out, she worried she might find Curtis among them.

And she did. Right there, across the boulevard, at the corner of a fancy restaurant, by the statue of a plump chef holding up a tray. Both frozen in place, both staring right at her.

"Lily?" Mary called.

Lily jumped, and realized she still stood in the crosswalk, with impatient drivers frowning at her. She hurried across the street, glancing over her shoulder. Curtis's gaze followed.

Lily almost smacked into the sand-colored stone that made up Mary's Home Furnishings. She gave one last look over her shoulder—yep, still watching—and hurried inside. The burst of AC did nothing for her sweating brain. Maybe Curtis wouldn't confirm it was her. Maybe he'd think he was imagining it.

Then her phone buzzed. A text from Curtis.

Feeling better?

Lily lowered the phone and looked around for an answer. This place always made her dizzy with all its everything everywhere. A half-dozen living room arrangements snuggled up in chic squares, each crammed with possibility. In the nearest, a white couch drowned behind matching pillows with lacy edges, sitting beneath a vast painting of blooming, white jasmines. The coffee table was more of an eggshell color, with crossing gold bars to make it look like a present. Atop that, a jar of flowers sat on a tray, alongside a thick, silver cross and a tiny frame that read, "Live, Laugh, Love." Add in two brown chairs with leather cushions and an end table with more flowers and a bronze candle holder, and you had Mary's Charming Main Room Number Four.

No customers right now. The store was closed, but Asher stuck around an hour later most nights, to wrap things up. He chatted by the sales counter with Mary, giving Lily a quick wink and a wave. Asher had done well with Mary's store. Maybe it was his tremendous height, or his crisp button-ups, always in gentle, friendly colors like powder blue or mint green. Or maybe it was how Mary taught him to help the customers rearrange the entire store in their own favor: this

117

couch with that ottoman, and this coffee table but that artwork. A customer could want a pillow, and walk out with a bedroom—and a smile, to boot.

Lily wished she had their gift for arranging the world right now. What pleasant, friendly spin could she put on this happy misunderstanding? Lily checked out the window. Curtis remained on the corner of the street, staring in her direction, his phone in his hand.

Who was she kidding? She was caught. Lily typed back, Sorry. My sister invited me out and I needed a break. She sent the message, then walked along a wall of pictures ranging from peaceful flower gardens to urban cityscapes.

A moment later, Curtis buzzed back. I feel that but why not just say so the first place?

Lily answered, I thought you'd be upset.

Curtis replied, You didn't think lying would bug me?

As usual, he was right. Lily frowned up at a gigantic print of a sad-looking water buffalo. Had lying really been necessary? But what could she possibly say now?

Fortunately, Curtis filled the gap. If you need a break just tell me. It's your book.

Lily read and reread that line over and over. Was he furious? Just annoyed? So hard to tell in a text! And yet, the invitation was plain as day. *Just tell me.* No shenanigans necessary. And then, *it's your book.*

Permission granted, and yet not needed. It tickled in her chest. It *was* her book. Why *had* she lied?

"Finally out of the house?" Asher asked, approaching her.

Lily pocketed her phone. "Yep." She checked the

118

window just past Asher. Curtis was gone.

Mary pointed to a cornflower-blue couch and said, "Please tell me this one sold today."

Asher peered at it. "Uh, no, why?"

"I don't like it."

"Really?" Lily and Asher both replied, sharing an incredulous look. Mary never stocked anything she thought was hideous.

Mary said, "I thought it was cute at first, but the more I look at it, the more it looks like the couch we had back on Westwood."

Asher said, "No way. This one doesn't have enough pizza stains."

"Or jam," Lily offered.

"Or eye makeup."

"Or—"

Mary waved her hands in the air. "Nope! We're past all that. Just discount the couch and move on." She walked away from the couch.

Asher watched her go, then muttered, "I run this place by myself most days, but sure, tell me how to do my job."

Lily nearly jumped out of her shoes, and stared aghast at her brother.

He had gone bone white, and the fleeting sideways glance at Lily told her Asher had forgotten she was right next to him. He threw on a Mary-like smile and said, "Ah, well. Mary knows best," then made a beeline for the back room.

Just like that, Lily knew why she had lied to Curtis. *My family doesn't like to cause discomfort.*

And yet...

Chapter 12

Curtis didn't bring the matter up again on Saturday. On Sunday, though, he did ask if he could come in the early afternoon instead of the morning, like they usually did on weekends. Lily never considered Curtis to be the religious type, especially since he'd missed church for two weeks, but she didn't argue.

Instead, she sat down in a pair of soft shorts and watched a couple Lifetime movies because it was her house and she wanted to, darn it. She planned on changing before Curtis arrived—these shorts really lived up to their name—but after the first movie ended, Lily realized she was still warm. What the heck?

Lily rose to check on the air conditioner. Seventy-four. Not terrible, but it was set lower. Lily checked the vents. Nothing. She lowered the temperature a little to kick it into gear, then turned on another movie.

By the end of it, Lily's thighs were sticking together and her shirt had adhered to her back. The air had never come on. And now, her so-called cooling system registered a temperature of seventy-nine. It was only noon. On a Sunday, when no repair service would pick up the phone.

"Aw, great." Well, Curtis was just going to see a little more leg today.

He didn't notice her legs when he walked in, just

reeled in the warmth. "Whoo, mind if we turn up the air?"

"Can't," Lily grumbled, "it's broken."

"Did you call a repair—oh. Sunday. Do you have any fans?"

"Just the one." Lily pointed to the ceiling fan, way, way, way above them. "I opened the windows, but no breeze."

"Maybe we should close the curtains, then, to keep out the sun."

Lily sighed, and shut out her view of the mountains.

It was a long, sweltering, mood-curdling day. The curtains blocked the sunlight, but trapped the warmth in a suffocating fog. The thermostat kept on ticking upward, and Lily just couldn't find a cool space in the house. The material of her living room couch sucked in heat, and Lily wasn't about to invite Curtis upstairs—not that it proved to be any nicer. They stayed in the kitchen all day, where they could at least refill their glasses with ice water, until it sweat down the sides, which felt lovely on the forehead.

As if that wasn't enough, the writing dragged. They'd reached what Curtis called the "apparent defeat," and Lily prided herself on knowing this part: when the protagonist thought all hope was lost. Elsa had tried to make the little town like her, but only stirred up trouble, and now Mitch had finally told her off for interfering. The pass was clear, and Dad was better; Elsa could finally return home.

"Good riddance," Lily muttered. She'd wanted this to be a gut-wrenching moment, where the reader looked through the rearview mirror as they left the sugar-cookie town for the bleak, gray-skied reality. Curtis, of course, had changed all that.

She had been excited when Curtis liked one of her ideas:

121

Elsa tries out a number of local Christmas traditions because she's so bored after her busy lifestyle. Lily had imagined a host of warm-hearted community activities. Ice-skating on the lake, then a cup of cocoa (with warm company, of course). Christmas caroling down the lamplit main street (Elsa couldn't sing, but Mitch sure could). A shop-local contest, where the people could enter a raffle when they bought Christmas presents from their neighborhood store instead of online. The winner got a free dinner at a local fine-dining establishment (which, of course, Elsa's dad would win and give to her, provided she take Mitch).

Curtis took all those ideas, threw them in a blender, and pressed "Subvert." Ice skating was now a dangerous activity the locals kept up despite accidents happening. Christmas caroling was now a money-grubbing exercise where the town extorted donations for "charity." And the shop-local raffle? Only included shops with owners on the town's "good" list. No wonder Elsa left.

"But why does it have to be all depressing?" Lily asked at the end of the scene.

Curtis sat up from his spot on the couch. He wore short sleeves, but still rolled them up to his shoulders, which only amplified his boniness. "Depressing? If these guys stayed in power, that'd be depressing, but they don't. Elsa comes back, shows everybody up, and changes things for the better. Mitch gets on Team Elsa, they kiss under the tree or the mistletoe or whatever, and best of all, Elsa has done the heroic thing of returning to do the hard work instead of returning to a life of comfort. Happy ending."

Fair enough, but couldn't he tell that story in the summer? Couldn't the Christmas story just be pleasant? Did Christmas really need a power narrative?

Lily kept it all to herself. Even if she could win the argument, which she doubted, it was too hot to argue. She put her dripping water glass to her temple, closed her eyes, and listened to the laptop's fan whir.

Curtis said, "You know, I really think we're going to make it."

Lily peeked one eye open. "Really?"

Curtis was leaning over his laptop. "Yeah. I'm looking at our layout, and we're about two-thirds of the way through. Today's the eighteenth, so I think we'll make it. You've got extra copies saved elsewhere, right?"

Lily nodded. "In the cloud and on multiple flash drives."

Curtis leaned back on the couch. "Yeah...yeah, we're gonna make it."

Lily slid her cold glass down to her chest, and watched the ceiling fan struggle. All this work, and it was actually paying off? "We're seriously writing a book in a month?"

"Amazing what happens when there's a deadline, huh?" But he was smiling. A real, even relieved, smirk, which seemed to be the most his red-splotched face could do.

Condensation dripped onto her skin, and the cool washed all over her body. "Then in that case..." Lily set down the glass and marched over to the freezer. She yanked it opened, and took a minute to let the frigid blast waft beneath her hair and down her shirt front, then picked out a gallon tub of ice cream.

Curtis's eyes misted. "Oh, yes. I will definitely take a bowl."

"Screw bowls. If we can finish a book, we can finish this." Lily grabbed two spoons, then took the tub to the couch. "Scoot."

Curtis slid aside, accepted his spoon, and helped her attack the gallon of cookies and cream. It only took seconds for the cream to start running. As Curtis lifted a scoop to his mouth, a splotch of spotted white leapt from his spoon and splattered on the deep purple couch.

"Shoot!" Curtis cried, wiping it with his hand. "Sorry about that."

Lily had watched the whole thing. Staring now at the smudge on her upholstery, Lily realized not one cell in her body seemed perturbed. "Whatever. I need to get a new one anyway."

"How come?"

"It's hard, it's too shallow, it's a bad color, and it absorbs heat." Lily shoved a massive spoonful of freezing joy into her mouth.

"Couch not what you thought it would be, huh?" Curtis guessed.

"Nope."

"Well, speaking of décor, I have been dying to ask...what *is* that?" He pointed with his spoon.

Lily turned and beheld the orange-on-green minimalist art thingamajig. "Oh, that. To be perfectly honest, I have no idea. I think it's a person with half a head asking a question. Or an orange slice precariously balancing on a papaya? No idea, and I'm not a fan."

"Then why did you buy it?"

"I didn't. My sister is an interior designer, and she owns that furniture store you saw me go into the other day. She does this kind of thing for a living, and I was struggling to write, so she took over the décor, and I never actually saw any of it until I stepped into my house for the first time."

"Huh. That explains a lot."

Lily looked up from her ice cream. "It does?"

Curtis gulped down a bite. "First of all, I've seen you walk around sometimes and just glare at stuff. Like that painting, or that exercise bike there. Or that light fixture in your writing room."

"Oh!" Lily growled. "I hate that thing! Every time I look at it, it stabs me in the eyes; I just wanna rip it from the ceiling!" She froze, then glanced at a wide-eyed Curtis. "Please don't tell your boss I said that. I don't want it getting back to Mary, and...erm, what was second of all?"

"Second," Curtis said, "it didn't seem like your style."

Lily sat up straighter and cocked her head. "You...know my style?"

"Well, I'm only guessing. You said you built this house, right? Like, chose the layout and roof and windows and all that stuff?"

"Right."

"It's got more of a cabin or a cottage feel to it. Not rustic, exactly, just earthy. And the décor is more...modern chic showroom."

It was almost chilling how accurate he was—if the stifling heat would allow such a chill to pass through her. Everything Mary chose, everything she owned and sold, seemed to say, "Look at me! Aren't I darling?" Lily had never cared to show off for strangers beyond cleaning the toilet. It was a house. Her house. Furniture, art, everything supposed to welcome her home, not dance in her face.

Curtis went on. "I kind of expected more of a relaxed, getaway kind of style when I saw the outside. Like, pictures of lakes and stars and stuff. Darker wood, maybe some older-looking lamps."

Another chill. Well, no, not a chill, exactly—not that cold. More like the wind finally rushing through the open window, tossing her hair on its stream. "Yeah, that would be better."

"And you can't just replace it all?" Curtis asked.

"Nope."

"Too expensive?"

"That, and my sister got it all for me because I asked her to. I don't want to thank her by chucking it all out the window."

"So…you just live with it?"

Lily sank further into her seat. "I don't know…"

Her buzzing phone cut the conversation short, not that Lily wanted these bats flurrying through her brain any longer. The text came from Mary. Hey, if it isn't too late can you grab two big bags of ice on your way over?

Lily's brain gear clicked over once. Then twice in the same span. Then four, eight, faster and faster her mind churned until everything fell into horrifying place. June eighteenth. Sunday. *Mandy's party!*

She gave a yelp and jumped up, standing on the couch with the ice cream tub under her arm.

"What?!" Curtis cried, staring up at her.

Lily checked the clock. Six-thirty. The party started at seven.

Lily looked down at her sweaty, short-shorted,

barefoot, frizzy-haired self and belted out a long, throaty wail.

"Seriously, what?!" Curtis shouted, leaping up onto the couch with her.

"It's Father's Day!"

"Uh, yeah?"

"You knew?!"

"What? Of course I knew! That's why I saw my dad this morning."

"I thought you were at church!"

"Oh, no, my dad's, like, a platinum-level atheist."

"I'm late!" Lily shoved the ice cream into Curit's hands, jumped right over the back of her couch, and bolted up the stairs. "Party! Family! Gotta go! Bye! Tomorrow!" She kicked her bathroom door shut, and had her shirt off before she heard the slam.

Lily cranked the shower on. *I can do this. Just be quick, get dressed, blame my lateness on getting ice.* Thank the Lord she'd already bought a dress. She only needed a—

—date.

Lily grinded her knuckles into her temples, screaming into her pinched lips. There was no other way. She hadn't even tried to find a date; she'd been too preoccupied with the book. And now, she only had one option.

She wiped the foam off her mouth, then darted back out of the bathroom, crashing into the balcony so hard she nearly flipped over it. "Curtis!"

"Yes? Oh…" Curtis quickly averted his eyes.

Lily looked down and saw her bra smiling back up at her. She let out a loud "Yarg!" and flew back into the bathroom. Flinging her sweaty, smelly shirt back on, she ran back out to the balcony. "Curtis!"

"Yeah?" he answered, still pointedly looking at the floor.

"Do you have anything formal you could wear? Tuxedo, preferably, but even a suit and tie?"

"Uh...yes, but why?"

That was an excellent question. Why on Earth would Curtis drop all his plans to attend the birthday party of a teenager he did not know, posed as a date for someone he didn't exactly like?

The clock was ticking. Lily pulled out old reliable: "There's free food."

He was back and dressed in twenty minutes.

Lily held up the hem of her dress as she scampered barefoot down the stairs. She could've had a knee-length, airy garment, but nooo, Mary had suggested the floor-length, burgundy, cling-to-the-sweat-of-your-legs ball gown. Pity's sake, it was *still* stuffy in here! Curtis had returned, and she gave him the briefest glance. Black suit, white button-up, black slacks, matching shoes.

She said, "Gorgeous, now help me."

Somewhere between cutting her thigh shaving, and blow-drying her hair while applying eye shadow at the same time, she realized she'd also forgotten to buy Mandy a birthday gift. Lily might have knocked out her own teeth if she hadn't remembered she had the perfect gift waiting in her writing room.

Carrying a ginormous, foam-filled grape was not easy, even with two people. They bonked the exploding light fixture once, and each of them squashed their fingers in the doorway, but Lily and Curtis managed to stuff the giant purple zit into her back seat. She dashed back inside for her shoes and purse, then hopped into her driver's seat, almost forgetting to wait for Curtis to get in.

As Lily tore around a narrow bend, her back tires kicking up pieces of gravel and shredded pinecones, Curtis grasped the door and the dashboard. "Hey, hey, if I'm gonna die, can I at least know what for?"

Lily rolled her eyes. The sun still shone, and the road was dry. What a baby. "We're late for a birthday party I should've been to by now." She glanced at the dashboard clock. Five-til-seven. Not bad, but she should never have forgotten Mandy!

"Okay, so I'm gonna die for being late to a birthday party. Friend of yours? Family?"

"Family. Name's Mandy, she's turning thirteen."

"Oh." Curtis glanced down at his fancy threads. "All this dress-up is for a teenager's party?"

"Her request." Lily's head was a blender right now, scrambling to figure out where to get ice, the shortest route to Mary's house, and how to explain everything.

"Is she high-maintenance or something?"

"What? No, she's super sweet."

"Then why are you freaking out right now?"

Lily realized she was squeezing her shoulders so tight that her armpits hurt. She relaxed, and applied the brake. She wouldn't be too late, and Mandy wouldn't mind. Mary would, but...

Lily took a little more care turning onto the highway, but made sure to still stay on the high end of the speed limit. "Sorry about that; I'm just upset with myself for forgetting.

Mandy's been going on about her birthday for over a month. Father's Day, seven o'clock, bring formalwear and a date."

"Date?" Curtis repeated. "Is...that what I am?"

Somehow, hearing that word from his lips made her neck prickle in funny ways. "It doesn't have to be a big deal. You don't have to, like, fawn over me or kiss me goodnight or anything. Just a one-night thing. If...that's okay. Something I should have asked first, probably."

"No—that is—yeah, it's fine."

"Good." Lily allowed herself to be just a tiny bit flattered by his stammering, then sank into deep thought. A date wasn't a boyfriend, but it wasn't a tagalong either. In Lily's mind, a date should be attentive, respectful, and pleasant company.

True, Curtis wasn't her favorite person, but he did have his upsides. Like how much work he'd put into her book. *Or how he knows my decorative style more than my own sister.* It was a little unnerving, the way Curtis could slice right through her layers and lay her insides bare. Sometimes, he was shockingly tender. Other times, he scoffed at what he saw.

Still, Curtis was a person. It wasn't fair to drag him along to a party with strangers just to make her look good. Lily resolved within herself to be a good date.

Her chance came at the gas station, where Curtis volunteered to carry the two floor-length bags of ice. They had to wait in line behind a grouchy, unshaven man buying a bottle of liquor, and two parents patiently explaining why their children couldn't have candy from the aisle *and* candy from the counter.

Rather than tap her toes in worthless impatience, Lily decided to use the moment, and the stark fluorescent lighting, to actually look at her date. She had to blink a couple times before she realized Curtis hadn't shrunk; she was just wearing heels. It was only a two-inch difference, but suddenly looking down made her belly turn.

Other than that, Lily had to admit Curtis scrubbed up nice. The simple black suit didn't hide his scrawniness, but somehow complimented it. The slacks made his legs look properly proportioned despite his height. And Lily had never been a fan of the bowtie, but Curtis actually looked dapper. He hadn't shaved, but the dark stubble balanced the soul patch so it wasn't so stark. Curtis's hair had also grown a tad, so it could sweep to the side instead of clawing down his forehead. All in all? Yeah, she could be seen in public with him. Maybe wear flats next time.

"You look nice," Lily said.

Curtis stared like it was the last thing he'd expected to hear from her. "Yeah? Thank you. Wore it to my big brother's wedding, and figured I might need it again someday."

"Well, it suits you very nicely." A date should compliment her partner.

And Curtis did grin, that boyish, chest-puffing smile only a nice word from a pretty girl could produce. "Yeah? You think your family will approve of your swagalicious new man candy?"

Lily snorted a laugh before she could cover her mouth. The children turned from their candy to gawk. "What?" she sniggered in a high whistle of a voice.

Curtis gave a sheepish shrug, rattling the ice. "I have no idea. I haven't been on an actual date in literal years, so I

131

apologize for the next several stupid things I say and do."

Years? Well, he wasn't the kindest soul. Kinda funny, though, which was another pleasant surprise.

But once they'd paid for the ice and returned to the car, the joke had soured in her mind. What would Mary and the others think when they heard their famous writer sister had hired in help? Lily also hadn't had a date in far too long, so her family would pounce like cats. The very first question of "How do you know each other?" would spill the whole story. And then the looks. The befuddled stare and dimming eyes of respect winking out.

"Curtis, I—"

"So is it—"

They both stopped, then Curtis said, "You go first."

"Okay. I was wondering...could we kind of downplay what we do? Like...maybe just say you're giving me advice?"

Lily couldn't check his expression while she made a turn across a busy street, but she could hear the way his voice slowed and deepened. "Are you...asking me to lie?"

"No, not lie. Just...okay, look, I haven't told my family how close I am to the deadline, or how much trouble I'm having. Not most of them, at least. I didn't want to worry them, because boy will they, especially my older sister. I don't want to make tonight about me; I want it to be a happy night for Mandy. So, can you help me do that?"

"So what am I supposed to say?" he asked with scorn in his tongue.

"Just say we've been talking. We met at the writer's

group and continued chatting since then, and you've been giving a lot of good advice. It's still true."

"By omission."

That hit her right in the diaphragm. Lily needed a second to catch her breath. "I just don't want to make a big deal of it. Not tonight." Then, she added, "Please?"

Curtis shuffled in his seat, then gave a low, "Fine."

Cold spiders walked up and down Lily's arms. She swallowed, then said, "So…what were you going to say a minute ago?"

Curtis hesitated, then said in a plain voice, "I was going ask if it's weird to say that dress makes you look like the world's finest bottle of wine."

Whoa, what? That splashed the top of her head, and spread across her shoulders, chest, back, and belly. It stupefied her for a moment, and made her miss her turn.

"No, it's not weird." An absolute lie. A compliment like that? Very abnormal. From Curtis? Apocalyptic. But if she played it normal, maybe he'd do it again.

Chapter 13

Lily thought Curtis summarized Mary's house quite well in one slack-jawed observation: "It has a fountain." Streams of water splashed in playful arcs down three tiers of flower-like bowls before plunging into the glittering pool below. Mary's driveway circled the feature, in case you didn't get a good enough look.

The circle drive had a second benefit: enabling visitors to make multiple rounds to ensure they were seeing this house correctly. An arched entryway tall enough to peer through the second story glass and the crystal-rain chandelier beyond. Oh, and another, skinnier arch on either side, with Grecian-vase flowerpots as big as a St. Bernard.

That was only the entryway. The rest of the house huddled up around like a family photo: the wrought-iron balcony, the bay window, the mini turret, garage, the curved side deck, all squeezed comfortably around the circle drive, dressed in their finest Sunday whites with black shutters, saying cheese through sparkling windows bathed in a shortbread-yellow glow.

Lily found a parking spot on the far end of the circle drive, but before she could open the door, a handsome teenager in a crisp, black-and-eggshell vest materialized and opened it for her.

"Oh, uh, thank you," Lily said.

"My pleasure, ma'am. Would you like me to take your ice?"

"Oh, yes, thank you."

Curtis thanked the ponytailed boy on his side, then said to Lily, "Your family's fancy."

"Not this fancy," Lily chuckled. "Mary's gone a little extra, I think." She ran a finger along the edge of her hair again, keeping strays in place. Three years she'd lived here, in that corner window that looked like it was trying to see over the garage's shoulder, yet she still felt the need to check a mirror before entering.

She finally did, whipping out a compact to gauge her hasty nude lipstick job and cheap eye shadow. By the time she'd dropped the compact back into her purse, Curtis stood at her side.

He was holding out an arm. *Right. Date.* Lily accepted it, and they walked in tandem to the door.

Another sharply-dressed high-schooler opened the door, and even bowed. Curtis gave a low "Holy crap" as he stepped into dueling rays of the chandelier's thousand lights, each one crossing beams between the cascade of crystals, and the zillion sequins of Mary's trim, golden gown. James stood next to her, just off to the side, beneath a curving, white staircase. His raven tuxedo and cleanshaven, movie-hero jawline almost dimmed the tired look in his eyes.

But just as Mary opened her mouth and spread her arms towards her sister, James's sleepy face jumped to life with, "Well, hey!" He lunged forward, arm outstretched, nearly knocking Mary aside before he clasped hands with Curtis. "I didn't know you were coming."

"Neither did I!" Curtis said, grasping his boss's hand with

an equal jolt of enthusiasm. "She said family, but I didn't connect that dots that you'd be here. This your place, man?"

"Yup. Every penny of it."

"Woof, nicely done."

Mary sidled her way into their powwow. "You two know each other?"

James said, "You've met Curtis before. At my office. Sorry, Curtis, you remember my wife, Mary." A certain, pointed look crossed from James's eyes to Curtis, though what it meant, Lily couldn't decipher.

Curtis shook Mary's hand more gently. "Mrs. Livingston."

Mary gave a brief smile, but then beamed at her sister, arms spread. "You made it!"

"Barely!" The ladies shared an embrace.

Mary looked Lily over and said, "Wow, you look gorgeous."

Lily brushed a molecule of dust from her burgundy hip. *Yes, I am a fine wine!* "I know, like a bottle of chardonnay, right?"

Mary gave a frankly pitiful smile. James bit his lip.

Lily sighed. "I got the wine colors wrong again, didn't I?"

"Well, fortunately it's a teenager's party, so you don't have to know alcohol."

Curtis raised an eyebrow, so Lily explained, "I never drink. I hate the taste, always have. Beer, wine, liquor, blech. So, yes, a teenager's party should have all my favorite drinks."

Curtis asked, "Why? Nobody's old enough to drive

anyway."

Lily actually chuckled at that.

James pointed to Lily and Curtis. "So how long as this been going on?"

They stared at each other. Lily would have been offended at the way Curtis leaned back an inch if she didn't feel her own back reclining, too.

Curtis said, "About, what, five minutes?"

Before he could give away Lily's forgetfulness, she jumped in with, "Curtis rescued me at the last second. For a while, I thought I'd have to go stag, but then...there he was! My hero."

Curtis looked caught between, *That didn't happen,* and, *Why yes, I am heroic.*

James said, "You said you met her, but I didn't realize it was anything serious."

They both stammered out a few word fragments.

James cut them both off by saying, "Lily, do me a favor. Get this guy to take a vacation. He's refused to take one for years."

Curtis gave a rueful smile. "Yes, yes, thank you, Jim."

Mary's smile twitched. "*Doctor Livingston* is so considerate, isn't he?"

While the smiles stayed on every face, the warmth went out of every one, leaving a chilly quiet in the entryway. Light music lilted in the next room.

Lily clenched and unclenched her bag, then said, "I got the ice by the way. But I think the, uh, car...boys took it. You have staff now?"

"Just tonight," Mary said. "Boy, do I wish, though."

James's eyes flashed with panic. Lily wondered just how

much they'd sunk into tonight.

Mary looked Lily up and down once more. "Did you bring a gift?"

Lily said, "Yes! It's in my car, and too weird to wrap. I figured we could just bring it in at gift time, or Mandy could come see herself."

"Sounds fun! Go see her by the way, she's around here somewhere."

Curtis and James gave each other a nod, then Mary gently ushered them into the house while turning to greet the next guests.

Despite living here for years, Lily could not understand modern housing. Everything was so vast and square and open that it almost looked like a warehouse. Almost. Mary had chosen simple, creamy white paint that conveyed a subtle warmth in place of a sterile pallor. And she'd filled every room with so many paintings, prints, couches, loveseats, lights, tables and pillows—good grief, the pillows—that the cavern actually looked snuggly.

The space did allow for a good twenty or more tweens to huddle in small groups, sitting stone-still on couches too prim and fluffy to seem inviting to outsiders. Most of the kids held drinks in a riot of colors. Nobody cringed at the taste, but they all drank with superhuman caution, their eyes immediately dropping to the carpet to check for drips. Pimply boys scratched beneath their clip-on ties. Gangly girls tugged at the hems of dresses that suddenly felt cheap. Many a curious eye reached across the room to some bashful other, but nobody would burst the bubble of murmuring quiet that hovered over all of them.

Except one brunette girl in a red halter dress that billowed about her knees like a rose. She hop-walked around the room, balancing a pomegranate-red drink, and headed straight for Lily.

"Oh, you're so pretty!" Lily hugged the now-official teenager as hard as she could. "Hap! Py! Birth! Day!"

Mandy smiled so wide it went from pretty to scary in a fingersnap. "Yeah, happy birthday to me! Let's freak out all my friends!" She glugged her drink.

Lily stared at the girl's manic expression for a minute before finding her tongue again. "Uh, what's wrong?"

Mandy pointed to an older teen standing attentively beside a wall. "See that guy? His name is Julio, he's a junior in high school, and he's been paid to fetch drinks for anybody who asks, like we're all too snooty to do it ourselves." Mandy dropped her voice. "I mean he's gorgeous, but still." Mandy suddenly seemed to realize Curtis was there. Her eyes bulged a moment, then an impish grin bubbled up her face as she switched her eyes to Lily. "Ooooh!"

Curtis leaned back. "Uh, what?"

Lily jumped in before Mandy could speak. "Oh, she's just giving me grief because I haven't brought a date in six months. Nine. Twelve. Twenty? Lord…"

Mandy stuck out her hand and said in a stuffy voice, "Mandy Louise Harper, mm, yes, charmed, I'm sure."

Curtis shook her hand, grinning halfway, like he wasn't sure he was allowed. "Ah, I'm Curtis Reynolds. You're the birthday girl?"

"That's what the cake says."

Curtis turned to Lily. "And I'm guessing she's

139

your…niece? Cousin?"

Lily and Mandy shared a look, their grins getting wider and sillier by the second. It was always so much fun to do this. "Actually," Lily said, "this lovely new bloom is my little sister."

Oh, yes, there was the stare. The blink. The jerky shaking of the head to rattle the beans into comprehension. Now if he'd only…

"Uh…wait, what?"

He did!

Curtis rolled up his tongue and said, "How old are you, Miss Harper?"

"Twenty-nine."

"And she's…?"

"Thirteen." Lily squeezed the girl hard from the side. "She was the best surprise our family ever got." She giggled to Mandy. "That never gets old."

Mandy smirked. "At least this party has one delight."

"Is it not going well?" Lily gazed across the room, at the pockets of clustered teenagers in formalwear, still and nervous.

"Everyone is too 'Whoa!' from how fancy everything is."

"You did ask for a formal attire."

"I know, but servants?" Mandy nodded to a stuffed charcuterie board on the coffee table. "Mouse-sized food I can't even pronounce? Whatever froo-froo thing I'm drinking right now? I look like some kind of wealthy heiress."

"And that's bad?" Lily asked.

"I wanted this whole date setup so I could get to

know Miguel better, but he keeps looking around the house like it's going to fall on him." Mandy indicated a Latino boy near the back door, who was indeed gaping at the ceiling—or at least chandelier number two.

Lily rubbed Mandy's shoulders. "Listen, the party's barely started. Everybody will warm up, and it will be a blast. Okay? Just relax."

Mandy took a deep breath. "Yeah. You're right. Mom and the rest are in the back yard, hiding from all the hormones, they say. I'm going to go tell Miguel a fart joke or something, let him know I'm still human." She downed the last of her drink, and soldiered on.

Lily tried not to laugh. "Kids, right? Always nervous about appearances."

Curtis was too busy staring at a sconce. "Are those gold flecks in the candles?!"

Forget the chandeliers, forget the frosted glass candle jars, forget the tumblers glistening with rainbow drinks; Mary's in-ground pool sparkled the most. Lily knew it was just the bottom of the pool and gallons of chlorine, but had nature every produced such a cool, gemlike cerulean? No ripples disturbed its glasslike surface, yet the tiki torches winked in its mirror sheen.

But Lily could only stand at the concrete edge, beneath the needling lances of the evening sun, and sigh.

"I know, right?" Curtis adjusted his midnight-black suit jacket. "Try wearing three layers."

"Try having nothing between you and sunburn." Lily

shrugged her bare shoulders. "You should have come last year; Mandy had a pool party."

"Oh…" Curtis watched the pool like a faraway lover.

"Yeah, you missed out on the chance to see me in a bikini." Lily pinched her eyes shut. "Which is an image I just put in your head."

Curtis cleared his throat, appearing to struggle against a smile. Lily decided to enjoy that.

"Lily!" a voice called. To her right, across the cobblestone patio, a square pavilion blanketed six people beneath white curtains. They sat on wicker sofas drowning beneath even more pillows. Strings of lights looped their way across the ceiling, while tall candles on a center table tried to match them from below.

"Hey, everyone!" Lily greeted as she stepped into the shadow of the pavilion. Still warm, but not blazing. "Curtis, this is my family."

"Whoa," he replied.

"Well, not all of them. The tall one there is Asher, and that's his wife, Godiva."

"Oh, neat name," Curtis said as he shook the thin, tanned blonde with sleepy eyes.

Asher put an arm around her and said, "Well, when you're a model and actress, you need to stand out."

The dark-haired Oak waved his hand through the air. "Four seconds. It took just four seconds for you to broadcast who and what dared to marry you." Godiva giggled, and Oak stood up to shake Curtis's hand. "I'm Oak, and this lovely lady here is Kimberly. Also a model, not that it matters."

The spiky-haired Kimberly chuckled. "Only for

stock photos."

Lily pointed to the mid-twenties girl with long, auburn locks. "That's my little sister Daisy. Don't let the sweet housewife look fool you; she's a graphic designer. And her husband, Jerome."

"*Captain* Jerome," Daisy said. "Don't let Mary hear you say it without the captain."

The broad-chested Jerome chuckled in a low timber. "I fly airplanes. Good to see you, Lily."

Oak's date Kimberly gasped. "Wait, Lily *Harper*? The writer?"

Oak gave her a puzzled look. "I told you she was my sister, remember?"

"I thought you said that so I would date you!"

"No! Well, yes, but it was true."

Lily kicked Oak's shin. "Don't use my name to get women!"

Oak waved hands over Kimberly's petite, curvy figure. "But the results!"

That got a laugh from most, and Lily made her way around the pavilion, hugging every one of her brothers and sisters, especially Daisy. While Oak and Asher lived nearby, Daisy was the only one to "officially" leave the nest.

"I hate that you're in Boise," Lily whined. "You haven't even seen my house!"

"I'm so sorry! It's been busy, and then *you've* been busy. And when your husband is a pilot, you live near the airport."

"There's an airport in Hailey, twenty minutes away!"

"A tiny one for, like, celebrity jets."

Lily turned to Jerome. "You. Start flying celebrities."

Daisy rolled her eyes. "Are you going to introduce us to

your date or do we just guess?"

Lily fought the blush. She had actually forgotten Curtis was there, patiently waiting, smiling awkwardly. "Sorry! This is Curtis. We...are both writers. He's been giving me pointers on my new book."

Kimberly gasped again.

Asher stood and shook Curtis's hand, then asked, "Have we met?"

"Not to my knowledge," Curtis said. "But I do work at Jim's office."

"Doctor Livingston," Daisy and Oak both intoned.

Asher shook his head. "Never been there, but you look familiar somehow."

Lily still agreed. By now, she could only guess that she'd seen him around their small town before. "Where's Mom?" she asked.

All three siblings frowned at once, and pointed behind Lily. Across the patio, on the opposite side of the cool, blue pool, stood several patio tables. Some teenagers ate and gabbed around one of them, but Mom sat at another.

Across from a man.

"What in the...?" Lily asked.

Asher said, "Mandy did specify that everyone must bring a date."

"Well, yeah, but..." The serpents in her stomach wouldn't stop wriggling.

Oak said, "She's too old to have kids now."

Daisy snorted. "We said that before with Mandy."

All the siblings here were only a few years apart, but there was a twelve-year gap between Oak and Mandy. They'd been shocked before, and by the dark glint in many eyes, they remembered what happened the last time Mom found herself a man.

And the time before that.

And the time before that.

Lily had fleeting memories of a sandy-haired man sitting next to her, watching *Sesame Street*, and then he was gone. Most people under this pavilion didn't even have that.

Lily swallowed hard, then said, "I'm going to go introduce Curtis. Be right back."

Curtis hurried to keep up with her, his shoes clacking on the cobblestones. "Wow, big family. That was, what, five siblings total?"

"Yeah. Six of us," Lily said, only half listening. The other half was sizing up the burly, gray-bearded man laughing with Mom.

"Holy crap. This dude your dad or…?"

"No. No dads. They all left."

"They…plural?"

She didn't have time to get into it; they were already approaching the couple—no, the pair. Lily wasn't about to call them a couple. "Hi, Mom."

"There you are!" Mom opened a thick arm, and Lily sank into its softness.

"Mom, this is Curtis. He's a writer like me."

"Oh! Sounds like you're the perfect man for my Lily, then."

Curtis smiled sheepishly. "I'm…not sure I'm quite that high up."

Lily raised an eyebrow at that, but brushed away any fuzzies it gave her. "Mom, who's this?"

"This is Cliff. Cliff, this is Lily."

The big man stood up and shook Lily's hand with his meaty digits. He had a kindly smile, though, beneath his watery eyes. "Lily. So…third-oldest, right?"

"Y-Yes. How did you know?"

Mom said, "With a family as big as ours, I've had to train him."

Cliff counted off on his fingers. "Mary, Asher, Lily, Daisy, Oak, Mandy. Did I get the order right?"

"Perfect!"

I wonder what the seventh will be called. No, no, she's fifty-two. Not happening.

"I see that look," Mom said with a rueful smile. "Don't worry, sweetheart, I've learned my lesson. Cliff is just a date. He's a trucker, gone way too much."

"More's the pity," said Cliff, and Lily swore she saw Mom grin.

Mom went on about how they kept bumping into each other, laughing at some inane details. The blood pounding in Lily's ears did not help her hear any of it. She kept a sweet smile, but slowly choked the strap of her purse.

Then, a hand rested between her shoulder blades, and she realized how close Curtis was standing. She glanced at him, and while he held up the same patient, friendly smile as Lily, his eyes watched her with a note of concern. Lily had forgotten how he saw through her. Yet while his hand was warm as anything else in this miserable sun, it somehow cooled her blood, unclenched her jaw, and uncurled her grasping hands.

After a little more chat, Lily made some excuse about

talking to her siblings again, and Mom didn't seem to mind being left alone with "just a date."

"Are you okay?" Curtis whispered as they left earshot.

"Yes. Thank you for that."

"Sorry if it was—"

"No, no, it was helpful."

"Okay…can I know what that was about?"

"Lily!" a voice interrupted before she could answer. Jim, James, or Dr. Livingston, one of them approached from the back door. "Mandy's decided she wants to do gifts first. Can you grab yours?"

"Yeah, but give me a minute, it's a bit unwieldy."

Curtis said, "We'll get it. Jim and I, I mean. You stay with your family. Jim? It takes two people."

"I'm game," James said.

Lily handed over her keys, then watched them go, wondering if she'd invited a stranger into too much. Even if she still felt his hand on her back.

Lily accepted a drink from one of the high-school servants, then returned to her siblings under the awning.

"Grossed out yet?" Daisy asked.

Oak said, "Grow up, you guys. Mom can have a boyfriend."

Lily and Asher shared a serious look. Only they really understood the problem. The others had been out when Mom promised it would never happen again.

Fortunately, Oak asked if Jerome had flown anywhere interesting lately, and the conversation returned to shallow waters. After a few minutes, Asher looked over Lily's shoulder and said, "Your date is back. Why does he look so familiar? It's driving me nuts."

Lily shrugged. "I don't know. It's a small town, so we've probably seen him around."

Then Daisy said, "Lily, he looks like that cartoon you used to have a crush on."

Lily hadn't taken a drink, but she choked anyway. "He—What?!"

Asher snapped his fingers. "That's it! The guy from *The Iron Giant*."

"Dean!" Oak cackled.

"Who?" asked every date, while every sibling burst into laughter.

Lily wished the mouth of hell would yawn beneath her feet and swallow her forever. She had forgotten all about her stupid, adolescent fantasy. Most girls crushed on pop stars or chiseled actors. Lily had swooned over a series of painted lines with a fake voice.

The worst part was...Daisy was right. As Lily shot a panicked look over her shoulder, she could see the resemblance. The short, black hair. The soul patch. The stubble on a pointed chin. Curtis was even an artsy-fartsy type. Why couldn't she have figured this out anywhere except a family party?

Curtis raised an eyebrow as he approached. "What'd I miss?"

The siblings laughed again.

"Nothing," Lily cut in. "Nothing, just...just an inside family joke you wouldn't get."

"Okay...uh, well, Mandy's about to open presents."

The group peeled themselves off of wicker and cushions, doing painfully bad jobs of hiding sniggers and sideways glances. Lily put her drink to her forehead, fully expecting the ice to boil. If it didn't, perhaps the chill would freeze her brain so it couldn't continue down this train of thought. Curtis did not drive a motorcycle or wear leather. Curtis wasn't casually cool and charming. And Curtis certainly didn't high-five billboard-sized robots.

So there was absolutely no reason for Lily to realize how smooth and thick Curtis's hair was tonight.

Chapter 14

Mandy adored her new foam chair, and when Mary gave Lily a questioning look, Lily replied, "I saw how much Mandy loved mine and realized it was the perfect gift idea." This smoothed the lines of worry on Mary's face. Although they seemed to move onto Curtis's for some reason.

With all eyes on Mandy's mountain of presents from friends and family, Lily had little need to defend herself against *Iron Giant* jokes. Mandy seemed delighted by her new shoes, gift cards, day pass to a local amusement park, and her favorite: books.

Mandy called from behind her stack, "I'd better get yours for Christmas, Lily!"

Lily gave her a thumbs-up.

But Curtis gave a bemused, "Huh."

"What?" Lily asked.

Curtis was staring at Mandy, or rather through her into the future. "She's going to read this book."

"Yeah, that's one reason I don't want any raunchy stuff in it."

"No, no, I mean the book we're working on right now, the one that isn't finished, someone is going to read it. Guaranteed."

Lily lifted her chin proudly. "Yep."

Curtis continued to look like he'd been hit with a

hammer.

"What?" Lily asked.

"I've just never had that kind assurance before."

She tilted her head. "What do you mean? You've put books out."

"Yeah, but it was only a vague hope anybody would care. You've got a contract already."

And just like that, she was three years younger. Same hardwood under her feet, same cloying potpourri in her nose, and the same spider-bites of worry in her brain. She could almost feel the gentle pressure across the soles of her feet, pacing circles around every room. She'd paced barefoot in those days as not to annoy Mary, who'd taken her in. She'd pace and wonder if she could repay Mary with that book. Would it sell? Would all her work amount to anything?

Would anybody care?

"I get that," Lily said, bringing herself back into the room. The cheap teenage perfume helped her remember she didn't live here anymore. She'd made it. Mostly. And Curtis was helping her keep it.

Perhaps that was why his look troubled her. His gaze had faded, his face blank. All that certainty while they were writing, all those absolutes of yes and no, but did he secretly doubt he knew anything?

Lily wanted to ask, but the crowd erupted in laughter at the reference on Mandy's new tee shirt.

As the hired teens swept up the last bit of wrapping paper, and the party guests quietly edged out of their way, Mary said, "Hey you two, let's step outside real quick," so Lily still couldn't talk to Curtis.

But Lily wasn't the only one who followed Mary. All the

siblings and their dates, plus Mom and Cliff came along, too. The rest of the teens stayed to talk as Mandy promised, "I'll be right back!" Right back from where? Had Lily missed a memo?

Mary led them back to the patio, past the cool blue of the mocking pool, to a firepit just outside the pavilion. One of the servants—still an odd word in Lily's head— had just stoked a roaring blaze. Thank heavens the mountains were tall enough to start hiding the setting sun, balancing the heat with first wafts of cool, evening air.

Mary said to everyone, "Okay, we'll be quick so we can get back to celebrating Mandy, but it's Father's Day, and we have a little tradition."

Crap in a bucket! Lily's brain roared. Shooting glances around the group, she realized every one of her siblings was holding a card, while her hands held nothing but sweat. What else would she forget tonight?!

Mary continued, "For those of you who are new, the Harper family doesn't really celebrate Father's Day. If you look around, you'll see why." The new faces all did, recognition dawning as they counted the number of dads in the pavilion on a closed fist. "Yes, our fathers decided they were better off without us, so we decided we are better off without them. Mandy was born on a Father's Day, so we are lucky enough to celebrate someone who's here instead of someone who is not. But about seven years ago, we found it kind of cathartic to do a little something nasty." She held up a card, with flowing, Hallmark script across the front. "We all find a Father's Day card, read it, mock it, and burn it. Because we do not need them; we've all made it just fine on our own, with just each other and

Mom."

"And a big sister," Daisy added.

"Amen," said Asher.

Others nodded. Lily would have joined if her brain wasn't sweating.

"What's up?" Curtis whispered so low that Lily could barely hear him as Mary went on.

"I forgot," Lily breathed back.

"Oh…" Curtis winced. So he, too, lacked the superpower of materializing a greeting card from moisture in the air. Now what?

Mary said, "I'll start." She flipped open her card and read in a bored monotone. "To the world's greatest dad. You are truly one of a kind, and I don't know what I'd do without you." Mary looked up. "Oh, wait, yes I do! Never mind!" She dropped the card into the bonfire.

Mandy said, "Ah, that was lame card anyway. Who writes these?"

Those words flicked a light switch in Lily's brain. "I'll write it!" she whispered to Curtis.

"Ooh, good idea," he said. "I think I have a pen…"

"Shh!" she hissed. Asher was stepping forward to read his card. Some kind of tongue-in-cheek jibe about being too "manly" to express emotions, so he'd say it through beer. Lily didn't hear the punchline over her muttering. "Hello, Dad, how have you been…yes, it's been a while…I'm all grown up and doing fine…and, uh…selling books with style. Eh, good enough. It's been so long since you called that…I…thought you'd been a-slumber…does that even make sense?"

"Lily?" Mary's voice chimed in.

Lily looked up and saw a dozen of eyes peeping back at

her. "Sorry! My turn? Right. Okay." She brushed hair out of her face that wasn't actually there. "So, this year, I thought I'd do something a wee bit different. We all know how cheesy and lame greeting cards can be—and this is the girl who watches Hallmark movies like they're going out of style."

The group chuckled.

"Right, so for the one or two of you who don't know, I am a writer." Lily heard Kimberly give a little squee. "So instead of giving Hallmark even more of my money, I thought I'd write a card this year. So...here goes." She cleared her throat.

"Hello Dad, how have you been?

Yes, it's been a while.

I'm all grown up and doing fine.

Selling books with style.

It's been so long since you called,

I thought you'd been in deepest slumber..."

Oh, no.

Lily cleared her throat to buy time, lips pinched in a fake smile. Why had she said slumber? What the heck rhymes with slumber? And this was where the punch line should go, so...

Lily faked a need for a drink, and sipped, thinking hard. Number? Bumbler? "Ahem. I thought you'd been in deepest slumber..."

Eyes like tiny spotlights criss-crossed Lily's face, scouring for the talent they'd been promised, burning her face, but freezing her blood.

Suddenly, Curtis stepped forward, holding out a wrinkled piece of paper. "You want your notes?"

Lily blinked, then took the paper. It felt like a receipt, and she could barely read his scraggled scrawl written at an angle. But she grinned.

"It's been so long since you called,

I thought you'd been in deepest slumber.

I only have one question...

Who the hell gave you this number?"

Everybody cackled—except perhaps Cliff, who looked nervous now. The group applauded Lily's latest work. Kimberly said she should write cards for a living, but Lily decided to stick to books. Rhyming was a nightmare.

The family kept the rhythm going, as Daisy recited her card in a flowing, posh accent, but Lily's brain seemed stuck on the stage. Her blood still raced from her belly to her face to her hands to her chest to her toes, and carried it all back to her brain with reports of alarm in every sector. That had been so close! She'd almost disappointed the entire family at once! Why wouldn't her hands stop shaking? Lily took a sip of her drink, but her face still steamed, and tears still pooled in her eyes. Why couldn't she calm down? It was just a moment of embarrassment, and it hadn't actually happened! They were family. They'd understand.

But you don't let the family down, scolded a voice in her ear. *You know the rules; we all work together. You can't be the only one—*

A hand touched her back. Curtis again, seeing everything she tried to hide. But the warmth of his touch reverberated through her nerves and veins, pulsing the message through her system, "It's okay." Her heart slowed, her blood eased into a normal flow, and her brain finally cleared through the alarm bells. Business as usual. Save for a confused bundle of nerves blushing between her shoulder blades.

Lily dared a glance, but Curtis was a good actor, watching the family and smiling along, never letting on what his hand was doing. Good idea, too. The last thing Lily wanted was for the whole family to go "ooh" and "aaah" and "Deeaaan." So, for subtlety's sake, Lily put a hand on his back, too, hoping that through the layers of thread and padding, something in his system would register, "Thank you."

For Oak's recital, he pretended not to know his card was actually a Mother's Day card because he was thinking of the parent who was actually there.

Then Mandy waved her card and said, "Dear Dad…" Mandy stared at the open card a moment, then turned to show it to everybody. "It's blank. Y'know, because I never knew him."

Everybody cringe-laughed, Lily included.

Asher said, "Ah, screw 'em all," which got a chorus of "Here, here," and a clinking of drinks. But Lily noticed an odd look on Mandy's face. Eyes averted, smile drooping, life and color paling. Mandy returned to her guests before Lily could ask about it. The rest of the family milled about, some seeking the cooler indoors while some remained in the open air. Servants came to collect and refill glasses.

Curtis's hand had left her back.

At some point, Lily and Curtis got separated. They chose the freon shelter of the living room, and Lily moved between family members, catching up with her many relations. She promised to sign Kimberly's copy of *Maple Leaves* when next they met.

The family made Curtis feel welcome, but he mostly talked with James. Or Jim, as Curtis said. Bizarre to hear him called that. Mary always said "James" with a subtle certainty, like one would say "bright" when talking about the sun. It wasn't something to question.

On the other hand, Jim and James seemed like two different people. When had James ever talked this much? He usually hung around the edges of the family. Friendly, loving, and helpful, but never so engaged. He still had a tired look crinkled at the corners of his eyes, but his smile was bigger—not broad, just solid.

Real?

Lily turned her attention back to Godiva and Asher on the opposite couch. Best not to think about such things. Mary didn't want to talk about them, certainly. When Lily peeked again, where the two men chatted with arms crossed, leaning against the far wall, Curtis seemed to be smiling more, too.

More than the rest of the partiers, at least. Yeesh, what was with these kids? Mandy had cut her cake about fifteen minutes ago, and everybody ate cheerfully, but they were all so stiff, glancing at the bow-tied servants like bodyguards who might toss out the riff raff any second now.

Lily was considering moving over to chat with three girls who looked like they were holding their breath, when Curtis made his way back over to her.

"Hey," he said. "Got a minute?"

"Oh? Sure, uh…" Lily scoured the house, but couldn't find a good quiet spot some teenagers hadn't claimed. Garage?

Kind of rude. Upstairs? Ha! She'd never live down the teasing. "We can take a walk in the backyard if you like." She turned to Asher and Godiva. "Mind if I slip away?"

Asher said, "Sure. You have fun with Dean—I mean Curtis."

Curtis raised an eyebrow. Lily made a mental note to give her brother poison ivy for Christmas.

Hallelujah, the sun had finally fallen behind the mountains. The whole earth breathed out a cool sigh, and sank into a sleepy purple tint. Some kind of stringed chamber music drawled through the outdoor speaker. *Really, Mary?*

Lily led Curtis off the back patio, into the manicured green beyond. Mary dreamed of making this space into a vast nature reserve, with great trees and bushes all around, with a walking path winding through it all. The flora was still growing, but the stony path did weave around many bushes and fledgling growths, allowing plenty of hidey-holes for weary heads and broken hearts.

"So, I have two questions," Curtis said as they rounded the first bend. "One, is there a particular reason most of your family has asked me if I've seen *The Iron Giant?*"

"No," Lily growled deep in her throat. "They're just idiots. Next question."

Curtis tapped his fingertips together. "Am I, uh, stepping on any boundaries?"

"What? No. What do you mean?" Also, since when did that bother Curtis?

Curtis said, "I mean about me putting my hand on your back. And also...doing it again later. We've been working together for a couple weeks, but skin-to-skin contact is kind of a leap."

Lily bit her lip. She would *not* put "Curtis" and "adorable" in the same headspace. "It's not like you groped my butt; it was just a friendly hand on my back."

"Good. Good. I was just slipping into the date role, and you looked a little upset both times."

So if I wear a dress every day, you'll be nicer to me? Lily fought not to giggle at the idea of hamming it up: falling onto the couch with her arm thrown pitifully over her eyes, her summer frock rippling in the wind. "Well, I appreciate you looking out for me. And I was upset, yes."

"How come?"

She crossed her arms, breathed in the musk of earth and pine. "Mom hasn't made the best choices with men, so we get a little jumpy when one comes into her life. As for the greeting card thing…"

"It bugged you about your dad?"

"Actually, no. I got over him years ago. I guess I was just upset that first I forgot my sister's party, and then I forgot the Father's Day ritual. I…just couldn't shake it off. I don't like upsetting my family."

"Why not?"

Lily slowed her gait to a ponderous pace. "You saw how we don't like our dads very much. In case you didn't catch on, each kid has a different dad."

"Whoa…"

"Yeah. And none of them stuck around. My dad stayed the longest, and only until I was about three. Mom struggled to provide for us all. We had to work together to survive. Share cooking duties, dishes in pairs, taking care of clothes so they'd survive as hand-me-downs, babysitting, working once we were old enough…" Lily rubbed her arms. Boiling all day, and now she was cold?

She thought she saw Curtis move his hands, like he was going to put an arm around her, then thought better of it. Maybe her imagination? *He must seriously love this dress.* Lily put that compliment in her back pocket, then turned to warmer thoughts.

"It made us all really close. Here…" Lily stood up on her tiptoes to see over a high bush. "See that top-right window? I lived there for three years. I was struggling to make ends meet, so Mary took me in. She was already housing Mom and Mandy. I helped raise Mandy, Mom would cook, Mary and James worked. Still a team."

Curtis nodded thoughtfully. "It sounds like Mary took on the matriarch role."

"Pretty much. Mom is still Mom, but Mary's the one at the head of the table in that Norman Rockwell painting. The one where the lady's serving a Thanksgiving turkey?"

Curtis smirked. "Nice. I think I'm also starting to see why your house is so important to you."

"Yeah, I'm tired of mooching off of my family's kindness."

"Plus, you've had to do a lot of sharing. Nice to have a space all your own."

Lily frowned. That wasn't…was it? Lily loved being part of the family team, but then again, she recalled spending plenty of time in this mini-forest. Sometimes, she'd weave through the enormous back pines to watch the sun set paint the foothills. Or she'd take a blanket and a book, and slip into any one of the bends in the bushes, surrounded by rose scents and the buzz of bees. Enchanting, really. And quiet. So quiet.

"Maybe," she said.

"It's no shame," Curtis replied. "Everybody wants to get away, have their own space."

Perhaps, but Lily wasn't sure that was the only reason. She could've lived anywhere on her own, or bought some existing property. Yet she bent to the dream of building her own house from the ground up. Besides, she hoped to get married one day and live in that same house, so sole ownership wasn't the full dream. So, what was it?

They were coming up on the end of the loop already. Lily thought of suggesting another round or two, maybe ask more about Curtis this time. But then, her eyes caught the twinkling of Mary's sequin dress. Mary was tucked behind one of the taller trees, its shadow making that patch of the yard almost black. Mary spoke into the darkness, her arms crossed, and when Lily looked closer, she saw Mandy huddled in the tightest, murkiest edge of the shadow. The darkness wasn't yet strong enough to hide the tears in Mandy's eyes.

Lily broke off from Curtis immediately, and hurried the short distance through squashy grass. "Mandy, what's up?"

"Ask *her*," Mandy groused.

Mary gave a long, patient sigh. "Mandy seems to think I've ruined her party."

Mandy didn't deny it.

Lily said, "That's a bit harsh, Mandy. What's the matter, exactly?" She heard the soft steps of Curtis approaching behind her.

Mandy swung her arms in every direction. "Mary blew

the whole thing into this…this elegant soiree!"

"You asked for fancy," Mary pointed out.

"I asked for fancy *clothes*! I didn't ask for servants and stupid, expensive food, or froo-froo violin music on the patio. What are we supposed to do, waltz? The decorations, the way you talk to everybody, it's all blown way out of proportion!"

Lily did agree that Mary had taken the theme a hair too far, but… "Mandy, what's really bugging you?"

Mandy paused, hugging herself. "Miguel can barely talk to me. Nobody can. Everything was fine at school, but now that they're here, they're all intimidated. Miguel seems to think I'm some rich white girl who's too good for every-body else."

"Mandy, no one who knows you would think that."

"Exactly! But they can't know me when I'm in this giant house with a friggin' hedge maze, surrounded by all this make-believe, fake upper-crust crap!"

Lily saw the flash of a match slicing across Mary's eyes. Mary said, "Nothing is fake. Yes, we paid for staff for a party, but that house? That's our real house. We live there. This landscaping? Ours. The pool? Paid for. And every one of us—Mom, James, me, Lily, Asher, everyone!—has worked our tails off so that we can live like this, and I will not listen while you call all that work fake."

Not one word sweetened the sour pout on Mandy's face. "Your *name* is fake."

Mary set her teeth. "It's just a nickname, *Mandy*."

"*You're* the one who insisted I go by that name."

There was a moment of quiet, punctuated by a high

laugh from Mom's patio table. Then, Curtis asked, "What's your real name?"

Mandy frowned at him and said, "Mandragora."

"Mom was on a plant kick," Mary instantly cut in, fingers reaching to the hair on the back of her scalp. "Flowers, trees, herbs, she named us all like that."

Lily glanced at Mandy, and her face dropped at once. Lily wondered if Mary really needed to add all that.

Curtis looked between the two sisters, then settled on Mandy. "Your name is Mandragora?"

"Yep," she said.

A little smile snaked its way up Curtis's right cheek. "Dude, that is awesome!"

Mary and Mandy both snapped their faces up to him. Lily thought she saw alarm on Mary's.

"R-Really?" Mandy asked.

"Yeah! You sound like some kind of magical super-spy."

There was certainly some magic sprinkling over Mandy just now. All that anger, all the disappointment and pain just disappeared. Poof! Lily couldn't tell that her sister had ever been upset, not with that wondrous gleam in her eyes. "Yeah, I…thought so too. Or maybe the witch all the broken-hearted girls go to when their boyfriends cheat on them."

Curtis said, "Ooh, I should write that book."

Lily swiveled her head back between the two of them, wondering which was more bizarre. Curtis, being so friendly and supportive, or Mandy being so…well, not more open; she usually spoke her mind. But there was something funny about Mandy's parted mouth, like it was tasting air for the first time.

Mandy took a slow breath, then turned towards the house. "I should get back. It's my party after all." She passed by

Mary, and her face contorted into a nasty sneer. "See you, *Rosemary.*"

Lily opened her mouth to call Mandy back and demand she apologize, then paused when she realized it wasn't an insult, not really. It was a name. One she hadn't heard since Mary began branding her interior design business a good nine or ten years ago. Mary regarded it like a horrible smell.

Curtis said, "Rosemary's a nice name, too."

She sent him a look that drained all the warmth from the air. "So is James." Mary spun with a swish of her hair, and marched away like an action hero outpacing the explosion.

The explosion was only in Lily's head. So Mary had overdone the party. Was that really a reason to be so upset? So Rosemary and Mandragora had nicknames; was that a crime? So Mary liked to put on a good front for guests. Didn't everybody? And wasn't it her job to rearrange homes to look more appealing?

But…that's furniture, not people. Lily had to blink a dozen times. Was…Mary…?

Curtis interrupted with, "So, uh, is Lily your full name or…?"

"Yes, just Lily."

Curtis nodded with a frown. "Okay, so *now* I'm stepping on toes."

"Maybe a little." Lily walked him back to the party, too dizzy for another loop in the hedges.

Chapter 15

Mary did make one change that finally livened up the party: she switched the outdoor chamber music to the same upbeat pop as the inside, and invited everyone to use the back patio as a dance floor. The two dozen teens abandoned the living room fast enough to leave a trail of fire. Fancy parties were foreign concepts, but a desire to show off, or possibly broach physical contact with that special somebody? Teenagers understood those things.

Mandy cheered up too, as she and her girlfriends gyrated in what only the gentlest soul would call dancing. Adults joined, too, but Lily had more important things to do than embarrass herself. First, she checked that Mary and Daisy were still showing up the teens on the dance floor. Then, she made sure Curtis was still focused on Captain Jerome's latest travels, and still writing down notes in a pocket book—story ideas, most likely.

Secured in this, Lily took a seat next to her brothers, plus their dates, back under the pavilion. The cushions were quite cool by now, and yellow light from the tiki torches danced on every face. Lily made some small talk for a second, then worked the conversation over to Mary. "Hey remember when she was still called Rosemary?"

Asher whistled. "That brings back memories. Not good ones."

Oak said, "I never called her Rosemary; just Rosie."

His date asked, "Why'd she change?"

Asher answered, "I think she was building her brand, and figured Mary sounded nicer than Rosemary. Not sure why."

Oak said, "Then she started asking everybody to call her that. Whole new woman."

Yes, Lily thought. *Whole new woman*. Rosemary had been stressed, scared, and constantly in need of a nap. Mary bled confidence, and transcended human needs like sleep. Mary dressed nicer to attract richer clients and thus pay the family bills. For a long time, Mary would come home, sashay in her business suit to their bedroom, and return as the bent, yawning Rosie in stained jeans. Over time, Mary would stay with them longer, perhaps enjoying a family dinner with a self-sure smile and promising that she'd take care of everything, so nobody had to worry.

One odd night, Mary went to bed with them, filling her sisters' heads with dreams of a better tomorrow. The next day, Mary was still there, listing off all the opportunities a day could bring, if one just looked for them.

But so what? Lily's brain argued. What was wrong with self-improvement? Mary never acted superior, just capable. No, she *was* capable. She made a new image and pulled her family into a new life.

Why did that bug her?

"I don't worry about it," Daisy said when Lily got her alone. "Rosie stepped up a notch, but she's still Rosie in my book." Daisy took a sip of her drink, then added, "Not sure she needs to call my husband 'Captain' all the time, though. Like, we know; we don't need to be reminded. Oh, well. Still raised us more than Mom ever did."

Lily winced, even if she had to agree. When Cliff excused himself a moment, Lily dashed into his seat to talk to Mom.

"I always felt terrible," Mom said. "A mother should take care of her little ones, but I just couldn't. I didn't have the strength. But I think Mary came out better than anyone could have. A good career, a good husband, a fine house, and she's still humble enough to look after her old mom."

Lily asked, "But do you think it's so important that she changed her name?"

"It's only a name," Mom replied.

"And what about Mandy? Nobody calls her Mandragora."

"Well, Mandy's a fine name. Sounds very put-together. I think Mary knows best."

So, there it was: image. Lily knew that already. Part of Mary's plan for everybody to get out of poverty was to transform their attitude. "Don't put your nose up, just your chin," Mary would say. Be proud, not snobby. Good grooming. At least one set of fine clothes. A tidy house and trimmed yard, as much as they could manage. Presentable.

But what's so unpresentable about Mandragora? It was an ugly thought, but a sticky one. Lily couldn't pick it out of her brain.

As the final, defiant flickers of the sun melted from the horizon, Lily found Mandy on one of the patio seats by herself, catching her breath. Lily took the seat across the table and asked, "Having fun?"

"Mostly," Mandy said. "Still waiting for Miguel to ask me to dance on a slow song."

"Why not ask him?"

"Meh. I'm thinking I might be done with him. If he doesn't know me by now, what's the point?" She still glanced towards Miguel, who laughed with his friends at the flailing of some other boys about to rip through their blazers.

"By the way," Mandy said, leaning across the table, "Curtis is way better than you let on."

Lily scanned the crowd and found Curtis back with James again. "Apparently, he's nicer as a date than a civilian."

"Then marry the guy so he's nice all the time."

Lily snorted. "Let's survive writing a book together first."

"How's that coming by the way?"

"Good! We just saw today that we're well on track to finish by the deadline. Barely." An old, weary knot mounted in Lily's neck, and she rubbed it.

Mandy said, "So what is—no, I don't want anything! Shoo!" Mandy waved off the confused teen with the drink tray. "So, what's the book like? Can I know?"

Lily couldn't see why not. "Well, it's still about a woman who comes home for the holidays, and decides to stay."

"No place like home, and all that?"

"Actually, it's a bit different now. The girl, Elsa, is a baker, this fancy patisserie artist, you know? Her dad gets hurt, and she has to stay to help him, so she gets involved in all the local Christmas things to pass the time."

Mandy grinned. "Sounds like something you'd write."

"Because it is! Anyway, the longer she's around, the less sweet and homey it all seems."

"Oh?"

"Mm-hmm. There's a lot of quiet oppression in the little town. There's this old-guard kind of group that decided what tradition should and shouldn't be, and any newcomers just have to play along. Everything's really skewed in the in-crowd's favor. Nothing changes because that keeps them on top of the social order. Meanwhile, everybody else, like the foreigners or the people with different political views don't get any support, so they just stay out on the fringes."

Mandy blinked. "Yeah?"

Lily paused a moment, then soldiered on. "Yeah, so Elsa tries to get involved and change things, show the crowd that the old ways aren't the only good ways, and that all the sweet Christmasy stuff can include everybody. Plus, obviously there's a romance. Guy named Mitch. He's a nurse, but his family wanted him to be a doctor because it's a respectable position, but he feels he's doing more good as a nurse, and likes the patients, so he stays. But he's also part of the old Christmas traditions because his parents are part of the town's head honchos, so he likes Elsa, but he's not sure he's ready to upset the power structure."

"There's a Christmas power structure?"

"Well...it's a town dynamic, really, not just a Christmas thing. Like, you buy out of Bob's auto part store, not Casey's because Bob is in the in-crowd, and if you buy from Casey, then Bob will tell everybody not to, like, support your bookstore or whatever. And he's got clout, so everybody pleases Bob, and Casey gets screwed over."

"Bummer."

Yes. Yes, it was. "But it's a happy ending! Elsa's going to come in and show the town how wonderful all the outsiders are. Like how their opinions actually make some sense, or the things they sell are good quality, and that they have some more inclusive ideas for Christmas traditions. So, yeah, Elsa sticks it to the man, wins Mitch over to her side, and starts up her own bakery right there in town. Happily ever after."

Mandy said nothing at all for a tellingly long time. Lily realized a slower song had started, and some of the teens were shyly melting into couples.

"What do you think?" Lily finally dared to ask.

Mandy chewed on her lip for a while. "It's different."

"Different bad?"

"No, not bad. I don't think so, I mean. I just never thought you'd get into, like, political stuff for a Christmas story."

"No?"

Mandy waved her hands. "Sorry, I'm saying it all wrong. I'm sure it's going to be awesome. It's just different, you know? It doesn't sound like your usual Lily Harper story."

No. No, it did not.

Flies buzzed in Lily's ears, and spotted her vision. She blinked. Blinked again. Still fuzzy. Mandy was only thirteen today. Even she knew Lily's style. If she could figure out that something was off, how much more would her usual followers? Kimberly, Oak's date? Lydia from the writing group? That lady at the book store? Mom? Daisy? Everybody? Would they say it's not your usual Lily Harper book?

Of course they would, she realized. *Because it isn't a Lily Harper book.*

Just then, a teenage boy approached Mandy. It was Miguel, swallowing and swallowing. "Um, do you want to...go out there? Together?" He gestured to the dance floor, where couples swayed.

Mandy blushed all over her face. "Yeah, like sure, okay, yeah, I'm good, if you want, yeah." She accepted his hand and left for the dance floor, throwing Lily an excited smile over her shoulder.

Lily flashed a quick grin, then let her mouth sink as low as her thoughts. She was ghostwriting her own book. *But it will keep the house, right? Isn't that the goal?* But what would the fans think? Would they ever want another book from her? Would they like this new, cynical style?

Do I?

No, her heart said instantly. *It's just not me.*

But it's what Mr. Gates wants. It's...

Presentable...

Lily leaned over her lap to stop the swaying in her head. How had all this happened?

The answer walked into her view wearing two shiny black shoes. Lily looked up and beheld Curtis, his lips pulled tight, and his hands fidgeting nervously in his pockets. "Hey, uh...you want to dance? You can say no, I just...thought it might be fun."

And what you say goes, huh? Lily thought. But some instinct made her say, "Yes." It was just too rude to refuse, her mind said.

Lily couldn't remember the last time she'd danced, but she felt no fuzzies in her tummy about it either way. Holding

Curtis's hand didn't make her feel funny, but she did fight the urge to slap him when he put his hand on her hip.

"You okay?" he asked as they swayed.

"I'm fine," she said, not looking at him.

"Because we can stop if you're not comfortable."

"I'm okay." Oh, who was she kidding? Curtis saw right through her pleasantries. "I'm just a little upset about some things, that's all."

Curtis nodded. "About your sister?"

She turned to him at last. "What?"

"Mary. Or Rosemary, whichever. You looked bothered after talking to her."

How true, and yet how false. "No, that's—Mary's fine."

"Really?" Curtis asked in a disbelieving tone.

Fire ants crawled across Lily's scalp. "Why do you say it like that?"

"After the conversation we had? And after what I've observed? I wouldn't blame you for having issues with her."

"And what *have* you observed?"

"A queen bee. Friendly, caring, but she's the boss, no question about it. Everybody has to live in her reality."

Lily reached down and pulled Curtis's hand from her hip to her waist. "You don't get it."

"Then help me get it," Curtis insisted.

Lily's eyes darted about the patio. At least a dozen couples, mostly teens, but Daisy and her husband danced only a few steps away, and beyond them, Mary herself with James. So Lily spoke through her teeth. "Mary rescued us! Six kids! Zero dads! Mary had just finished

172

college when we found out Mom was pregnant with Mandy. She could have flown off and forgotten about us, but she didn't. She got two jobs and suffered so that we could all eat. None of us would be here without her!"

Curtis replied, "So that gives her the right to unquestioned rulership? To change peoples' names so they look better on a pedigree? You have to live forever with décor you hate because Mary's feelings are too precious to—"

"I want to stop," Lily blurted out. Her face boiled like the sun had shot back up.

"What?"

"You said we could stop any time, and I want—" Lily let go of Curtis and stepped back. "I want to stop."

Curtis froze, arms still out for an invisible dance partner. Then, he stowed his hands in his pockets. "All right, that's fine."

Lily spun and marched back to her seat, eyes blurry again, though they did register many couples watching her go. Mary caught her eye as she passed, brow crinkled with concern. Lily waved her off. Funny. Lily had just defended her big sister, but right now, she couldn't fathom talking to her.

Lily didn't speak to Curtis for the rest of the party, nor anybody else. She suddenly didn't want input or opinion; she wanted to be left alone with the voice in her head. Even if that voice did nothing but whimper and bite its nails.

The sky had finally turned black, and the air gloriously cool, when parents and big siblings lined up to take the party guests home. As the first headlights swam up the dark drive,

Lily told Curtis, "We should probably go. We still have work to do tomorrow."

He simply said, "Okay." He was obviously troubled, but Lily didn't ask. It had been an impossibly long day, and Lily just wanted to go to bed and forget every minute of it.

Lily made her rounds, saying goodbye to every sibling, in-law, and fresh face. Mandy, at least, seemed happier than when they'd arrived. She gave Curtis a hearty handshake and said, "See ya, Curt. Stick with this girl; she's a good one."

Curtis cleared his throat, while Lily flashed a sickly-sweet smile. She bade her sister one last happy birthday, then passed back through the house. Teens in vests were cleaning up plates, wiping down tables, and starting on dishes, some of their refined demeanor breaking down as they shared stories of the night, chuckling in low tones. Lily passed under the gigantic crystal chandelier, wondering at how ostentatious a light fixture could be, and then left the house.

Mary stood at the circle drive, gabbing with a mom through the car window. Lily caught her saying things like, "Oh, they had a great time," and "It was spectacular." *Do the guests not get a say of their own?* Lily wondered.

James shook Curtis's hand one more time and said, "See you tomorrow. Lily, take this guy somewhere for a weekend to give him a rest."

Another *ahem*, and another plastic grin. Lily couldn't even blush anymore.

Mary gave her sister a hefty embrace, though Lily

struggled to return it. Mary asked, "Everything okay?"

"I'm just tired," Lily said.

"Well, drive safe. Thanks for coming! Wasn't it fun?"

Lily gave her usual smile because it was the silent option.
Were my lips always this tight?

But this was definitely not the time for an argument;
Lily's brain felt like monkeys were scratching their way out.
Curtis and Mary gave each other frosty goodbyes, then the
couple headed to their car. A servant opened the door for her.
Thanks, or whatever.

Ten minutes never passed so slowly. Curtis looked out
the window with his chin on his fist. Did he feel upset that
she'd cut off their dance? Was he grumbling to himself about
Lily's family like the asshole he was? Or was he just thinking
about the story? She decided to care tomorrow. Every mile
made her eyes sting more, and it was strangely difficult to
breathe.

At last, Lily parked her car in the garage. "Well, I'll see
you tomorrow," she said.

Curtis answered, "Gotta get my stuff."

Crap. Oh, well. As she grabbed the doorknob, Lily could
at least comfort herself with the thought that she was home.
MY home.

Until she opened the door. Sticky heat barreled over her
so fast that Lily nearly choked. She'd forgotten about the
broken air conditioner. And in her haste to leave, Lily had also
forgotten to open the curtains so air could flow in.

She let out an angry growl as she marched through the
house, yanking open all the curtains, flinging open windows,
and silently demanding that the heat and pressure leave her
house immediately. Then, in the middle of the living room,

Lily stopped, and growled some more.

There was that wonky, orange-and-green "art" piece, its vaguely humanoid figure tilting its head in puzzlement.

Curtis shrugged on his backpack, eyeing her. "What?"

"Nothing."

Curtis followed her gaze to the picture. "Oh. Not exactly a welcome sight when you first come home, is it?"

"Nope." Lily did not want to chat right now. Her brain was already in an ice-cold shower upstairs, and the very idea of her bed made her eyelids droop.

Then Curtis said, "There is one simple solution." He walked over to the picture, picked it up off the wall, and slid it behind the treadmill, facing away. "There we go. It's only temporary, but at least you don't have to look at…" His voice trailed off as he gawked at Lily.

Except Lily wasn't home anymore. Something else had burst into Lily's brain, something huge and black and hideous, with wings of fire burning all the doilies and plush pillows of her mind, and kicking up ash in a blinding, choking cloud. It plucked its way through her eyeballs, tore through the front of her face, and screamed.

"Who the hell do you think you are?!"

Curtis leapt, literally left the floor as he sprang backwards, bumping against the television. The burning thing loved it.

Lily shouted, "What makes you think you can just walk into someone else's life and start moving things around for your convenience? Were you born a douche bag or did you go to school for it?"

Curtis threw up his hands, his eyes the size of plates. "Whoa, okay, I'm sorry. I—"

"You don't get to do this!" Lily marched around the coffee table to get up in his face, blissfully happy that she still wore her heels, and had a good inch or two on him. "This is my house! Mine! You don't just walk in and do what you want and say what you want and make everything perfectly happy for you! I'm sick of it, and I'm not doing it anymore!"

"I—"

"And you *don't* get to tear open my book and just...just rip out the pages you don't like and put in your own things! It's my book! You stole my book!"

"Hang on, you asked me to—!"

"You stole my voice!" It echoed now, bounding and rebounding off every wall and rafter, swallowing whatever words Curtis had planned to say, and muting him for several seconds afterwards.

Lily cleared her scratchy throat, and wiped something that was pooling and stinging in her eyes. "Just...just go! Get out of my house. Go home!" She pushed him around the couch and towards the door. "Go! And don't come back! Don't ever come back!"

Curtis stopped at the door. "But what about—?"

"No! We're done! You're fired! The book is over!"

It's what?! Wailed something beneath the flames and ash. The burning thing stomped it flat, watching logic gush out like blood from a burst tick.

Lily ripped open the door, fully expecting it to fly off its hinges. "Get out! We're through! I never want to see you again!" She hated the sound of her own voice. Despite how angry she was, despite how loud and authoritative the words might be, it still came out high and nasally. Whiny. Seconds from a complete, sobbing breakdown.

Curtis took a step towards the threshold, but couldn't go through. "Look, Lily—"

"Oh, now I have a name?!" Lily shoved Curtis through the door and slammed it before she could see if he fell down the porch steps. She turned the lock, fumbled with the deadbolt, and spun around, still hot, still smoking, still eager to burn.

Then, she saw the light in her writing room, every bulb stretching in a different direction, chaos and negligence made manifest. Lily made a noise somewhere between a scream and a roar, then turned and ran to the garage. When her heels tripped her, she snatched them off and threw them at the kitchen. One hit the hospital-white cabinets, the other smacked the coffee maker.

The garage's cold, concrete floor did nothing to cool her mood. She grabbed the entire toolbox her brother had bought for her, and hauled it into the office. Lily grabbed her office chair, stepped onto it, then stabbed a screwdriver into the light fixture's weak point.

"This is my house!" Lily skewered the screw, twisting, stripping, scouring it. "It's the one place I have any say in my own damn life, and I say get! Out!" One by one, Lily threw aside the screws until the light fixture finally fell off the ceiling. About an inch. It dangled there on its wires, gently swaying in its mocking way.

Lily grabbed the entire fixture and ripped it down as hard as she could. Wires snapped in blinding flashes. She could only hear the light shatter on the ground as the power cut out through her entire home, leaving her in utter blackness.

Lily didn't mind. Darkness was the perfect place to cry.

Chapter 16

"What…happened?" asked the electrician. He was a squat, burly man, three feet wide and all muscle. He stood on a stepstool, gawking at the fried wires poking out of the ceiling of Lily's office.

Lily rubbed her eyes, but it only made them drier. "I was careless."

"It looks like you ripped the whole thing out."

"Can you fix it and get the new light in?" Lily indicated the box in the corner of her office, boasting a simple, warm dome light.

The electrician said, "Yeah, I think I can salvage it. It'll take a while…" He trailed off the way all servicemen do when the job gets more expensive.

"That's fine. Excuse me." She yawned for the tenth time in two minutes. It was shaping up to be a three-coffee day, and it was only one o'clock.

Lily estimated she got four hours of sleep last night, all in pieces no bigger than thirty minutes. That burning, billowing beast in her brain just wouldn't stop screaming. It railed against Curtis, against Mary, against Mr. Gates, against Lily herself. She couldn't even remember half the things she'd cried about last night. There were few images, few thoughts, just wails from some burst vein of sorrow deep below the skin.

And when the sobs died down and her brain started

churning again, Lily remembered she only had twelve days to finish her book, and she had to do it alone. That thought alone peeled her out of her tear-stained bed. Lily was two-thirds done. Surely she could stitch together some kind of ending, right?

Except she didn't want to finish this story. It wasn't hers. How could she Scotch-tape some hollow ending onto somebody else's book and expect it to stand? Who would read that? Lily considered making changes, but pulling at any thread seemed to untangle the whole mess, and she didn't have time to write another book.

So instead, Lily swept up the broken glass in her office, went out and bought a new light fixture, called an electrician, and got to work on a different project.

A knock sounded on the front door. Lily excused herself as the electrician got to work. Lily wiped the sleep from her eyes and the sweat from her brow—the air conditioner people said they couldn't even come out until tomorrow—and opened the door.

A mid-thirties man and woman stood on the other side, both blonde, both tan, both in athletic wear. "Hi, Lily?" said the woman. "We came about the treadmill?"

"Come on in," Lily said, trying not to giggle with vindictive glee.

One thing that kept sleep from her last night was wrestling over the issue of Mary. Was it Mary's fault for buying all this ugly crap? Lily's for delegating that responsibility? Mary's for blocking all negative speech with her stonewalling smiles? Lily's for never even trying? Or Curtis's fault? She didn't know why it was his fault, but it seemed easier to blame him for some reason. She'd finally found a few minutes of slumber when she came to the only conclusion that mattered: all this décor had to go.

The explosion light was already dead. The rest, Lily would put up for sale on the internet. Maybe Mary wouldn't find out, maybe she would, but Lily's sleep-deprived mind could only handle one issue at a time right now.

"Anything wrong with it?" the man asked, playing with buttons on the treadmill.

Lily said, "If there is, I don't know it because I never used it. I prefer to run outside."

"In this heat?" the wife asked.

"Even in this heat. Side note, sorry about the temperature in here. AC is busted."

"Can we try it out?"

Another knock rapped on the door. Lily told the wife, "Go ahead, see if you like it," while heading to the next visitor.

A squat Hispanic woman stood on the other side, her sleeveless top revealing biceps so hard they could have only been sculpted by lasers.

"Here for the weights?" Lily guessed. The woman nodded.

Lily showed her the rack, once again attesting that she'd never used them. A part of her felt bad for selling all this stuff. Her whole family chipped in for these as a housewarming gift, but Lily had the distinct feeling Mary had headed that discussion, as she headed everything else. Maybe Lily would repay her family. Otherwise, she'd use the cash to pay off Mary's interior design bill. Either way, someone else could use all this way more than she could.

Another knock sounded. Was it the lady who wanted the yoga mat and medicine ball for her studio? The weird dude who actually wanted her minimalist art thing? The air conditioning people coming a day early because this world was full of hope after all?

Lily just called "Come in!" and turned back to the Hispanic woman. "Yeah, I can sell them individually if you like. I just want them off of my hands."

"I might do that." She put her hands on her hips and thought hard.

Lily took the opportunity greet the third buyer coming through her door.

Except it was Curtis.

She gasped so loud that the whole room heard it over the treadmill's engine. Everybody spun to her. Even the electrician called from the office, "Everything okay out there?"

She couldn't tell. Everything below the neck had gone numb. Fortunately, her mouth still had its old reflexes. "Yes! Sorry, just…startled me, that's all."

The feeling seemed mutual; Curtis stood with only one toe in the living room, breathing through a barely-open mouth. His hand jittered on some kind of tall box, tapping out an SOS. Everything else was cool and stiff, or perhaps frozen. Should she feel guilty or delighted that he looked so nervous? Lily doubted she'd feel either one beneath the white noise in her nerves.

Lily forced her jelly-legs to walk until she was within whispering distance. "What are you doing here? And what's this?"

Curtis took a deep breath, then tapped the box. "This is

my peace offering so you'll let me stay long enough to apologize."

Not one word of that made it past Lily's preconceived filters. She blinked a bit, then said, "Aren't you supposed to be at work?"

"Lunch break." His button-up was actually tucked in today, and Lily finally comprehended the badge on his shirt pocket. Curtis Reynolds, Patient Support Specialist, Requesting Permission to Apologize, Apparently.

The dark and burning beast began to stir in her mind again, snarling and snapping at the very sight of him. But the ashes had grown thick and suffocating by now, so it only stirred up all the fears that had settled like a carpet on her brain. The book was dead. What was she going to do? The beast refused to ask for help, but the ashes refused to pretend she didn't need it.

She averted her eyes to find something that made them sting less, and saw the Hispanic woman trying to get Lily's attention. Lily said to Curtis, "Kitchen," then hurried to deal with a problem she could actually fix.

The woman did indeed want all the biggest dumbbells, and paid cash. When Lily asked if she needed help, the woman said, "No. Training starts now."

As the woman left, Lily checked the road for signs of her next potential buyer, but the pavement was empty. The athletic couple had switched out, the husband testing the treadmill, so Lily had no choice but to actually deal with Curtis now.

He leaned against the fridge, but straightened up when she came. "Selling a few things?"

"That's none of your business. What's this?" But

from this angle, she could see the picture. It was a fan. One of the skinny, bladeless models, tall as her collarbone.

Curtis said, "I figured the AC repairmen probably wouldn't come right away, so this would come in handy. It's a good one. High-power, minimal noise. I have one just like it, so I can vouch for it."

Lily wanted to shove it up his nose, but her lower back was already starting to sweat, and it was only going to get hotter. "Fine, I accept your peace offering. Now what do you want?"

"To apologize."

That word still did nothing for her. She could feel the disbelief twisting her face. "Why?"

Curtis needed a minute to speak. His fingers kept drumming on the stupid fan box, his eyes fixed on the tile floor. "I lost a lot of sleep last night thinking about what happened. The way you yelled, the things you said."

"Am I supposed to say sorry?" Lily could feel the apology crawling up her throat already. She didn't even know why. She swallowed it down.

"No," Curtis said. "That's my job. The reason I lost sleep was because I was arguing with myself, and in the end, I lost that argument. You said I stole your voice. I stole your book. Well, you're right. I did. I tried to tell myself I didn't, but…" He let the sentence hang.

Lily's stomach traded blows with her lungs. He was sorry? He was admitting fault? "That's quite the turnaround," she said.

Curtis clicked his tongue once, then looked at her at last. "I sent a story in to an agent once. He said he loved the concept, but get rid of this, this, this, and this. All the lifeblood

185

of the story, in my opinion. He just wanted the next YA dystopian-turned-blockbuster. I've never been madder at the publishing industry. It felt like they were kicking me out of my own book to make it something they wanted." Curtis nodded slowly. "I'd forgotten that. Until last night. So, I'm sorry."

His words were like snow in summer. Lily gawked, shaking her head, trying to comprehend what was happening. She'd yelled, kicked him out of the house, and he was apologizing? Wasn't he furious? Wasn't he going to come back with a guilt trip about how much he'd helped her? Remind her how she couldn't even start her book without him? Lily had at least expected the silent treatment, dragging out those miserable, wordless days until she had to beg him to come back with all manner of apologies.

"Also," Curtis continued, "I wanted to say that, if you can forgive me, I'd like to help you finish the book."

Lily staggered backward and banged her hip on the counter. She cursed behind her teeth, glared at the counter, glared at Curtis, glared at the fridge because it looked smug. She had to turn, to mobilize her thoughts with a walk around the flat, ghostly-white island counter.

She spotted the couple now standing beside the treadmill, waiting. "Like it?" she asked, the switch in her voice flipping to "cheery."

"We do," the man said.

The woman raised a finger. "Question, where did you get this couch?"

"It was a gift," Lily said, "but they got it at Mary's Home Furnishings."

"Oh, I love that place. Just can't afford it."

Lily's chest swelled with hope. "I'm actually selling this one. Name your price!"

It was sold in seconds.

No other buyers came as the athletic couple hauled out the treadmill. Time to talk to Curtis again, to put some effort into comprehending this...miracle? Agony? Lily couldn't even name it.

She stood on the opposite side of the kitchen island, arms folded, glowering. "Why? Why do you want to help me? Is it the money?"

Curtis said, "I can't deny that's part of it. But that's not all. For one thing, I feel like I owe you. We spent all this time writing; the least I can do is help you cross the finish line. It's also about what I said last night: I see why your house is so important to you now: you wanted to make something *your* way. Besides, I'll be damned if I'm the reason somebody loses their home. If you want me to leave the fan and get lost, I get it. But I figured I'd at least offer. So, what do you want to do?"

How in the world could she possibly trust him? Sure, he sounded contrite, but could someone seriously turn around that fast? On the other hand, if he was truthful, then she had her Christmas miracle six months early. He'd help her finish the novel, she'd send it to Mr. Gates, he'd write the check, and Lily would keep the roof over her head while she worked on book number four.

She pondered her options. Curtis waited without a word. The electrician squeaked on his ladder now and again from the other room. For one minute, Lily entertained the notion that Curtis was seriously sorry and seriously ready to help her finish the book her way. If that was true, then it was because she had yelled at him. Her voice was the only explanation. How? No clue.

By some alien means, Lily had used her voice, and the world had changed around her.

If all that was true, then there was one way to test it, and one way to move forward from this point. It wasn't by thinking of the right thing to say. Instead, Lily opened her mouth and said what was on her heart.

"I want to start over."

Curtis inclined his ear, stupefaction etched on his face. "Start...over? The whole book?"

"Yes." She clenched her teeth to keep them from rattling.

"Miss Harper, that's—"

Lily scoffed. "You get onto my sister for changing names, but you can't use mine?"

Curtis froze. A moment later, he spoke again. "Okay...Lily. You said your editor wants the book on the thirtieth. That's less than two weeks to work! Even less if we want any edits or rewrites!"

Lily hugged herself, rocking left and right. "It's not my book."

"I admit that," Curtis said, "but it would be easier to make changes and a new ending than to start from scratch."

"It's not my book."

"Lily—"

"It's not my book!"

Curtis went silent.

Lily realized then that perhaps yelling wasn't the only way to use one's voice. "I'm not saying it's an awful book. I'm sure it's a hard-hitting commentary, but that's not what I want to write. I don't want the little town to be a place of hidden evil and prejudice. Our whole world is full of that already! I want to write the kind of town that I *wish* was real. I want to write a story where people can just unload their things, kick off their shoes, and rest for a while. And maybe, if I'm lucky, when the book is over and they have to go back to the real world, they'll feel a little stronger. Like they can make it one more day."

None of the Harpers talked about the past anymore. Mary didn't like the subject; she said it made them all sad. Better to enjoy where they were, how far they'd come. So, Lily never had to explain just how much even the fluffiest, corniest novel helped her escape that tiny, stuffy bedroom with its ceiling fan that never cooled anybody. With the screeching newborn in her ears. The stench of sweat building because they couldn't afford to run the water very long. Lily had walked miles to the library in her garbage tennis shoes, just to borrow one more gasp of air so she could hold her breath a little longer.

I help people breathe. Don't you dare take that from me.

It took ages for Curtis to decide. Lily debated whether she should keep talking or stay quiet. It used to be an easy choice, now she just couldn't tell.

Curtis rubbed his hand across his soul patch. "You know…your brother-in-law has been trying to get me to take a vacation for years. I bet I could wrap up my stuff today and start a break tomorrow. That way I could be here all day if need be."

Half of Lily froze. More Curtis? More arguments and frustrations? But the other half of Lily melted. *He'd do that for my book?*

189

Then, Curtis thrust his hands into his pockets and looked her firm in the eye. "I have one condition. I don't know if I have the right to say that, but here it is: I won't get in the way of your voice, but I won't stand idly to the side either. I still care deeply about art. You want to make an escapist novel and give people rest? Fine. But cliché characters and familiar tropes only empty the brain; they don't fill it back up with anything good. Good art does. Writing that's fresh, real, and alive does that. I said I want to help you, and I mean every word of that, which means pushing you to the best of your ability. But yes, I promise it will still be your book."

Ooooh, it was so tempting to throw the Keurig at him. *He apologizes, then makes demands? Insufferable asshole.* Too bad he was right. Lily didn't want to be the cheap filler Mr. Gates expected. But there was a bigger reason Lily shoulders started to unclench: Curtis had listened. That meant he was serious. That meant he'd changed.

That meant no hissing tongue in her ear. Just a gentle hand on her back.

Lily asked, "How much longer do you have for your break?"

Curtis replied, "About fifteen minutes, not including drive time."

Lily walked into the kitchen. "Let's think of some meal plans for the next week and a half. I'll go shopping today to get a truckload of food, plus whatever else we need so we don't get interrupted more than necessary."

"So…we're doing this?"

Lily took a slow, shaky breath. A whole novel in

twelve days, maybe less, stuck in a hot house with a man she both despised and needed. But it would be *her* novel. Her voice.

"Yes, we are." Lily picked up a pad of paper and started to write.

Chapter 17

Okay, Lily said to herself as Curtis pulled into the driveway, *showtime*.

Lily had spent all day preparing for this moment. First, she hopped onto all social media saying she'd be gone writing until July first. Then, she sent the same message to all her family via text. After that, shopping for a mountain of food, everything from frozen broccoli to popsicles. Finally, Lily had started planning for Curtis's inevitable inquiry.

She waited at the front door for three reasons. One, it was creepy to just watch someone through the window. Two, she itched to properly welcome Curtis in, rather than him simply inviting himself. Three, it was still hot as hell, and the outdoors offered at least a kindergartener's effort of a breeze. Lily stood barefoot at the entryway in shorts and a forgotten-number-of-years-old Anberlin tee shirt. She'd shaved her legs, and Curtis was lucky he'd get that.

Curtis, of course, still wore the same button up at this afternoon, but he'd untucked it and removed his hospital ID. Yet Curtis had added one item to his getup that made him several notches more attractive: he'd adorned his hands with a ginormous pizza.

"Evening," he said, squinting in the sun. "Can I come in?"

"Sure." Lily stepped aside.

Curtis slowed as he walked through the living room. "Wow, you cleaned house."

Sort of. Lily had sold all the exercise equipment, the couch, and even that ugly minimalist art. She had another woman coming tomorrow for the over-eager coffee table, and another for the furry, black-and-white-stripe rug on which the table and couch had sat. Still, after packing up all the cringy knick-knacks for a yard sale someday, Lily thought the room looked almost bare.

"I'll fill it out one day," Lily said, "but not while I'm writing eighty-thousand words in eight days."

"Eight?" Curtis asked.

"Yes. We have twelve days until July, but I figured we'd spend tonight planning, then get cracking tomorrow—if not tonight—on about ten thousand words a day. Then, we have a few days to edit and rearrange things if we have to."

"Solid plan, if a difficult one."

Lily went to the cabinet for some plates as Curtis laid out the pizza. "Worse comes to worst, we can make it a shorter book. Mr. Gates might argue, but...well, at least it will be a complete book." She returned to marvel at dinner: half veggie, half meat. "There's a metaphor there," she said.

Curtis chuckled. "Two very different styles squeezed into the same box."

Yeah, but I've tried yours. Have you even tried mine? Then she thought, *No. Say it out loud.* Lily swallowed. "I've tried meat. Have you tried veggie?"

Curtis gave her a narrow, scrutinizing look. "Not really my style, but I'm guessing you're still being metaphorical."

"A little. Also, veggie pizza is amazing."

Curtis sighed, and plopped a veggie slice onto his plate. "I am willing to try it. Will your book have this much symbolism in it?"

"Yep."

"Like what?"

"Pizza."

He actually grinned, then sat down. "Okay, Miss Har—Lily—tell me what you've got so far."

Lily heard the heavy clunk of a spotlight flipping on. She took a deep breath, then spilled out what she'd rehearsed. "It's the same premise: woman reluctantly returns home for Christmas, and ends up staying. But this time, the town really is as good as it seems. Elsa doesn't buy it at first, but finds peace here. She's the one who has to change, which means she's the one with the character arc, not the town." Lily was particularly proud of that last bit.

Curtis still sighed.

"I know it's fake," Lily said, "but that's the point, remember?"

"But where's the conflict? With a sugary-sweet town where everything is perfect, the plot can just coast by on ice skates. And if it's such a lovely place, why doesn't everyone move there? How is it still small?"

One of Curtis's many good questions. Fortunately, Lily had been neurotically predicting them all afternoon. "It's slow and poor. You won't really make it big here; there's no big tech company, farming is so-so, it's all mid-tier local businesses at best. You do it because you love the work or not at all. And there's not a lot of money in it. The richest guy is, like, the bank manager or something.

"But that's *why* it's such a beautiful community. Because they don't have much, they all band together and support each other, and as I said, they do the work because they love the work, not for the prestige or riches. That sugary-sweet small-town feel came out of necessity, not plot convenience."

Miracle of miracles, Curtis didn't counter her. He sat with his palms down on the hickory-brown tabletop. He'd furrowed his brow, like he was trying to find holes in her idea.

Then, with a significant look, he picked up his slice of veggie pizza and took a bite.

"Good?" Lily asked.

"Surprisingly, yes. Not great, not my style, but yes, I can stomach it."

Pretty weak compliment, but Lily's lungs opened wider anyway. Curtis had promised to help with her story, not his own. So far, he'd been true.

Suddenly, Curtis's eyebrows bounced up into his hairline. "You know, that kind of setting actually lends itself to a character flaw for Elsa: she's hooked on the status and the money for—oh, no."

"What?"

"Would Elsa really make a lot of money as a baker?"

Lily would have dropped her jaw if she wasn't eating. "Oh, no," she mumbled.

Curtis clicked his tongue at a woodpecker's cant. "Maybe it's more about prestige? She starts off at a snooty, upper-crust place where the menu is in cursive, then moves to a town that only understands two kinds of cake: chocolate and plain. Hard to stand out like that...except she would. Rats!"

Lily chewed that one bite like a cow with a cud. After

hours of planning, she'd lasted four minutes before proving why she couldn't do this. She tried to tell herself it was just a slip-up. Every author does it. But those authors had ages to correct them. Lily had days. Lily felt like she'd been carrying an enormous boulder. She'd only slipped a little, but even that tiny twist of the ankle shot a chain-explosion of shame all the way up her legs.

Curtis must have sensed it, because his voice grew softer, but he sat up straighter, hands folded, like a lawyer trying to rescue a client from too much evidence. "Okay, let's think about this. What's a career you can take anywhere in the U.S., something where you can rake in the big bucks or chug along with nothing but smiles for fuel."

Lily grumbled, "Author."

Curtis chuckled without an ounce of mirth. "Maybe something in the medical field. Does the town have a hospital?"

"More like a clinic."

"Hmm. Could still be helpful. Or maybe some kind of specialist practice, something she can do with limited equipment and space. Let's see…"

A grumbling rattle cut him off. Lily's phone glowed with a perfect circle of Mary's face.

Lily stared back, trying to chase the fuse that had lit in her brain, then scurried across every node and cortex. She managed to stamp out the flame just before it blew up an entire box of How-Dare-You.

"I remember that look," Curtis said, leaning slightly away.

"I told her not to call," Lily muttered dumbly. Maybe

196

it was an emergency. She hoped so. She hoped not, too.

"Want to ignore it?" Curtis asked.

Like nobody's business. But Mary would call again. And then she'd just come over. "It'll be faster if I answer. Excuse me." Lily picked up her phone and ran somewhere private and unused: her writing room.

"Hello?" It was a genuine question.

"Hey, sweetie," said Mary's voice. No shaky tone, no choked tears, no hyperventilation. Not even the sickly-sweet overcompensation. So, not an emergency.

Then why are you interrupting me? her brain cried. Her lips, on the other hand, said "Hey! What's up?" *Traitors.*

"Oh, not much. I just wanted to call about your text that asked everyone not to call."

Lily's mouth stammered silently. *Did you seriously just say that sentence?* "Oh?"

"Yes, I just wanted to make sure everything was okay."

"I'm just getting dangerously close to my deadline, and I have a ton of work left, so I pretty much need to disappear until July so I can get it done."

"Oh, I'm sorry, sweetie. Anything I can do to help?"

Lily rolled her eyes up to the ceiling, and spotted her new dome light, sleeping serenely. "No, thank you. I've got it."

"You sure?"

"Yes, I've got it."

"Okay, I'll bring over dinner one night."

"No, no, I've got everything planned for the next two weeks."

"Oh, it's no fuss at all."

That's not what I said. Lily fixed her eyes on the plain, non-eye-gouging light she put in. "Really, I've got it."

A pause this time. Or something like it. Pauses didn't have eyes that pierced your clothes, and they didn't have claws that lacerated their way up your back. This did.

It only lasted a second before Mary spoke again, a twinge of confusion in her voice. "Are you...sure?"

"Positive. Don't worry about me; it's just two weeks. Not even that. I promise to come up for air."

"Okay...if you're sure you don't need anything."

"I'll be okay. Thanks for checking in." Lily's finger crept close to the End button like a teenager going for a kiss.

"It's just..." Mary said.

Lily grinded her teeth together and stomped her foot. "Yes?" said her pleasantest voice.

Why do you keep talking so sweet to her? asked that burning, ashy thing.

I don't want to upset her, replied a tiny voice the size of a mouse.

So she can't be upset but I can?

Mary continued, "Something James said has been bugging me tonight."

Actual curiosity cooled the steam hissing from Lily's ears. "What did he say?"

"James said he talked with Curtis today, and apparently Curtis was some kind of big jerk to you last night."

Lily heard James's voice call from the background,

"Tell him I said sorry!"

"Oh, shush," said Mary. "And that's the other thing! Are you still seeing him after he was such a jerk to you?"

Lily leaned against the bookshelf for support. She was exhausted already. "We're not an item. We're just collaborating. He's a writer, so he's giving me advice."

Mary replied, "It sounded like a big fight."

"We worked it out."

"In one day?"

Lily admitted that was strange. "It's not like we were repairing a marriage. We just had to be civil."

"Are you sure? I didn't like the feel of him last night, and I really don't like someone being a cretin to my family."

"You're sweet, but I can take care of myself. Don't worry about me."

"But I do worry."

Every part of Lily huddled around the phone immediately, as if to cuddle it, stroke its casing, and whisper that everything would be okay.

Then, she paused and wondered why. Why was she taking up so much time soothing Mary's worry? She un-huddled, feeling a hundred pins and needles travel down her spine, but her lungs stretched again.

Lily said, "Mary, trust me. I've got everything taken care of. I'm going off the grid for the next several days so I can focus. If you really want to help, take me out somewhere on July first. Okay?"

Another pause with teeth. Another uncertain twinge in Mary's voice. "If you're sure. I just worry about you."

Lily almost coddled the phone again, but then she realized there was nothing in that statement for her. "I've got to get writing. See you on the first. Love you."

"You too…" A nervous tone lingered on the line.

Lily pressed End.

Eels, serpents, and lizards all swarmed her flesh, making Lily dance in discomfort. Why had she left it at that? It was so rude!

But why? I had to go; I told her not to call.

I could've been nicer.

But why? I didn't insult her, and I'd asked to be left alone.

She's my sister. I should be nice.

But why?

Lily took sharp breaths through her nose, swallowing the stale, hot stillness of her writing room. A dainty breeze tickled the curtains, but did nothing more. Lily flicked on the light. A simple, soft, homey glow poured across the room like honey. She walked circles in the sweet goop, bare toes digging into the rug. She yanked a beach picture off the wall and set it on the floor, facing away. She snatched the fake books out of the shelves, and the seashells, and the little inspirational sayings. It all went to the trash. Mary had tried to be kind. That didn't mean she had succeeded.

Just then, Curtis poked his head in from the living room. "Everything kosher? Any emergency you need to attend?"

"No," Lily said. "Just trying to make my sister hear me."

"Ah." He didn't say more. Good call. Lily's arms still itched, and she worried she'd punch somebody.

Then, Lily remembered something. "Actually, I have

a question for you."

Curtis stepped into the writing room, taking a moment to look at the light. "Oh, you fixed it. Nice."

"Thank you. Apparently, James told Mary about our blowout last night. What did you tell him?"

Curtis put up his hands. "Nothing bad. I told him we had a fight, and I wanted to take my lunch to apologize. And then when I came back, I said that you convinced me that I need a vacation, and that I had some personal things that needed attention, so could I have time off ASAP? I didn't mention the book."

She pondered her next words carefully. "It sounded like you told James you were in the wrong."

Curtis slid his hands into his pockets. "Well, I was, wasn't I?"

Yes. Except... "But I yelled."

"Yeah, but that's probably because I didn't listen when you whispered."

Lily suddenly felt farsighted, and had to step backwards to really look at him. "Curtis, I don't understand you. Sometimes, you're...you're..." She bit her lip, but Curtis waited expectantly. *Okay, then.* "...mean and...harsh and critical, but then other times you're insightful and attentive and considerate, and I... you scare me. I feel like I've put so much of myself into your hands, and I just don't know what those hands are going to do."

Even saying those words felt like prying open her eyes in a dustbowl. Curtis didn't reply for some time, didn't even seem to be trying to search for words. Maybe he didn't have any. At one point, his eyes dropped to the smartphone in his hand, and then, he held it up.

"Would it help to know that I may have found a job for Elsa?"

Lily allowed one finger to tap on her crossed arms. "What job?"

"I stuck with the medical field, but I was wondering, what's a job every town needs, but not every town has? Some kind of specialist position. I did a little scrolling, and long story short: pediatric dentist."

"Huh?"

"Think about it: every town has kids, every kid has teeth, but not every dentist specializes in kids. So maybe this town has a local dentist, but he's focused on grown-ups, and is busy with pretty much everybody in town already, so the parents have to drive an hour to a good specialist. She'd just have to take a step down to a slower pace and smaller paycheck."

Lily took in a slow breath, letting the wind cool her brain. "She got into the business for the smiles and the kids, but somewhere along the way it became about the status. She was talented, and had referrals coming out her nose."

Curtis nodded along. "Her schedule got full, and it became a kind of game: how many patients can you Wonder-Woman your way through without messing up?"

"She got faster and faster, the number one kids' dentist in the city, always busy, always beloved. But when she comes to the new town, she's forced to slow down, and that helps her to enjoy the time with the kids instead of powering through it!"

"*Voila!* Character arc."

Lily drew one more breath, stretching her lungs so

wide that her ribs bent backwards to make room for more air. Then, she let it back out, and all the knots and kinks and shaking left through her lips. Lily didn't fully understand it, but she believed it: Curtis had come back to help her. And on her terms. She'd just opened her mouth, and the fabric of reality altered. Just like a novel: pour out a few words, and a universe takes shape.

She walked over to her desk, and took a seat in her high-back chair, gripping her armrests like an embrace. "Bring everything in here, would you? I've always wanted to write a novel in this room."

Curtis gave a friendly salute, then headed back to the kitchen. Lily's eyes fell on the empty space where the bean bag chair had been. She'd have to replace that. Plus her couch. And explain the changes to Mary one day. Plus, you know, writing a book less than two weeks.

There was so much to worry about. It was nice to know that Curtis was no longer one of them.

Chapter 18

11 Days Left

Lily may have trusted Curtis by now, but when he showed up the next morning with a box of chocolates, she had to pause. "Uh…"

Curtis smirked as he slid past her into the house. "I may be partial to hickory tresses, but this is for work. There are twenty candies in here. Every ten thousand words, we get one, which leaves some extras for celebrating the end."

"Ah! Sounds great." Her hand slid through her hair. "Better put them in the fridge, otherwise we'll be able to drizzle them across ice cream." The windows were open to let in the crisp morning air, but Lily knew the dew would soon sizzle. It was only June…

Pacing didn't help cool things off, but Lily felt like she'd chugged ten energy drinks, using a power line for a straw.

"You okay there?" Curtis asked after an hour of her scuffling across the floor. They set up in Lily's office, dragging a chair from the dining room to replace the purple foam sack. Lily had removed so many pictures that the walls shivered in their bare whites, but without a horrid light fixture shooting sunrays in every direction, it wasn't so blinding.

"I'm just worried about the deadline," Lily said.

"I hear that."

"You don't look worried."

"I never panic until it's too late. Glad one of us is sensible."

Lily gave a chuckle that came out manic, then returned to pacing and blurting out ideas as they came.

Protagonist Elsa had six birthdays off screen to account for her DDS and all her experience in the shiniest, sleekest, most sci-fi dental office in the country. With a zip and a whir, cavities met quick and merciless ends. Despite her sudden thirties, Elsa didn't worry about marriage or kids because that would require time to analyze her life. Her longest partner was her sickle probe, and pets were just one more thing to distract from the rush of a crammed schedule of five-star reviews.

All in chapter one, which ended with Elsa's first call from Mitch, middle name Boyfriend, last name Material. Not that she knew it yet. All Elsa knew was her dad had been badly injured. Elsa raced through a shook-up snow globe—Lily still liked that one—and found Dad with a crushed leg, a dislocated shoulder, and a paper cut for good measure. He'd recover, of course, but not before Christmas, and certainly not before the pass filled with snow.

No way home. No way to leave Dad by himself. No caseload. No sickle probe. Just faded brick Maw-and-Paw shops behind a gray gully of slush piled along the edges the town's only highway.

"*Elsa had never been irritated by her own heartbeat,*" Curtis read, "*but with no other sound in this frozen little hamlet, she was constantly aware of the loud, gulping tremor in her ear.*"

"Gulping?" Lily repeated.

"Kind of sounds like that through a stethoscope, I think."

"Huh." Lily was too distracted watching the repair man tinker with the AC unit in her backyard. It was one o'clock sharp, and everything was sticky with heat. Lily didn't know if the rancid body odor in the air was hers or Curtis's, and she didn't want to know. She just hoped the repair man could chase it away.

They needed to rewrite the descriptions of the town to be less sinister, but Lily struggled to describe a winter wonderland when her bare feet left damp imprints on the hardwood. They jumped around to indoor scenes instead. A cozy bake-off at the church, where Elsa could meet Mitch by griping about how much sugar damaged your teeth—only to find out Mitch made those winning brownies.

At Curtis's begging, Lily had agreed that Mitch would not be Elsa's childhood sweetheart. Instead, he was like her, a city slicker who'd been forced here by circumstances, but never left.

"But how'd he get there?" Curtis asked.

Lily replied, "He ran out of gas a mile outside of town. He asked for help, and the locals were so friendly that he never left."

Curtis's eye twitched.

Lily didn't care because at that moment, she heard a click, and then a whir. She turned her gaze to the vent in the floor, all her hopes in her throat. She ran a hand across the vent and chilly tendrils wafted around her fingers. She gasped, then buried her face in the cold wind.

The repairman said something about a wire, then something about a bill that he put on the counter; Lily barely heard or cared. She just wanted him gone so she could stand over that sweet coolness again. Curtis didn't correct her either; he was lying next to another vent, frosting his face. Lily knelt in front of her own vent and pulled her shirt forward to let cool air waft away all the stickiness.

And then, as her sweaty skin started to shiver, Lily closed her eyes. Cold wind. Darkness. Foot stepping forward, the tiniest crunch of snow that the shovel had missed. Ears stinging, pull down the fluffy hood. Exhale into the scarf for a cloud of warmth, immediately chased away by—

"In your happy place?"

Lily jumped, still on her knees, releasing her shirt so the cool fabric snapped back onto her belly. Curtis stood against the wall beside her, watching with curious bemusement. She was sweltering again, but only in the neck and cheeks. "I was…just…"

"What?" he asked.

Lily rolled her jaw around a little, then said, "I was picturing the town. You know, with the cold."

Curtis looked back and forth between Lily and the vent. "Oh. Like, a winter thing?"

"Yeah. You don't…do that?"

"Can't say I have. Is that something you usually do?"

"Sometimes, yes." She ducked her head. "Sensory stuff. Like…sticking my feet in sand to picture a beach. Or crunching leaves in my hands to get that fall sound." Lily tangled a finger in her hair. Why was she telling him all this? *Because it's less bizarre than getting high off an air conditioner.*

When she dared to look up, Curtis was still staring, brow a hard line of thought, mouth puckered to the side. He slid down against the wall until he was seated next to her and asked, "So what do you see?"

Lily wrapped her arms around herself. "Oh, just…winter stuff, you know?"

He shook his head. "No, I don't. Tell me."

Lily reminded herself that Curtis was on her side now. *Okay, then, time to be a little weird.* Lily pulled her long, sweaty hair back, then leaned over the vent again, eyes closed.

"It's just wind at first. Dark. Nighttime. But then I feel myself walking through it. Boots pressing into the sidewalk, tiptoeing around icy patches. I come to a crosswalk and have to hobble across a pile of slush that's been shoved aside by the plows. Boots clack against the black pavement, splotched with yellow reflections of streetlights. There's a stop sign, frosted on the top, dripping icicles like…like drooling teeth." Was that stupid? God, she sounded stupid.

"Keep going," Curtis said from somewhere to her side.

Lily decided to use that voice and materialize Curtis walking beside her, just to keep the vision going. He had a good-fitting peacoat, and he'd traded the soul patch for a full beard, not that he needed to know those details.

She said, "We cross the street to a warmer block. Well, not warmer, just shielded from the wind. And the storefront lights are a kind of toasty yellow, you know, like an oven in your mind. One's a barbershop. The barber is yawning by his empty chair. Slow day, but he's

208

thinking about a roast chicken at home, so clocking out early sounds nice. Next one's a realtor's office. The realtor, a woman, talks with her secretary. They're laughing about something we can't hear, drinking decaf coffee. Next is, uh..."

"What is it?" Curtis asked, in her ear. In her mind, he tipped his head at her, eyes curious beneath his cabbie hat.

Lily licked her lips and let the vent freeze them. "There's no building next, just an empty lot on the corner. There's a fence around the edge, with rainbow lights hanging in waves. In the center, there's this Christmas tree, a real one, three stories tall, been around for ages. Every inch of it is wrapped in white lights—bright ones, like a chandelier. They call it the Glass Tree because the light makes it look like that." She peeked one eye open to see if he was gagging.

He wasn't; he was taking notes in a little pocket notebook.

Lily balked. "What are you...?"

"My memory's not *that* good," Curtis insisted. He finished scribing, then said, "Okay, I'm caught up. Tell me more."

"Seriously? You don't think this is weird?"

"I think it's bat-crap bonkers. But it's working."

"It's not poetry or anything," Lily muttered. "Not like you can do."

Curtis replied, "Way too many people think they can write a book, but precious few have the ability to actually get inside one. If this is how you do it, then I won't knock it. We can work out word choices later. Right now, just close your eyes and get back on Main Street."

Lily toyed with her hair once more, inhaling the cool, breezy idea that she was doing something right. Maybe something better. Something her own. "It's Pine Street, actually. Main is much prettier."

Lily spilled out as much as she could, and Curtis copied it to the computer with a little refinement. After that, Lily could feel the sweat and grime of the day weighing her down, so she excused herself to take a shower. Rinsed clean, wearing a fresh set of clothes, she realized she was actually having fun. Her book. Her way.

She let herself smile. Even let herself sing a little as she cooked up some pasta for dinner. At least, until she remembered Curtis was at the dinner table with his laptop.

"Sorry," she said quickly.

Curtis looked up. "Doesn't bother me. You're not bad, actually."

"Oh, pshaw! You're biased."

"Actually, I'm exceptionally picky."

That was the other thing: Curtis was acting a lot more like date-night Curtis. All compliments and tenderness. Lily didn't get it, but she lifted her chin and accepted it.

By late evening, Lily was pacing her office with a confidence she hadn't had since her house's blueprints were complete. She was buffered from the scorching orange rays of a grumpy sun by the crisp, lilting air swirling all through the house, putting her in enough of a good mood to try pushing Curtis one step further from his comfort zone.

"What are some sweet and cheesy lines we can add to this scene?"

Curtis slowly looked up from his chair by the window, eyes pinched as if in pain. "Is that necessary?"

"C'mon, it's the first date scene! We need something adorable."

"Adorable, fine, but cheesy?"

"Just a sprinkling. Something to make the audience go, 'Awww.'"

Curtis sighed. "Yes, yes, but please don't try to sound too clever."

"What do you mean?"

"I mean don't be one of those writers who tries to reinvent the genre by blowing everybody's mind with a massively awesome line that just sounds like you're trying too hard to sound massively awesome."

"Uh, example?"

Curtis clicked his tongue a dozen times. Yep, still irritating. "'I didn't believe in a soul until I met you.'"

"What?" Lily snickered. "Is that a real line?"

"Yeah, I saw it in a movie once. Can't remember which one, but trust me, it's not better with context."

"Oh, I saw something once that made even me gag. It was this corny Christmas chick flick—shocking, I know—but the guy said to the girl, 'You're my fuzzy white Christmas blanket.'"

"Ew, what?!"

"I know! It was so clunky!"

Curtis snapped his fingers. "My mother is a fan of those kinds of movies, so one day she watched a Valentine's Day one while I was over. I don't know what I did to make her torture me like that, but I was very sorry by the end of it."

"Ha."

"Anyway, it's about a girl who enters an archery contest, because Cupid, you know? But at one point, she's falling for her competitor, and says to him, with a completely earnest face, 'I always aimed for the prize. This time, I aim my arrow for you.'"

Lily jumped. "Wha—is that flirting or a threat?"

Curtis laughed, a much deeper timber than his normal voice, a bit odd for his face, but a far pleasanter sound than scoffs and clicks. It made another knot come loose in Lily's shoulders. She suddenly realized how heavy her eyelids were, and felt the snowy fuzz at the edges of her brain. She was awful tired for only eight o'clock. Wait...

"Oh! It's eight. That's when you're leaving, right?"

Curtis leaned to see the clock on Lily's desk, then sat back and rubbed his eyes. "Wow. That actually went by quickly."

"Yeah...yeah, it did." Lily marveled. A day full of writing. Characters, adjectives, visualizing, plot holes, backstories, yeesh, it made Lily's brain fry just thinking about it. But doing it had been strangely easy. Even enjoyable. Like it used to be.

Maybe better?

Lily raised her arms in a long, tip-toeing stretch, giving her new light a friendly wave before she came back down. "Okay, you hop on my computer and check the final word count. I'm going to grab the chocolates."

She found them still in the refrigerator, but cold chocolate was still chocolate. Lily tore off the packaging and day-dreamed about a salted caramel bursting in her mouth as she skipped back into the office. "So did we actually get more than ten thousand or right at the mark?"

Curtis leaned over the desk, still as stone. "We didn't make it."

Lily's foot skidded mid-skip. "What? Well, how close are we?"

Curtis turned in the chair slowly, as if using the last of his strength. "Sixty-five hundred words."

Her legs almost gave way. Sixty-five hundred. Just under two-thirds of their daily goal. Her eyes fell down to the chocolates in her hand, but peered right through them, to the dark pit opening in her rug. "That's not possible."

Curtis rubbed his brow. "Maybe it will be a shorter book. We talked about that."

"Maybe, but we're barely on the first date! We haven't even met all the characters yet, it's…it's only a couple chapters in! And we skipped a lot!"

Curtis winced. "I could stay later if you like."

"No." Her tired bones shot the message through her mouth. "No, it's been twelve hours. And it's gonna be twelve hours tomorrow, and the next day, and the next and…" Lily's eyes stung, and her teeth chattered. She slammed the chocolates on the desk, not caring for the clattering sounds within. "I was having fun! I was actually making my own book my own way with some real help, and we…you laughed! Just a minute ago! It was a good day today, and now you're telling me that actually enjoying myself is not enough?"

Lily threw herself into the computer to check Curtis's numbers, nearly knocking him over on the way. Yep. Six thousand, five hundred and twelve. She hung her head below her shoulders, legs twitching under the weight of it all.

"Lily?" he asked in a soft voice.

"Hmm?" she croaked.

"Would you like to watch a cheesy romance movie?"

Lily puffed out her lower lip and nodded.

Curtis patted her hand. "Come on, let's go cringe."

He really sat with her, too. At least, she was pretty sure he did. They put the TV on the floor since Lily didn't have a couch anymore, but at least they had the furry rug—the buyer had never come. They started up some corny Christmas love story Lily had never seen, but halfway through, Lily's head got so heavy that she had to lie on the rug. The film became blurry after that. She thought she saw the credits at one point, but didn't remember shutting it off. She only had the dim recollection of a blanket on her shoulders, and the soft click of a door closing.

Chapter 19

10 Days Left

Lily wanted to flay herself for wasting time on a movie, but she had to admit she felt a lot better in the morning. Energy was high, and the bitter aroma of coffee from her French press nearly made her float. *I really need to sell that stupid Keurig.*

Curtis knocked before entering, yanked his laptop out of the backpack and said, "All right, I've had four Pop Tarts and a Mountain Dew; I'm ready to roll!"

Lily observed the eye twitch and said, "Maybe I should type."

Type she did, until the laptop bled ink, and her fingers went numb. Lily hammered out any idea, any string of words, just to get the word count back up. Editing could come later, she reminded herself. Just get the ideas out there.

Lily forgot that sometimes, words don't come in any form. Writer's block? It felt more like writer's constipation. She could only glare at the screen, clenching her brain muscles until, mere seconds before the aneurism, she could type a five-letter word.

"We had a whole book," Lily griped at ten a.m. "Why can't we make this work?"

Curtis replied, "You said you wanted to start over."

Lily didn't dare answer. This was his fault, and she might just let him know it. She let the keyboard do the talking instead. She still couldn't get more than snippets of a scene, but she could at least plan out all the ways she could cleanse Curtis's old ideas until they became her own.

Jed the Rancher went from a power-hungry homophobe to a jolly, Santa Claus stand-in who loved filling his snow-hardened fields with festive partiers dancing around colossal evergreens, swinging glasses of eggnog in one hand, and courting with the other. Maria the Doctor no longer leered at her patients with a smile of icicle teeth as she discussed payment first and medicine second. Now, she worked long hours to research the auto-mechanic's chronic pain, then went home and shed weary tears on her soft-armed husband, who seemed to solve all life's problems in half an hour of cuddles. Xander the nineteen-year-old no longer mooched off his dad's money while pretending to be an Ivy League elite. He used that money to take care of Mom after her stroke, selling fan art online to give the income a little boost.

"Fan art?" Curtis read over her shoulder.

Lily's eyes flicked to him like switchblade. "Yeah. Like characters from movies or TV shows?"

"I know that, but is that realistic?"

"People buy it."

"Not very—"

"It's all he can do! He was just drawing for fun when the car crashed, killing Dad and crippling Mom."

"I thought it was a stroke."

"I'm changing it! It's allowed!"

The tendons in Curtis's neck bulged, thick as guitar strings and just as tight. "I'll get us some lunch." He left halfway through the sentence.

She checked the clock, then her word count. Ten thousand and two. Lily grabbed the chocolate box from her desk and popped a victory snack into her mouth. Her tongue tried to wriggle out of her mouth when it tasted the sunscreen tang of coconut. She choked it down, then started on the next ten thousand.

She only made eight thousand by quitting time that night. All that typing, all that anger, a headache in every pore across her skull, and she was *still* behind!

"We're doing better, though," Curtis said. "Only two thousand behind instead of three-and-a-half."

"That's not exactly helpful," Lily groused. She hadn't smiled since this morning, and her cheeks ached something awful. Or maybe it was the underuse of her mouth, considering she let Curtis do most of the verbal brainstorming, and either agreed by writing what he said, or disagreed by writing something different. *Let him figure out which was which*, the smoldering beast crowed from its perch of pain.

He gave a tired sigh. "Right, well, just trying to end on some positivity. See you tomorrow."

"Oh, I can't wait!" she said in a shrill, sardonic voice.

Curtis shoved his laptop and cords into his backpack in a clunky mass, then flung it over his shoulder. He marched to the door, opened it, then stopped.

"I know I messed up," he said, "but I'm doing my best."

Lily stared back through stinging eyes. "So was I."

Curtis let the door slam behind him.

Lily crawled into bed while it was still daylight, and cried until the orange rays across her carpet darkened to nothing. She pulled out her phone, and had Mary's number up before she froze. *No. Mary can't help me this time.*

After soaking the last dry corner of the comforter on her eyes, Lily switched to Curtis's number and texted two words: I'm sorry.

He didn't reply.

9 Days Left

Lily rolled up her sleeves and made the best biscuits and gravy she could muster before Curtis came over. She nearly collapsed with relief that he really did show up, wearing a faded tee shirt and stained shorts.

"Hi," she said feebly. "I made breakfast. Want some?"

Curtis glanced at it. "Uh, no thanks. I had cereal. I thought we ate breakfast alone."

"Yeah...I...forgot to tell you in advance." She sighed over her creation, the milky gravy still steaming, with bits of sausage shooting their husky aroma though the kitchen. Lily bowed her head, and silently filled her own plate.

When she dared a peek, Lily saw the bruise-colored rings under Curtis's eyes. "Can I get you some coffee?"

He shook his head. "Not a coffee guy. I prefer tea."

"I have some of that, too."

"I've had some."

"Okay..."

They slogged through the words. This wasn't a story, it was a swamp, knee deep and fighting every inch of movement. When they reached twenty-thousand words by noon, Lily shared the chocolate box. Dark chocolate ganache, *too* dark.

Curtis leaned on Lily's desk as he hovered his finger over the chocolates. He picked one up and bit it. Some kind of pink cream on the inside. He frowned the whole time, like his face was set in concrete.

"Are you still upset?" she asked in a faint voice.

"Hmm?" He blinked at her. "Oh, no. Well, a little, but…I just slept like crap last night."

"Did something happen?"

"No, I was just thinking about the story in an endless loop 'til two in the morning."

Lily's lips slowly drifted apart. He'd tossed and turned for her story, while she slept like a baby. Before she could think about it, Lily shot out a hand and grabbed Curtis's. His fingers were long, bony, and warm.

"I'm glad you're here," she said as he stared at their hands. "I know I may not act like it sometimes, and I'll probably get nasty again this afternoon, but…but I'm glad you're with me."

The edges of his cheeks seemed to soften. The wrinkles in his brow smoothed and faded, and a shimmer of sunlight caught in his eyes.

Curtis squeezed her hand back. She could still feel every ridge of his bones, but it didn't hurt at all.

8 Days Left

They still weren't making their daily quota. Even looking at the book layout, they weren't on track, no matter the word count.

So, they wrote.

And kept writing.

When they ate, they brainstormed, wiping hands on napkins before typing anew. They paced, discussed, checked the story layout, made little adjustments, then sought the words to give it life.

Curtis kept rubbing his eyes. Losing sleep, probably. Lily kept wanting to ask him silly questions. What are you writing lately? Were you born in Idaho or did you move here? Did you know the stubble works better with the soul patch than the soul patch by itself?

But those had nothing to do with writing, so she ignored them. Ignored him, really, which soured in her belly.

Maybe later…

7 Days Left

They wrote the ending because it was the only thing that came easy. Until neither of them was happy with it.

Lily sulked again, but kept her tongue civil. Curtis blinked a lot, and frequently stirred, as if waking up from wide-eyed sleep.

Only two thousand words short this time…

6 Days Left

Type. Delete. Type.
Repeat.
Still two thousand short.

5 Days Left

"Something's wrong," Curtis said.

Three in the afternoon. Or something. Lily's phone was on the dining table, but she herself lay on the furry rug where the couch used to reside, reconsidering her plans to sell it. It made a soft nest for weary heads.

Curtis paced next to her, jeans shuffling by her head. "The flow of the story's off. It's fighting us at every turn."

"How?" Lily asked the ceiling. "We've got the through-line: she comes eager to leave, learns to slow down, finds love in the process, and ends with a simpler, but happier life."

Curtis sighed, and tried to rub the black out from under his eyes. No success. "Room for two down there?"

Lily shifted to the edge of the fuzz, then he laid down, his left side pressed against her right. It made her freeze for a second. The last man to make this much contact was her body pillow. She turned her head just a little, and watched his jaw move as he spoke.

"Something in the story is fighting us. Or not helping. Or...something. Nothing is happening as it should. Do we have enough conflict?"

"I think we do. Elsa chafes against small town life, she has to work her way into Mitch's heart, she has to let him into hers, she argues with Dad, she fights with her schedule and the weather, she's fighting everything."

"But to what point? Is it really pushing the story along?"

Lily thought it over. They had plenty of scenes of Elsa speed-walking through town because she had nothing else to do. Of small-scale Christmas parties where people didn't want to talk about work. She was just starting to warm up, though, thanks to some ice skating on the lake, the closest thing this town had to excitement. Made a perfect excuse for Mitch to come up and make full-body contact.

Kind of like Curtis right now, Lily noted. She decided to sit up.

Curtis snapped up right beside her like a human mousetrap. "It's the guy!"

Lily jumped, then let her breath out. "It usually is. What do you mean?"

"He's not really involved in the story. Not enough, at least."

"What? He's the guy who took care of Dad in the hospital. And we have him checking up now and then, too."

He waved his hands in circles as he spoke, nearly bopping her at each revolution. "He's only popping up when we need him. He dips in and out of Elsa's story; he's not actually part of anything. Honestly, I think it's his job. We made him a nurse because in the old story, his parents wanted him to be a doctor, but he found satisfaction his own way. But now he's an out-of-towner; his parents aren't in the story, so that whole arc doesn't work. He needs a new job. Or maybe just a hobby. Something that fits his character and plays off Elsa's so they weave together more naturally."

Lily considered that, and found Curtis to be right. Mitch tended to stand off to the side of the story, waiting for his next scene. Then, he'd step in, be adorable but frustrating, and vanish until he could do it again. "Okay," Lily said, "so what should he be doing?"

Curtis thought on it.

Lily thought on it.

It took them two hours to realize they had no idea—and no words in that whole chunk of time. They'd moved to Lily's office, each sliding off their respective chairs. A faint buzzing swarmed through Lily's ears: the chatter of a brain burbling everything and nothing at once.

"I'm sorry," Curtis muttered.

Lily let her head flop around her limp neck, and spoke above the droning in her mind. "Sorry for what?"

"I promised to help, but I'm not doing a good job." He wasn't looking at her, just staring into space, his body a limp sack of meat, his skin sporting an odd, waxy sheen.

"You're doing your best," Lily said. "I'm the one who insisted on changing everything."

"And I'm the one who bent it out of shape in the first place."

True. And sometimes, she wanted to scratch his eyes out for it. Other times, like right now, she just wanted to hold his hand. Her arm wasn't long enough, though.

Curtis peeled himself from his chair with the limp

stiffness of a marionette. "I'll get some dinner going. We're just doing leftovers, right?"

Lily leaned forward, the buzzing bees stabbing her eardrums. "No. We're going out."

"Oh. I don't remember that on the calendar."

She rose at once, eyes boring straight ahead, Curtis a little to the side of her infinite gaze. "No. No, we're going out. We need a break."

"A break? Lily, we don't have time."

"We don't have *energy*! Curt, if we don't recharge, all the time in the world won't matter." Her voice was half passionate, half desperate whine.

Curtis folded like wet pasta. "Yeah, okay. I'm too tired to fight you."

Lily said, "We'll grab some dinner, go for a walk, just get some fresh air."

"Okay, I'll buy."

"It's a date."

He scratched his stubbled cheek. "Two in one week. I must be doing something right."

Chapter 20

They settled on a local bar and grill that hit all the right notes. Close to home to minimize travel, fancy enough to feel like a treat, but not so fancy that they had to change clothes—or feel like Cupid was floating over their table.

It was an old place, old in the dashing, silver-fox way. The bricks were faded, and chipped around the corners, the wood dark as a smoking parlor, and scuffed to a fuzzy sheen. The pictures on the wall had an ancient feel to them, an autumnal simplicity too shabby for modern photography, and the fishing spots they showed had probably been choked with suburbs by now. The restaurant had just enough modern touches to feel like part of the real world: computerized point-of-sale, wi-fi, and pretty waitresses in tight, black clothing. But the country music on the speakers had a slow, wistful quality to it, not too loud or twangy, and all the lights were simple, soft, and dimmed just enough to hide you from the world.

Mary didn't care for it. She thought it was too rustic, even if the menu did feature grass-fed beef and wines nobody could pronounce. Mary preferred polished tables and white walls, saying the family "deserved it" after all they went through. So, Lily always went alone.

Or, once in a great, blue moon, with a date. Which made bringing Curtis very odd. Not unmanageable, just like a picture tilted ever so slightly to the left. He did pull the chair out for her, though. *I forgot: date-night Curtis is best Curtis.*

The hostess sat them upstairs, by an enormous window. Fortunately, the evening sun scorched the opposite side of the building, so they had a cool view of Ketchum, trimmed with brushstrokes of goldenrod light. Lily loved her house, but the streets and signposts were a welcome reprieve from her own four walls.

After the hostess sat them, Curtis leaned forward and said, "So about Mitch's career, are we thinking some kind of—" He pulled back, waving his arms in front of his face. "Nope, nope, no writer talk. Cleansing the brain."

"Right," Lily said. "Let's talk about something else."

"Agreed."

He closed his mouth, and waited.

Lily waited, too. For what? She didn't know. A conversation fairy to grace them with a topic, perhaps. How could she have spent the better part of the month within slapping distance of this man and have nothing to talk about but the book? What did he like? What was he doing with his life?

I don't know anything about him. It seemed a good place to start. "So, where are you from?" she asked.

"Iowa," Curtis said. "Type in 'Nowhere' on Google Maps, and I'm ten miles east."

Lily chuckled. "So, what brought you to Idaho?"

Curtis crossed his arms and smirked. "Like most people, I thought Idaho and Iowa were the same state, so I was coming home from work and wound up in potato country."

"Oh har-har. Seriously, what brought you here?"

The smirk slid a little. "Uh…chasing a girl."

"Ooh! Saucy."

"Heh, the most G-rated online dating story ever. She was from Twin Falls. It's, like, almost two hours south of here? Anyway, we hit it off, so I flew out to see her, and about a month later I visited again, only this time I used a truck because it was easier to carry all my stuff."

"Whoa!" Lily opened her mental notebook for recording story ideas. "She must have really been something!"

"Yeah." Curtis watched a bead of moisture spill down the side of his water glass. "Yeah."

Oh. Lily could guess how well that had turned out, and Curtis didn't seem interested in telling what happened. She wondered if her voice would even reach him anymore.

Lily fumbled. "Did you, uh…ever think about going back to Iowa?"

"No," he said in a low, but present, voice. "My parents followed me out west a year later, and my brother is in New Mexico, so I've got nothing back there."

"Oh…" She couldn't think of anything to add. They just listened to the next table over argue about a baseball game.

Curtis suddenly sat up straighter and looked her in the eye. "And how about you, eh? Any crazy love stories?"

She scoffed. "I wish. I'm afraid I'm a boring romance writer. I've had three big relationships, but nothing crazy happened in any of them. One was my best friend in high school, but we only dated three days before we realized it was kind of gross. I did have a sad breakup in college, though. He moved to New York to work in a hospital there, which was really great for him, but I hate huge cities, so we ended it. I cried a lot, but never chased after him or had a stupid rebound or anything. And then there was my boyfriend of six months just before I became a writer. We had some fun, but agreed it wasn't going anywhere, so we had a very grown-up conversation and parted like two mature, confident adults."

"And not one of them had a name, which I guess was the point."

"Oh, shut up. You never said your special girl's name."

Curtis's hands flinched, curling almost into fists.

All the air left Lily's lungs. "I...I'm sorry, that's clearly sensitive. You can forget—"

"Mel," Curtis said. "Or Melody, but she preferred 'Mel' because she had no musical talent whatsoever. Her words, not mine. True words, though. I used to call her 'Cara-Mel' because she was so sweet."

Lily scoffed. "Okay, the next time you make a remark about my book being too saccharine, I'm going to bring that up."

Curtis smiled, quick as a flash, then dropped it. Or maybe it was another flinch. Lily bit down on her lip. *Pete's sake, Lily, bringing it up is the opposite of helpful. Change the freaking subject already!*

Lily said, "Mine were, uh...Duncan, Joey, and Nolan. In order, if you cared to know."

"Nothing since becoming a writer?"

"Nothing serious. I got absorbed in writing, plus getting my house. This right here is the longest relationship I've had in three years."

Curtis leaned closer, and took both of Lily's hands in his, holding them up at face level. "Lily?"

Ev. Ry. Thing. Froze. "Wh-What?"

"You're too good for him. This is an intervention. We all love you, and we think you could do better. I mean look at the guy! He's white as milk and has all the body mass of a dehydrated pretzel!"

She nearly spat all over him as her shoulders heaved with laughter. She bit her teeth down hard to keep in the noise, but the it just made her squeak like a kettle. She ducked her head to her chest. And snorted.

Fortunately, Lily was able to gain control of herself just before a skinny, brunette waitress walked up. Lily realized she was still holding Curtis's hands, and dropped her grip like a hot plate.

The waitress grinned. "Sorry to break up the cute couple."

Lily cleared her throat. "No, no, we're, uh, not a couple."

Curtis said, "Yeah, celebrities are a bit out of my league."

"Celebrity?" the waitress asked.

Lily flashed him a hot look, and Curtis said, "Uh, never mind." Lily loved her fans, but boy was she tired.

The waitress listened to their orders, scribbling with quick and flourished strokes, but kept glancing at Lily, as if trying to remember her.

Lily concluded by turning to Curtis. "Split the cheesecake with me?"

Curtis replied, "If you're quick enough, you might get some." He pinched his eyes shut. "That came out ruder than I intended."

"It's okay," she replied, waving him off.

The waitress spoke as she wrote. "Cheesecake. Is that all?"

"I think so," Lily said.

The waitress nodded, but hesitated as she turned. "Sorry, are…you that writer who lives in town? Harper?"

Rats! But Lily gave her best smile. "Yes, Lily Harper."

"Oh, yeah. I'd heard there was one who lived here. What do you write?"

"Romance and girly stuff."

"Mm."

Lily smiled a little more. "Not much of a chick lit gal?"

"Not really, no offense."

"None taken. Everybody has their own stuff. What do you enjoy…" Lily checked the name tag. "…Sasha?"

Sasha cringed. "Movies, mostly. Big, dumb action flicks or braindead comedies." Lily swore she heard Curtis choke. "I've started an online grad degree, and I read a bazillion words a day, so novels aren't exactly fun anymore."

"Oh, no, nobody wants to read after all that. What are you going to school for?"

"Psychology. Geriatric care. My grandma had dementia, so I got interested in how the brain works."

"Aw, you're so sweet. You must be passionate about the subject."

"I am! When I'm not drowning in citations, I mean. So, yeah, I spend my free time emptying my brain."

Lily nodded. "You need an escape. That's why I mostly read fluffy stuff that doesn't question the nature of existence. I've got enough of that in my head already."

Sasha said, "Yeah, escapist stuff. Is that what you write?"

"Mm-hmm. Beach trips, cozy bookstore romances, and coming soon, Christmas in the mountains."

Sasha considered a moment, then asked, "What's the bookstore one?"

"It's called *Maple Leaves*. It's about a girl, Mabel—yes, it's a play on the title—who's struggling to save the little New England bookstore her family owned, but after she takes on a truckload of debt, she suddenly realizes she may not want to be in that business after all."

"Oh!"

"And she's partnering with the only guy who seems to truly care about the store, so there's a friends-to-lovers story alongside it."

The corner of a smile flickered on Sasha's cheek. "That's actually…is it in the library? Sorry, I'm poor."

Lily chuckled. "Yes, the library has some copies."

"Cool." Sasha glanced down at her notepad. "Sorry! I'll go get this order to the cooks. So sorry!"

"It's okay!" Lily called as Sasha sped away. "She's sweet."

Curtis was gawking at Lily, with two fingers pointed in the direction Sasha had run. "How the hell did you do that?"

"What?"

"She had zero interest in your book, and you got her from 'Never' to 'Yes, please!'"

Lily grinned. "She wasn't interested in my book, but she *was* interested in rest and escape. That's what I'm selling, not just novels."

"Oh, so that was planned? You made it sound so natural."

Lily gave him a level stare. "It *was* natural. I was just making conversation. She mentioned she was overwhelmed,

231

and I empathized because she's the kind of person I write for: the one whose world is so batty she can't take one more second of reality, and just needs to breathe for a few pages."

"Yeesh," Curtis breathed. "When you're done with your book, come sell mine, would you?"

Lily laughed, but then gasped. "Hey, maybe I could! You know, as a thank you. Once I'm done, I mean. And, you know, I should probably read it first."

"It'd probably help."

Lily folded her hands on the table and adopted a perky, managerial smile. "So, Mr. Reynolds, tell me about your book."

Curtis looked like he'd just been asked to disarm a bomb. "Oh…uh, right, book. It's a sci-fi story. Aliens come to Earth, and they seem nice, but not really. Well, that all happens before the story actually starts. It's about a group called the Truants—I call them that because they never attend the kinda-sorta schooling the aliens impose, but they're smart enough to get away with it and…that's rambling. Um, so the Truants are outwitting the aliens who are trying to tell humans how to human, which they don't like, obviously, which is a commentary on humans not knowing how to human either and…uh…"

He cursed under his breath, and dropped his eyes to the table, fingers balled into fists. Cutlery clattered in the background. Some Southern beau on the speaker crooned about a girl he lost. Lily didn't have anything more clever to say.

"I can write," Curtis insisted. "I can plot a story, sling some winter-crisp dialogue, I can go on and on about the importance of art and truth and beauty and all that, but ask me to tell somebody why it's worth their time, and I just...can't form the right words."

Lily leaned a little closer and asked in a soft voice, "Why do you write?"

He met her eye immediately. "To tell the truth. That's why I write sci-fi. Fables tell the truth better than lectures. And when people read about a fake world, maybe they'll start wonder if they're living in one, one manufactured to sell people instead of grow them."

So sharp. So jaded. And yet, so passionate. Why couldn't he describe his story with such gusto?

I guess some people weren't raised in the art of telling people what they want to hear.

Curtis suddenly snickered, and gave Lily a sad smile. "We're talking about books again."

She shook her head. "I guess it's who we are."

"Yeah..." He looked at her face for a reddeningly long time. "Yeah, I guess it is."

Lily had forgotten how hot it was. Even with the sun on the other side of the building, when they left the restaurant, she choked on dry, hot fog. Like walking into her own mouth.

"Blech," she whined. "I'm more of a cold-weather girl. That's why I made my home in the mountains."

Curtis donned his sunglasses. "Mountains are closer to the sun."

"Yes, thank you. Why don't we find someplace indoors to meander?"

He scoffed. "Where?"

Lily scoffed back, gesturing to the dozens upon dozens of shops lined up in neat rows across the main drag. "Anywhere? C'mon, let's look."

Only a block or two later, Lily quit laughing. Ketchum had a great many stores, but it was nearly six o'clock on a Sunday. Nothing but "Closed" signs written in swirly hipster fonts.

"Not really anywhere to go anyway," Curtis grumbled. "This town is nothing but overpriced clothing stores, trendy sports equipment, and kitschy tourist shops."

Lily crossed her arms, frowning all the way down to her neck. Sure, the town had a lot of same-y, upper-class baubles, but there was more than that. What could she show Curtis? Surely something was open that wasn't a restaurant...

She snapped her fingers and said, "Come with me."

Just a few blocks down, at the base of a three-story building of classic red bricks, Lily led Curtis into the pungent scent of hops and hardwood floors. The modest brewery/restaurant was still pretty new, but the full tables said good things about business.

Lily walked up to the bar, and an upper-thirties woman with hair in three different half-finished styles beamed bright beneath tired eyes. "Miss Harper!" she called in a too-loud voice. "What can I do for you? Drink? Fries?"

"No thanks, Harriet." Lily looked about the tables to see how many people were staring. All of them, of course. "I was just wondering if I could head upstairs. I want to show my new friend the view."

Harriet nodded so hard her hair bounced everywhere. "Of course! Let me know if you need anything else!" She motioned towards a back door, and Lily entered, with Curtis close behind. They stepped briefly into a stainless-steel kitchen so clean the reflections nearly blinded her. But Lily quickly took another door that led to a darker brick stairwell, immediately drowning out the noise of clattering pans and sizzling grease.

"This place used to be a bookstore," Lily explained.

"I remember that. They moved to Hailey, didn't they?"

"Yep. I made friends with the owner, and she used to let me come up here all the time. Then she moved out and the brewery took over. The new owner is more into bad-boy billionaire bodice-rippers than snuggly romances. However, she loved the idea of having a local celebrity frequenting her store, so she lets me continue the tradition, and I eat here now and again."

Curtis said, "I thought you didn't like alcohol."

"I don't, but the fries are really good." She passed through a barren, musty room with no lights except that which came through the windows. Her shoes clomped across the hardwood floors, then she opened one last door, letting in the traffic noise. "After you."

He stepped out, and Lily followed him out onto a narrow turret balcony protruding from the third floor. Even at that height, she could see most of the roofs, glistening black in the evening heat. Yet a breeze blew above the streets, tossing her hair and washing the warmth away.

"It's not much," Lily admitted, "but it's kind of breathtaking in its own way, I think. I love just looking out over everything for a while."

"Yeah, you can see a good chunk of the town," Curtis said.

She leaned on the railing, sighing to the west. The orange sunlight traced the edges of the mountains, casting them in dark greens. "Isn't it beautiful?"

He took a long time to reply. "It's nice in its way. I mean aesthetically, it's a nice town, got a bit of an old-timey look to it, which I'm sure was your point, but..."

"Go on," Lily prompted gently.

"But I'm afraid this place lost its luster long ago for me."

"Why?"

"You just saw it. It's not a town, it's a tourist trap. Half of it is food and clothing, all catering to the ultra-rich. The other half is realtors, but God help me if I know who they're selling to because the prices out here are catastrophic. Nobody can afford to live here, nobody can afford to shop here. People pass through on vacations, but the locals who live and work and die here? They suffer. Even you can only afford your house because of your ridiculously-high book sales. This isn't the charming mountain vista it pretends to be. It's a bunch of stuck-up, gentrified, posh, high-heeled elitism that put on a flannel shirt for better marketing."

She folded her arms across her stomach. "I can't deny a lot of what you said. I will argue there's good to be had here, and little gems that are worth it. However, that's not what I was looking at."

He turned to her. "What were you looking at?"

Lily pointed to the ginormous range of mountains

dominating the horizon, the sentinels of the west, prickled with evergreens, and sighing in their soft green hue. "You know what I think when I look at those mountains? They'll never conquer that. Suburbs may overpopulate other places, and tourist traps will climb as high as they can, but those mountains are too big, too steep, too rocky, and too beloved to become another paved boulevard. Think of how much it would cost! For just one of those mountains! My street may be overcrowded one day, and the fields might all be torn up, but those mountains? They will always be wild, always a bastion of fresh air and natural beauty. And you know what? It's free. Everybody gets to enjoy it."

Her stomach shook as she said it. She'd always believed that, but something about it rang new today. They'd never gloss over the mountain, never make it pretty or perfect. They could try, but it would resist. It would outlast.

Lily said, "They'll always be themselves."

She watched the mountains for a while, ignorant of the rumble of traffic and chatter of humanity, hoping to draw a little of that solidity into herself. When she turned around, Curtis was watching her, but quickly flicked his gaze up to the mountains.

"What?" Lily asked.

Curtis shrugged. "I have to admit your optimism is refreshing."

"You don't strike me as very optimistic yourself."

"In my experience, optimism is equated with ignorance. Living in a fantasy land, wishing on a star that problems would magically vanish, that sort of thing. Yours is a bit...sturdier. I mean you built a home on a dream, but you're working to keep it that way."

"Trying to, at least. I just want a peaceful place to live, near my family, where I can always go and rest from all the craziness of life and…and…" Lily squinted at the mountains, her gaze tracing the empty trails between the evergreens, the switchbacks of ski runs, now green and dry. "He's a ski instructor," Lily breathed.

"Who is?"

"Mitch! The boyfriend! He's a ski instructor!"

"Eh, sounds kind of Hallmark-movie to me. Fall in love with the ski instructor?"

Lily shook her head hard, lightning shooting through her entire being. "No, listen! Elsa's hooked on the speed and business of her old life, right? Well, what's the fastest thing to do in a snowy mountain town?"

Curtis turned his face to the mountain, thoughts washing over him. "Skiing."

"Right! So it becomes her one source of fun, and a way to talk to the guy, get to know him, because she thinks he's on her level since he likes the thrill of skiing, too. But in reality, he's the type to go home and settle down afterwards, but Elsa would keep skiing all through the night if she could, just to keep up that sense of movement."

He leaned his hip on the railing, clicking his tongue. "She keeps picking harder slopes. Faster, more dangerous, when she's not ready for them."

"Ooh, I like that!" she said. "Mitch tries to talk her down, but she won't listen. That's conflict."

"Until one day she gets in over her head…"

"And gets hurt! Now, instead of slowing down, she has to stop entirely!"

"Ooh-hoo-hoo, she would hate that."

Lily put her hands on her hips and puffed out her chest. "It brings the character to her knees, not in a way that's too horrible or depressing. It's not a permanent injury, and she won't lose her job or anything. It just forces her to face herself and how she hates the quiet moments because they're so empty. Until Mitch and Dad and community all fill the gaps. Then, she doesn't ever want to speed up again because it will push them all out."

Curtis tapped his foot like he wanted to pace, but only had two steps of balcony to work with. "The action matches the theme. The physical crash foreshadows the total-life crash she's headed for, but Elsa learns her lesson, and joins a smaller dentistry so she can really appreciate the kids she's working with instead of speeding through them to bump up her numbers."

"She kisses Mitch under the mistletoe, and they all live happily ever after. The end." Lily gave a giddy squeal.

Curtis laughed with her. Then, he paused, staring back at her for a moment, before lowering his eyes, the smile starting to melt.

"What's wrong?" Lily asked.

"Nothing wrong," Curtis said. "I just...feel the need to apologize."

"Curtis, you've apologized a hundred times by now. I've forgiven you."

"No, that was for taking over your story. This goes deeper."

"What do you mean?"

He wriggled as though he had garden snakes in his jeans. "Look, I'm a bit calloused. Don't gasp, it's true. I've met a lot of so-called writers who think that just because they have a semi-interesting idea, they should be published and famous, without actually learning the craft. And I've seen way too many published authors chasing trends, pumping out books meant to push the right buttons in the brain, not wow or challenge people. And the romance genre? Blushes, corsets, and physical tinglies, no depth or complexity or anything worthwhile."

"I assume the apology is coming?" Lily said in a wry voice.

"My point is I…underestimated you. I thought you were another hack writer pumping out fluff for idiots so you could cash a paycheck and smile for Instagram. But I was wrong. There's a lot more too you, and I'm sorry for judging and dismissing you. You're a real writer."

It was twin bee stings in the eyeballs. Lily spun away from him as her guts tried to explode. She covered her mouth as moisture poured unbidden down her face.

"What'd I do?!" Curtis exclaimed.

"No, it's not you, this is…something else." Lily wiped her face, gasped deeply, and swallowed down all the sobs that had sprang from some well she didn't realize she had. "Let's just say you're not the first person to think I'm a fluff writer who's only good for bringing in money to fund real writers." She hadn't heard from Mr. Gates in some time, but his words still echoed down the hall of her mind. *It's like you're a real writer…*

Curtis cringed. "Do you want to talk about it?"

"Actually…" Lily spun back to him, fire scorching in her face. "I want to go home, finish this damn book, and prove them all wrong."

He nodded, his face like stone. "Then let's go kick some ass."

Transforming Mitch into a ski instructor proved to be the exact fuel the story needed to function. Sadly, that meant going back and changing everything that no longer fit the new plan. It meant shredding the first cutesy date scene they'd slaved and laughed over. Lily despaired when she saw the clock strike eight while their word count was still in the red.

"I can stay later," Curtis said.

"Are you sure?" she whimpered, hoping he'd stay, and hating that he'd need to.

"C'mon, we're on a roll!"

Lily sighed out a thank you, and kept going until nine.

Ten.

Eleven.

Her eyes were starting to blur. If she rubbed them, they stung. The glare of the screen made the words all run together, but she typed on anyway. They were a third of the way through the book, tracing a new river of story through the fields of old ideas, cutting new waterways as needed and damming up old ones. Forty percent through.

Midnight clicked on the clock.

Curtis finally stepped away from Lily's writing desk and collapsed onto his own chair, rubbing his eyes with his palms. She nearly dozed off just watching him.

"I need to go to bed," he said.

Lily started to reply, but a yawn interrupted her. "Will you be okay to drive?"

"Yeah, yeah, just gotta get home, collapse, try to shove breakfast down my throat, and hurry back over. Maybe shower, if I have brain cells."

"You look like you'll fall asleep at the wheel."

"I'll be okay, it's just a matter of working up the energy."

"Curtis?"

"Mm?"

"I have a guest room. You can sleep there if you want."

Curtis blinked his bleary eyes at her. "That would be awesome, actually."

Lily stood and stretched, waving her new office light again. It was becoming a habit. "Come on up, I'll show you where it is."

A short jaunt up the stairs and to the left, Lily opened her neglected second bedroom. It was a modest space, recently freed from most of Mary's chic accessories, but Lily did keep one beach picture on the wall and a big seashell on the night stand. It made the room look quaint and escapist, instead of showy.

She pointed and said, "Bathroom's right there, and if you get up before me, help yourself to whatever food we still have."

Curtis leaned on the doorframe and said, "Start work at eight like normal?"

"Yep."

"Sounds like a plan."

"Good. Sleep well. See you in the morning."

"Night."

Curtis leaned in, they shared a quick kiss on the lips,

and Lily lumbered into her bed, so tired that she fell asleep before she realized what she'd just done.

Chapter 21

Wait, what?

The question lanced through her sleepiness, brighter and sharper than the morning sun slicing through the edge of her window shade. *Did I kiss Curtis?*

No, that was dumb. Kissing required two people who were more than "tolerable acquaintances." And yet, the memory didn't have the fuzzy quality of a sleepless hallucination. And Curtis was more than tolerable by now, right?

Lily checked the clock. Seven-thirty. She had to get up and write. She hurried into the shower, then spent five straight minutes massaging shampoo into her hair. *But who kissed first? He had leaned in, hadn't he? And why?* The implications made her head spin.

Finally clean, Lily stood for another five minutes in front of the mirror, holding a towel that was supposed to dry the beads of moisture splattering onto the tile floor. *But if he leaned in first, why did I kiss him back?*

Another five minutes choosing between her last pair of jeans and the exact same pair as option one. *Does he think something is happening between us? Is there? What does it mean?*

There was no more time to think. Eight o'clock had

struck. Lily softly pulled her door open, peering through the crack until she could see the other room. Open. She crept out, tip-toeing across her own upper floor until she could see over the balcony. No one in the living room, but she did hear the clinking of a spoon in a cereal bowl.

Her belly gurgled. Between hunger and the book, she had to go down there, had to see Curtis. And what? Ask if he remembered the kiss? What if it really had been a hazy dream? First off, *why, brain?!* Second, forget the kettle, she'd be able to boil the water for her coffee on her own face! Too vulnerable. Way too vulnerable. She didn't even think of Curtis that way. She was tired. In fact, he was probably tired, too. He certainly didn't like in that way.

And that fact certainly did not pull down the edges of her mouth.

Lily trotted down the stairs like a grown woman, crossed her living room, and walked right into the kitchen like she owned it. Which she did. Yet Curtis looked so dang cozy, cross-legged by the breakfast bar, scooping his cereal into his unshaved face, short hair splayed about in a boyish, sleepy way. It was almost like he belonged.

In MY house?

He wore the same wrinkled clothes as the night before. *Good Lord, I let him sleep in my house! Sure, it wasn't my bed, but it was my house! MY house!*

But it got worse. The sleepy eyes, hand-swept hair, all those pre-caffeine, unpolished trappings? It was…he was…oh dear Lord…*cute*. Curtis was *cute*. Not in the childish way, more of the not-quite-handsome-but-damn way. Open. Comfortable.

Safe?

245

Lily shook off the thoughts and continued to the cabinets with an airy, "Good morning!"

"Morning," he said in a sleepy tone.

Lily filled her electric kettle and flicked it on. "How'd you sleep?"

"Like the dead. Thanks for the bed."

"Any time." *Excuse me?!* "Er...you know what I mean."

Curtis nodded, chewing thoughtfully. "I think we can get a lot done today, now that we're over that hump."

"Me, too." Lily picked up the cereal box and poured her own bowl.

"Lily?"

"Yes?"

"Did we kiss last night or did I dream that?"

Lily spun towards him, flinging cereal in a perfect Froot Loop rainbow across the counter, floor, island, stove, and sink.

Curtis marveled at her handiwork. "Wow, it's like you were making a fairy ring."

Lily didn't have the breath to laugh. "You... remember it, too?"

Curtis picked up one of the far-flung Froot Loops and nibbled on it. "Guess that answers it."

Well, there it was, out in the air. Two kissers who kissed. They hadn't even thought about it, just done it.

Still clutching the cereal box into an awkward oblong, Lily blurted out the first thing that came to her mind. "How tired were we?"

"Very!" he cried in a high voice choked with relief.

"So tired! That's...what it was."

"Absolutely." He picked up his spoon and poked at the floating rings in the bowl. "But, ah, according to the events in my head, I was the one to, uh, move in first. So, for that, I...sorry."

Lily's stomach twisted, and she didn't want to examine why. "Well...you can't kiss with just one person, so apparently, I responded."

Curtis gave her a very funny look.

She half-shouted, "So tired!"

"Ridiculously!" Curtis barked back with an idiotic smile. He grabbed his coffee cup and gulped. Then, he gagged and nearly threw up on the counter.

Lily suppressed a grin. "I thought you were a tea guy."

"I am." He rolled his tongue around his mouth, as if trying to wipe off the taste. "But I need caffeine, so I played with the coffee maker."

"I have tea if you want some."

Curtis shook his head. "You know me by now: insufferably picky. There's only one flavor of one brand I actually like, and it's back at my place."

She nodded, then knelt down to scoop up her mess from the floor. "You know, we do take breaks. You could always run back to your house and get your tea if you want it."

"Why, am I staying another night?"

Lily paused with a fistful of Froot Loops. Her mind said to laugh it off, perhaps make some awkward joke. Instead, she rose to meet him, and said, "Maybe you should."

"Uh, what?" Curtis asked, his face absolutely blank.

The butterflies flittered throughout her brain, but the pieces kept adding up. "We only have four days until the deadline, and we are still..." Lily pinched her eyes shut and gritted her teeth. "...still behind schedule. If we're going to finish this, we need to pour everything we have into it. If we go to your place and pack a suitcase for a couple days, we can make everything that much faster. You can stay in the guest room, and we'll punch through this thing once and for all."

Curtis still had a spoon halfway to his mouth. He finally lowered it, and said, "You serious? I mean, are you comfortable with that? This is your house, after all."

Yeah...

Lily crossed her arms. "If I want to keep the house, I have to finish the book. If that means I have to let you sleep in my own bed, so be it." She paused. "Just for the record, that was hyperbole. You sleep in the guest room."

"I figured. I mean, if you're okay with it, so am I."

Strange as it sounded, and as loud as Mary would gasp if she ever found out, Lily found she really was okay with it. If nothing else, his unpolished casualness fit better than anything Mary had bought.

Lily figured it was only fair she got to see Curtis's place, too, so she rode shotgun in his little, eco-friendly car, past the edges of the city limits.

They didn't talk about the book. Lily couldn't tell what Curtis was thinking, but her mind kept going back to that kiss. It was almost upsetting that she could barely remember it. A quick peck, nothing more. No fireworks, no teenage shivers, no gag-induced regret. The kiss told her nothing about her own feelings.

So, she was forced to gather all her innards and ask them, "What do I feel about Curtis Reynolds?"

Ew, said one eye, *we are not kissing Captain Soul Patch again.*

But, said the other eye, *his hands are really handsome. Thin, but strong.*

Her back added, *And they're comforting, too!*

Her ears shrieked, *He clicks his tongue incessantly! How can we spend even more time with that?!*

Her stomach gurgled, *Too fast. Way too fast. We don't really know him.*

Her hands twitched. *I wonder how his hair feels.*

Her chest constricted. *Too close! He's way too close! He's in our house! In our work! In our dreams! In our life! I can't breathe!*

Lily finally turned her focus to the elder statesman. The heart thumped, *Yes-no. Yes-no. Yes-no.*

Curtis then asked, "Did I ever tell you I live on a ranch?"

Lily swung her head so fast she hurt her neck. "What? No, you don't."

"Scout's honor! It's called Golden Ranch."

"You make fun of cheesy romances when you could live in one?"

Curtis grinned far too wide.

"What?" Lily asked.

Curtis pointed as they turned off the main road. Lily saw a sign that read, "Golden Ranch Townhomes."

"Oh, very funny," Lily scoffed, trying not to be too disappointed.

Curtis parked in a cracked lot with grass growing between sidewalk slabs. The townhomes looked sturdy, if old, their siding faded from white into a wheat-yellow. Curtis turned his key in a small, one-story dwelling stuck on the end of a row of townhomes.

"Please be clean, please be clean, please be clean." He opened the door. "Ha-ha! Nothing in the sink! Oh, that table, though…" Curtis scrambled to clean up yesterday's breakfast. It was a quick task, considering how close the table was to the sink, and everything else in the kitchen. The table itself was pressed against the wall, beneath the window. It only looked big enough for two. Three, if one unfolded the extra chair against the wall.

"I'll be quick," Curtis said. "Make yourself at home." He passed through a living room, and disappeared into another door. Lily could see the edge of his bed, and one side of a desk. Lily was curious about his writing abode, but decided not to pry, contenting herself to the living room.

It didn't look like a bachelor pad. No clothes strewn about, at least, and no crumbs on the thin carpet. It didn't smell like body odor either; more like…absolutely nothing. How odd. The only other door led to a bathroom, and it looked clean, too. A small place, but well-kept. Lily might even call it homey.

Lily looked around for a bookshelf, but found none. Probably in his room. Darn, she couldn't judge his tastes! She did see a small DVD collection by the TV. *Star Wars*, the new *Dune* movie, some TV show called *Firefly*…and the 1995 *Pride and Prejudice* miniseries starring Colin Firth and Jennifer Ehle. Okay, she was absolutely going to razz him for that.

She meandered a bit longer, searching for anything

that might help her know the man she'd kissed. He was clean and tidy, which didn't leave much. He had a couple pictures on the wall, all sketches and paintings. One was a color-pencil drawing of a wolf, but the fur on its left side stretched into something else. Lily tilted her head and saw it was a misty evergreen forest. Lily had seen that artist at a local show. The painting of the Snake River looked familiar, too. Was every painting local? That did seem like Curtis. *Buy local! Down with the man!* Lily snickered.

The sound died in her throat when Lily saw a shelf in the corner of the room, and a framed picture of a red-haired maiden.

What hit me? asked her stomach. *Shock? Jealousy?* Perhaps both. She was a pretty lady of soft points: pointed nose, pointed chin, pointed look in her sparkling, coffee eyes. She looked like an elf. She was nearly as short as one, too, judging by the picture where she had both arms around Curtis's belly, the crown of her head just brushing his chin. Her smile was enormous, though. Hers, and Curtis's. Lily had never seen that smile before.

And two more pictures showed her why. In the first, Curtis wore a sharp, slim, black suit. The girl wore a dress of lacy white. In the last picture, printed on a folded pamphlet, the lady grinned impishly above the words, "Melody Elle Reynolds: 1993-2021."

Soft footfalls, muffled by carpet, sounded from the bedroom. Lily whirled around. Curtis flashed a smile as he dragged a small suitcase on its wheels. "Nearly done, just gotta—" All the color fled his face, and every light died in his eyes, as he spied Lily by the pictures.

Lily wondered if she should apologize. But why? The

pictures were in public view. So why did it feel so wrong to know? Maybe it was the hollow, ghostly look on his face. Like she'd thrown the grave open again.

"Forgot about that," Curtis muttered. "Ought to take it down, really." There was no urgency in his voice.

Lily flitted her eyes to the elfin girl once more. "What happened to her?"

Curtis spoke in a near whisper. "COVID. Three years ago."

Lily gasped and gazed at the picture again. "She looks so young!"

A little smile wriggled its way up Curtis's mouth. "Yeah, she always looked seventeen. Or younger, which made people look at me very strangely. I used to tell people, 'She's an adult; she's just pocket-sized.' She hated that, but she hated it with a smile. Yeah, she was young…"

"Was she sickly?"

Curtis shook his head. "She was a nurse at the hospital. In the ICU. I know she was safe. I know she was careful. But she liked helping the sickest folks, and…" He leaned back against the wall. "I blamed the doctors. Then I blamed the government. Then China. Then God. Then pretty much everybody else. In the end, though, I think the only culprit was bad, rotten luck."

Curtis looked around the little townhome, a dull, faded amusement barely flickering in his eyes. "We bought this place when I moved out, six years ago. Barely graduated. We both worked at the hospital, her as a nurse, me as an office jockey under some oncologist who asked me to call him Jim. It was supposed to be temporary until

I became a world-famous writer. We struggled in those days, but it was romantic, you know?"

Lily didn't answer. It felt wrong to.

"Obviously, that plan didn't work out. But she always believed in me. So, when she died, I used her life insurance money to pay off this place and keep trying." He took a breath so slow, so ragged, he may as well have been breathing thumb tacks. "She told me not to compromise. That was the last thing she said. 'Write what you believe in, not what someone says you should.' So I have. I've tried. No matter how many heads I have to bite off in the process."

Curtis rubbed the bridge of his nose. "God, I'm confused."

"Why?"

"Because I thought I knew what good art was. I thought there were writers and hacks, with great big walls between them. Now it's all blurry."

"How do you mean?"

Curtis brought his eyes up to hers, and Lily felt that gaze all the way to the back of her head. "You. I'm co-writing a paperback romance novel, and I'm not sorry. Not embarrassed like I should have been. In fact, I'm impressed. Seeing you work, seeing you push through complacency and become something great. It's impressive. And I…" His neck tensed, like there was something stuck inside. "Listen, I know I shouldn't have kissed you like that, without asking, without even thinking. It just happened. And if it bothered you to have some dude kiss you out of the blue, then I'm sorry. I don't want to be the guy stealing kisses and calling it a favor. But…if it didn't bother you…then God knows it didn't bother me."

Lily had written about love for over three years, and read about it for more. She knew that love was tactile: hots and colds, pinpricks and butterflies, goosebumps and blushes. Sometimes, of course, love was a sound: a jackhammering heart, a tearful gasp, or a soul-deep sigh. On rare occasions, love could have a taste: the sweetness of wedding cake, dry tang of lipstick, or the bitter-sweet burn of cologne on a collarbone.

Never once did Lily hear that love could be seen. Oh, sure, a gesture might indicate love, the old ring on the finger or tickets to a far-off hideaway, but that was an action, requiring movement of some sort. Curtis didn't so much as twitch. But what else could this be? What else could muster the sheer bravery of complete stillness? Such utter refusal to blink, to look away from her face, to allow any intrusion into this steel-solid moment?

Lily couldn't measure up to it. She trembled too much, tried to look at anything but Curtis. When she gathered the strength to look back at his eyes, they were too open, too steady to meet, and she had to shift her gaze to the eggshell paint on the wall.

She had no script, no scene construction, no carefully-planned dialogue to fill this moment. What could she say? What did she want to say? Working with Curtis had taught her it was okay to just speak. So, she did.

"I think we should focus on finishing the book. I don't...really have the brain space to think about anything else right now."

Curtis broke his pose at last, shoulders sinking a single inch as his breath fell from his lips. His gaze finally shifted to the right, just over Lily's shoulder. It lingered there a minute, then fell to the carpet. "Yeah, my head's spinning, too."

Lily turned her eyes to the right, but did not move her head, did not want to see that impish grin of victory on the shelf.

Curtis finished packing in no time at all, and soon, they were driving back as silently as they'd come. A sluggish, muggy, gray sky crawled across Lily's vision. She wanted to go back to bed, to figure all this out, but the book would not wait. She'd just have to deal with it.

Lily rolled down the window, knowing it would be the only time today the still, heavy air would caress her face. That little sensation made her realize that while she'd considered the opinions of her heart, head, stomach, and various other bodily representatives, she'd not yet heard the voice of her lips.

You know, they said to her, *I'm not sorry either*.

Chapter 22

3 Days Left

There's tea in my coffee cabinet. Lily tried not to read into that, but it was *in* the cabinet, not *on* the counter. Putting something on the counter meant it was temporary, a rental space soon to be evacuated. The cabinet was a home. *Curtis is in my cabinets.*

A bizarre thought, perhaps, but working nonstop until midnight—again—caused a few logic cells to snap. Lily became hyper-aware of how much Curtis was…*here.* His clothes in the guest room. His toothbrush on the sink of the guest bath. His Pop-Tarts in the cabinet—yet again, cabinet not counter.

Lily wondered about that as she pushed down her French press. It's not like he was in *her* room, or *her* bathroom, despite every room in this house being, legally, *hers.* And even within the confines of his (her) room, Curtis wasn't wrecking the place or throwing his things everywhere. And his tea cozied up right next to her coffee, so everything was still accessible.

"Pardon me." Curtis slid past Lily to grab the sugar from the countertop.

First my cabinets, now my bubble.

But that brought up the oddest thing of all. His smell just was not right. Personal experience had taught Lily that men smell like sweat, teenage cologne, or rectal gas. Curtis smelled like practically nothing. Soap, maybe, and clean cotton. Not absent, but not intrusive either. It just said, "Hey, I'm still here."

Lily gave a friendly, good-morning smile, and he returned it. No significant glances, no expectations. His laptop sat on the dinner table, plugged into an out-of-the-way port. Shoes by the door, unlikely to trip anybody. Backpack in the office, tucked beside his chair, taken from the dinner table, but she didn't need that many anyway.

How did having a second human in her house take up no more space than usual?

Curtis interrupted her thoughts by asking, "So should we keep the scene of Mitch and Elsa out at dinner? I think we should because it's still relevant. It's a humble, simple restaurant, but it makes Elsa feel oddly welcome."

Lily nodded vaguely. "Yeah, she's surprisingly comfortable with it."

So, their conversation returned to the book. Lily couldn't believe how wearying her writing had become. Just as shocking was her ability to keep doing it! At times, she'd sit and sigh about how exhausted she was from constant, twelve-hour days of writing and talking about writing—those days now reaching sixteen hours—and then she'd sit up and type out some more words as if her fingers hadn't listened to a thing she'd said.

Mitch had a new job. A couple of them, actually. Odd jobs filling out this or that. Some part time nursing, some ski instructing, some helping in Dad's auto garage—Dad fixed cars now. An easy change, considering Lily had never gotten around to actually showing Dad's ranch, much less a single horse. Elsa's growth on the slopes provided some natural progression of the story, as well as opening up opportunities for her and Mitch to be together.

Better than that, Lily's friendly community was starting to come to life. The rancher's son delivered Dad's groceries, then stayed to chat for a few minutes. Elsa marveled at how he didn't immediately rush back for his next delivery, but the youth replied that there weren't many to make, and what was the point of delivering if you weren't going to be friendly, too? Mitch and another car-savvy fellow followed Dad's instructions so he could keep up with some of his work while remaining in a chair. Elsa approved of this work ethic, but Dad said, "It's not work ethic. Corrie needs her car running so she can get to work." Everything the characters did had a people focus, a humanitarian gem, dipped in just enough dust and sweat to feel realistic.

Greater than even this, Lily and Curtis were well beyond the halfway point. In fact, they were about to hit the two-thirds mark. By noon, they were only five hundred words behind their daily goal. A mere page! Lily could stay up past midnight for a final page.

They took their lunch on the porch to best enjoy the gusty afternoon that rocked the evergreens and tickled the tall grass. Great, poofy clouds made the sun work for his burns, but even when his rays slipped around the frayed-cotton edges, he couldn't reach his fingers under the porch awning to the two picnickers swaying on the swing.

Curtis still had his laptop out, but Lily wanted five minutes to just enjoy the coolest day in weeks. For that reason, it sent a jagged thorn of hate right into her heart when her cell phone buzzed. Such a grating, bleeping, techno-warble against the friendly whoosh of the wind. It had been days since Lily heard her phone go off. Most people had respected her boundaries, and even Mary only sent encouraging texts that were easy to ignore. Lily growled as she picked up the phone, hoping her big sister wasn't pushing the limits again.

She wasn't. It was Mr. Gates.

"Oh!" Lily jumped to her feet.

"What?" Curtis cried.

Lily reeducated herself on how to breathe. "Nothing, probably. It's my editor."

"Oh, probably checking in."

"Most likely. I need to take this." Lily swiped the green icon. "Hello?"

"Hey, rock star," said Mr. Gates' baritone. "How's Idaho?"

"Windy!" She cupped her hand around the microphone to block the noise.

"Same in New York. After all this damned heat, I'm not going to complain."

"Right?"

Mr. Gates said, "I just wanted to check how progress is going. I haven't heard anything for a while."

"Nose to the grindstone and all that," Lily answered.

"Yeah? Nothing big to worry about?"

"Not at all. Making sure everything is perfect."

"I like that. I just wanted to be sure since you're usually more vocal about your progress, and since the deadline is Friday."

"Don't worry, I'll have it to you on…wait, Friday?" Lily

ran through her mental calendar. "That's the thirtieth."

"That's right."

"I thought you wanted it on July first."

"No, I wanted it *before* the first. On the thirtieth."

Lily's bowels dropped to the floor. Her voice leapt to the ceiling. "Oh! Ha! My mistake. That's no problem, though. I can still get it done by the thirtieth." She gave Curtis a tight-lipped smile.

Curtis blinked stupidly at her, then his eyes roved about, likely doing the same math she was doing right now.

"Good," said Mr. Gates. "Say seven o'clock? I want to get a head start with some evening reading."

Lily pinched her eyes and her windpipe. "Yep. Seven in the evening."

"That's five o'clock Idaho time."

"Yes…five…our time…"

Lily watched Curtis age before her, his cheeks sagging and going gaunt, while wrinkles appeared under his eyes. She felt her posture stooping. She leaned on the railing. The breeze had slowed, leaving only the stuffy heat.

"All right, then," Mr. Gates said. "I just wanted to triple check. Glad I called! I'll see the full manuscript on Friday evening, by seven New York time?" Lily heard the upward swoop of his words, his voice a metallic ring along the scimitar's edge.

"Absolutely. Seven your time. Friday."

"Glad to hear it!" His voice resonated with sudden glee. "I'll let you work. I can't wait to read your next bestseller!"

Lily couldn't muster a goodbye, but the line was already dead anyway. She lowered the phone towards her pocket, realized her shorts didn't have pockets, and placed the phone on the railing instead, where the glare from the camera reflected the sun into her eyes.

"Does he want the book a day early?" Curtis asked in a hollow voice.

"It's my fault," Lily said. "I messed up the deadline."

"Aw…" He leaned his head back against the swing, biting his lip hard.

"I'm sorry."

He didn't answer.

Lily didn't want him to. He was overly honest: he'd tell her that they were no longer five hundred words behind schedule, but eight thousand. Or more. He'd tell her that was a good chapter or two ripped right out of the back of the book. He'd tell her it would be a story with no ending or a story with a missing middle. He'd tell her they were already working from eight in the morning to midnight, that they couldn't stretch themselves any further, or that if they did, they'd be so sleep-deprived that they'd flub the story. He'd tell her the only possibility was to drop the editing days and just write a rough draft and submit that. Then, he'd tell her that was the most idiotic thing a person could send to a publisher. He'd also say that they couldn't ask for an extension because Mr. Gates had been generous already, and that one delay in the publishing process started a domino chain of delays, and Lily's Christmas book wouldn't come out until January.

She didn't want him to say any of those things. She already knew.

Lily turned and walked into her house, closing the door

behind her. If Curtis wanted in, he was intelligent enough to operate a knob.

She walked through her whole house, though it felt more like swimming, pushing through some thick ether, wobbling in the current, suffocating. She waded into her office, then back to the living room, then the kitchen, then back to the living room. Downstairs bathroom. Living room again. Kitchen. Garage. Living room yet again. Lily jogged up her stairs to the second story, glancing up at the rafters. Their crossing beams narrowed their eyes at her, like debt collectors waiting for payment. Lily wandered into her room, her master bath, back into the hall. She even walked a loop through Curtis's room, still neat and tidy and smelling of nothing but linen, as if he was just part of the room, not an addition to it. Back to the hall.

And everywhere she went, Lily muttered so low even she barely heard it, "I'm sorry."

Lily leaned on the balcony overlooking the living room. Still so bare. Mary's touches scrubbed clean, the couch sold, yet Lily never got around to putting herself into the place, so nothing filled its emptiness.

Except Curtis, looking up at her with sad, tired eyes. His jaw was more beard than stubble now, and his hair a mess from all the times his hands ran through it in frustrated furrows. His thin lips pressed together, no commentary, nothing.

"I don't think I can do it," she confessed. It felt more like vomiting. "It's too much. I'm too tired. I can't keep running this ragged. I'm further behind, which means working even harder, which..." Lily grabbed the edges of her hair. Then, she stormed downstairs. "I just need to do it. No sense whining; I'm wasting minutes."

But Curtis stepped in front of her before she could slip into her office. "Hold on a sec."

"I don't have a sec!" she barked. "I can literally hear them ticking away in my head!" Lily pushed Curtis away and stormed into her writing office. She jerked her chair out from under the desk, utterly furious with its audacity to require moving. Lily punished it by slamming her rear down with all the force she could muster. Then, she turned to the laptop.

And stared.

Her brain couldn't take it. All words, all vocabulary, had been locked behind Fort-Knox-thick panic doors. She could bang all she wanted, but nothing would come.

Curtis gently—or maybe cautiously—approached from the side. She left him in her peripheral. "Lily…"

"I need to do this," she choked. It was so hard keeping her face from splitting open and spilling out all the tears and madness. Why couldn't he just leave her alone?

Whatever his reason, Curtis said, "You look like you need to cry."

"No."

"Why not?"

"Because if I cry, I'll fall into your arms, then then I'll probably kiss you again, and then tomorrow morning you'll say, 'What did it mean?' and I'll say, 'I don't know!' and we won't be one word closer to completing the book!" Lily slammed her laptop shut, some part of her wincing as she thought she heard a crack, then shoved it away so it knocked against a lamp. Lily's head fell on her arms, and there she stayed.

She said the only thing that gave her any semblance of

peace. "Just put your hand on my back and don't say anything, don't do anything else, okay?" Curtis had about six seconds. *She* had about six seconds.

He only needed two. Lily had four full seconds of composure before her back nearly shook Curtis's hand off.

Oh, to be a movie heroine right now. To have no "real" tears, just sweet, poster-worthy, lazy rivers of emotion traveling serenely down their pre-laid path. Shallow rivers, at that, nothing to threaten makeup. Her eyes might redden a little, just a little, but all in all, she'd look like a proud, confident young woman simply having a setback.

She wouldn't bawl, loud in the back of her throat. Her mouth wouldn't stretch past her teeth, as if to let more sound out, and then the noise wouldn't get strangled in her gargling throat, until it finally burst forth in another five seconds of coughing, gagging wails. There would be no gasping, no genuine wondering if she would choke to death. And not once would she ever feel like a lump of human pieces, a soggy, unassembled un-person.

Most importantly, she'd be able to stop. To wipe her eyes and say, "I'm okay. I can do this." Lily cried for over thirty minutes without more than a few seconds' pause. It actually hurt; her thighs, her butt, her stomach, her neck, her back, her throat, her nose, so much squeezed and heaved and clenched that she begged her own heart for relief.

Only one space of Lily Harper did not suffer: the palm-shaped area just below and between her shoulder blades. An island of…not happiness, but solidity. A rocky island lashed by the storm, but unmoved. Curtis didn't speak, not once. How could he? He did not believe in false platitudes. His lips could not lie. But his hand could. His palm, somehow warm and cool at the same time, could soothe her tears with empty hope.

Lily's mind orbited around that idea more and more as longer breaks spread out the tears. It was stupid, honestly, thinking that one part of Curtis could lie and another could not. Every part of him longed for truth. But neither was this solidity a lie; she felt it, an anchor holding the rest of her together. Maybe she'd misjudged the message, then. Maybe he wasn't saying it would be all right. Maybe that solidity itself was the message. *I am here. I am still here.*

She held it. Not the hand, but the idea it poured into her. She grasped it in her heart with tear-slicked fingers, and wrapped all her limbs about its promise: I am here. I am still here.

And so am I.

Lily untangled her the limbs of her soul, reached one hand above the other, and started to climb that anchor. Link by link, she rose above the torrent, above the crashing waves and salty spray. She swayed once or twice, when the wind slapped her anew, but Lily grasped all the tighter. Then she relaxed, and climbed again. Above the wind. Above the lightning and rain. Above the clouds themselves.

In the real world, Lily raised her head, feeling every vertebra crack. Her arms were sopping wet, so Lily grabbed a dozen tissues to clean herself off. It was still bright outside, only one o'clock. She'd expected the sun to be setting for some reason. Lily took several great gulps from her water bottle, and then she gulped the air around her. Both came cool and sweet. Lily caught the faintest whiff of mustiness from her bookshelf. And clean linen.

She turned slowly in her chair. Curtis's hand slid off her back, leaving a cold imprint. He still had the same tired, ashen look as before. The same as her own.

"We may not finish it," Lily said. "It may not work."

Curtis looked her firmly in the eye. "It may not be exactly as we want. That doesn't mean it won't be finished."

Lily shook her head. "We're not cutting anything."

"No?" Curtis asked.

"No. I'm writing *my* book. Not the book that works for someone else."

Curtis watched her for a long moment. "You're not playing."

"No."

"You're either crazy or badass."

She could only give half a rueful smile. "You still with me?"

He gave the other half. "Win or lose."

Lily wanted to ask why, but feared she already knew. *One thing at a time.* "Let's finish this."

Chapter 23

~~3 Days Left~~
2 Days Left

Lily began a sentence, and only put a period on it at eleven at night. One long tangent of paragraphs and chapters in chronological order. Instead of eight thousand words, Lily counted eleven thousand.

Was it perfect? She had no time to check. But it existed, which was a vast improvement. A breeze of hope cooled her panicked face as she lay down for bed that night. Maybe she would finish it after all. They were getting quite close...

There were times, in the space between breaths, when terror clawed at her throat. When she feared that the story she wanted to tell would not be enough to keep her home above her head. That all her talent had come days—no, months—too late. When that happened, she looked to Curtis.

It didn't make a lot of sense. True, Curtis did help; he always had some turn of phrase, some insight into the exact way a character would speak a line of dialogue, so he did keep the sentence going when Lily felt her breath run out. Yet he couldn't make time sit still; couldn't even type at the same time as Lily. They pored over every scene together as one; dividing and conquering was too dizzying at this point. So all in all, Curtis couldn't make this happen any more than she could.

But he was there. It solved nothing, but it made everything better.

1 Day Left

Lily had not slept well. Everything wobbled. The coffee pot wobbled over her cup. Her foot wobbled into a wall. Her skull wobbled into Curtis's. Not half as romantic as movies made it look.

"Do you need a nap?" he finally asked at one o'clock. Curtis. Whose eyes were so black underneath that any doctor would screen for trauma.

"No!" Lily snarled in an oddly nasally way.

Curtis put two fingers on her forehead and pushed with enough strength to flutter a napkin. Lily stumbled. "Uh huh," he said. "Go take a nap. I'll work in the meantime—"

"No! It's my—"

"—and run it by you when you wake up."

Lily glared at him, but she could barely see him through her eyelids. "One hour. Wake me up in *one* hour! Not two! Not one hour and ten minutes! Not one hour and one minute, not—"

"I got the gist. Go beddy-bye now."

Lily literally did not remember doing so. She had the vague idea that she climbed the stairs, then suddenly awoke in her bed, with Curtis shaking her shoulder. Lily groaned, rolled over, and stretched. Curtis watched, and swallowed.

It made Lily check her outfit. Tee shirt and shorts, everything covered. So why the stare?

Curtis cleared his throat. "It's, uh, been an hour."

"Thanks. I'll be right up." Lily yawned.

Curtis left her room, but his feet moved funny, as if they were stuck to the carpet.

Lily quickly ran her hands through her hair, wondering what kind of mess she looked like when she first woke up. Wondering why she cared.

At exactly midnight, Lily Harper remembered something critically important. She had not given herself twelve days to write. She'd given herself eight, with four days to edit. She'd lost a few days, but...

"Did we just finish?!" Lily screeched in a raven's voice.

Curtis blinked at the page. "That depends. Are you one of those writers who puts 'The End' on the last page?"

"No."

"Oh." He looked affronted. "Then we're done."

She trembled from shoulder to fingertip, from hip to toenail. "Oh...Oh my God."

"Aaaand save," Curtis said, clicking the keys. "Aaaand save to a second location. Aaaand save to the flash drive." Curtis whipped a second flash drive out of his pocket. "Aaaand again!"

Lily laughed harder than the joke deserved. "We're done! We..." She started to cackle. "We did it! We're—"

Curtis held up a finger. It had all the appearance of a colon cancer screen, and just as much stopping power. "Almost.

We're almost done. We still have edits to do. You know how Elsa had that nasty phone call with her boss at the end? He wasn't nasty in chapter one."

Lily dumped the tea she'd just made, and tossed the cup in the ever-rising sink. "See you in the morning, soldier."

Last Day

In reality, Lily saw very little of Curtis, despite sitting either a few feet away in her office or directly across at the table. Both had their screens up, reading their copy of the book. They had no time for fine-tooth edits like spelling errors, a fact that made Curtis pull a few hairs out.

But reality was reality. They could only mend the story inconsistencies, and scratch whatever comma splices they happened upon in the process. And even that was skimming.

Five o'clock pounded on her door before she knew it. Lily sat in her office chair, chewing her last good fingernail. "We still didn't fix Paulie."

Paulie was a minor character, a volunteer fire fighter who wanted to retire, but couldn't find a suitable replacement, and feared leaving his little town undefended in an emergency. The poor old man was strained, and had tried to recruit half the town throughout the book. Then, he'd been forgotten by his creator.

Curtis watched the second hand spin on the wall.

"He'll have to stay on duty for a while longer."

"So…we just turn it in like this?"

Curtis sighed, the last dregs of effort leaving his lips. He leaned on the side of her desk, either staring at her computer or the wall beyond it or nothing at all. "We're out of time. He's a minor character. Maybe we can fix him after your editor gives it a go, but…we're out of time."

Lily bent her spine, and deleted the last note she'd made for herself. One last lightning-speed scan for any red marks unattended. Nothing. Lily saved the file, opened an email, attached the story—double-checking it was the right document—and then took one last deep breath as she clicked the send button.

All was quiet.

She didn't tremble this time—well, her hands shook, but they'd been doing that all day, as six cups of coffee will do. Beyond the caffeine shivers, Lily found herself eerily still. Her brain agreed with her hands: we have to move! We have to plan! We have to do something!

The "Message Sent Successfully" screen rebuffed her. As did the great, white, five-zero-zero on her phone.

"Man." Curtis's words hardly left his lips. He trudged the whole four feet to his window chair. The carpet was furrowed from his constant shifting. "So, what happens next?"

Lily forced her brain to think past the writing stage, and into the future she could finally believe in. "Mr. Gates will read it. If he likes it, he'll accept it, though that still means I'll likely have a few changes. If he doesn't like the book as a whole…well, he either accepts it out of desperation or pushes the book out until next year or…I don't really know. I still have a three-book contract, but I'm sure there are ways he can get out of it."

"Lily, you're a known author. Selling one of your bad books will make him more money than putting out nothing."

Lily winced. "I don't like that. I don't just want to make people money."

"I know. Sorry, I didn't mean it like that."

Lily dug rows in the carpet with her toes, trying to get some feeling back in her flesh. "Anyway, if he likes it, then it will come out in November so that it's got a good window for Christmas. I'll get my check, and then I'll write yours. Fifty-fifty."

He chuckled, a low, toneless clucking from the bottom of his lungs.

Lily grinned at it. "Delirium finally catching up?"

"No, I've just never written anything so certain of being accepted."

She smiled even deeper. And then, though the words made her eyes well up, and though it felt like being naked in Times Square, Lily said, "Curtis, I could never have done this without you. I just want you to know that, whatever Mr. Gates says, I'm so grateful."

Curtis smiled, too. It began as a smirk, the safe and familiar turn of the lips, present, but uncommitted. Like an indoorsy child forced out into the heat for a pool party. A quick dip in the shallow end, compliant enough to appease an audience. Until the child lets the cool, wet drink wash over him, and suddenly he's diving into the deep end, searching for treasures on the hard, blue bottom. No one can watch him down there; he does it for himself. So deep went Curtis's smile: back to his ears, up to his eyes, and down to his throat.

"So am I," he said.

"Really?" Lily asked.

"Yeah. I wrote something I believed in."

Lily's smile dove in after his, to that deep, cool place where no eye could see from the surface. Only they knew its depths.

But then, Curtis suddenly came up for air, his grin dripping away. "I suppose I'll get out of your hair, then."

Lily blinked. Blinked again, acclimating her eyes to the future, where the work was over, and Curtis was no longer required. "Oh…"

He hesitated.

She paused.

At length, he rose. Curtis hoisted his chair off the carpet, and carried it back to the dining room. It belonged there. Not here. It had only rented the space until Lily found a better window seat for reading. Still, she stared at the four pockmarks it left on the carpet.

Lily heard him trot up the stairs. She stood at last, left the room, but paused at the threshold of her office, near the steps. She leaned on the frame, ear turned so slightly upward. Distant, muffled footfalls. The scuff of pant legs rubbing together. A light clatter in the guest bathroom, like a toothbrush giving the sink a goodbye tap. More footfalls. Soon, a slow, mournful zipping. And the echoing thumps of her heart.

Curtis hauled his suitcase downstairs, but opened it again in the kitchen, removing his little snacks and preferences. Pop-Tarts, cinnamon-plum tea, his favorite mug with the fat bottom. Not a lot, really. Yet the cabinets yawned, suddenly cavernous.

He packed his laptop last, strapping the bag over his chest, then looked to Lily.

"What will you do next?" Lily asked, just to fill all the space he seemed to empty.

Curtis shrugged. "Go back to work on Monday. You?"

"Uh...sleep? Go hiking again, maybe. Or just sit by the phone until Mr. Gates calls. Oh! I'll likely need help on some edits."

His eyebrows popped right up. "Yeah! Call me when you need me."

"I will." She nodded a lot.

Curtis nodded back. "All right, then, uh, see you...later."

Sure. Maybe. Lily just kept nodding.

Lily followed him to the door. He opened it, and a sticky warmth spilled into the house. He stepped out, then turned. "Bye."

"Bye," she said in an oddly small voice.

Curtis adjusted the weight of his suitcase, then turned.

And stopped. He seemed to mutter something to himself, then he swung around to face her again. "Look, Lily, would you ever want to be with me in a non-literary context? No work, no book, just...people in a place performing agreed-upon activities?"

Lily's brain declared that was the dumbest way to ask for her time, but her mouth was already saying, "Yeah!"

Curtis's eyebrows jumped again. "That was quick."

"Uh-huh." She bit her lip hard as punishment. She

did want to see him again, odd as it was after ten days of constant there-ness. Still, what exactly was he asking for? Lily decided to pull the reins a bit. "Well, I still need a couch. Can you help me get it? Then…maybe sit in it and, I don't know, watch something? Something you like this time?"

"Yeah, sounds great."

"Sunday?"

"Yeah, Sunday…Sunday works."

"All right. See you, then."

He gave a nervous smile. *Cute*, her brain said before she could stop it. Curtis turned away at last, and Lily decidedly closed the door instead of watching him leave.

She couldn't move for a while. What was there to do now? Every nerve said to write, but there were no more words to type, and her weary brain couldn't possibly start something new. Twitchy, anxious, and oddly cold, Lily went around the house making a list of furniture to buy. The place was just so empty.

Chapter 24

"Here's to the three-time author!" Mary called.

Lily raised her orange juice, and clinked the over-sparkly glass with Mary's, Mandy's, Mom's, and Oak's. Asher had work, and Daisy lived too far away, but it was still a Harper family reunion in Lily's tired eyes.

"To be clear," Lily said, "my editor has not said yes yet."

Mary said, "You had the contract before you started the book."

"A conditional one."

Mom wrapped an arm around Lily and said, "I'm sure your editor will love it."

Lily rested her head on Mom's. It was good to be home.

Well, not home. Mary had invited everybody to Aurora's, a small but shockingly swanky breakfast-and-lunch eatery off the main drag. Only a handful of tables, but they didn't seem like they were meant to be used anyway. The white of the tablecloths bamboozled the eyes, and scoffed at the mere mention of crumbs. The tall glasses winked at each other through their chandelier gleam. Any drink poured into them looked tamer somehow, as if they'd buttoned-up their colors and tucked in their textures to be more photogenic.

Not Lily's favorite place; it always made her cut her

eggs into even portions before she ate them. But pancakes were pancakes, and she did like the dark reds and blacks of the well-mannered berries upon them, sprinkled with an orderly dashing of powdered sugar.

Lily had spent the entire time filling her family in on what the book was like, how many pages it might be, whether it would become a Lifetime movie, how cute was the main boy (Mandy's question). Now that the food had arrived and Mary had given her toast, Lily said, "And I am officially done talking about the book. I haven't seen you all in forever! I want to know what's up with all of you?"

Mary spoke first. "Not much on my end, I'm afraid. Just work and home."

"That's it?"

Mary snickered. "It's only been two weeks, maybe less."

Lily's jaw fell into her syrup. Somehow, despite the knife of "only twelve days" being at her throat, Lily had forgotten that "only twelve days" was, indeed, only twelve days.

"Woof," Lily said. "Okay, Oak? How about you? Anything interesting happen?"

Oak shrugged. "Not really. Get up, go to work, crunch some numbers, come home, tell my roommate that I'll put his nose in the blender if he doesn't clean up his crumbs, and go to bed."

Mary elbowed him. "What about that promotion?"

"Oh!" Lily exclaimed. "You're up for a promotion?"

Oak looked as though he'd meant to blow a bubble gum bubble, but swallowed it instead. "Well, I...sort of, but..."

Mary rolled her eyes in a big-sisterly way. "He's putting his name in for a supervisory position."

Lily gasped. "Wow! Already?"

Oak could only muster a tenth of the smile everyone else had. "Maybe. I'd be still doing the same accounting work, but, yeah, also supervising some people. If I do it."

Again, Mary rolled her eyes. "You have what it takes, brother. Don't doubt yourself."

The corner of Oak's mouth twitched, a feeble attempt at a grin.

Lily stared. "What's wrong, Oak?"

Oak sighed through his nose. "Okay, so…remember that girl I brought to Mandy's party? Kimberly? I met her because her brother Freddie works at the same firm I do. Freddie is up for the position, too."

"Oh, awkward."

"A little, but…if I'm honest, I think he would do a better job than me."

Mary scoffed. "Don't be crazy. You said yourself you're the best accountant in the whole company."

"Yeah, best with money and spreadsheets and stuff. Gimme a box of jumbled receipts and I'll set it straight. But supervising people? Freddy actually has experience in that. And he's better with people in general. So maybe I should stick with the accounting side of things and—"

"Oak, don't doubt yourself. You're talented, you're a quick learner, they'd be stupid not to have you for the job. Never underestimate your potential."

Oak gave another one of his almost-smiles.

Lily watched her younger brother poke at his bacon, and wondered if this was less about doubt, and more about strengths.

So…say something? a voice in her brain chimed in.

Her stomach snorted. *And make the whole table*

uncomfortable? I came here to have fun with my family.

That in mind, Lily turned to her youngest sister. "So Mandy, what's new with you?"

Oak whispered something that sounded like, "Brace yourself."

Mandy stuck up her nose and said, "Actually, I prefer to be called *Mandragora* now."

"Oh?" Lily glanced around the table. Mary's smile was tighter than a corset in denial. Mom gave a weary little sigh. Lily caught Oak's eye, but his gaze said, *Don't look at me! I've been holding down the fort for two weeks; your turn.*

Lily said, "That's…" and paused. Any answer she gave would sour the mood at the table. She withdrew, and danced around to a different line. "How come?"

Mandy—Mandragora—gave her a dead-eyed stare. "Because it's my name."

"Right, right, but…why the change?"

"Because I think it's badass, and I think I should be called what I am, not what's comfortable to others." Her voice lifted into a snooty octave, and she sipped her juice with all the showy poise deserving of a restaurant with napkin rings.

Embers glowed in Mary's eyes. "I think it's a bit of a mouthful."

Mandragora replied, "Take it up with Mom; she named me."

Lily winced.

Mom's mouth made a lot of funny shapes, but in the end, she said, "Mandy, listen to your sister."

Boy, did it get quiet. Nothing but clinking silverware and the sound of judgement from the artsy sconces in the wall.

Lily fought for a new subject—anything. "So, Mand—

sis—that's a cute shirt."

Miraculously, Mandragora actually glowed, tugging at her soft, Easter-blue top with frilly sleeves. "I know, right? I'm super proud of it."

"Proud?" Oak asked. "Did you make it?"

"No way, I suck at sewing. I haggled for it at a yard sale."

Mary choked on her cranberry juice. Drops of red splashed on the white tablecloth, Lily swore she heard it gasp in indignation. Mary dabbed her mouth, then said, "Y-Yard sale?"

"Uh, yeah." Mandragora blinked back at her. "When I went on a walk yesterday? I passed a yard sale and got this bad boy for five bucks."

Mary kept her fingers at her throat. Lily had heard of fancy ladies clutching their pearls, but she'd never actually seen it. Mary finally smiled again and said, "If you needed clothes, you could have asked."

Mandragora shrugged. "I didn't need them. I just saw this while I was walking and I had a few bucks, so I haggled for it."

The word "haggle" seemed to stab Mary in the eyeballs. "What I mean is, you don't have to go to yard sales and thrift stores and things like that."

"I…know? I just saw it and wanted it. What's wrong with that?"

"Oh, it's not wrong, I don't mean that. It's just there are so many stores around…"

"Yeah, if you want to spend two hundred bucks on a tank top."

"Well, we've come a long way; I think we can afford

it."

Oh…I get it now. Lily stuffed her mouth with pancakes, and tried to find interesting shapes in her syrup.

Mandragora leaned on the table and asked, "Come a long way from what?"

Age lines ripped through Mary's foundation. "From our old lives."

"You make it sound like we crawled out of a ghetto."

Oak showed his teeth. "You wouldn't remember. You were too little."

For a second, it seemed to sink in, but then Mandragora said, "Okay, fine, tell me about it, then."

Mary waved her fork with a smile sickly-sweet enough to pour on waffles. "Ah-ah! We don't look back."

"But we never talk about it!"

Mom frowned. "Those were lean, hard days, sweetie. You're so lucky you've only known plenty."

"I don't feel like I know anything!"

Lily tried to squeak her voice in. "Oh…what's there to know about those days anyway?"

Mandragora scowled. "Uh, my dad? The guy I write a fake card to every Father's Day, but no one will tell me anything about?"

Lily and Mary locked eyes, a tunnel of ice between them. Mom had asked Lily and Asher not to say anything, but Mary had gotten it out of them.

Oak had not. "What's there to tell? He ditched, just like all the others."

Mandragora opened her mouth, but Mary jumped in first. "That's why we don't talk about it. It doesn't do any good to stir up a bunch of bad memories for everybody. This family is on a much better track to a brighter and happier future. We don't need to remember people who don't matter, we don't need to scrimp and save for pennies for yard sales, and we don't look back."

Oak said, "Damn right."

Mom said, "Hallelujah."

Lily could feel Mandragora's eyes on her, begging for an ally. Lily's lips moved, and words dribbled out like spit. "Pancakes...are good."

"Aren't they heavenly?" Mary asked.

Everyone returned to the food. Awkwardness averted.

Mandragora picked her fork back up and stuck it into her sausages. "Yeah, it's pretty good. Sorry we couldn't go to Lucy's House, Lily, I know that's the restaurant you really like, but Mary decided this place was more appropriate."

Lily could hear the gasp from Mom, just above a whisper. She saw Oak suck in his lips, gaze glued to the plate. Red-hot daggers seared from Mary's eyes.

Lily's smile bounced right up like a trusty spring. "It's fine!" The perfect tone, not so high as to sound fake. "I'm just here to see my family again. Thanks for breakfast, Mary, it's really good."

Mary's eyes cooled, and her sugary smile returned to its rightful place. "Oh, don't mention it. Family deserves the best."

Mandragora's face fell, and did not look up again.

Lily spent the rest of the breakfast wondering who had just spoken through her lips.

*
**

"Is that why we drove two hours away to buy a couch?" Curtis asked. "To save money without Mary finding out?"

Lily ran her hands along a furry black sofa, shaking her head as she thought of how hot that would be. "It wasn't two hours; it was an hour and forty-five. Besides, there aren't that many furniture stores by us."

Curtis followed Lily to the next possibility. "But you didn't pick a regular furniture store. You picked a discount warehouse." He waved his hand around the cavernous, one-room block. Industrial-steel rafters above, bathroom tile below, and miles of savings for all your home décor needs in between. No music, but there was a nice, artificial breeze coming straight from the North Pole to coerce people into quick, thoughtless purchases.

Lily considered a beige couch, but it looked hard as iron. "My house won't pay for itself, and Mr. Gates still hasn't gotten back to me." It had been over a week since she clicked that Send button. Not a peep. "I have to save money until then. Besides, this place has good stuff."

"And if you happened to see Mary walking through that door over there?"

"What?! Which door?" Her heart scrambled up her spinal column and hid behind her brain before she registered that the question had been rhetorical.

"Wow," Curtis said.

Lily folded her arms tight across her chest so she didn't punch him for something he didn't really do. "Okay, fine, I'm a baby, I'm a coward, I'm a ten-year-old little sister in a grown-woman's body." She flopped down into a poofy, chocolate-brown leather sofa. "Actually, this is nice. Sit down, tell me what you think."

Curtis sat, wriggled his butt into the cushion, then said, "I think it's too soft. I also think you give Mary too much power over you. So what if you want to save money by getting a shirt at a yard sale or a couch at an outlet place? Isn't it wise to save?"

"Mary saves," Lily said in a pathetic voice. "It's just not secondhand."

"Why does that bother her?"

"I think it gives her flashbacks to when we were poor, and clipping coupons to save five cents on groceries. Those were hard days, and she never wants to go back. Heck, I don't want to go back either. Mandy just doesn't understand that fear. She was super young when things started turning around. But you're right. I wish I could have said something to defend her. You should've seen her face; she looked like I rejected her! But at the same time, she was so dang spiteful about it!"

Lily slapped the couch and jumped up, marching to a pearl-white couch across from the coffee table—*40% off!* said the sign. "Mary sacrificed a lot for us. Yes, she's too controlling, Yes, she's blowing money on image. Yes, I'd wager she's constantly dealing with low-grade anxiety behind that plastic smile. Yes, sometimes I want to grab her by the ears and just pull."

Curtis asked, "Is there a 'but' at the end of this?"

"You'd think so. Sit. This one's firmer."

He did. "It's pretty darn good, but what do you think?"

Lily wriggled a bit, then said, "It's too deep; my feet

are barely touching the floor."

"Then let's keep looking."

They slouched across three others. Too short in the back, too expensive, too much of a couch-shaped black hole sucking every living thing into its cushions. All the while, Lily fussed about Mary's overbearing control, and her own inability to do anything but smile.

"I guess I just need to grow a spine." Lily sat in one more couch, a simple, gray-brown three-seater. It didn't buckle beneath her, didn't resist her with a board for a backrest, but seemed to welcome her figure into every surface. "Ooh, this one is nice. Have a seat, tell me what you think."

Curtis gave her an odd, curious look, but obeyed. He adjusted his position a few times, then nodded. "Yeah, it's a nice one."

"Not too expensive, either," Lily said. "I can see myself watching corny movies on this. Can you?"

There was that odd look again. "I don't watch a lot of corny movies, to be honest."

"Honey, I've got a whole catalogue to introduce you to. Seriously, do you like it?"

"Yeah, but do you?"

Lily nodded. "It's cozy! I'm about to fall asleep already. Do you think we should get it?"

Now, he stared, his mouth pulled down in befuddlement.

"What?" Lily asked.

Curtis ran his hand up and down his pant leg. "Uh, you're being kind of funny."

"How?"

"Well, you asked if 'we' should get it, even though it's your couch."

Lily's heart hid behind her lungs this time, and squeezed them so tight she couldn't speak.

Curtis continued, "You've also been asking my opinion on every single couch. I mean, I'm okay with it, but…like, are you expecting me over a lot or…what?"

Several wonky things bounced around in Lily's tummy. Her eye muscles strained from trying not to look and see if anybody was overhearing them, and her brain crunched out several calculations and schedule arrangements to determine just how many times Curtis could, and *should* come sit on her couch.

She didn't answer. She just sat, blinking stupidly at Curtis's armrest.

He scratched behind his ear. "I mean, you know how I feel, so…" So nothing. He just squeezed the armrest, rubbing furrows in the upholstery with his thumb. An odd thing to find enticing, but there it was.

He waited with the patience of a saint. Lily knew it was her time to speak, but how could she tell him what she did not know herself? She didn't know the meaning to all these feelings and mental babblings. She didn't know why she'd automatically placed him in the furniture of her mind. She didn't get how anything could happen so fast, could so violently pivot from loathing to longing.

And then, Lily remembered that knowing and understanding are two different things.

Lily scooched herself to the middle cushion, eyes on the rug beneath them, keenly aware of the arctic chill of not-my-home, and the voices of customers and salesmen discussing payment plans somewhere. All that in her mind, Lily slouched to sit lower in the seat. She loosened the muscles in her neck, tilting her head to the left, until it rested on Curtis's shoulder.

Bony.

Until his cheek rested on her head. Soft. Shaved, finally, save for the soul patch. That's life for you, this weird roller-coaster where the thing that once repulsed you could become the very thing you grew to depend on.

"Is...this okay?" Lily asked in the tiniest voice.

"Yeah," he replied, scarcely any larger. "I mean the workers may ask questions, but I'll tell them they're getting a sale."

Lily held back the chuckle. "No, I mean...is this okay? Do you..." The words came out of her throat like razor blades. "...still think about Mel?"

Seconds pass like hours when you're vulnerable. Lily waited days for an answer.

"No," Curtis said. "I find myself going multiple days in a row without thinking about her. I'm trying to feel guilty about it, I really am. I used to be pretty good at that. Lately, though, I can't muster the shame. I'm too...happy. And I know she wouldn't want me to feel bad anyway."

So...then it was okay to wriggle her head and nuzzle her cheek into his collarbone? That space was open? She did so either way. It was less bumpy here somehow. In fact, Lily swore the groove of his shoulder fit her head just right. Curtis's head turned, and Lily felt his lips kiss her hair.

Lily was sold; she could definitely fall asleep on this couch.

A thunderous buzzing growled between them, coming from Lily's pocket. She sat up with a scowl and fished out her phone.

Curtis said, "Looks like Mary tracked your location."

"It's not Mary," Lily gasped, showing Curtis the phone: Mr. Gates. Curtis straightened up like he'd been electrocuted in the butt. Lily took the biggest breath of her life, then swiped to answer.

And since they were already so close, Lily leaned into the side of Curtis's head, and put the phone between them so they could both hear. "Hello?"

"Hey, rock star, how's Idaho?" His voice was too neutral! Too vanilla!

"Uh, still hot. New York?"

"Still polluted. I finished your manuscript."

Lily's free hand grabbed Curtis's. He grabbed back. "Yes?"

"I have edits," he said. "A few things to tighten the story. Like that storyline with the fireman, that went nowhere."

"Yeah," Lily groaned, squeezing Curtis's hand tight.

"But considering it's the best thing you've ever written, I'd be an idiot to pass it up."

Lily jerked so hard she clacked her temple against Curtis's. She clenched her teeth, shook off the stars in her eyes and said, "Really?!"

"Absolutely. Congratulations, three-timer!"

Lily pumped her fists as much as she could without elbowing Curtis, feeling like a shook-up soda bottle with nowhere to pop. Curtis himself was all aglow, his excitement caught in his jaw, straining the muscles in his neck to be silent.

Lily leaned right in and kissed him on the lips. She didn't care who saw. Didn't care if Melody herself streaked down from heaven with a holy lance of vengeance. Lily had done it. *They* had done it. The house was safe for a while longer, and Lily Harper was a real writer.

And *man*, his lips were warm. And soft.

"Yello?" Mr. Gates said.

Lily squeezed close to Curtis so they could both hear again. "Sorry, I'm in a public place so I can't scream with joy!"

"Ha-ha, I get that."

"Thank you, Mr. Gates. Thank you, thank you, thank you."

"It was my pleasure. Seriously, it's a good read. You've bumped up your game. How'd you do it?"

Lily flitted her eyes towards Curtis. "Well, I had a bit of help. This fellow writer came over and helped me to shine."

Curtis squeezed her hand again. Lily couldn't turn to see his face without losing the phone, but she could feel the warmth on his cheek, and kissed it to cool him down. It seemed to make things hotter, actually.

Mr. Gates was quiet a minute, then asked, "What, like a co-author?"

All the warmth in the air froze. Lily's innards see-sawed over the question. Co-author? Lily Harper and Curtis Reynolds? Harper and Reynolds? Well, it sounded authorly, but wasn't this her book? Then again, without Curtis, she wouldn't be having this phone call. Or would everyone think Lily Harper had hired on an *actual* writer to help her sorry self?

His hand remained tight in hers, and his body had stiffened.

Lily licked her lips. "Is that, like, a bad thing?"

Mr. Gates didn't answer for a bit. When he did, his voice sounded much closer to the phone. "Lily, what exactly did you promise this person? Co-authorship? Royalties? Publication?"

"I-I, no? I paid him for his time—er, I'm going to pay him out of my advance. It was contingent upon publication."

Mr. Gates sighed, low and slow. "Thank God."

Lily didn't look at Curtis. Couldn't. Dared not. "Is it so bad as all that?"

"Mm, it's not preferable. Your name is the known name; if you bring in an unknown, who knows how that will affect sales? Though I guess it depends who they are. What's the name?"

"Curtis Reynolds." Lily spelled the last name.

"Curtis," Mr. Gates chewed on the name. "Man's name. Not a lot of men in the romance genre."

"Well, there's Nicholas Sparks. He was pretty famous." Lily neglected to mention that she had never read one of his books because—her stomach curdled—he was a man.

Mr. Gates gave an unimpressed, "Hmph. Let's see, Reynolds. Skinny guy? Soul patch?"

"Yep." Lily gave Curtis's quick kiss on the chin.

Curtis flinched, all his focus on the phone call.

Mr. Gates said, "All I'm seeing is sci-fi."

Lily felt her heart sinking, an elevator dinging lower and lower into realization. "Yeah?"

"And what is this, self-publication?"

"Yeah. He's…"

"That doesn't give me a lot of confidence. And

anybody who Googles his name is going to wonder who this guy is and why he's in the romance world, riding on your coattails."

What? "But...he's a good writer! You've seen his work. You liked what he did to my book."

"Have you read any of this guy's books?"

Lily cringed. "I've been busy...I got behind on the deadline." Lily rubbed her thumb on Curtis's by way of apology. He rubbed back. *Thank goodness.*

Mr. Gates said, "Well, if you haven't read them, how do you know it's not your good work shining through?"

Her head became fuzzy. "But he...taught me a lot of principles."

"Principles? Let me guess, John Truby's *Anatomy of a Story*? Stephen King's *On Writing*? Lily, I don't know how much you paid this guy for his time, but you could've gotten the same education for forty bucks on Amazon.com."

It was like watching somebody get whipped with barbed wire. Lily wanted to look to Curtis, to assure him with her eyes that Mr. Gates was wrong, but she didn't dare take her ear from the phone. Besides, something about seeing the whip crack and the blood fly, it made Curtis seem more...mortal, somehow. Could she really have taught herself all this?

As the wells of her heart shouted, "No!" Mr. Gates's voice drowned them out. "My advice, Miss Harper? Cut and run. Pay the guy what you owe, heck, write him a nice thank-you in the dedication page, then say goodbye. You're going places, he's not."

Whip-crack! Lily squeezed her eyes shut. She could feel her grip and Curtis's slipping away. "I...isn't that kind of unfair?" she asked.

"You promised money, right? Pay him and all is fair."

"Sure, but…" Not going places…but could he? With her help? Hadn't Curtis earned that much? Didn't she believe in him? Surely Mr. Gates was overconcerned, right? Her name could still sell plenty, even with another attached.

"Miss Harper…" Mr. Gates' voice came through lower and firmer than a moment ago. "I'm telling you, putting this guy's name on yours is a wild card. Anyone who likes it will think he's the star when it's really you. Anyone who doesn't like it will say you're a sellout and he's a leech. You put his name on your book and you won't get near the same level of love as you did before, not to mention sales. It's your book, Lily. Protect it."

Protect it. Lily saw an immense gate closing around her book, banning entry. Except she was on the outside, reaching through the bars for her story. And as she reached, a primal desperation came over her, numbing her to the pain of her ribs breaking, her shoulder dislocating, the fibers of her arm snapping free of her torso, all to gain one more inch. The smoldering thing in her mind arose, stretching its wings of ash and flame. It screamed in cinders.

Lily spoke with a wobbly smile. "I mean, if you say so."

"Atta girl!" The gaiety in Mr. Gates's voice told Lily she'd said the right thing. Even if her suddenly-cold grip said her hand was now empty. "I'll send over my suggestions, you get the story back to me ASAP, and we'll get the contract squared away."

He kept saying things like that: contracts, marketing, advance, distribution. Business words. Heartless. Fitting, since Lily couldn't feel her own anymore. Did a heart attack make your ears ring? Something was doing that. Perhaps the silence that filled the absence of Curtis's breathing.

It took forever for Mr. Gates to finally say goodbye. When he did, Lily set down the phone, and looked to Curtis. He looked like a writer, leaning on the armrest, hand under his chin, one finger curled against his lips, his face in profile, eyes distant, his mind somewhere far, far away.

The warehouse lights seemed brighter somehow, a sickly, hospital-white. The air conditioner even colder. Icy, sterile.

Lily had to breathe several times before her throat could be convinced to speak. "I'm so sorry about all that."

"Mm-hmm?" He was so still, the voice may have come from the couch itself.

Lily tried again. "He was so rude to you."

His gaze snapped to hers, like a knife across a throat. He remained there, boring her with those eyes that saw no deception. Others glared daggers; Curtis glared wind, a polar gale right into her soul.

It stirred the searing beast within. "He wouldn't have published it!"

"No?" Curtis asked with detached dullness.

"He...he said it would have messed things up."

"And that was too much of a risk for you." Another teeth-chattering gale.

Lily's mouth burned straight into her brain, boiling everything but speech itself. "It's not like we planned on sharing credit! That's not what this was!"

And then, it was gone. All the flame in her whole being,

spent in seconds. It left Lily with ash in her mouth and a cough in her throat.

Curtis didn't even seem burned. He remained as icy and solid as ever, as if no heat could ever touch him again. "You're right. This was always a transaction. Forgive me; I forgot that."

With nothing left in her to burn, Lily could only recoil, duck her head into her neck to hide from the chill. Why did he speak so quietly? Why couldn't he bark at her, call her names? Why did she want him to?

Instead, Curtis stood. "I'll take a bus home. Enjoy your couch."

He left without another word.

Lily stared after him, planning on chasing, on calling, on something. But her joints were frozen. Lily already knew there was no point. Stories are driven by conflict, and Curtis didn't want to fight anymore.

Chapter 25

Lily sat on the couch exactly once, then decided her bed soaked up tears just as well.

She'd bought the couch without thinking; eager to get out of the store before breaking down. When the delivery van came days later, Lily pointed to the empty living room. It wasn't until she sat on the right side that she looked at the left, and realized she would always see Curtis there, thumb drawing lines in the armrest, hand reaching for hers.

Why did it hurt this much? She'd known him for a month, and hated him for half of it. So why the ache, this physical, visceral ache as if her ribs had all been ripped out by a machine?

Her exposed heart said, *Don't play dumb. You know why.*

"It's stupid," she muttered to the couch as she walked circles around it, a full week after Curtis walked out of her life. "We weren't together, not really. He wasn't my boyfriend. We weren't anything."

I know, her heart whispered, *we never even got that chance.*

Lily wept for an hour after that.

Then, back to work. Perhaps that was the reason she couldn't instantly recover from Curtis's loss: she had to drag herself back into the writing room to work on Mr. Gates's edits. Alone. They weren't even hard edits! Give the fireman more of a story. More Christmas-y descriptions in these scenes. Simple. They just interrupted the grief, stretched it out into pockets of sorrow that burst into her throat at random points so she'd have to stop work to squeeze the tears back in, then remember what she was writing, then get frustrated and start crying, and then squeeze again.

Lily thought about watching a cheesy movie to ease her mind, but took one look at her couch and turned back into her office, the one with the empty space where Curtis's chair once sat. She could still see the indents in the carpet.

One evening, Mother Nature had a mood swing. A vicious thunderstorm snapped at the sky, gobbled up the sun, and stole thirty degrees from the air. Rain slapped the windows, wind pummeled the trees, and Lily saved her work to the cloud every five minutes, just in case a power surge should wreck her computer.

It was a nice distraction, though. Lily watched from the back windows by the kitchen, feeling her mood sour by the second, yet getting a strange, macabre joy in that sourness. This was some high-quality thunder, real punch-you-in-the-chest kind of sounds. The sun wouldn't set for hours, but that sky was half-black already, and those clouds weren't really clouds, just one unending sheet of lead.

Perfect bad-mood weather. Nobody could tell her to quit crying in this. No one could wipe her tears and say it was okay; the gods demanded sorrow. Smiles not allowed. Or rather, smiles not required. This is a day to be morose and glum, without shame or explanation. Lay down your pretense, all ye heavy hearted, and find rest.

Lily sank into a numb thickness, dense as the storm

clouds, heavy as iron. She stood against the window, head resting on the cool pane, letting herself zone out into a blank and empty stare.

Until a knock came at the door. Lily peeled her mind out of the muck and stared at the door, a strange terror shooting up her back. *What? But no! This is my sad time! I don't have to explain myself to anybody. Go away...*

They didn't; they knocked again. Who would come here during a storm? Unless maybe...Curtis?

Lily's brain got stupid again. It kept showing her images of a windswept Curtis, rain dripping off his soul patch, desperation clouding his eyes. She heard vague apologies from both of their mouths, and felt the heat of a thick, biting kiss beneath a thunderbolt. Being a writer put crazy ideas into one's head.

Lily didn't know who might actually be on the other side of that door, but she certainly did not expect a sodden, soggy Mandy dripping absolute rivers onto her porch.

"To be fair," Mandy said before Lily could ask, "it wasn't raining when I left."

"What are—? Why? Get in here!"

Mandy took a moment to wring out her hair and shirt on the porch, then stepped inside. She was still dripping buckets, from her fingers, her shorts, her...backpack?

"What happened?" Lily asked, then ran upstairs for a towel. When she returned, Lily repeated the question.

Mandy dropped her backpack with a squishy thud by the door, then dried her dripping locks. "I was walking over here, and then the storm popped out of nowhere." Mandy slipped off her shoes and socks with wet squelches.

"But why were you walking in the first place?"

"It's not that long."

"What's with the backpack?"

Mandy paused at that question, a thundercloud covering her face. "Can I stay with you for a while?"

Lily needed a minute to recover from the implications of that question. "Mandy, did you run away?"

"It's Mandragora."

"Answer the question! Did you run away? Does anybody know you're here?"

Mandragora crossed her arms with a huff. "I was going to text them."

Lily grabbed the sides of her head. "Are you...what is going on?"

Mandragora stomped her foot, splashing more water onto the floor. "Look, if I had to spend one more minute with Mary and her perfect, photoshopped life, I was going to stab somebody."

"So you just left? Why didn't you tell anybody?"

"Because they would have stopped me, duh!"

Lily pointed her finger in Mandragora's face. "Do *not* be glib about this! People could be panicking right now."

Mandragora leaned against the wall, then jumped back up and dried the spot with the towel. "I don't care if Mary worries."

"And if *Mom* worries?"

By the blank look on her face, Mandragora clearly had not thought that far ahead. "All right fine, I'll text her, but what do I tell her? Can I stay?"

A sudden meanness rose up in Lily's throat. *You ask*

me that after you're already here? Soaking wet with no ride? Thanks for the manipulation, brat! Fortunately, Lily swallowed it back. "Yes, fine, you can stay the night, but you call Mom right now. Call! Don't text."

Mandragora gave a pouty nod, then picked up her backpack. The whole thing was shiny with rainwater. "Can I use your dryer on my…probably everything?"

Lily rubbed her temples. "Yes, fine. You can pick out some clothes from my room in the meantime. It should fit close enough. But listen, I'm doing edits for my book, so I'm going to go in my office, and I need some quiet, okay?"

"Quiet as a mouse. Thanks, sis."

"Call Mom."

"Calling."

Lily marched into her office and flopped into her writing chair. Well, this was just fantastic. It wasn't enough that she could barely scrape two words together, nor that her heart had fallen out and left an aching hole, now she had to babysit a teenager, which had to mean listening to more whiny drama about Mary.

She chose to focus on writing. She'd talk to Mandy— Mandragora—later. Lily put her hands over the keyboard, and hovered there a moment.

Her brain was being stupid again, but stupid in a way that made sense this time. Lily got up, marching past Mandragora, who paced on the phone, leaving wet footprints everywhere. Lily grabbed one of the dining table chairs, hauled it into her office, and plopped it down by the window.

It was just easier to concentrate with that nearby.

*
**

By late evening, the storm had quit, Lily had finished her edits for the day, and someone was knocking on the door yet again.

"If it's Mary, I'm not here!" Mandragora's voice sounded like it came from the kitchen. Lily checked the time. Eight at night. She hadn't eaten since lunch. She stood from her chair and rubbed the kinks out of her back. She had barely moved, and had not talked to Mandragora about her ditching home, other than to double check she'd called Mom—which she had.

Lily sighed, once more wishing Curtis was here for comfort. Well, she could do this on her own. Lily answered the door.

Once more, the person on her porch surprised her. Not Mary at all, but James, looking wearier than ever. The porch light highlighted the gray streaks above his ears.

"Hey," he said with a half-smile. "Mandy here?"

"Mandragora!" the girl shouted from the kitchen.

James nodded, and asked Lily, "Can I come in?"

"Sure." Lily moved aside for him. James stepped carefully across the living room, like one might approach a frightened cat. Mandragora watched him from her seat at the kitchen table, her back to the wall, the table between them.

James sat down on the opposite side. Lily stepped into the kitchen to watch from the sidelines.

Mandragora glared at her. "Did you call him?"

"No," James answered. "I offered to come myself. I figured you'd be more likely to talk to me than Mary right now."

Mandragora huffed and stared down at an empty plate with indiscernible crumbs. "I'm not going back."

James said, "Okay, then what's the plan?"

Mandragora looked to Lily.

Lily narrowed her eyes right back. "How long are you wanting to stay?"

Mandragora's shoulders lifted and dropped. "A while?"

"Like a week? A month?"

Another shrug.

Lily slowed her breathing. "Listen, I've got to know why."

"Because Mary wants to control every aspect of my life! Remember when I got that shirt from the yard sale? Two days later, she buys me three brand-new shirts and says, 'Isn't that better?' Like, who cares?! And when I said I didn't want them, she called me ungrateful. I didn't ask for them! Plus, she's already telling me what classes to take in the fall so I can 'secure my future.' It's eighth grade! What, is some CEO going to go back to my book report on *Harry Potter* to see if I got what it takes to be businesswoman? And she never, *never* calls me Mandragora! It's always, 'Mandy's a nicer, prettier name.' It's my name! I'm not even changing it! It's literally the name on my damn birth certificate! She's the one who wants to change me, and make me all perfect and presentable for our perfectly presentable family joke."

Whoa. Lily knew things were rough between her sisters, but Mandragora had turned redder and redder throughout that speech until Lily saw edges of purple on the girl's neck. Mandragora had pounded the table so hard that crumbs had bounced off her plate and fallen to the floor.

Mary had five siblings, but this was the first one to react

like this. Lily had been sixteen when Mary took over, and observed all of her brothers' and sisters' reactions to the coronation. No fuss. No fights. A few little arguments, some frustrations and fussing, sure, but nothing like this. Everyone followed Mary because everyone knew they'd succeed with her help. What was Mandragora's problem?

James listened to the whole thing with attentive indifference. Lily could see why Curtis and James liked each other, that mutual ability to remain cool under pressure. "Yeah, Mary likes to interfere. She has her ideas and thinks they're the best ones." A grayness shadowed his face for a moment, then passed just as quickly. "But you said something that went way over the line, didn't you?"

Lily stiffened. "What did you say?"

Mandragora looked away.

"Mandragora. What did you say?"

She slouched in her seat, and kept her face to the wall. "I told her that if she'd stop stressing over me, she'd probably be able to actually have kids of her own."

Lily gasped so loud she startled her sister. "What is the matter with you?! You know how much that bothers her!"

Mandragora slouched further and scowled at the table. "How should I know that if she never talks about it?"

"*Because* she never talks about it," James answered. "Everybody has something they don't like talking about. Dragging it into the sun won't make them like you any more."

"She doesn't like me at all, so why bother?" Those

words came out quieter, more from the throat. Mandragora pinched her lips tight.

Lily wanted to say that wasn't true, but struggled to come up with examples.

James broke the silence a moment later by turning to Lily. "It's your house, Lily. It's up to you."

She could imagine Mary sweating through her makeup to know there was a sibling out of her reach. And Lily did not want to add herself into this drama. Then again, would Mandragora run away again? To a friend or some unknown person? At least here, the girl would be safe.

Lily sighed. "Yes, you can stay for...a while." Such a long word for only five letters.

James nodded. "Okay. I'll have your mom pack you a suitcase."

"Thank you," Mandragora muttered.

James rose from the table. "I'll head back. Lily, do you have a sec?"

"Sure." Lily followed James out the front door. It was a sultry night, thick and sticky. Even the crickets barely chirped. "What's up?"

James toyed with something in his pocket for a while. "I'm probably being nosey, so you don't have to answer if you don't want, but I was wondering about Curtis."

"Curtis?" Lily's heart jumped, and stayed in the air.

"He's been gloomy lately, and he says you two had some kind of fight."

Fight? More like a fizzle, a bad firework crumbling to embers before it ever even popped. "What else did he say?"

"Nothing," James replied. "Just that you two kind of broke up even though you weren't together. Something happen?"

Oh, yes. Mr. Gates happened, and said he didn't want to risk having Curtis's name on the book, and Curtis got his feelings hurt and blamed me. What was I supposed to do? Tell Mr. Gates no? That all the work I put in meant nothing? That I didn't want to be a writer after all, thank you very much?

A nice argument, if Lily could actually push it out of her mouth.

James gave a rueful smile. "It's okay, you don't have to tell me. Just a bummer, that's all."

Lily shrugged in a very Mandragora kind of way. "We weren't even together."

"Yeah. Shame." He bade her goodnight, and left Lily with her big argument stuffed in one cheek, and all her counterpoints in the other. She managed the swallow the whole lot, but it made her stomach sick the rest of the night.

Chapter 26

The edits only took two weeks. Mr. Gates set the machines of publication in motion, but Lily was left with an empty calendar. She could write a new book, but her mind was still mud. She could watch television, but she still didn't like sitting on that couch. She could spend time with Mandragora, since the girl was still living here, but that always ended with whining about Mary.

In truth, there was really only one thing that could cheer Lily up for any length of time.

"Daisy Dinner!" Lily and Mandragora cheered from their seats at the breakfast bar.

Daisy smirked as she stirred mushroom sauce on Lily's stove. While every Harper could cook, Daisy outstripped them all. With her husband out flying so much, Daisy often had no one to cook for, so she'd travel to the valley and make dinner for one of her siblings every week or two.

Unless that sibling had locked herself away for weeks on end.

"I seriously missed this," Lily said, leaning over the bar to get a better whiff of the garlic and thyme dancing with the mushroom aroma. "I could never make pasta this fancy."

Daisy replied, "You could if you actually used the recipes I give you."

"But that would deprive you the joy of cooking."

Daisy pointed her spoon at Lily, paused, then returned to

stirring. "Yeah…"

Mandragora propped her chin on her hands. "What kind of stuff did you make when the family was still poor?"

"Pfft, nothing like this. But I did learn a super cheap garlic…bread…" Her spoon slowed to a crawl.

Lily had only just realized it, too, and it stopped her breath.

Daisy glanced at Lily, then gave an awkward shrug and smile. "We don't really talk about the old days, though."

Mandragora pouted. "Why? It's not like Mary's here."

"Well, I don't like talking about it, either. I have *way* better meals to make."

An odd thought shot through Lily's mind. *Does Daisy love to cook because it reminds her how far she's come?*

"Besides…" Daisy dropped the spoon and let the sauce simmer. "I have something to talk to you guys about."

Lily gasped. "You're pregnant!"

Daisy stammered and gaped. "Jeez, Lily, I didn't even get to announce it!"

Lily shrieked in sisterly bliss. "Yay! I'm sorry, but yay!" She ran around the counter to drown her sister in a hug—careful to avoid the belly, of course. Daisy was still slim, but then again, Lily's embrace was bordering on boa constrictor.

Daisy only got out of that embrace—and Mandragora's—by choking out the word "Sauce!" Lily and Mandragora released her at once, and Daisy stirred a little more.

Lily clapped her hands. "Who else have you told?"

"No one. You two are the first."

Mandragora pumped her fists in the air. "We're number one!"

"Besides Jerome, of course."

"Oh. We're number two!"

Lily was practically dancing. "I want to know everything! Do you have names picked out? Do you need help getting a baby room together? Are you having the baby at the hospital or at home? Sorry! I know I'm being that creepy over-involved person, but I'm excited! You're the first one to have a baby!"

Daisy kept stirring. "Yeah…that's what I wanted to talk to you guys about."

"What do you mean?"

Daisy stirred, and stirred, and stirred. Then, she stuck the spoon straight down into the sauce, and turned to Lily. "How do I tell Mary?"

Lily came down off her tip-toes, striking the earth with a bone-shattering thud. "Oh…"

Daisy sighed. "Mary wants kids. In fact, don't tell her I said this, but I think she wants kids way more than she lets on."

"Yeah…"

Mandragora frowned. "But that's not fair. Why shouldn't you get to celebrate just because Mary's sensitive?"

Lily glowered at the girl. "If your best friend in the whole world just had the best kiss of her life with that guy you really like, would you be able to celebrate with her?"

There was an argument in Mandy's eyes, but it never made it to her lips.

Daisy finally took the sauce off the burner, giving Mandragora a long look. "Well, I'm seeing why you're staying with Lily and not Mary anymore. By the way, what does Mom think of you living here?"

Mandragora shrugged. "She's okay with it. I mean, she misses me, but we see each other a lot, and talk and stuff."

"Huh. You'd think she'd be more eager to get you home."

Lily said, "Well, it's Mary's home, so…"

Mandragora added, "And Mary thinks she *is* my mom, so…"

Daisy gave Mandragora another long look. "That's because she *was* our mom."

Mandragora furrowed her brow. "No, she wasn't. You guys still had Mom."

Once again, Daisy opened her mouth, then froze. She shook her head and said, "Never mind. It's in the past. Anyway, dinner is ready. Lily, can you sort everything? I need to use the bathroom."

"Get used to saying that," Lily joked.

As Lily and Mandragora set the table, Mandragora dropped her plates with grumpy thuds. "Why does no one ever talk about that past?"

Lily's spine was starting to stoop from all this whining. "Why do you *want* to know? It's not like we're keeping secrets of murder or treasure or anything special. It's just bad memories of hard times."

Mandragora slammed her last plate with both hands.

Before Lily could shout at her, Mandragora said, "Do you know what kind of food Daisy used to make when you were all poor?"

Lily crossed her arms. "I'm not talking about that."

"I'm not asking you to talk about it. I'm just asking yes or no."

"Then yes."

Mandragora shoved a finger into her own sternum. "I don't! You guys all have these memories of being a family, while I'm just off to the side smiling and nodding." She stomped back into the kitchen for utensils and napkins, saying nothing.

Lily didn't move, too anchored by Mandragora's words. Was she right? Was she somehow missing out on being part of the family? Lily would have killed to only have good memories. And yet...there really *was* something special about the way Daisy would spend twenty minutes in the spice aisle of the grocery store, holding her lemonade-stand money, trying to think of the best combinations that would make off-brand spaghetti taste gourmet. Or how when they went to the library, Lily would scour the fiction section while Daisy leafed through cookbooks for cheap meal ideas. She'd been too young to work, but she wanted to help her family, so she'd given them something tasty now and then.

But we don't look back... Lily decided to say nothing. *The story of my life.*

Lily said, "I need the advice of someone older and wiser."

Asher nodded, pretending to stroke his non-existent

beard. "I wisely suggest that you ditch that little sissy car you drive and buy American."

"Shut your face, butthead."

Lily had made sure to visit Asher in the shop after closing time so that she could call him whatever childish name she wanted. Asher stood behind his sales counter, shrugging off the insult with a smile. "Everybody wants my advice, but nobody wants to hear it."

"I asked for advice on Mandy, not macho machines."

"Is Mandy—I mean Mandragora—just being a pest?"

Lily sighed, sinking deeper into the chocolate-brown display chair. "No, not most of the time. She's actually trying to be a good house guest. She does her homework quietly, cleans everything, she's even cooking now."

"Cooking?"

"Yeah, Daisy came over a couple days ago, and Mandragora took an interest."

Asher gasped. "You got a Daisy Dinner?"

"I got a Daisy Dinner!"

"Aw, I get one next Saturday." He wiped his mouth just thinking of it. "Anyway, I can take Mandragora for a couple days now and then if you want, but nobody's home most of the time."

"Maybe. I just wish I knew how to make her and Mary play nice again." Lily slouched even more into the upholstery. "Side note, this chair is shockingly comfortable."

"You want it?" Asher asked. "It's on a Mary Sale."

"What the heck is a Mary Sale?"

"It's when Mary comes in and decides we need to

clear something out. It hasn't even been here that long, but Mary said no, so I guess that's the breaks." Asher's mouth twisted into sour shapes.

"Is Mary being bossy?" Lily asked, centipedes crawling in her belly. Why were there so many grumpy family conversations lately?

"Not really. She's usually not here, but when she is, it's like she has to dictate something. I used to think she was being controlling, but…it's like she feels she *has* to do something or else she's not contributing."

"The *owner* of the store thinks she's not contributing?"

"That's what I said. I told her the other day, 'Sis, chill, I can take care of this place.' Heck, if she'd let me, I'd take full control, and let her relax for once. She can still get an owner's cut for all I care, just sit down for once in your life, you know?"

"What did Mary say?"

"Not to worry about her. 'I've got everything covered.' The usual." Asher leaned harder on the counter, his face suddenly serious. "Did Daisy tell you…anything special?"

Lily caught the look in his eye. "She told me a special announcement, if that's what you mean."

"And asked how to break the news to Mary?"

"Yep. Any ideas?"

"Tell her it's a win for the Harper Clan."

Lily blinked. "That's…brilliant, actually. You think she'll still be hurt?"

Asher shrugged. "Probably, but there's no avoiding that. Actually, that's my point. If Mary could just sit down, she might be able to finally have the kids she wants."

"Mandragora said that. Not kindly, though."

311

"Ouch."

Speaking Mandragora's name brought Lily back to her original reason for coming. Or rather, the true reason, even if Lily hadn't been able to admit it until now. She slowly stood up, and tip-toed to Asher's counter, looking around to make sure the shop truly was empty. "Asher?"

"That's me."

"Do you ever think that Mandragora is…out of the loop?"

"Kind of. It's not surprising; she's way younger than we are."

"Yeah…Asher?"

"Still me."

"Do you think that…maybe…we should tell Mandy about the old days?"

Asher visibly paled. "You mean, like…at the Westwood house?"

Lily toyed with her bracelet, circling the wrist over and over. "I don't like reliving it either, but I feel like we all got closer through that experience. Like…" A silly grin forced its way onto Lily's face. "She doesn't know what it's like to see her brothers put on a two-man play because you can't afford a television."

Asher reeled. "Ugh, you remember that?"

"Yeah."

"Oof, go drink or do drugs until you forget my terrible acting."

Lily's shaky hands started to strangle each other on the counter. "But see, that's the thing. I don't want to forget it. It made me so happy to see you guys trying to cheer us up. I hated those days…but there are some things from back then I don't want to forget."

Her breath came in shivering staccato. Could she possibly mean what she'd just said? Was there really beauty in that bog of memory?

Asher's big hand closed around hers. Soft, warm. "I remember the day you came home with a backpack so full of books that the zipper started to break. You knew I needed some research for a class, so you surprised me by getting some books for me. Fat, heavy books."

"Anything for my brother."

"What you *didn't* say was that you hadn't gone to our local library, but the one in Hailey, which I wager is a good hour or two in one direction on foot. Probably longer if you're carrying eighty pounds of books."

Lily winced. "You knew?"

"I saw the library receipt."

"Oh. Ours didn't have what you needed, but the librarian said the Hailey branch would."

"Mm." Asher squeezed her hands tight.

She squeezed back.

"The thing is," Asher said, "I think Mandragora, of all people, would benefit from staying ignorant." He gave her a hard look, one only he could because only he had been there with her.

If she focused, Lily could still feel the ache in her palm from squeezing the knife too hard. "Maybe...but do you think she's ready to hear other things?"

Asher asked in a quiet voice, "Are we?"

313

Chapter 27

The world was on repeat.

Lily noticed only pieces of it before, like how Mandragora kept staying the night for weeks, and then months. October spread its pumpkin hues across the city, and still she remained. Every time Lily broached the subject of returning to Mom and Mary, Mandragora gave an indecisive shrug.

Part of Lily wanted to force her back home, but then the girl would bounce back here in a month. Besides, Lily found herself busy with another circular duty: marketing. Mr. Gates liked the revisions, and now she just had to promote her new book. The days became cycles of social media posts, writing updates, reaching out to old contacts with platforms, and touching base with her editor.

She should have been happier. Fans crawled out of the woodwork to gobble up any scrap of information on Lily Harper's new novel. Lily had been so buried in the keyboard that she almost forgot how many fans and followers she actually had. The problem was the questions. One fan jokingly asked, "How'd you write it so fast?" A blogger asked in an interview, "Does your latest book offer anything new?" and a more hard-hitting podcaster asked, "How does your book stand out from the other Christmas romances out there?"

Every answer pointed back to Curtis. Sometimes, she

answered with pure honesty. "I wrote so fast because a friend pushed me." Sometimes, she pushed him to the side. "Someone recommended a few literary techniques with this book, and so far, people have enjoyed them." Other times, she ignored him altogether. "I wanted to try a more structured, classic-story approach that keeps the feel-good snuggliness of Christmas but also pushes a solid arc."

Lily never quite knew how to feel about that. She told herself Curtis had done his job, and now it was over, but that made her throat hurt. On the other hand, the deed was done: Curtis was out of the book, so bringing him up would only bring awkward questions. Promoting her book quickly became an exercise in shaky smiles, clever wordplay, and antacid pills.

One day, the oscillating seesaw hit Lily in the face.

"Lights, camera, action!" Mandragora tapped the record button on Lily's phone.

Lily grinned at the lens. "Today's the day! It's finally here!" Lily waved her hands over the nondescript brown box on the floor. She knelt in front of it in her writing office, trying not to tear the thing open like an animal.

Lily continued to the camera, "I know I've done this twice already, and I know we've all seen the mock-up of the cover art, but folks? This is still an early Christmas present to me. Shall we?" She picked up the kitchen knife. "You'd think I'd own a ceremonial box cutter or something by this point. Nope! A boring knife with a tomato-juice stain."

Mandragora giggled silently, but kept the camera steady.

Lily cut through the tape, flung open the box with a dramatic flair, and beamed. There they were: her books. Early author copies just for her. Lily dropped the knife and slowly reached into the box, like each book was an infant in need of cradling. She scooped up the first book and let the joy crawl all over her face.

Two-dimensional covers were apparently the rage, so rather than a photorealistic scene, Lily's book boasted a flatter, yet fittingly colorful image. A great, green-gray mountain with an ice-cream peak rose up through the royal-blue background. Beneath it, a woman in a Santa-red coat walked away from the reader, head hunched, hands in her pockets, whirling snowflakes dancing around her. She walked down a simplified main street of an old-timey, Dickens-style town, just beneath a classic lamp post with a wreath. Yellow lights spilled out of the windows before her, like constellations beneath the mountain base. Sprawled across the top in white, swirling letters read *Escape from Christmas.*

Lily forced herself to take a breath to avoid passing out on camera. "Oh, boy, you never get used to this feeling. Seeing your work for the first time is...is..."

Fog clouded the edges of her brain. The room became a vague something in the background. Her eyes stuck on the Times-New-Roman print of her name: Lily Harper.

And only Lily Harper.

Yes, seeing your book for the first time would be...but Curtis wouldn't be able to...

A gear in her brain clicked, and Lily snapped back into reality with a hard blink. It let loose the tear hanging on her lashes. A cold storm tore through her tummy, but Lily was well-versed in sudden smiles, so she beamed at the camera and wiped her face. "Sorry, it's always so emotional. I really wasn't sure this one was going to make it, but..."

But...?

"But it did...miraculously." Her tongue felt thick and furry saying it. Lily shook off the daze and held up the book for the viewer to see. "There she is! *Escape from Christmas* launches on November seventh. That's only a few days away, so preorder your copy while you can! Link in the description. Thank you all so much for believing in me."

Pause. Mandragora hit the end button, then gave her sister a curious look. "You okay?"

Lily waved her off. "Yeah, yeah, just...emotions." *Should I try it again? No, the box is already open. It's okay. They'll believe it.*

Lily stood up, book still in hand. "Think you can upload that on your own? I just, uh, need a moment."

Mandragora said, "Okay. You want to watch a Christmas movie later? I know it's not even Thanksgiving yet, but still."

Lily sucked on her lips. "Maybe. I'm a little busy."

Mandragora shrugged, then left.

Lily set her new book on the shelf, on a special out-facing display, right next to her first books. The displays were the only new thing in the office besides printer paper and a few pens. Lily wore jeans now instead of shorts, and long sleeves to shield her arms from autumn winds, but that was about it. She had not replaced Curtis's chair with anything comfier. She had not replaced Mary's pictures and knick-knacks with her own—not in this or any other room, and so they always seemed bare. Lily had received her advance from Mr. Gates, so her house was safe for the moment. Just empty.

Some nights, after Mandragora had gone to bed, Lily

would circle the couch she still couldn't sit in, wondering why Curtis had such a hold on her brain. It had been four months since that horrid day, but time had stopped for Lily Harper. She ached just as badly; she was just better at coping with it.

"Why can't I forget you?" she asked the empty night. Lily missed him, sure. Missed that comforting hand on her back, missed his obvious yet unintrusive presence, even missed arguing about the book. But this was more than sad longing. It stayed in the pit of her stomach and kicked, like a hamster on the wheel. She couldn't sit still anymore, couldn't feel the peace and rest that came with completing a book. Lily blamed it on marketing and the craziness of the launch, but Curtis had nothing to do with those things. So why did she always think of him when she couldn't sit down?

At last, the book did launch. Mandragora surprised her sister with donuts. Lily shot internet fireworks across all her social media accounts. Friends, family, and fellow authors praised her latest success. Mr. Gates sent an email congratulations, plus a note that pre-orders had exceeded her last two novels. Her biggest hit yet—so far.

So, when Mary took Lily out for drinks that night, Lily celebrated as hard and fast as she could swallow. Even after Mary gave many confused and concerned looks. Lily didn't remember much after that, except when Mary drove her home and insisted on getting Lily into her bed.

Lily suddenly remembered that Mary had not yet seen the un-Mary'd house. Lily had found many convenient excuses to have their get-togethers elsewhere.

The panic nearly sobered Lily up, and helped her form intelligible words.

"No, no, it's fine. Mandy's inside, so she'll make sure I don't fall down the stairs or whatever. I just don't want you guys to fight. It's been such a great night, so can we please end on a high note, not a bitter one?"

Mary gave a genuine smile, and consented. Lily went to bed with an ache in her belly, but that wasn't new.

Lily continued her whirlwind of signings at libraries and bookstores, ask-the-author events online, small-time interviews, anything and everything to get her book out there. Even then, he loomed. A goateed man asked Lily to sign a copy of the book for his girlfriend, and she wrote, "To Venus. Your name is awesome!" Which made her think of how Curtis redefined Mandragora.

Those local events made Lily shudder with fright. What if Curtis showed up? He never did, but Lily did see two familiar faces while signing books at the library: Josie, who headed the local writing group, and Lydia, the blonde fangirl, each holding their own copies of *Escape from Christmas*.

Lily apologized for disappearing from the group, and both women told her it was fine, and that they already loved the new book. Lily focused on the smiles, and the chatter, told herself she would not, under any circumstances, ask about a certain someone else in the writing group.

But Josie asked, "So, do you remember Curtis? The guy who criticized your chapter?"

Every day. "I think so. Why?"

"He actually likes this book."

Lily dropped her pen mid-signature. "He…read it?"

"Yeah, I had the group read your first chapter just to talk

319

about how far it had come from when you first showed it to us. He said it was good, but he seemed pretty grumpy about it. Sore loser, I guess."

Lily could barely keep even a fragment of a grin. What must he have felt to read that chapter again, in front of everybody, knowing he could never tell them he helped write it because they would never believe him? What kind of torture…?

Then Lydia said, "I'm surprised he came back. He vanished for a few months."

"Really?" Lily asked in a hollow voice.

Josie nodded. "Yeah, but honestly? He's more tolerable now. I don't know where he went, but he's not as critical as he used to be. And his writing is different, too. Nicer."

"Could…you maybe send me something he wrote?"

Why had she asked for that? What possible good could it have done? Lily didn't know, and she regretted it bitterly. Josie sent Curtis's short story, a speculative fiction of a group of men scouring a darkened forest for a hidden world, where giant koi fish floated in the ether, denizens of some ancient and unknowable place. Lily could see Curtis's type immediately: a metaphor of humanity reaching beyond its grasp. Most of the expedition team grew madder by the minute, ravenous for answers to the universe while their own world burned.

Except one. One explorer did not question the flying koi, did not try to step into their world or take from it. When the ancient beings asked him why he had come, he sat down, and said that he just wanted to see something beautiful. He was the only one to return from the forest, smiling, and inspired to try again to help his corroding planet.

"A happy ending," Lily muttered into her tear-stained pillow. "How very Harper of you."

The crowning gem to Lily's misery came in the most ordinary place: the milk aisle of the grocery store. Her cheeks were starting to hurt from all the smiling she had to do. The book launch brought out more fans looking for autographs, or just a "Hello" from a local celebrity. Lily loved her fans, though, so she massaged her face and kept laughing with them, and recommending her own favorite reads.

While trying to decide if she wanted a half-gallon of chocolate milk or all of the chocolate milk in the aisle, Lily's phone rang, with Mr. Gates's name on the display. Lily sequestered herself in a cold corner to not bother anybody, and answered, "Hello?"

"Miss Harper!" Mr. Gates boomed like the most self-assured car salesman in the world. "I have news so great, you'll want to fly to New York and kiss my toes in person."

Lily resisted the gag. "Uh, what?"

"I got you an interview on live TV."

Lily jumped right off her toes. "You what? How? Where?"

"That's the best part: it's *The Carla Ramirez Show*."

Her legs genuinely failed her, and Lily fell backwards against the edge of the aisle, grabbing the shelf of two-percent to steady herself. "You...are serious, right?"

"I am!" Mr. Gates laughed. "It took a few favors and some begging, but Carla Ramirez liked the idea of a rising

star's Christmas romance right around the holidays.
They're going to contact you also, but I wanted to be the
first to give the good news. You'll be live on November
twenty-eighth, part of Carla's big Christmas push. You.
Are. Welcome."

Just enough of Lily Harper remained aware of her
surroundings, so she squealed at an indiscernible pitch,
rocked her knees instead of dancing, and hugged herself
instead of random strangers. "Thank you, thank you,
thank you!!"

"Congrats, Miss Harper. Welcome to the big
leagues."

Big leagues. After an episode on *Carla*, when people
Googled "romance novels," her name would appear on
page one. Nora Roberts, Danielle Steele, Lily Harper. In
that order, of course.

Lily finished the pleasantries with Mr. Gates, hung
up, and allowed herself one whisper-screamed, "YES!"
before she turned and saw Curtis Reynolds pop into the
aisle.

He jerked backwards at the sight of her, at her
upraised arms and giddy smile, all of which dropped the
instant she met his eyes.

"Uh, hi?" he said.

"Heh. Lo. Hello." Lily's tongue had frozen, and all
the joy with it.

Curtis glanced at the phone still clutched in her hand.
"Good news?"

Lily pressed herself against the milk aisle, as if she
could crawl under the shelves and hide behind a gallon of
skim. "Yes…"

He looked at her with those same hard eyes. His writing may have changed, but his appearance had not. Not his bony body, not the soul patch, not the closed, level gaze of one who's given up. "Well, good for you." He reached past her to grab a gallon of milk, then said, "Take care."

"You, too," she whispered.

Curtis made it two steps, then said over his shoulder, "Congrats on the book." It even sounded half-sincere.

The icy ledge bit into Lily's legs, but she could not feel them anymore. Or much else below her neck.

She took a different checkout aisle from Curtis, and tried not to look at him, tried not to see how hard he tried not to look at her. Lily made pitiful small talk with the cashier, ever glancing over the woman's frizzy bun, to the back of Curtis's dark head. He took one exit, Lily took the other.

She drove all the way home thinking of Curtis instead of Carla Ramirez. In place of all the dreams of dazzling lights and overnight fame, one thought dominated her mind: he won't be there. It didn't matter that he had pushed her to learn more about the craft of writing. It didn't matter that he contributed half the words in every chapter. It didn't matter that the book would not exist without his presence being her constant ally in those hard, hard days. Curtis Reynolds did not get to come to the big times.

Lily passed her evening in a fog. She made dinner and ate it. Mandragora wanted to watch a Christmas movie. Lily said she was busy, and closed the door to her office. She sat in her chair, trying to think of new story ideas, something she could claim as her own. She could only spin in circles.

After Mandragora went to bed, Lily paced around the couch yet again. This time, she looked up at the rafters, wondering why she'd built them so high. Or the living room so long. Or the windows so tall. It was so big for just one person.

Thoughts dissolved into ideas. Ideas melted into feelings. Feelings slithered into mush. At midnight, Lily finally gave her aching feet a rest. Behind the couch, a bit of the furry, tiger-stripe carpet still showed. Lily lay down on it, barely thin enough to fit. She pressed her back to the couch, nuzzled her face into the rug, and let every part of her shut down.

A bitter musk rose through Lily's nostrils and slapped her awake with promises of endless bliss. It turned out to be a coffee cup in her face, held by Mandragora, who squatted next to her on the floor.

"Morning," Mandragora said. Daylight shone through her giant windows in a downward arc, right on Lily's spot on the floor, judging her.

Lily groaned as she sat up. Her back was sweaty from being pressed against the couch, and her shirt clung to her skin. Her hips and shoulders cried out; the furry rug was no replacement for a mattress.

"Hi." Lily's voice croaked. It felt cracked and dry. She'd slept with her mouth open. She accepted the cup and gave it a sip. Boiling hot, but the cream was just right. "It's perfect. Thank you."

Mandragora sat back against the base of the stairs, across from her sister. "So, you're not okay."

Lily used the smell of coffee to assist with the smile.

"Oh, I'm fine. Just wore myself out."

Mandragora leveled steely eyes on her, eerily reminiscent of Curtis. "Don't do that."

"Do what?"

"Don't talk like Mary, pretending everything is perfect and rosy when it's not."

Lily pondered this a moment, a little stung, honestly. Then, she decided that one sip of coffee was not enough to maintain the façade. "Fine. I'm not okay. I'm grumpy, I'm tired all the time, and my brain feels like it's stuck in traffic."

Mandragora gave her a pitying look. "Is the book not doing well?"

Lily laughed in a nasty tone. "Actually, Mr. Gates says it's doing great! I'm breaking all my old records! Well, not by much, but still, it's a hit. Reviews are generally good, sales are good, the world agrees that this is Lily Harper's good-est novel ever."

"And yet when I asked if you wanted to watch a movie about a lady who runs a New York hotel, and has to rediscover the magic of Christmas, and choose between the handsome chef or the handsome prince, you said no."

That made Lily chuckle for real. "That does sound like a movie I'd like. But then I'd have to drag a chair over to see the TV."

Mandragora cocked her head. "Why? Why not sit on the couch?"

Lily closed her eyes. It sounded so stupid in her head. Would it sound any better out loud? "Because Curtis and I picked this couch together."

Mandragora's eyes sparkled at once. "You did? Why?"

"Because I thought he'd sit on it more. I thought he'd sit

on it at all."

"Hang on...do you love him?" Mandragora leaned closer.

Lily dropped her eyes to her coffee. "I don't even know." She took another sip. Still too hot. "Mostly, I just feel guilt."

"Guilt? How come?"

"It's complicated."

Mandragora frowned. "I'm not a kid anymore. You can talk to me."

"I changed your diapers. You'll always be my baby sister."

"I'm serious! What happened with you two? Why isn't Curtis sitting on the couch and watching bad movies with us? I mean with you, and me in my room? Well, I say I'm in my room, but I'm actually on the balcony spying."

Lily chuckled again. For a second. "It's complicated."

"Then explain it to me."

"It's complicated."

"C'mon!"

The beast burst into flame. "Mandy, sometimes people don't want to talk about stuff, and dragging it out of them only makes them resent you!"

Mandragora froze for a second, then burned. She leapt to her feet, stomped up the stairs, and called over the balcony, "It's Mandragora!"

Lily sipped her coffee and let it singe her tongue. "Whatever."

Chapter 28

The Harper Family Thanksgiving had one rule: no fighting. No arguments, no loud disagreements, no conflict of any sort. It was a day to be grateful, knit together in unity and harmony.

I wonder how long that will last? Lily had apologized to Mandragora, but the girl still had beef with Mary. Could Mandragora keep her tongue? Would Mary let matters lie? Would be bees buzzing in Lily's brain burst out and sting everybody?

The whole clan came together, dressed in their finest. Lily and Mandragora each wore mid-length dresses and leggings, Lily a dark red on burgundy, Mandragora a cream on black, hair brushed and necklaces sparkling. Daisy, Mom, and Asher's wife, Godiva, all shone in their own dresses, while Asher, Oak, James, and Daisy's pilot husband, Jerome, looked more relaxed in good slacks and button-up shirts. Even the golden retriever had been bathed and groomed.

Mary outshone them all in her fitting, burnt-orange, off-the-shoulder dress that showcased her still-tan shoulders.

"She looks like a pumpkin on a hot date," Mandragora muttered when she first saw it.

Mary stood at the head of the table, with a glass of wine in her hand. The meal was already conquered, the ginormous turkey picked clean to the bones, the stuffing bowl reduced to crumbs, the army of rolls whittled down to a few browned casualties, the cranberry sauce an oozing remnant of its former glory, and the green beans curiously untouched. The dog waited with practiced patience.

"It's been a red-letter year for the Harper Family," Mary declared. "Asher, Mom, and I have both had our best years ever at work."

Asher chuckled, "With the sweat stains to prove it."

Mom chuckled, but Mary gave Asher a cutting look, and he fell silent. Mary continued, "My darling Doctor Livingston was voted Best Oncologist in Southern Idaho. Again!"

James crossed his arms with a very real grin.

"Our famous sister, Lily, published her third book, and will be on *The Carla Ramirez Show* next week!"

Everybody applauded, and Lily smiled as sweetly as she could through the scraping in her chest. *If nothing had happened, would Curtis be sitting next to me right now?*

Mary said, "And let's not forget Daisy, who will be going by 'Mommy' in a few months!"

Daisy blushed and touched the four-month bump under her dusky-blue dress. Jerome kissed her cheek. Mary genuinely looked happy for her.

"And Oak, who got promoted to supervisor!"

Lily watched her brother with a critical eye this time. She remembered how hesitant Oak had been to take the job, and while he gave a smile worthy of an Oscar, Lily thought she saw a few spider's-thread cracks.

At last, Mary turned to the youngest of the bunch. Lily watched the girl on her right, who sat neat and straight and pretty, save for the clenched jaw making lumps in her cheeks.

Mary gestured towards the girl with her glass, and the smile seemed to stretch, like a prisoner on the rack. "And our dear...Mandragora...finally turned teenager. All grown up!"

Lily exhaled slowly. Mandragora's jaw loosened, and she nodded her thanks to the eldest.

Mary said, "Onward and upward. To the Harpers!"

The whole table called "To the Harpers!" with a loud clanking of glasses.

Lily gave Mandragora a significant look. *See? Mary can listen.*

Mandragora rolled her eyes and stuffed sweet potatoes into her pouty mouth.

After everybody helped clean up the table—except Daisy, by virtue of being pregnant—the family scattered to different parts of the open room. James, Asher, and Jerome took up spots in front of the TV to watch the football game, though they seemed to enjoy arguing about it more than watching it. Oak never got into sports, so gave the dog exercise outside with a frisbee. Godiva bedazzled Mandy with stories of her latest modeling shoot.

Lily joined Daisy and Mom at the dinner table where they'd spread out a puzzle of a farmstead in full, colorful glory.

Daisy quickly sat back in her seat and rubbed her stomach. "I can't lean forward as long as I used to. I'm only four months in!"

Mom said, "You just take care of yourself, we'll move it closer if you like." Mom beamed at the belly bump. "My first grandbaby!"

Lily said, "My first niece or nephew!"

Daisy smiled, but then it halted. Despite her complaints, she leaned forward again and lowered her voice. "It's still really weird to be the first one with a kid. Mary's been gracious, but I can tell it stings now and then."

Lily nodded with a deep frown. She'd lived with Mary for three years, and had...suspicions. They were close enough sisters for Lily to know—perhaps too well—that intimacy wasn't the problem, at least not back then. But that was where conversation always stopped. To ask what the problem was meant admitting a problem, something Mary would not do. Lily asked, "Mom, do you know anything about...that?"

Mom made a quick look-around for eavesdroppers, then said, "She won't say. Mary never does let us worry about her issues. But if you ask me, it's stress. That girl works a million hours a day, and then with Mandy...she doesn't rest."

Lily whispered, "Asher said the same thing."

"He and I have talked about it, too. The last time she took a vacation, she worked the whole time. Either tapping away on her laptop or organizing day trips or whatever else. And..."

This time, Mom made a more careful sweep of the surroundings, then leaned in very close. Lily and Daisy did the same, with Daisy holding her tummy. "This doesn't leave the table—Lily, do not tell Mandy! But I've heard Mary and James arguing."

Lily sucked in a breath. "How bad?"

"Well, that depends. It's not often, maybe once a day, if that. And they don't yell or anything. But they've never been like this before. They've always been so calm together, but lately, they just bicker, or they avoid each other." Mom's eyes fell to the half-finished barn. "And I just watch."

"Aw, Mom…" Lily took her mother's doughy hand. "It's not your job to fix things."

Mom replied in a timid voice, "Isn't it?"

"What?" Lily glanced at Daisy, who returned her concerned look.

Mom rubbed Lily's hand a minute, then asked, "How is Mandy? I mean, Mandragora? Mary's not the only one still adjusting to that."

"She's…okay. Content, I think." Lily scanned the room, and found Mandy gabbing with Godiva about beauty tips. "But every time I talk about her moving back in here, she clams up."

Daisy asked, "She's that mad?"

Mom answered, "They'd been at each other's throats for ages. Mandragora doesn't like Mary's ways, and Mary is used to getting her way."

Lily twirled a puzzle piece between her thumb and forefinger. "I need a deadline for this kid. I can't raise her forever."

"You shouldn't have to," Mom said in that same small, brittle voice from before. "Mandragora shouldn't have to choose which of her sisters raises her. It shouldn't be a sister at all. Oh, I'm sorry. Just seeing Daisy's baby bump has me thinking about motherhood. Don't be sorry, Daisy, it's not your fault. It is what it is. At least, that's what I usually say. But when I see my girls fighting and I know I can't stop them, when I see my youngest being raised by siblings, when I see my oldest suffering alone, I can't help but feel guilty. Mandragora should be fighting me, not Mary. Mary should be the fun sister, the one who lets her do all the things Mom won't. Mary shouldn't be so burdened with a child that's not hers that she can't have any of her own. I shouldn't have abdicated like that. I should have stepped up."

"Yeah, you should've," Daisy spat.

Mom and Lily both jumped.

Daisy's hand flew to her mouth. "I'm so sorry! I didn't mean that! I don't know why I said..." Daisy broke off, one hand on her chest, the other on her stomach, pale as a bedsheet.

Mom replied with a soft, sad smile. "It's okay, sweetie. I know."

Daisy didn't respond. She stared down at the puzzle, a tear slipping out the corner of her eyes.

Lily felt her back bending. Her vertebrae pushed against her shirt, desperately pulling her away from the table. Lily said, "I have to...check on Oak...been out there a while." She peeled herself from the chair and made for the back door. When she dared to look back at Mom and Daisy, they were holding hands, some wet, wordless voice passing between them.

Lily shivered as she left the house, and not from the weather. The air was brisk, but bright, the sun counterbalancing the cold into a comfortable coolness.

Lily brought the chill herself, and tried to shudder it away and focus on another relative.

Oak stood on the edge of the patio, just past the pool, with a high collar and a low glass of red wine. The dog had decided to keep the frisbee, and lounged across the grass. Oak gazed over the long, green lawn, and the winding path between the firs at the edge of the property. At least, that's what his body faced. When Lily drew near, Oak's eyes seemed much, much farther away.

"Hi," Lily said.

"Hey." Oak came to with a long breath, then offered Lily a smile. "What do you think Carla Ramirez will ask you about?"

"Uh, the book, but that's all I know. I have a phone meeting with my editor on Monday to talk about possible pitfalls. I've done interviews before, but not in front of so many people, and never live."

"I'm proud of you. Really."

Lily hugged Oak around the side. "Thanks. By the way, how many of those have you had?"

Oak pulled the wine glass from his mouth and considered it a while. "Take this from me."

"Yoink."

"Thank you."

"What's bugging you?"

Oak crossed his arms, and tapped one shoe that may have been a passive-aggressive stomp. "Mary bringing up my promotion. It's been months; I thought I'd have a better grasp on the job by now. I mean, I'm doing all right, but, I'm leading staff meetings and doing paperwork and, and…I had to fire someone last week, right before the holidays, and that sucked hard. It needed to happen, but I haven't been able to shake it off."

Lily rubbed Oak's back. "That's hard."

"I want to help people with their money, not have livelihoods in my hands."

"What made you decide to go for the promotion?"

Oak shrugged. "It's a good career move. Upward and onward." A zombie could not have been more monotone.

"So," Lily had to ask, "is it?"

Oak took ages to answer, so long that Lily thought he may be ignoring her. Yet finally, with his dull eyes still staring somewhere in the backyard, Oak spoke in a brittle tone, the same tone as Mom. "Look, Lil…if I tell you something, can you promise not to tell anybody?"

The chill returned, like frozen ants beneath Lily's skin. Mary always said, "Secrets are like termites; they'll eat our home alive from the inside." Then again, Lily had a whole house of things Mary didn't know. How could she have secrets and refuse Oak's?

"Sure…if you want."

Oak gave a longing glance at the wine glass in Lily's hand, then shoved his hands into his pockets. "Last Thursday, when I fired that guy, I talked to Freddy, the guy I mentioned before?"

"The guy you thought might be better at the job?"

Oak nodded. "We were having lunch in the break room, and I was just whining about it. I told him he would have been better for the job, and he said, 'Hey, we can still switch if you like.' He was joking—I mean, halfway joking—but I kept thinking about it. Yesterday, I asked my boss if Freddy and I could switch. Not saying we should, just asking if it was possible. She said yeah, if I want to."

"And do you want to?"

"We're Harpers. We don't look back," said the zombie voice.

Lily knew how to translate that: Mary would have a fit. A part of Lily, the burning, beastly part, said, *So what?* The other part said she'd be a hypocrite to say Oak should do something Lily could never do herself.

But the beast would not be quiet. So, it transformed from a soaring firebird to a slithering serpent, winnowing between the cracks of logic. "What if," Lily whispered, putting an arm around her brother's side, "you switched jobs, and then just…didn't tell Mary?"

Oak's side turned to stone beneath Lily's palm. He needed a moment to speak. "How long could I do that?"

That was an excellent question. Lily had only one answer. "I mean…I undid a lot of the interior decorating that Mary did to my house four months ago, and she hasn't discovered it yet."

The way Oak gasped, Lily was cheating on Mary with another family. But Oak didn't reprimand her. Didn't say anything, actually.

Lily added, more slowly, "And…that includes all the workout equipment you guys got for me. I'm sorry, I just don't use that kind of stuff. I can pay you back."

Oak replied, "Actually, I knew you wouldn't use it. You're more of an outdoor exerciser. Asher told Mary the same thing when we bought the treadmill, but you know Mary. 'Our sister deserves the best.'"

"Ah…" It was the only nice thing Lily could say.

"So don't worry about the money. I mean, we're the ones who let Mary have her way." Oak sighed, low, deep, and cold. "Why are we so scared of her?"

Scared? That was a barbed-wire word. Mary was not cruel; she was sweeter than sunshine. Then again, humans didn't just build shelters to protect them from storms. The sun could be just as fierce.

Lily tip-toed back inside, for fear of falling through one of the hollow gaps beneath her, the tunnels between the underworlds of the Harper family. Where Daisy hid her resentment. Where Mom hid her guilt. Where Oak hid his job. What did Asher hide in those caverns? What of Jerome and Godiva who married into this family? Were they forced to dig a ditch beneath their lives, bury everything of themselves, and cover it with dirt when Mary walked by? What of James?

She didn't ask. She didn't want to know how far these tunnels stretched.

Unfortunately, that only left one person with whom to speak: Mary herself. Lily wandered to the kitchen, where Mary set out the pies, a creamy-orange pumpkin, a sticky-brown pecan, and a flaky apple. James stood behind her by the kitchen island with a stack of bowls.

Lily quipped, "How'd you get James to leave the TV?"

Mary said, "Easy. I just asked him to help me with dessert."

James peeled the top off a massive tub of mint-chocolate-chip ice cream. "We all have our price."

Mary cut the pumpkin pie into pieces so even she could have been a machine. "Excited about going on *Carla*?"

Why did the simplest questions turn into *Sophie's Choice*? Lie, and keep the party going? Or tell the truth in however many fragments you can carry without cutting your fingers?

Secrets are like termites...okay, let's test that.

Lily answered, "Kind of?"

"Kind of?" Mary asked. "What's the matter? Nervous?"

"Well, yeah, but it's more than that."

Mary scooted the pumpkin pie aside and slid the pecan closer, fishing out a clean knife from the drawer. "C'mon, tell big sis."

James glanced at Lily, then the ice cream he was still supposed to help with.

Lily decided to say it anyway, while everybody else was just far enough from the kitchen that they couldn't eavesdrop. "I've been feeling funny lately. Guilty, if I'm honest. And every time I talk about that book, the knife just twists tighter, and speaking about it in front of a massive audience just makes my stomach feel like it's sitting in the electric chair."

Mary chuckled. "Electric chair? That's why you're the writer and I'm not. But why are you feeling guilty after all your hard work?"

Lily licked her lips. *Here goes nothing.* "Because it wasn't just my hard work. Curtis helped me, too."

"Do you feel bad about breaking up with him right after?"

James turned at the waist, an ice cream scoop in his hand. "I never said they broke up. I said there was an argument."

Mary ignored him, and regarded Lily with a knowing

337

raise of the eyebrow.

Lily played with her thumbs. "It was pretty much a breakup. A breakup of a four-minute relationship."

"I had a feeling."

"How come you never asked?"

"I figured you'd tell me in your own time."

Mary's words soaked into her, like butter into warm bread. And seeing Mary serve up dessert after serving up dinner and making her whole house presentable for so many people, Lily remembered the days when it was safe to tell Mary anything.

"It wasn't just a little help here and there. Curtis was with me from start to finish. I mean, if he was instrumental to the whole story—and he seriously was— is it...right...for mine to be the only name on the cover? Should he be there, too?" Lily stood on her tip-toes, the butterflies in her stomach nearly achieving liftoff.

Mary had stopped cutting the pie, watching Lily with a vapid, dizzy look. Lily thought she saw dots connecting in those irises, piecing together the date of the book launch, and the date of this conversation. James just stared with a curious frown.

Finally, Mary picked up her smallest smile. "Did...he...come up with the story?"

"No," Lily's mouth snapped out the word. "No, the story was mine, right from the start."

Mary's smile bounced up to normal size. "Oh! So, he just helped you tell it right?"

"Uh...yes, but that's a huge part of writing, too. Is it fair that I'm getting all the credit?"

Mary looked back down at pecan pie, slicing a long,

clean line between halves. "Are you feeling guilty because you promised him credit and didn't give it to him?"

Just like Mr. Gates. "No, I only promised half my advance."

"Yikes! That's a good payment for, what, a month of work?"

Lily's heels slowly found the floor again. "And that's enough?"

Mary pulled the last pie closer. "Sweetie, you gave him what you promised. If it bugs you that badly, support his books. Help him write one, too, then promote the Dickens out of him. Return the favor, then you'll be even, right?"

That did make a funny kind of sense. Why share her own book when she could help Curtis with his? Get him his own platform, his own fame. There was room enough for both of them! But would Curtis want her help? Maybe, if she could word it right. It wouldn't be easy of course, but she could try, try just as hard as she had with own book. Lily thought she may have found a solution at last.

Then, James said, "That was foul, Lily."

"James!" Mary gasped, whirling around and slicing a wonky angle through the apple pie.

Lily blinked at her brother-in-law, too stupefied to be hurt.

James glanced at his wife, then turned his eyes to Lily. They burned like the sun. "He gave you what you couldn't get on your own, but you're the only one who gets to be on *Carla?*"

"James!" Mary hissed his name through all her bared teeth, her patented smiles and softness stretched tight across the bone.

"Oh, what?" James rounded on her with a quiet nonchalance. "We disagree on things. It's allowed." James snatched up a bowl of ice cream and left the kitchen at once.

Lily's mouth hung wide open, but only a wisp of breath came in.

Mary stood with her back against the kitchen island, one hand grasping the edge. She seemed paralyzed, jaw locked in staggered horror. She looked like a woman who'd walked into her house, and found the windows smashed in, the furniture flipped, and every drawer hanging open. One hand squeezed the knife. The other leapt up to her hair, without Mary seeming to even notice. She grabbed a knot of her own hair, at the base of her skull, grasped it into a ponytail shape, and just squeezed.

Just then, Mandragora's voice cried from the living room, "Whoa, hey! Is that ice cream?"

Mary dropped her hair, and whirled back around to face the curious eyes of her family. "And pie! Sorry about this one, my hand slipped."

Oak made a joke about how food is food no matter the shape, and the family laughed, a canned track suitable only for a dried-up sitcom. Even the dog barked on cue. Lily ducked through the other side of the kitchen while the family converged on the dessert. She dashed into a bathroom and stayed there for twenty minutes, already making up excuses about a bad stomachache, some flu going around.

An ironic lie, considering it was the truth that made her vomit into Mary's sparkling toilet.

*
**

Everyone bought Lily's illness story, of course. She'd told so many just like it over the years. "Oh, it's nothing." "I'm fine." "This discomfort you see is absolutely unrelated to anything happening right in front of your eyes."

Thanksgiving was perfect. So many smiles, a great big photo of the entire clan, sweet goodbyes as the sun began to set. Indeed, another red-letter year for the Harper family. Not a complaint from anyone that could be heard through the layers of dirt.

"Ignore James," Mary whispered as she hugged Lily goodbye. "He's just upset about something else."

"Like what?" Lily asked.

"Oh, don't worry about that. We'll figure it out; we're fine."

Half of Lily wanted to squeeze her sister's hand and tell her she didn't have to go through anything alone. The other half wanted to dig her nails into Mary's cheek and just rip. Neither side won, of course. Lily just smiled. As always. As expected.

Mandragora slid into the passenger seat of Lily's car and said, "That wasn't so bad. At least Mary used my real name."

Lily tried to cling to that. Mary extending the snapped-off twig of an olive branch. Progress. Good. But she kept thinking of all those tunnels snaking under their lives, hollowing the earth until there would be nothing left to stand on. What would happen when they all fell through?

"Can you believe her at the end, though?" Mandragora scoffed. "Family photo time! Like we did on Halloween. And in the fall. And summer. Nothing's changed, Mary, just look

341

at the old photos. At least then I wasn't fat on pie. She always has to look our best."

Steam hissed from Lily's nostrils. Something hot and smoky was snorting in her brain. At Mandragora. At Mary. At herself.

Lily came to the highway and flipped on her right blinker, waiting for a chance to turn. She looked to her sister, gazing out the window, daydreaming about something or nothing. The beast in Lily's mind snarled ash. The blinker went *click-click-click*, ticking down the time bomb. What was about to come out of her mouth? The volcanic burst that had burned Curtis? Or the craftsman's flame that shaped him?

The last car whooshed by. Lily switched her blinker to the left, and took her opening.

Mandragora popped out of her daydream. "Where are we going?"

Lily said, "Do you want to know who your dad was?"

Mandragora recoiled against the door. "Do...what?"

"You want to know what happened back then? You want to know why we all suck up to Mary? Why we let her decorate our lives with a smile?"

Mandragora gaped, eyes wide with confusion, and a dash of terror. "Yes?"

Lily nodded. "So do I. We're going home."

Chapter 29

Lily had forgotten how short the drive was. Mary always spoke of the past as if it were on the other side of the country. Lily made it in twenty minutes. The little town of Bellevue stretched across the highway, then promptly went back to sleep. It had been a Wild West town at the end of the Wild West, so it was born old. The white paint on a brick building had chipped so badly you could barely make out the auto-parts logo from 1979.

"Mary doesn't like coming back here," Lily mused.

Mandragora said, "Yeah, too many poor people to scuff her boots."

"Stop it." Lily turned off the highway. "Mary knows firsthand what it means to be impoverished, and she's not ashamed of the poor. It's just that these streets hold a lot of bad memories for her."

"Why?"

"You'll see in a minute."

One minute exactly, it turned out. Just a few blocks from the main road, really. Lily breathed through her mouth as she turned onto the old street. Westwood. It wasn't too bad a neighborhood, really. Great big trees everywhere for plenty of shade, even if they hadn't been pruned in a while. A few cracks in the sidewalks, but nothing dangerous. The potholes had the dark patches of recent fillings, so that was nice.

But then...oh, how Lily's fingers curled around the

wheel, how her muscles squeezed each other for comfort, how her very bones bent in on themselves. The house. It was so much worse than she remembered.

The weathered paper on the front door was too far to read, but Lily bet it said "CONDEMNED." The body almost looked okay. The siding was still straight, and the eggshell paint, while yellowing, had not flaked too badly. But that roof was so frayed and warped that it almost looked furry. The wood of the porch had bent inward, and Lily thought she saw a few missing planks behind the battered, rotten railings. All the grass had been gobbled up by weeds as tall as the porch, save for the bald patches of dirt splotched across the front yard. Tangles of sage swallowed what had once been a driveway. Even the curb had a weathered, brown-gray malaise about it.

Lily parked in front of the woebegone curb, facing the wrong direction. She doubted anyone would care; clearly no one had for many years. She tried to imagine would could have happened in a scant nine or ten years, but she didn't want to think what black growth might be eating away at the inside of the house.

Mandragora leaned past Lily to take in the ugly hag of a house. "Wow. Okay, sure, it's nasty now, but I bet it wasn't that bad when we lived there."

"You're right," Lily said. "But it only has two bedrooms and one bathroom. And seven people."

The girl's eyes bulged all over again, and she gave the house another look. Spruce up the paint, wake up the grass, and change out the wood, the house was still only a thousand square feet. Maybe. "All of us?"

"Not at first," Lily admitted. "Mom bought the house

with a guy straight out of high school. You could do that back then. Sort of. He didn't want to get married, and she said that was okay. The house was already old, so it was cheap, but they made it work. But then Mom had Mary—well, Rosemary back then. Or Rosie. Either way, the guy decided this wasn't in his future, so he up and left.

"Mom was torn up, of course. One day, while a friend was babysitting Rosie, Mom went out and got both drunk and pregnant. We still have no idea who Asher's dad is."

Mandragora wrinkled her nose. "Really?"

"Really."

"How'd Mom pay for two kids?"

"A work-from-home job, some nice neighbors, and a whole lot of luck. Grandma and Grandpa were alive back then, too, but Mom wanted to hang on to the house. Besides, Mom met my dad after Asher. His name was Zack, and of all the dads, he stuck around the most. He got Mom pregnant fast, but he decided to step up. He made good money, something in accounting, I think. I guess one day, when I was three years old, Zack wondered why a man of his standing should slum it out in a tiny house with three kids, two of which weren't his own. So, he left Mom some money and vanished."

Lily wondered if this was how war veterans felt. You take a shot in the arm or the leg, and it's the most blindingly painful moment of your existence. Then, you do the hard work of healing and you can finally get around all right. One day, you put too much weight on it, and it explodes through you like it never healed at all.

"Why do you want to know all this?" Lily asked, her forehead in her fist. "Do you think you'd be better off having these memories? To remember being abandoned like an outdated magazine?"

Mandragora had to think about that one. At least she'd learned some sensitivity. "I don't know about that. But I do know that our whole family revolves around all this. We don't talk about it, but it touched everybody. I feel like it's defined my life and I don't even know what it was."

Lily nodded into her fist. She was right. This was why they were here. Lily decided to skip the days and months of toddler tears, and how nine-year-old Rosie, not Mom, had been her biggest comforter.

"Mom kept falling into this cycle of getting over-whelmed by everything and leaning on a guy to solve her problems, then giving him everything he wanted, and ending up with one kid and zero dads. Daisy's dad was an airline pilot on leave, and Mom was still pretty. Poof, there was Daisy. Poof, there went Mr. Airplane."

Mandragora said, "Hold on, Daisy's dad was a pilot? And she married a pilot?"

Lily smirked. "Yeah, that caused a few heart attacks. But Daisy was smart, and waited to see if he'd really stick around. Obviously, he did. Mom wasn't so bright." Lily bit her lip. How to tell this story without bad-mouthing their own mother? Maybe she couldn't. Maybe that was the point.

She tried anyway. "Oak's dad was a sleazy conman. He made nice to every one of us, and for a while, we all loved him and fell for it. Turns out, he was just trying to get government money for all us kids. Plus the one he had with Mom so he would have a legal reason to cash the check."

"Did Mom see through him?"

"No. She just smothered him, so he dropped Oak shortly after he was born. After that, Mom finally seemed to have realized that men were not the answer. Of course, it was too late by then. Five kids, one Mom, limited income, and worn-out allies. We were on our own."

Mandragora asked, "What about, like, child support?"

Lily sighed. "Maybe if Mom had pursued them. Or if she knew where half of them were. We all just learned how to rely on each other and do without. Peanut butter and white bread became our daily protein. Canned peas, spaghetti with no sauce, boxed mac and cheese, and not much else. We were well known at the grocery store. The poor children of the town slut. Eventually, we'd go to the store without Mom because she couldn't take the shame. We'd walk down with our backpacks and stock up on the same five things we did last week, and the cashier would give us all the look that said, 'Oh, still poor, are you?'"

Lily kicked open the car door. "Come on."

Mandragora followed Lily into the thick jungle of sage. Lily had no machete, so she stomped, kicked, and shoved, heedless of the scratches on her hands, or the tears on her nice Thanksgiving dress. Lily brought Mandragora to the back-corner window, and peered inside.

Gutted. No carpet anymore. Copper wires ripped from the walls. Wooden floors scuffed and dusty. A cemetery for dead bugs filled the window sill.

"Take a look," Lily said. "That was our bedroom. Three girls stuffed into that tiny room. No closet, just a great big chest of drawers for all of us. Yeah, try being fashionable when you only have two or three of anything. I remember

Rosie started wearing thong underwear because it fit in the drawer better. And if you wanted personal space, you sat in your bunk bed." Lily shuddered. "God, that room smelled so bad in the summer. No…it smelled bad any season."

Mandragora stared into that room for a long, long time, her mouth turning in disgust. "How did it all get better?"

Lily barked out a bitter laugh. "Better? It got worse! I mean for a minute, yes, things improved. Rosie worked her ass off and paid her way through college. She went to community college by day and worked as a waitress by night. She was pretty and personable, so she got a lot of tips. She was also brilliant, and scoured the world for a handful of scholarships that added up to just enough to go to a real college. She'd made friends with a gal who had parents in Boise, so Rosie stayed in their guest room and continued waitressing to pay rent. That opened up room for us in there." Lily tapped the glass.

"But then, the last year Rosie was in school, Mom did it again."

Mandragora tensed, knowing who was next.

Lily crossed her arms, thinking of all the things Mary would say to stop her. Lily brushed them off. They were this far in; may as well go all the way. "His name was Tom. Tom Yarhouse. He didn't come by too often because, well, five kids. And we didn't all like him. By that point, most of us knew what happened when Mom met a fancy man.

"One day, Tom came over. Mom sent the younger kids to the park. It was early fall, so we had the windows open. It actually felt really good. Asher and I had stayed behind. I was cutting up some carrots for dinner, and suddenly, we heard a lot of shouting from the bedroom. Mom had told Tom that she was pregnant. First, he accused her of cheating on him. Then, he accused her of using the baby to rope him into paying for her whole family of…rats or brats, I don't remember."

Lily checked on Mandragora. The girl had paled, but stood firm.

She barreled ahead. "He threw Mom against the wall. Asher and I told him to get the hell out and never come back. He listened."

"He did?" Mandragora breathed, face a mask of shock.

"Asher was always tall, and he played a lot of football back then, so he was pretty scary when he was mad. I wasn't, but I still had the kitchen knife, so that sent a message." Lily uncurled her fist, dropping the imaginary knife, and put her hands on Mandragora's shoulders. "Are you okay?"

Mandragora nodded slowly, like a machine with a loose spring. "So my dad was a prick?"

"You see why we didn't want to tell you?"

Mandragora stared at the wall for a while, then said, "No."

"No?"

"My big sister and my big brother are heroes who probably saved my life and I'm just not supposed to know that?"

Lily had to take a moment to breathe that in. Thirteen years, and she'd never been called a hero. Never been called anything. They'd buried the whole story under shame and regret.

Mandragora stomped a sage bush. "Argh! That's why this ticks me off! Who is Mary to decide that I just shouldn't know these things? That I should just accept my family as God, but never tell me why?"

Lily said, "Actually, that one was Mom."

"Mom?"

"Mom asked me and Asher not to tell anyone about what Tom did. I think she was too humiliated to admit she'd roped one more bad guy. We made up a story that he took off. Everyone could believe that. But Mom was pregnant again. She asked us not to tell Mary—Rosie— for as long as we could. She was finishing up her schooling.

Lily disentangled herself from the sage bushes, and stood in a dirty patch in front of a window closer to the curb. She had to squint to see through the dust and the fading light. The living room inside was as barren and stripped as the last room. The kitchen was simply gone. All the cabinets and fixtures torn out, leaving nothing but outlets and a few pipes sticking out of the drywall.

Lily drew in a long, dusty breath. "I can still see it plain as day. I was sixteen. Mom was four months pregnant, like Daisy is now. We were all setting up the little, plastic Christmas tree for when Rosie got home. But suddenly, there she was, busting through the door with a smile as big as Texas. She'd finished early, then bummed a ride home to surprise us all. For one second, there was a big, blissful gasp that sister was home and we'd all have Christmas together. And then, Rosie saw Mom's baby bump. And everything just got quiet."

Mandragora seemed to look at the window, not

through it. Her mouth hung open, just a hair, but enough to tell Lily that the girl was putting the pieces together. Lily didn't want her to feel guilty for being born, but Lily thought she'd let the girl feel bad a little longer, for no other reason than to let her in on the family's pain.

Lily peered through the window again, reconstructing the scene. "Rosie got this look on her face that took me years to figure out. It wasn't anger, wasn't sadness, wasn't even fear, not really. Maybe a little at first. She knew, like we did, what this meant. But something else came over her a minute later. I think she looked at Mom, looked at us, looked at the house, and finally put the pieces together in a new way: Mom could not take care of her own children. She was overwhelmed, and ran to men to save her, and they never did. Rosie was the oldest. Rosie had a degree now. And Rosie had already proven her ability to rise above. She knew she had to be the one to save us.

"So, she put her arms around each of us, and she said, 'It'll be all right. We'll all make it through together. I promise.' Then, she went over to Mom, took her hand, and said, 'Don't worry, Mom. I'll take care of everything.'" Lily made sure to face Mandragora again. "And then, she put a hand on Mom's belly. Rosie said, 'Don't you worry, little one. This will all be over before you know it.'"

Mandragora crossed her arms. The scowl came easily, but Lily swore she saw something wet in her grump. "Yeah, okay, so she did it for me. So that I'd never know hardship, I heard that part."

"She did it for all of us," Lily corrected.

"Well, what did she even do?"

Lily rested a shoulder on the old house as she thought.

"Mostly, Rosie organized us into a family unit. Everybody contributed. Mom got a better job outside the home to make more money. Asher went to community college and also worked part time at a bank. Daisy and Oak went to public school, but also helped with laundry, yard work, all that good stuff. And, of course, Daisy became amazing at cooking. I was Babysitter in Chief. I started homeschooling because I could be done quick and still keep an eye on everybody. When Mom had to go on maternity leave, I got a part-time job at the grocery store, and she took over babysitting. But really, you were the only one to look out for. Oak was eleven when you were born, so we were a pretty responsible bunch."

Mandragora said, "But what about Mary? You haven't told me what she did."

Lily replied, "Everything else. She kicked off her interior design business right then and there, but it was slow going, so she also worked at this clothing store, which gave her ideas for the furniture shop later." Lily frowned with thought. "Actually, I think all of that wove together. Rosie worked and directed, but really, her big job seemed to be uplifting all of us. She sat down with Asher and grilled him on what he wanted to do with his life, then helped him get there. Before I even finished high school, Rosie did the same thing to me. Didn't work as well, but it's not her fault. She helped us to plan ahead and find the best life that suited us.

"But it went beyond that. Remember how I said our room smelled horrible? Well, add a baby in there. For a while, we just got used to it, but Rosie thought that wasn't good enough. She bought a scented candle and lit it every night. You would not believe how much that little candle changed things. We all went to sleep so much easier. Actually, no! We stayed up talking to each other, just laughing about stupid things or planning ahead. I remember we'd put you in the crib, but then you'd pull yourself back up and start babbling to us. Like you were trying to join the conversation. It was adorable. All because Rosie bought a scented candle. She knew how to rearrange our lives and make them better."

Suddenly, a pit opened in Lily's stomach, and the candle in her mind snuffed in a wisp of smoke. "I caught her crying one night. Rosie, I mean."

"Why?" Mandragora asked.

"She wouldn't tell me. She just wiped her eyes and said, 'Oh, don't worry about me, I'm fine.' I think it all just got to her. She was in her twenties, but she was the matriarch of our whole family. She worked so hard, trying to start one business, then another, just to get us out of poverty. Every cent she made was for the family as a whole. Not just her, of course; we all put our resources into a pool that paid for what we needed. Then again, we all had Rosie to lean on. Rosie didn't have anybody."

Lily rubbed her suddenly-cold arms. True, Rosie had the best chance in life, and true, she was the oldest, but Lily had been seventeen that night. Surely that was old enough to be a shoulder to cry on once in a while. Or Asher. Or Mom. Somebody? *What about James? Does she cry on his shoulder?*

Mandragora kicked loose a dirt clod. "So, what happened? How'd things change?"

Lily answered, "Slowly. We were still poor. A bag of chips was a Sunday dinner. But Rosie was brilliant. She knew that poverty was more than money; it's a mindset. She found simple ways to rearrange life so it didn't seem so bad. Like the scented candle. Or she bought us all a cheap pack of clean, hole-free tee shirts. We did laundry constantly, but we finally had good clothes. I mean, we looked like a sports team because we all matched, but still. Later, Rosie made sure we all had one nice outfit. We could take it to church, to dates, whatever. They probably cost ten dollars at the thrift store, but we felt like a million bucks."

Mandragora gave a nasty little smile. "Ooh, Lady Mary shopped at the poor people store."

"Yes," Lily said in a waspish tone. "Because she had to. It wasn't a choice she made out of many; it was the only option she had. If Rosie wanted a new pair of jeans, she crossed her fingers and hoped she found her size. Thrift stores and yard sales weren't some fun way to save a few bucks; they were an absolute necessity, and a constant reminder that she could not give her family what they needed, only what was available."

That shut the girl up. Mandragora went back to digging up dirt clods with her toes.

Lily sighed and ran her fingers through her hair. "We still suffered. We were hungry. We had no air conditioning. And do you think any of us even dreamed of a thirteenth birthday as massive as yours? We still had to scrape quarters off the sidewalk because we wanted a new home. Rosie made our lives better with little designing touches. Paint for the house. Hair ribbons. A couch with a hide-a-bed so Asher and Oak could sleep in the living room and Mom could take the other bedroom with you, clearing up more room for the rest of us girls. It was window dressing, but it made us all feel like we could get out of our circumstances.

"Eventually, it started to happen. About two years into it all, Rosie hit her stride. She had enough money to invest in an old, outdated furniture store, so she took it over. Asher wanted to go into business management, so she put him in charge while he finished his degree online. Mom ran all the secretarial things. Rosie sold, while still doing her interior design gigs. I don't know how many hours she worked, but I do know that's around the time she started calling herself Mary instead of Rosemary." The memory made Lily's shoulders sag.

"The store was a hit, so we put away more money for the house. I went to college and worked, and shared babysitting duties with Daisy. But most importantly, Mary met James. She avoided him at first because she needed too much time with her family. The rest of us pushed her into him though because we felt she needed some fun. Eventually, he agreed to be part of the family, and all that it meant. James was hitting his stride as a doctor, and we'd saved up quite a bit, plus we all worked. Together, we were able to afford that big, beautiful house you live in now."

Lily closed her eyes, reliving that first cold breeze of air conditioning. "I can't tell you what that was like. It was...life-affirming. Completely rejuvenating. I felt like a zombie who'd come back to the living. We had multiple rooms. Multiple bathrooms. We could breathe for the first time instead of sharing oxygen. And it only got better. The store grew, Mary's business grew, James kept going up. Eventually, Asher could support himself and his new wife. Then Daisy got married and moved out. Oak found his own apartment. And now I have my house. And you had a bigger thirteenth birthday party than all of our birthdays combined."

Lily stopped to breathe, dizzy with recollection. Being here again, the bare dirt on her shoes, legs still itchy from the sage, beside a blackened, moldy window, Lily wanted to take a shower, to wash this place off of her. No wonder Mary refused to look back.

Mandragora stepped up to the window and looked inside once more. "I remember a little. I remember playing under a blanket with you and Daisy. Or hide-and-seek with Oak. He had a dramatic side, and I thought it was hilarious. I don't remember...the rest."

"Mission accomplished, then," Lily said.

Mandragora shook her head. "But here's the part I don't get: we're not there anymore. So why does Mary still act like we are? We're not in poverty, in fact Mary and James are friggin' rich! So why do we have to keep climbing the ladder and acting like some top-tier, bourgeois white family that's above everything? I don't need all that. I know my house is awesome, I know I've got it good, so stop telling me that I need to keep pushing higher, and acting like who I am isn't good enough for your stupid paranoid dreams!"

She drove her fist straight into the window. It didn't even crack. Mandragora bounced backward, spun in a circle, then held her wrist, eyes bulging wide. "Ow. Ow. Why did I do that?"

Lily examined the girl's hand with a sigh, deciding not to voice a metaphor about lashing out. No cuts, no bruises, just an owie. Yet Lily kept looking the girl's hand over, giving her brain time to digest Mandragora's cries. "You should say all that to Mary."

Mandragora yanked her hand back. "She wouldn't listen. Besides, it doesn't answer my question. Why does Mary act like we're still climbing out of a hole?"

"I don't know. Maybe she can't see that we're okay now." Lily's gaze listed to the dry fragments of grass. "Maybe *we* can't see it. Maybe we're scared to step out of Mary's net, that we don't think we can really do this. That we're not enough without her. Mary rescued us, so maybe we're afraid we'll crash and burn if we go it alone."

Is that true? Do I not think I have what it takes? Well, I didn't, did I? I needed Curtis. But that's Curtis, not Mary. Then, another thought hit her. *Did I drop Curtis because I wanted to prove I could go it alone? But do I really want to be alone?*

"But we're not alone," Mandragora said.

Lily pulled herself out of her thoughts and looked at her sister. "What's that?"

"You said that if we don't have Mary protecting us, then we're alone. I think that's stupid. Just because she's not Mom doesn't mean she can't be there. And there's freaking seven of us. Ten, if you count in-laws. I mean, we're…" Mandragora had to gather her thoughts a minute, a minute she spent staring into the disemboweled old house.

At last, she spoke, her back straight and face steady. "We're Harpers. We don't do 'alone.' We've already proven that we can stick together through anything. But we're Harpers, not Marys. Mary needs to become one of us again."

Lily had to take a step backwards. *Mary needs to become one of us again.* That was exactly it. Mary had taken the

Harper family out of the depths, but somewhere along the way, she painted them in her own tribal colors. Why? Because she was just as much of a victim as the rest of them. Mary had been frightened, and now she laid out her own little world where she'd never have to go back to that awful place where her youth had been stolen. And she'd brought her family with them because she never, ever wanted to lose them.

But they weren't Marys. They were Harpers. She couldn't hold on to them like this. How to make her see that?

Lily said, "You're pretty bright for a teenager."

"Yeah."

Lily gave the old house one more look. What a sad, sorry thing, fading to black in the encroaching dusk. Maybe somebody would save it. Maybe they'd knock it down and start over. Either way, it wasn't her problem. "C'mon, let's go home."

"Definitely. This place is creepy." They crunched through the sage and dry grass. Suddenly, Mandragora grabbed Lily's hand. "Thanks. For everything."

Lily squeezed back. "Don't mention it. Er, I mean, you're welcome." Lily exhaled, long and slow. All the dirt and must and mold she'd breathed in fled from her nostrils. When she breathed again, the November air was crisp and clean.

Mom waited for them on the porch when they returned home. The sun was fading fast, a waning yellow yolk breaking over sea of darkening blue, and Mom had wrapped herself tight in her jacket. Lily and Mandragora shared a curious look as they parked in the garage. They walked around the house, rather than through it, to meet Mom on the porch.

"What's up?" Mandragora asked.

Mom stood up with a friendly smile, but also an odd look in her eyes. A kind of darkness, not gloomy, just dusky as the sky around them. "First of all, we had extra pie." She handed Lily a Tupperware container, which Lily snatched right up.

Then, Mom turned that dusky look to her youngest daughter. "Mandragora, it's time for you to come home."

Mandragora's face instantly melted into a wax mold of disgust. "Why? So I can take orders from Mary again?"

"No," Mom said, "so you can take orders from me."

Mandragora looked to Lily for answers, but Lily was just as baffled.

"And my first order," Mom said, "is to go inside and pack up all your things. Lily has sheltered you long enough; it's time to give her some space. Mary has plenty of it, so you can I can be very comfortable without disturbing her."

Lily's breath caught in her throat.

Mandragora blinked. "Wait. Are you...?"

Mom nodded towards the house. "Go on, young lady. Pack up."

The girl blinked again then muttered something like "Yes, ma'am," and made for the front door.

Lily would've followed, but her feet had glued themselves to the porch. "Mom?"

"Yes, that's me," the matron said. "And it's high time I acted like it."

Lily's brain swam. Mom as a mom. What did that even look like? "Do you want to come in?"

"No, thank you. I like the cold, and it's a nice night. The air smells clean out here."

"Doesn't it?" They remained on the porch as they waited for Mandragora, breathing in the dewy mountain air, watching the old day fade away.

Chapter 30

The only good thing about flying to California was that Lily's publisher paid for it. Dashing to the gate only to be told to sit and wait? Choking on dry cookies in turbulence? Sitting in a cab that smelled like last night's beer vomit, with nothing to drown out the noise of the political AM radio except the endless cacophony of honking horns? Lily wished she could do this over the internet, with a cup of coffee on her right, and the sun-kissed mountains in front of her.

At least the hotel was nice. A king-sized bed and a hot tub almost made up for the journey.

Lily barely had time to think in the five days since Thanksgiving. Having her house to herself again had been fun, but since that day, everything had been a series of checks. Check the email from *The Carla Ramirez Show* to make sure she knew what to do. Check her social media to ensure the information was correct. Check her outfits to see if she had anything suitable. Check the store to see if *they* had anything suitable. Check her bank account to see if suitable was something she could really afford.

Check the car, check the departure time, check her luggage, check into the hotel, check her itinerary for tomorrow, check that she had everything she needed, check the maximum recommended dosage of melatonin so she could sleep through the nerves.

The day of the show, Lily was only interested in checking

her phone. She had called Mr. Gates several times, to the point where his secretary not-so-kindly told her not to call again. He would contact her when he was ready.

But what if he was too late? Lily had a plan to make everything better, but it hinged on Mr. Gates picking up his darn phone *before* the show!

Every social media beep, every buzzing text of "Good luck!" from family shot a jolt of lightning up her spine like the carnival game with the hammer. *Ding!* It never came back down. It just stayed there, so when the next jolt shot through it, it joined its comrades and they all had a buzzing, nerve-tingling party in her brain.

Clothes on. Hair groomed. Taxi ready. No call.

Another honking ride in inch-an-hour traffic. No call.

"Gates, you better have been fired," Lily snarled. What if he didn't call? She couldn't do it on her own!

She forgot Mr. Gates for a little while in the flurry and hurry of the production crew. From almost the instant she entered the deceptively-plain studio building, Lily found herself ushered through a hundred hallways by a hundred red-eyed crew members sweating through their black turtlenecks. *Here's where you go, but not now. Here's where you go after the time that is not now. Here's where you don't go ever, we just wanted to show you anyway for some reason. Here's a hand to shake. No, not his hand, he's too important. Here's a glass of water, now here's the clock, oh look, you're late.*

Lily finally sat and caught her breath in the makeup room. The glaring lights around the mirror made her looked washed out, but the makeup girl swept in with all the tricks and tools to make a woman visible through her own pallor.

Still no call.

Lily set her phone on the makeup table and took the chance to breathe. The hairstylist, a redhead with a face so youthful she could blend in at a junior high, worked Lily's dark hair into a splendid sheen, tumbling in thick waves down her left shoulder.

"Very nice," Lily said.

"Thank you," the girl said. "I loved your book by the way."

"Oh, that's sweet."

"I haven't read the others, but everyone tells me it's your best."

"Yeah..." Lily sighed.

A call rang.

A call! Lily snatched it with a gasp. "Excuse me, sorry, this is super important." Lily disentangled herself from the chair and found a quiet corner, away from the chatting turtlenecks and the whiny pop diva in another chair. "Hello?"

"Hello, big star in t-minus-however-many minutes!"

"Yeah, hi, I—"

"How's California?"

"Way too hot to put me in a Christmas mood. Listen, um, there's a bit of a problem."

"Problem?" His voice finally assumed a serious tone. "Something wrong at the studio?"

"No, that's all fine, it's just something about the book that's bugging me."

"Go on."

Okay. Now or never. Lily took a breath. Nothing happened. She tried again and got a squeaking puff in her lungs. It would have to do. "Remember back when I said that somebody helped me write the book, but you said that we should just keep my name on it? I...think we made the wrong choice."

The silence on the other line gave Lily plenty of time to hear what she'd just said out loud for the first time. Why, exactly, was this supposed to convince her editor to make a massive change?

At length, Mr. Gates replied, "Ah, it's a bit late for that, don't you think?"

"Maybe, but maybe there could be a reprint or a...second edition?" Lily cringed at her own request.

"A second edition less than a month after the first? Miss Harper, I think the nerves are getting to you."

It was just condescending enough to ignite the beast in her brain. "Mr. Gates, I don't think it's fair that Curtis should sit out while I bask in the glory."

"Miss Harper, what exactly are you wanting?"

"I want his name on the cover, too." *It took me months to admit that. Don't take it from me.*

Another pause. "Look, Miss Harper—Lily—I'll say it again: it's too late for that. The book is printed and published. *Escape from Christmas*, a novel by Lily Harper. Only Lily Harper. That's what's in stores, that's what's on Amazon, and that's exactly what Carla Ramirez is about to hold between her enormous, fake fingernails."

"I know, but—"

"So, what do you think it looks like if you suddenly start saying there's another author involved, huh? What do you think people will say?"

Lily froze. "I…"

"Yeah, it's as bad as you're imagining."

"But…maybe if I make a good statement, everybody will think it's noble or—"

Mr. Gates laughed through his nose. "Noble? Lily, what do you think the internet loves more? Honesty or a scandal? Your career is about to launch into space; don't shoot it down with a hasty decision."

Her lip quivered. "I get that, but—"

"Miss Harper, the answer is no. I'm not risking my career or the integrity of this publishing company to satisfy your conscience. Just go out there, smile for the camera, and enjoy the big times, okay?"

Lily's mouth kept moving, but her tongue had gone completely dry.

"Okay?" he repeated.

"O…kay…" She crumpled into herself, leaning her forehead on the wall.

"No more crazy ideas?"

"No…"

"Great! I'll be watching you from my office. Have fun!" The line went dead.

Lily pulled her phone from her ear and stared at it. So that was it? All that moral wrestling and Mr. Gates shot it down from the other side of the country? He says no, and that's that?

Well…whose fault is that?

Lily sulked back into the makeup chair. The cherub-faced hairdresser had to start over; Lily didn't realize she'd played with the ends of her hair through that entire call. Lily worried they would sizzle, her face burned so hot.

Another buzz shook her phone. A text from Mary. Good

365

luck! We're all watching you!

"Yeah, I bet you are," Lily scoffed. Watching to make sure she put on a good image and told a nice, sweet story. So many people had a hand in her words. Why did they get to decide what she said?

The question swirled through Lily's mind through the rest of her makeover. It swirled as she walked through more hallways to the green room. It swirled as she sank her fingers into the armrests of her leather chair, with seconds left until her call.

Why did they get to decide?

Why did they get to...?

...did they get to...?

Lily had imagined the words since book one. She'd even responded to them in her head on numerous occasions. Once or twice, when no one was looking, Lily would speak them into a stirring spoon, just to make the daydream more real.

But they sounded so much better from Carla Ramirez's voice: "Please welcome our next guest, Lily Harper!"

Whoa, those lights! Watching from behind the curtain did not prepare Lily for the silent *whoom* of sunburn-inducing floodlights. Everything beyond them was a fuzzy, black-and-yellow haze, but Lily could hear the chattering applause very, very well. *Also* better than the daydream. Assuming, of course, that *this* wasn't the daydream, with that constant floaty feeling in every limb and organ.

Whether walking or floating, Lily crossed the immaculate white carpet, and there she was, Carla Ramirez herself, dominant yet gentle in her midnight blazer and floral blouse. Her ruby lips smiled beneath the swoop of her strong cheekbones. Her deep brown hair glowed bronze in the halo of stage lighting. Carla shook Lily's hand in both of hers, every finger topped with a long, crimson nail. Strong grip, soft palms. Lily would never wash her hand again.

Carla motioned for her to sit, and Lily did. For some reason, she'd expected the tan, low-back couch to be hard. Nope. Soft enough to sleep in. Carla sat in her own chair, one leg crossed, shoulders squared, hands clasped, the benevolent queen.

And of course, the book, poised and upright on the circular table between the seats. Its adorable blues and yellows popped against the sandy table and pale couch. Lily swiveled her head to absorb every detail from the other side of the screen. A bit less magical, to be sure, with all the metalwork above, the cameras staring blankly at her, and the dull glow of the exit signs between audience bleachers.

As she took it all in, breathing in the reality she'd only dared to dream, Lily's eyes fell on the empty cushion to her right. The floating stopped, and she sank further into the couch. *Would he be here if I'd fought for him? Would I be here if I'd included him?*

"So, Lily." Carla Ramirez! Talking to her! Lily spun back around with a showstopping grin. None could say what might have happened, and she could argue more with Mr. Gates another day. Right now, this was her one moment of glory.

Carla said, "Your first book was a summer beach story,

then autumn in New England, and now Christmas in the mountains. What's in mind for spring?"

Lily laughed, her voice so dang loud against the audience's rapt silence. "Oh, I'm not sure yet. Maybe a...flower girl who wants to make the church look nice for Easter, and falls in love with the pastor. Oh, actually..." Lily didn't mean to put her finger to her lips in such a posed thoughtfulness. It just happened! Carla laughed either way.

Lily nearly missed the next question thinking about that book. *Themes of revival mix with spring and the church. Her mom could be dead and this is the flower girl's way of keeping her alive.* Lily had a modest Christian following already with her wholesome books. Maybe...

Focus!

Would Curtis have had some ideas?

FOCUS!

Carla charmed the audience with some light questions. Favorite character? Elsa's dad; he was sweetness personified in flannel. Was the town based on anywhere real? No, absolutely no real place she could see outside her window every day. Do you prefer paper books or e-books? Hey now, don't get me in trouble on live TV!

Carla laughed. The audience laughed.

Lily could only muster a decent grin. Curtis kept popping into her head, saying that Elsa was his favorite character, not Dad. And e-books were not real books, darn it! He should have been here. *I should have fought for him.* Lily blinked the visions away. It was too late; she'd made her choice and now she had to live with it.

Forever.

Finally, Carla crossed her other leg, and gave Lily a knowing smirk. "So, Lily, confession time: you've slipped under my radar twice before. I'd heard your name, heard good reviews, but each time I let it pass. This time, however, everyone from my manager to my nail stylist said that this book was your best ever, so I thought I'd be a fool not to ask you onto my show."

Lily almost melted into syrup. *Carla thinks I'm cool!*

Carla touched her cheek with a lacquered nail. "I'm told this book is richer than your last two. All the seriousness of literature with the charm of a paperback. Tell me, what made this book so different from the last two?"

Lily sucked on her lip gloss. There it was. The one question she could not answer. "Ah, well, it was pretty tricky, and...almost didn't make the deadline." Lily stared at the blank, white carpet, scouring her brain for an answer as her mouth stalled with babbled nothings. How could she answer this question properly? What story could she possibly spin?

Why do I have to spin a story anyway? How did I get myself into this web? Why didn't Mr. Gates listen to me? I could have announced Curtis on the freaking Carla show! Why can't I ever say what I want to say?

Lily envisioned Curtis again, only this time he was cowering. Her throat was scratched and scraped as she screamed. *You stole my voice!*

Suddenly, it was Mr. Gates's face, reeling as she wailed. *You stole my voice!*

Now, it was Mary's, her perfect makeup cracking with fear. *You stole my voice!*

And then, they were gone, all of them, like wisps in her

mind's eye, leaving just one face: hers. It was a pinched, angry face, the cheeks splotchy with hate, and eyes gleaming with tears. She was screaming.

You stole my voice!

It vanished. Stage lights seared through her mind, and sharpened the edges of every couch cushion, every thread of carpet, every one of Carla Ramirez's still-smiling teeth. No words, not in her ears, not in her head. Nothing but a silent moment, waiting for Lily Harper to fill it.

Lily spoke. "The truth is, I had a lot of help."

Carla tilted her head. "Friends in the industry?"

"No. It was a local author, Curtis. Curtis Reynolds. He helped me bring the book to life. I was up against my deadline, and he helped me see where my story could go. And he pushed me to think critically about my book. Not just about what I could write, but what I could *say.*"

Stop there! shouted something in her mind. *That's plenty! You dropped his name and still looked good. Now stop!*

It was impossible. Lily had let the truth into her mouth, thinking it would be sweet or savory, like a delicious morsel. No, it was like air. Like breath. She had to breathe again.

"Honestly, this book would not exist if not for Curtis. I had the original idea, I pushed for a sweet, wholesome Christmas story, and God knows I hunched over that screen until my eyeballs nearly fell out, but Curtis gave it all structure, and pushed me every inch of the way. He lost sleep right alongside me, and gave up weeks of his time to focus exclusively on my—on this book."

Carla Ramirez narrowed her eyes, but kept her smile. Her gaze flitted to the novel on the table, basking in the light of the stage, and then back to Lily. "You make it sound like his name should be on the cover, too." Such a light, friendly tone for such a powerful sentence. Like a razor wrapped in silk.

And yet, Lily smiled. She could see the cameras in the periphery of her vision, broadcasting her words around the country, but her lungs never felt so full. Any frightening chill that tried to crawl up her spine melted under the nestled flames of a simmering beast in her mind, grunting its approval.

"He should," Lily said. "He should have from the start, but I didn't want to admit how crucial he was. I started alone, and I wanted to continue alone, you know? But the truth is I wasn't alone, not this time."

A spark lit on her tongue. Now *this* was delicious, even if it forced her to once again choose her words carefully—not to weave a lie, but rather a truth she didn't yet know how to make real. A promise. "In fact, I'm working to change that. I'm in talks with my editor, and the hope is to get a reprint with Curtis's name alongside mine so that the cover is more accurate."

A low, "Oooh," went through the crowd, the first sound in ages.

Lily kept up her smile. Oddly, it took no effort at all.

Carla's smile turned into a wry smirk. "Well, isn't that something?" Carla turned to beam at the cameras. "There you have it, folks, a smart and charming new Christmas novel available right now: *Escape from Christmas* by Lily Harper and...?" Carla raised an eyebrow at Lily.

"And Curtis Reynolds."

"Curtis Reynolds. We'll be right back."

371

The audience applauded dutifully. A crewman made a signal, then someone shouted, "And we're off."

Lily's smile, shoulders, and energy all fell with a crash. *Holy crap, what did I just do?*

Carla accepted a cup of water from a stage hand. "Well, that was gutsy."

"Yeah?" Lily said in a small voice.

"Mm-hmm. Not sure everybody's going to like it, though."

Lily sighed. "I'm sorry."

Carla gave her a quizzical look. "Sorry? Don't be. I love a good ratings boost. Worry about yourself, *chica*. Good or bad, you can't take that back."

Chapter 31

"What. Was. That?" Mr. Gates's low, even voice sliced through the swearing of Lily's taxi driver. They had barely left the TV studio.

Lily took another breath for courage. How was confessing the truth to millions on live television easier than one phone call? "It wasn't right, Mr. Gates."

"Wasn't right?! And telling millions that you stole somebody else's work is?!"

"I did not. Steal. Anything. I wrote that book, and Curtis did, too."

"You said we were changing the cover!"

"I said I was in talks with my editor. I made sure not to promise anything."

"Oh, sure, and the entire audience of Carla Ramirez isn't going to expect an immediate turnaround!"

"I'm truly sorry for the inconvenience."

"Inconvenience?! My boss has his fist halfway down my throat!"

"And that's my fault. I should have said something long ago."

"You should have kept your mouth shut! Miss Harper, you are in violation of the contract that said you were the sole author. And, you made us both look like liars!"

Lily crossed her legs, trying to mimic some of Carla Ramirez's queenly energy. "We *are* liars, Mr. Gates. We buried Curtis for our own selfish gain."

Mr. Gates barked out an ugly laugh. "That's right, Miss Harper, I'm a big fat liar, and as a big fat liar, I cannot wait to hear your next book proposal!"

Lily's phone gave a pleasant *beep-a-deep* to let her know the call had ended. She lowered it to her thigh and tried to focus on the traffic. *It's okay. He's just one editor. There are other publishers out there. I'm still a known name, right? Someone will want my books. In fact, maybe the company will gently push Mr. Gates aside and assign someone else to me. I've made them a lot of money, after all.*

Lily caught her reflection in the rear-view mirror. *Yeah, and maybe Mary will shop at the dollar store.*

She set her phone to do-not-disturb. She had a feeling she'd be plenty disturbed soon enough.

Lily didn't really want to talk about it. Not yet. She wanted to buy an early ticket and fly home to forget, but after a possible career fission, this didn't seem like the time for discretionary spending. She passed the evening in her hotel room, watching bad movies and just trying not to think about anything.

The next day, Lily got ready. The journey home was another train of stop-and-go, from the taxi cab traffic to the delay at the flight gate. This time, however, she used those moments to send several text messages. She had an idea of what was coming, and she wanted to be prepared.

Lily thanked the Lord she wasn't famous enough for

paparazzi. A movie star would be swarmed by now, but a novelist, even after *Carla*, could slip by unnoticed. Mostly. She got plenty of curious stares and pointing fingers, but kept her eyes behind sunglasses or her nose in a book, ignoring everything and everyone. On the plane, Lily wrote up a blog post to share all over her platform about who Curtis was, why she'd come out about his help, and what this meant moving forward. It didn't make her sound any more innocent, and she didn't know what "moving forward" even meant.

She feared for her career, feared for her name, and feared for her house. Yet as Lily closed her laptop and looked out the airplane window at the carpet of clouds beneath the crystal-blue sky, Lily couldn't help smiling just a little. The lie was over. She no longer had to dance around half-truths and fake smiles.

She was free.

Once she landed, Lily picked up her car from the airport and raced home. Good ol' Idaho, with its long, empty highways. The mountains rose around her, enveloping her in their rocky folds. They'd stood forever. Maybe she could, too.

Lily made it home in the gray evening. As she entered the Wood River Valley, a gentle snow began to fall. She paused at a red light to watch them tumble, fractal flakes floating on a light breeze. The car behind her had to honk before Lily realized the light had turned green. She'd been lost in the air, a frosty wind dancing with the snowflakes. Free.

The grass outside Lily's house had a light sugaring by this point, like a field of spearmint gumdrops. Her roof had paled, and the snowfall was thin enough that Lily could see the cut of the mountains behind it. God, she wanted to take a picture and make a puzzle out of it.

But Mary's car was in her driveway. By the dusting of snow, it had been there for a bit. Yet the driver's seat looked empty. She'd seen no one on the porch. So where…? Surely Mary didn't…

Lily hurried into the garage and hoisted herself out of the car, legs thick and heavy from unuse, back cracking. She snatched her suitcase out of the car and rushed into her house. Through the kitchen and yes, there was Mary, standing in the great, wooden living room, a single lamp straining to light the high walls, and the muddy shadows clouding far more. Mary stood with one hand on the back of the couch, the other on the hip of her jeans. Coat and scarf on the rack, no snow in her hair, no ruddy glow to her cheeks. She'd been in this room for a while.

"We need to talk," Mary said.

The fiery beast would rather scream, but Lily took a centering breath instead. "How did you even get in?"

"I have a key, remember?"

Lily pressed her tongue into the floor of her mouth and rolled her suitcase to the base of the stairs.

Mary said, "I watched your interview on *Carla* yesterday. I thought we talked about—"

"You can't do this," Lily interrupted, glaring down at her staircase.

Mary balked. "What?"

Lily took one more breath, then spun to face her sister. *I'm ready. Let's do this.* "You can't just walk into my house like you own it."

Mary crossed her arms. "I needed to talk with you. It's important."

"Then wait in the car. Or on the porch. But you cannot just enter *my house* when I'm not here."

Mary's mouth parted a fraction of an inch. She snapped it shut immediately, and waved a finger about the room. "Well, I can see why."

Lily didn't need to look around, but she did anyway. Hard-back purple couch: gone. Hideous orange-and-green wall art: sold. Exercise equipment: sent to a more loving environment. Various pillows, sea shells, inspirational posters, and coffee makers: AWOL. Lily felt the apology rising like vomit, and swallowed it back. Twice.

That left Mary to speak first. "You asked me to decorate for you. 'Surprise me,' were your exact words. That took work, Lily. And time. And expense."

"I'm paying for that," Lily interjected. "But it wasn't me or my style."

"If you wanted a certain style, why not tell me? I did exactly as you instructed."

"And that's my fault. I own that. I was overwhelmed by the book, and scared to get in the way of your process, so I surrendered to you what I should have done myself."

Mary frowned at Lily's new couch. "It just seems a tad ungrateful."

Lily's exhale came out like a bull's snort. "You're right: I'm not grateful. I'm not grateful that my house was filled with things you found appealing, not me. I'm not grateful that you convinced my family to buy me a treadmill I never wanted. I'm not grateful that my preferences are somehow seen as inferior to what you think I should have. I'll say it again: I'm thankful for the effort and attention, but it didn't work out. If you're looking for an apology, then I'm sorry I pretended everything was okay when it wasn't. But I'm not sorry that I finally made this house feel like mine and not yours."

Mary's mouth spread wider this time, and her nose wrinkled in disdain. "Well, tell me how you *really* feel."

Lily almost laughed. "How can I when you react with *that* comment?"

A curious change broke over Mary then. She'd already been upset, but in a high-nose, stuffy sort of way. Now, Mary's chin dipped, her hips squared, and she glared at Lily through an iron brow. This was no high lady about to criticize; this was a woman about to fight.

"You want to rearrange your furniture, go ahead. It's your house. But when your actions harm the family, that I can't overlook."

"What are you even talking about?" Lily couldn't deny the tingles of fear riding up her back, like long, skeletal claws.

Mary answered, "You are the most famous of us. And you just got more famous. But what you do won't affect just you; it makes an impression on the whole family. So how do you think it makes our family look when the biggest of us stands up on live TV and says that she stole somebody else's work?"

Lily nearly spat fire then. "I said that because it was true. Yeah, I wrote half or more, but I didn't write it all. I lied as long as I could, but I just couldn't anymore."

"I'm not asking you to lie, I'm—"

"Yes, you are! You're asking me to cover things up to make myself—our family—look better, but that's still lying! I don't *want* to lie anymore! I don't want to pretend things are perfect when they aren't, and I don't want to screw over somebody I care about anymore. I messed up. That's the truth. Now I'm sorry if someone looks down on the rest of the family because of what I did, but I am done faking my way through life."

Mary lunged. She jabbed her finger within an inch of Lily's face, and when she spoke, it was all teeth. "*That's* what bothers me. You say yourself that your actions could have consequences for the whole, but you still don't care! You'd rather do what's good for you. We. Are. Harpers! We stick together; you can't just go off on your own!"

Lily needed three deep breaths for that one, or she was going to snap Mary's finger in half. By the third breath, the beast had calmed, and she could speak in a low, mellow voice. "I'm not on my own."

Mary put her hands on her hips, scowling through a loose thread of blonde hair. "What is that supposed to mean?"

Lily walked over to her purse and took out her phone. "I sent out messages today. In the cab, in the airport, whenever I could. Everyone knew what had happened, of course, but I explained it anyway. I told them I messed up and that I had to come clean, and that the way I did it may have ramifications for them. And that I was sorry I disappointed them.

"I said to Asher, 'I'm sorry if someone doesn't want to buy from the shop because of me.' Asher said, 'It's cute how you think you're a better furniture salesman than I am, but I appreciate the thought. The truth is, I'm too proud of you to be mad at you. That took guts to do on live TV. Love you, sis. Don't worry about me; I doubt this will be too serious for us. Let me know if you need anything.'"

Lily paused to gauge Mary's reaction. Befuddled. Good.

Lily continued. "Daisy asked if she could meet me for a bite at the airport, but our schedules clashed. So she said, 'I'll come visit next week if that's okay. I'm not mad; I just want to make sure you're okay and I hate doing it over the phone. Don't worry about me; I don't think anybody even connects us together since I got married. Side note, if your publisher really does drop you and you need a graphic designer for your next book cover, hit me up, sis!'

"Oak has 'demanded' that I come see him tomorrow, but he said, and I quote, 'I'm not mad at you or anything. Actually, I am worried for you. Come over, I'll make you dinner, or at least call Daisy and get her to make dinner. You can tell us everything and we'll see how we can help you.'

"Mandragora said, 'I'm on every social media site playing up how awesome you are. I mean, that'll only reach like two hundred people, but that's something, right? Don't worry, sis, I'll get you more book sales!' Mom said, 'Honey, I am so proud of you. You were more honest in public than I've been able to be in private. You're an inspiration to the rest of us.'"

Lily dropped her phone on the couch like a microphone. "I didn't text you because I was working on what to say, and I knew I had to speak in person anyway. But it sounds to me like the Harper family is still together. The question is: where are you?"

Mary huffed out a low, gargled breath. Her fingers squeezed, somewhere between claws and fists. Then, they leapt up to her hair, raking up her scalp and pulling at her roots as Mary snorted fire. "Okay," she said. "Okay,

okay." Mary finally wandered to her purse and pulled out a hair tie. In frenzied seconds, flying fingers yanked her hair back into the messiest ponytail Lily had ever seen, all snagged and frayed. "Okay, so now we come to the truth."

Lily glanced at her phone, only to remember she'd already used up her greatest weapon. Seeing that mess on Mary's head, and the bulging in her eyes, Lily's breath came in shallow gasps. This was a face Lily had not seen in years, and it forced her to take a step backwards.

Lily had planned ahead for how to fight Mary. But she had no idea how to defeat *Rosemary*.

"I never thought about what I could have been," Mary snarled. "It was too depressing. If Mom had known how to actually take care of us and keep her skirt down, where could I have gone after college? And it didn't matter anyway; I love my family. I would die, starving and thirsty, before I let any of you wither away."

Lily decided to try a gentle approach. "I know."

"No. You. DON'T! Think back, Lily. Did you ever see me eat lunch?"

"Wh-What?"

"Think on it."

Lily scratched her head, as if that would wake up the memories. "I can't—"

"That's because I rarely did. In the morning, if I had work, I'd pack a lunch, then sneak it into someone else's bag. If it was a weekend, I'd say I ate already, even though my stomach was gnawing on my liver!"

Lily gasped.

"That's right!" Mary said. "And do you remember the day I bought everybody a pack of tee shirts? They were only a couple bucks, but remember how good you all felt when you finally had clean clothes?"

"Yes," Lily said.

Mary shrugged. "Did I get any?"

Lily hesitated.

"No. Mom left us in such a hole that I could barely scrape enough for you guys. I had one good outfit, and I had to wear it almost every day. Every day, I'd wash it, dry it, sew up any loose seams, and do it again tomorrow. But you know what? Every time I got depressed, when my knees hurt from kneeling in front of the tub as I washed that stupid dress, I thought of how loud you all cheered when you got those five-dollar shirts. I thought of how proud you were, how carefully you all ate so you wouldn't spill spaghetti on your silly, cheap, white shirts. It made me so happy that I'd start humming to myself, and my knees wouldn't hurt so bad."

Lily had no argument for that. In fact, she remembered painfully searching through the flea market for a simple, beige bra that wouldn't show through the white cotton shirt, so that she could keep wearing her clean clothes. Who knew you could love a tee shirt so much? Rosie did.

Mary…Rosie?…tapped her finger on the back of Lily's couch, harder and harder until the knuckle bent backwards. "Do you know how much debt I went into to buy that house where we could all live? Where Mom could retire with dignity? Where Mandy could grow up in safety? Did you know that James feels like I'm just using him for his money? As if I don't cry myself to sleep when I go to bed and he's already snoring? I am *still* sacrificing for this family and I am *proud* to sacrifice for this family."

Now, Mary bore her finger into the couch. Lily swallowed when she saw the nail crack. "So, imagine my surprise when I hear that a member of *my own family* is going *behind my back* and trying to turn my family away from me!"

Lily saw no point in playing coy. She just stood her ground, hands squeezing her pants, trying to decide whether she feared this iron-jawed, disheveled wretch...or missed her.

Mary thundered on. "First, I find out that Oak has given up his promotion. He's back to doing grunt work while someone else rises. Now, why would he do that? I can barely get a straight answer out of him, but one thing I did get was that he talked to you. Curious. But then Mom starts contradicting me in front of Mandy, telling me *she's* going to be in charge of Mandy from now on! Mandy barely listened to me in the first place, and now she won't listen at all! Why is Mom doing this? Why this sudden sense of obligation she didn't have for the last thirty-five years? Well, apparently, it started when she talked to you on Thanksgiving.

"And, of course, there's Mandy herself. Acting all nice and calm and even friendly, ever since she got back from your house. I ask her what her game is, and do you know what she says? That *you* took her to the Westwood House. That you laid out every horrible thing we went through, everything we swore, all of us swore, she would never, ever know. I have given that girl every drop of blood in my veins to protect her, and you sneak behind my back and drag her through it all!"

Lily bit back, "Mandragora left that house more grateful than ever before. How can she be part of this family if we all block her from the very things that *made* us a family? That's my opinion."

Mary crossed her arms and shifted her weight to the other hip. "Your opinion? Your opinion just proved very destructive. I told you to just play it cool about the book, and let it all wash over, but no, you had to shoot your career in the head."

"You don't know that," Lily said, more to herself than to anyone else.

"Don't I? Just this morning, do you know what came up on my newsfeed? A video titled 'Romance Writer Admits Copyright Fraud,' and trust me, it doesn't get any kinder after that."

Lily would have gasped if her throat would open. Someone had written that? That hateful, half-truth? She clenched her stomach and squeezed out a few words. "It sounds like a trashy gossip site."

"It doesn't matter," Mary said. "It has thousands of views and hundreds of comments. That's what people are hearing about you, and that's what you've done to yourself. So, forgive me if I don't think your opinion is good for this family right now! Why, Lily? Why go mess everything up? Why not just smile for the Carla show and let me handle everything else? Why couldn't you just keep your mouth shut?!"

Lily had to look at the floor, fearing that her gaze might set something on fire. The beast in her mind raged, *Keep my mouth shut?! You'd love that wouldn't you, Mary? Love to wrap your claws around everybody so you can show off your perfect little dolls with no personalities of their own!*

That kind of talk won't work, said a quieter voice in

her head.

Then what will?!

An excellent question. What string of words would make the great Mary bend her ear and actually listen? Well, not quite Mary anymore. Lily lifted her eyes to her sister. Still watching with her brows up, impatience and pride personified. But that hairdo, that fire in her eyes. Rosie...

Lily suddenly found that she didn't want to fight. What a cruel trick this creature played; show Lily her sister and rob Lily of her will to continue.

Unless...unless Mary had just revealed her greatest weakness...

"Well?!" Mary demanded.

Lily thought fast. No time to edit or refine. No Curtis to help her say it in just the right way. One shot. This would either make everything better, or so much worse.

"You want to know why?" Lily took a great, steeling breath, and began. "Let me tell you a story."

Chapter 32

"Once upon a time, there was a girl named Rosemary. Her dad left before he could know her, and Mom couldn't handle that. Mom kept finding the worst men, and had five more babies, all dirty and ragged and fighting for a scrap of food. With a family that big and a mother that weak, Rosie had to fend for herself.

"Fortunately, Rosie was no ordinary gal. She was smart, resourceful, pretty, fast, funny if you let her be, and far stronger than her skinny arms let on. She picked up every person in that poor, bedraggled family. She fed them, cleaned them, then let them climb on her shoulders, one by one, so that they could reach the stars. The family was so happy to have Rosie there to save them.

"But somebody else was watching from the shadows. Someone watched as Rosie pretended to eat so her family would have more. Someone saw Rosie crying in the dead hours of night after everybody went to sleep. One day, that someone saw her chance. Rosie was kneeling on the hard tile of the bathroom, scrubbing the only dress she had, watching the fabric tear and the color fade with each wash, wondering what she could possibly do once it finally died. The Someone slipped out from a crack in the floor, crawled up Rosie's aching back, and whispered into her ear.

"'Hello,' she said, 'My name is Mary. I see how tired

you are. I've seen how much you sacrifice for them. But dearest, who looks out for you? They can't help you; they're weak and broken and reliant on you. I can help. I can make you feel strong, invincible even. And I can lift your family to a high place where no wickedness in this world can harm them. All I ask in return is your name.'

"And Rosie, desperate for relief, agreed. Mary entered into Rosie, just a little at first, no more than a drop of blood in Rosie's veins. It was enough that Rosie could smile more. And when she smiled, others smiled. And Rosie found she didn't feel so poor and small anymore. She felt grand, proud, and capable. Soon, her neighbors who'd known her all her life asked who this elegant young thing was, she answered, 'Mary.'

"'Mary. Mary. Mary.' Every time the name was spoken, the drop of blood in Rosie's veins grew. First a murky blob, then a cloud, and soon, it became a stream that pulsed through every part of Rosie's body. It no longer mattered that her family was fed and happy. As Rosie looked for a new home for them, every house seemed tiny and dingy, no matter how new. She wanted nothing less than a castle.

"One day, she met a handsome doctor. He wasn't funny, but when he tried to be funny and failed, Rosie still laughed. She liked him. But Mary feared. Mary liked to hear the word 'Doctor' from everyone who met him, had to hear it again and again to assure herself that she was among those who never starve.

"With his help, Rosie built her castle, built its walls high with bricks of gold and green. She dug a moat a mile wide, and filled it with accolades and opportunities. She raised her gates as high as the mountains, but with everything Rosie made, Mary feared it would disappear. Mary wanted more, always more. Happiness was not possible in the hot, dusty earth; she demanded the sky, so she built, and built, and built.

"Rosie looked, but could not see her family anymore; they were hidden behind pillars of smoke and walls of mirrors. When she reached for them, chains sprang from her fingertips and bound them, every one. But Mary kept building. The chains pulled taut, stretching Rosie like a rack, tearing the very muscles from her arms.

"Rosie cried, 'Stop! This is far enough!' But Mary was no longer a shadow; she was a storm cloud whose lightning flashed in diamonds, and whose thunder drowned all other sound. Mary bellowed, 'How dare you? Doesn't your family deserve the best? You would rob them of all they could become? How will you ever protect them without me?!'

"But just then, another sound rose through the wind and thunder. It was quiet, so quiet that Rosie had to strain her ears to hear it, but it had the strength and timbre of many voices in one. It called, 'Rosie.' Rosie looked down. From the end of every chain, Rosie heard the voices of her family, crying out, 'Rosie…let go.'

"It was then that Rosie saw two more chains, stretching out from Mary's neck. One chain ended in Rosie's right hand, the other in her left. The chains were so interwoven with her family's bonds that Rosie couldn't release one without releasing them all. And still, her family cried, 'Rosie…let go.'"

Mary eyed her sister with the gaze of a cornered beast. Hard, still, unblinking. Yet tinged with a certain tension around the eyelids, scanning every inch of Lily's face to see if this strange, new creature before her could be trusted.

Lily's mouth had gone dry, all the moisture redirected to her eyes. *Please hear me.*

Bright fingernails tapped across a tanned arm, one-two-three-four, one-two-three-four. At last, her mouth opened. "So, what does she do?"

Lily shook her head. "I'm not that good of a writer. I can't finish this story on my own. Will you help me finish it…Rosie?"

The pretty face in front of her twitched, mouth turning down into her throat. "Rosie was a scared, underfed little girl." She reached for her ponytail with fingernails pointing like claws.

Lily snatched the hand and held it firm. "You don't need Mary anymore. None of us do."

"Oak is stuck in that little apartment, Mom has a terrible track record with raising kids, and you? I know how much this house costs; if your popularity drops even a little, you won't be able to keep it up!"

"Oak will be fine. Mom and Mandy will be fine. I will be fine, you know why? Because even if I have to sell this house, I won't go back to that cramped, overcrowded place I used to know because you brought us out of it. We aren't there anymore! We don't need a hero to come rescue us because we are already strong enough to get through anything. You did that. We don't need Mary anymore. We can all take care of each other now."

"Well, good for you!" Spittle flew from Mary's mouth. "I'm so happy you've all decided that you're perfectly fine without me. I hope you all have wonderful lives together without a giant house you can't afford and a husband who's ready to walk out! You're all fine and dandy taking care of each other, well, *who's taking care of me?!*"

Lily counted to three, just so Mary could hear that question hanging in the air. When her eyes dilated, when Mary began to breathe through her mouth, in that one second between realizing what she'd just said, and drowning it in the answer she'd always given, Lily reached through, putting her hands on her sister's shoulders, and looking deep into those wide, pleading eyes.

"I will. I'm not sixteen anymore; I'm twenty-nine. I can work, vote, cook, and pay bills. I read books because I like them now, not because I need a place to hide." God, she hadn't planned to cry, and with her hands occupied, Lily couldn't wipe her face. "You made me strong. You don't have to hold me up; I can hold *you* now. Rosie, let me go. I promise, I won't leave."

Mary's eyes darted everywhere except to Lily. Her face remained as tight as a prison lock, but the violence had gone from it, leaving only confusion, doubt, and fear. "You...can't, you have your own...too many things to worry—"

"Then we'll all hold you! Mom, Asher, Daisy, Oak, even Mandragora. You have six people waiting for you to join us! Come out of that house, Rosie. You got us out, now it's your turn, but we can't help you if you keep wrapping us in chains. Let go of Mary. She could never love you like we can. Please, Rosie, let go."

She didn't. Maybe couldn't. If anything, her sister held tighter, every fiber and sinew clenching at the same time, veins popping, teeth grinding, squeezing herself together.

But Lily was out of words. She stammered and choked, but nothing felt right on her tongue. She could see the iron fortress rising higher, the walls slamming shut impossibly fast. She was losing her.

So Lily grabbed her sister. She threw her arms as far around Rosemary as they would go, grasping and clutching skin and sweater alike. It was like holding a statue. An inhuman, inanimate *thing* that no chisel could crack.

Only one sentence came to mind. Lily threw all her hopes on its words. "Don't you worry, Rosie, we'll take care of everything." She kept hugging her sister, feeling her go rock solid beneath her embrace.

And then, every part of Rosie went limp. Lily gasped as her back gave way, but she clasped tighter, and let herself fall. They hit the ground, and Lily winced at the explosion in her kneecaps, yet she held. Held something soft. Something flesh.

Hands climbed up Lily's back. Fingers grabbed through her shirt, into her skin, pinching, poking, and squeezing. Arms compressed Lily's ribs, and stifled her lungs. And a squeak sounded in Lily's ear. It rose to a whine, and tumbled into a thunderous crash of falling notes and broken wheezes.

Rosie wept up a storm, a burbling mass of noise and water. She rumbled and shuddered and threatened to reel right out of Lily's grasp, but Lily held fast, and never let Rosie fall. Lily blinked through her own mist, and whispered into the mess of blonde, "It's okay, sis. I've got you."

*
**

At some point, Rosie stood, tried to walk, and fell again. Lily caught her. And the time after that, too. The third time, Lily was able to guide her sister to the couch, where they could both collapse with ease.

Not one word passed between them, just tears and tissues. The floor was littered in sodden puffs. Lily didn't have to grasp quite so hard after a while, so her clutching fingers relaxed into soothing hands that stroked the head that lay on her chest. Through the window, Lily watched the gray sky fade to black. Flecks of white still waltzed around her porchlight.

Then, at some unknown hour, Rosemary spoke in a thin rasp. "What did the house look like?"

Lily didn't know which way this talk would go, so she just told the truth and hoped for the best. "Awful. It's condemned."

"Condemned?"

"I guess the people who bought from us were worse off than we were."

"So, it's dead then."

Lily pondered that word with a grim nod. "Yeah, it's dead."

At last, Rosie pulled herself off of Lily's chest. She peeled her matted hair off her cheek. The pony tail had given up a while ago. "What did Mandy think of it?"

Finally, Lily had some good news. But rather than share it, Lily said, "I think you should ask her yourself. And when you do, tell her that Lily *insists* she tell you exactly what she told me."

Rosie frowned at that curious reply, but did not pursue it. Instead, she laid back on the cushions, sighing herself into a boneless lump of flesh. "Your couch sucks by the way. Mine was prettier." The corners of her mouth betrayed the edges of a smile.

Lily said, "Your face sucks. And your coffee maker. But I do have a French press if you want some decaf."

Rosie shook her head. "Do you have any tea?"

"Sure do." Lily pulled herself from the couch, and spied the dancing snow starting to pool at the bottoms of her window panes. "Actually, how about cocoa? The weather's perfect for it."

"Oh, yes, I'd love some." Rosie's eyes grew distant. "It always seemed like too much of an indulgence..."

Lily swallowed the lump in her throat and made them both a perfectly-hot cup with milk, cinnamon, a tiny splash of vanilla, and extra marshmallows. Rosie did not wait on the couch, but meandered around the living room a while, then stood by the back door, watching the thinning snow swirl against the night. Even when Lily brought the drink, Rosie did not move. Lily decided to join her, gently blowing the steam from her mug.

Rosie suddenly said, "James says he wants to go to marriage counseling."

"Oh," Lily said. "That's good."

"Good?"

"It means he wants to fight for the marriage, right?"

Rosie's frown softened. "Huh. That's a better perspective on it than I've had." She blew on her cocoa. "Do you think I should do it?"

"Why not?" Lily asked. "Don't you want to?"

"Yes. But...he wrote his vows to Mary. I don't know if he'd even like Rosie."

Lily paused to process that one. "Well, if he doesn't, then he's stupid. Rosie is the best. Send him my way and I'll set him straight."

Rosie gave a fleeting smile. She took a drink of the cocoa, sighed all over her body, and said, "This place is beautiful, Lily. The house, the view. It's wonderful. I'm really proud of you."

The words warmed her far more than the cocoa did.

Lily finally took her eyes off her sister, peered through back window, and gasped. The clouds were breaking, and the snowflakes faded to a spotty mist roiling in the moonlight. The moon revealed the mountains cutting across the horizon in an obsidian saw. Snow padded the earth in a thin, white carpet.

"All I need is to start the fireplace," Lily said. "Then, I'd be living in my own book."

Rosie chuckled, but then grew quiet, frowning at some thought in her head. "Lily?"

"Yeah?"

"Did you mean it when you said you'd help me?"

"Of course I did! Why?"

Rosie traced the rim of her cocoa with her chipped fingernail. "Do you think I could stay with you for a couple of days? Maybe…a week? No more, I promise. I just…I think I need to get away from all that…Mary stuff…back home."

Lily nodded without even thinking about it. "Sure. But what will James say?"

"I'll talk to him. I'll run home, pack a suitcase, and tell him I'm willing to do therapy. I just need to hunker down with myself for a little bit." Those poor, dry, scarlet eyes had never looked more worn and weary, not even in the old days.

"You've got it. But every time you insult my couch, I dock an hour of stay time."

Rosie laughed, not the tittering silliness of Mary, but a real, if tired, laugh. "Thank you. I'll go pack, then."

"Take your time."

Rosie finished her cocoa, then grabbed her coat and opened the front door.

Curtis stood on the other side, hand raised to knock.

Chapter 33

"Wark!" cried Lily.

Curtis jerked in place, shaking some of the snow off his coat. "Bad...time?"

Yes, it *was* a bad time; Lily's heart had stopped and she needed a transplant!

Rosemary looked from Curtis to Lily, and back again, watching all the silence pass between them. "I...was just leaving." She squeezed out of the door. "Curtis."

He nodded. "Mrs. Livingston."

Rosie's shoulders drooped. "Ugh, that sounds so old." She sulked a trail of footprints to her car.

Curtis remained on the porch, and Lily's brain remained on Neptune.

"Can I come in?" he asked.

The chilly air made Lily's decision for her. "Yes."

Curtis stomped his boots on the welcome mat, then stepped inside, only as far as the foyer. He closed the door, but kept his coat and hat. Lily backed into the living room.

Then, they stared. Not one thing had changed about him. Still skinny, unless that coat was more than padding. Still had that ridiculous, pretentious soul patch running down his chin like a fuzzy black arrow. And even though Lily had *watched* him come in, even though he stood with the boots and coat and hat of someone who would not stay, Curtis *still* somehow looked like he'd been in this room the whole time.

Curtis eyed the floor behind Lily. "It snowed in here."

Lily whirled around and spied the carpet of tissues. "Augh!" She dashed through the room, snatching up the mess. "Sorry, had a bit of a family drama."

"That explains it." Curtis pointed to Lily's shirt. Splotched with wet spots. Lily didn't want to guess which fluids were which.

"Yeah, I'm a bit of a mess right now." She was still in her sweatpants for pity's sake.

Curtis pointed to the door. "Do you want me to leave?"

It was tempting to say yes. Lily had just endured an emotional whirlwind; did she really have the brain or heart space to look at his face again? On the other hand, may as well get all the drama done at once. "No, please stay. I'm glad you came. Wait, hold on. Why *are* you here?"

Curtis thrusts his hands into his coat pockets. "That is quite the story! It begins yesterday when my mom calls me in the middle of my shift. She's a big fan of *The Carla Ramirez Show*, and she says, 'Curtie—' that's what my mom calls me, '—didn't you help that local author with her book? Because she just said your name on TV.'

"Well, I'm at work, so I can't exactly turn on daytime talk shows while Mrs. Patient is having a panic attack over her bad mammogram. But just a few minutes later, I get a beep on my phone. It's your sister, Mandragora, who apparently follows me on social media now, and she says that I need, need, *NEED* to see today's *Carla* episode, and that I should just trust her on that.

397

"Side note: did you know Carla Ramirez has a livestream? I didn't, but it came in handy because we don't have a TV in our office. I had to tool around with the time, plus stop and attend to patients, and Jim could tell I was distracted, so I told him what happened. Then *he* says that Mary texted him, saying you did something dumb on live TV. So we close his office door and watch the darn thing together. And there you are, killer in blue by the way, seated in front of a book I've avoided for the last month, telling the entire galaxy that Curtis Reynolds not only exists, but that he deserves to be on the same book as you."

Curtis paused, just staring at Lily. Melted snow pooled around his boots.

Lily could only nod.

He plunged ahead. "And then that evening, I get a call from a New York number. I ignore it. They call again. I get curious and answer. The guy on the other line says, 'Hello, Curtis, my name is Mr. Gates.' That's what he calls himself by the way: Mr. Gates. No first name. He says, in summation, 'We have been informed that you were the co-author on Lily Harper's latest novel, *Escape from Christmas*. We would like to apologize for not contacting you before, as we had no idea that Miss Harper had partnered with anyone."

"What?!" Lily snapped. "He did too know!"

"I remember, and told him, 'You didn't hear Lily tell you about me that day you told her the book was accepted?' He got real quiet, then changed the subject. He said they're going to issue an immediate reprint, and would I please confirm how I'd like to spell my name?

So, I tell him how to spell 'Curtis Awesome-Sauce Reynolds,' and he said they'll be sending me fifty percent of the author profits from here on out, plus backpay for books already sold."

Lily groaned. "Backpay that will come out of my royalties, I bet."

"Probably. And all I had to do was e-sign a document that says all is forgiven, and lawsuits are the furthest thing from my mind."

She gave a little chuckle. "Good for you, Curtis. I wasn't sure if Mr. Gates would actually change anything."

Curtis nodded, then stared at his boots for a moment. He finally took off his hat. Lily sighed at his black hair. So ruffled. So boyish. When he ran a hand through it, she nearly cried. *Did I seriously miss him this much?*

He said, "So, uh, naturally I wanted to talk to you, and it seemed like an in-person kind of chat. I texted you when I saw you were home, but I got no answer."

Lily glanced at the phone on the end table. "Yeah, sorry. Family meltdown. Actually, how did you even know when I was coming home?"

"Well, obviously, I drove by your house every couple of hours like a creep with too much time on his hands." Curtis spread his arms wide. "I have no defense for that one."

Lily grinned and shook her head. "Well, here I am. You found me, now…what did you want to say?"

A hundred answers raced across Curtis's features. Then, a cloud covered them all. "I'm just a little confused. Why did you do that?"

She said, "Because it was the right thing to do. I'm just…I'm so sorry it took me this long to figure it out. I'm sorry I didn't believe in you after you believed so much in me.

I'm sorry I didn't take that chance with you. I'm sorry that…I'm sorry I stole your voice."

He remained a mask. "But what changed? Why share my voice now?"

I got sick of lying. I got sick of being miserable. I dove into my past and discovered a pattern of make-believe that nauseated me. All true, but Lily found an answer that was even truer. And scarier.

"Because I really missed hearing it."

The cloud broke instantly. A warm waft of air seemed to fill his lungs. Curtis drew it in through parted lips. "I, uh…missed yours, too."

Now it was her turn to breathe, a warm, balmy breeze that turned her insides all toasty. "Yeah?"

"Yeah. I lied about avoiding the book. I bought it. And read it. Then tore it up. Then bought a new one. I was…conflicted. But I think I missed your voice more than I resented it."

Resented. Lily blinked away the stinging in her eyes. "Can you ever forgive me?"

Curtis's right cheek went up. Then his left. "I asked Jim if I should. He said, 'Brother, if a girl is willing to risk her career and reputation for you, that's a pretty good sign of repentance.'"

"Kinda." Lily hugged herself.

"What's wrong?"

"I don't regret confessing, but is it wrong to still be worried about my future? About my house?"

Curtis gazed about the room. "Honestly, I'm not sure how much you need to worry."

"Mr. Gates said I violated my contract."

"But he's adding me on as an author, right? And I'm only getting fifty percent, so you must still be getting the other fifty. I'm betting you'll be fine."

"I wish I could believe that, but Mary—Rosie—said she saw some website that just tore me apart."

Curtis held up a hand. "Wait. Was the title something like, 'Famous Author Admits Fraud'?"

"Something like that."

"If it's who I'm thinking of, then screw that guy. I flicked through his website, and it's nothing but shock value and click bait. 'Big-Time Actor HUMILIATED by Racist Slur,' with 'humiliated' in all caps. Or, 'Disney Going Bankrupt After Box Office Failure' two minutes after the movie premiers. Conjecture and algorithms; ignore it."

Lily said, "Maybe, but he still has a lot of followers."

"But Carla Ramirez has more followers. Do you read what she said?"

"What?"

Curtis smirked. "I'll have to find the exact phrase, but she put out a thingy on the internet that said something to the effect of, 'It takes guts to admit what Lily Harper did. I wish more people were as compassionately honest as her.'"

Blood rushed to Lily's head so fast she nearly passed out. "She said that?"

"Something like it."

"Oh my gosh…but do you think it will be enough? This house isn't cheap."

Curtis rocked in place for a minute, then said, "Maybe I can help."

"Help?" The back of her neck was suddenly ticklish.

"Well, I haven't spent much of that big fat check you

wrote me. Just your usual post-breakup comfort food. And apparently, I'm going to get some royalties soon. Mr. Gates said your preorders were fantastic. I can invest it into this place."

Lily's face didn't burn; it sparked. Sweet lightning snapped across her pores and she swore that she glowed. "Oh! Oh, no, Curtis, I couldn't ask you to do that. It's my house; I should be responsible for it."

Curtis said, "But my house is paid off, remember? Mel's insurance."

"But wouldn't you like to get a house of your own one day?"

Lily swore his eyes glanced to the living room before answering. "Yes…but…I like this place. I like your dream."

"You're a sweetheart, but it's *my* dream, not yours. Why not spend some money on your dream?"

Curtis fell quiet again. He suddenly looked very fragile. Lily started to ask what was wrong, but then he spoke. "My dream is to write a hundred books with you."

Lily had written romance for the past three years. She knew how the heart could flutter or jackhammer with delight. She knew how it could freeze, overwhelmed by joy. She'd never read how it could stay perfectly calm, steadily beating, as if had finally found normal again.

"That's not an exaggeration, by the way," Curtis added. "One hundred books. Dream big."

"You'd go through all that again?'

"A hundred times. Well, ninety-nine. We already did the one."

Lily started to giggle, then choked. "Will any

publisher accept us?"

Curtis blinked at her. "Y–You're Lily Harper! You were on *Carla*!"

"But my editor was furious with me. And I don't think publishers like a writer who passive-aggressively maneuvers them like I did."

He frowned. "Have I taught you nothing about the bottomless greed of the entertainment industry? *Someone* will pick up a name that was on national television."

Lily gave him a dirty look. "That's not exactly inspiring."

"Okay, then we self-publish. I know some tricks, and you know how to make people actually like you. Cater to the crowd that admires your honesty. In the meantime, we'll type up another masterpiece. In fact, I heard you tell Carla about your idea for a springtime novel, and, well, my head is bursting with thoughts. I'd love to talk it over with you if you have time."

Okay, *now* her heart was hammering like a woodpecker. Another book! Another journey! And yet, she hesitated. "Can I be honest?"

"Of course."

"I've just had a plane ride, a long drive, and a family crisis, all on the tail of flipping my career in the air like a coin. Plus, there's the emotional roller coaster of seeing you again. I'm exhausted. All I want to do is order some takeout and watch a movie with zero narrative tension and more Christmas trees than actors."

Curtis nodded. "I hear that. Okay, I'll step out and let you rest."

A chill ran over Lily's heart. "Or...you could take off your coat and watch the movie with me. I'll let you make fun of it. Occasionally."

The smile filled Curtis's whole face. "I'd love you. To! I'd love...love to."

Sparks burst in Lily's face again. "I'd love ...to...too."

Lily ordered Thai, and asked Rosie to pick it up on the way back. Then, she threw the shoes off her feet, changed clothes, and curled her stocking toes on the fuzzy, tiger-stripe rug, cooing with delight. Curtis shed his coat, boots, and gloves, then took up a seat on the left side of the couch. Lily sat on the other side, trying to decide if she wanted to watch the movie or Curtis.

When Rosie arrived, she took a seat in the chair by the couch, then they all dug in to the food, laughing at corny dialogue, then giving a tearful *Awww* at equally trite lines a moment later—at least the girls did. Curtis politely held his tongue.

In truth, however, Lily could barely focus on the film. With food in her belly and all the adrenaline finally leaving her system, she kept drifting in and out of sleep. At one point, she woke to a bleary image of Rosie giving her a funny, knowing smile. Lily wanted to ask why, but she was already fading again. Curtis's shoulder was far too comfortable.

The End

Acknowledgements

A book is rarely created in a vacuum; so many people helped bring this book to fruition and we're so thankful for each and every single person who helped us.

We want to thank all our lovely beta readers. Your feedback made Lily stronger, Mary fuller, and you even cut out a character for us (sorry, sister Fern, you weren't as necessary as we thought you were). This book wouldn't be nearly as solid and impactful without your thoughts.

We also want to thank our street team. Advertising as an indie is so very difficult, but sharing the load with amazing people like you makes it much easier. You guys are rockstars!

And our lovely readers! Thank you for taking a chance on this little indie book about two authors, written by two authors. We write for you, that you may find rest, empowerment, and delight through fiction.

Finally, we want to thank God. He gave us the talent and know-how to write our books, and we wouldn't be doing this without His inspiration and help when the writer's block sets in.

About the Authors

For years, Mike wrote on his own. Di helped with story construction and being "Watson," as Mike affectionately called her, for her ability to happily sit and listen to story ideas for hours on end. In 2023, they decided to join forces and write together.

They live in southern Idaho with their two boys and a crazy cat, crafting worlds and new friends for their readers, all to bring rest, empower, and delight.

See their other books, upcoming projects, and more weirdness at mdblaylockauthor.com.